NETHERSPACE

NETHERSPACE

ANDREW LANE AND
NIGEL FOSTER

TITAN BOOKS

Netherspace
Mass-market edition ISBN: 9781785651861
Electronic edition ISBN: 9781785651854

Published by Titan Books
A division of Titan Publishing Group Ltd
144 Southwark Street, London SE1 0UP

First mass-market edition: March 2018
2 4 6 8 10 9 7 5 3 1

A CIP catalogue record for this title is available from the British Library.

Printed and bound in the United States

Did you enjoy this book? We love to hear from our readers.
Please email us at readerfeedback@titanmail.com or write to us at
Reader Feedback at the above address.

To receive advance information, news, competitions, and exclusive offers
online, please sign up for the Titan newsletter on our website:

TITANBOOKS.COM

To the memory of Craig Hinton. Be proud.

For Tara and Sacha.

"IF A LION COULD SPEAK, WE COULD
NOT UNDERSTAND HIM."

Ludwig Wittgenstein,
Philosophical Investigations (1953)

"WHAT WE'VE GOT HERE IS A FAILURE
TO COMMUNICATE."

Prison captain in *Cool Hand Luke*
(1967), screenplay by Donn Pearce
and Frank R. Pierson

THERE ARE FOUR STEPS AWAY FROM OUR LIFE
THAT WE SHOULD CONSIDER:

- Different carbon-based chemistry in an
  Earth-like system, such as another nucleic
  acid configuration, or different linear
  chemistry altogether instead of DNA.

- Different metabolic circumstances around
  carbon-water-based life, such as sulphur
  instead of oxygen, different amino acids
  and proteins, or metals as support at
  temperatures above 300 °C.

- Different chemistry altogether, perhaps
  based in silicon and silicones – or perhaps
  chemistry we haven't thought of, for
  instance in Jupiter's atmosphere or core.

- Totally different recursive systems
  altogether, from reproducing tori in
  stellar atmospheres to complex systems
  of subatomic particles on the surfaces of
  neutron stars.

Jack Cohen and Ian Stewart,
What Does a Martian Look Like? (2002)

On 15 April 2019, at 14:12:15 GMT, the ninety-three-kilometre-wide lunar crater Copernicus turned sky blue.

A minute later it changed to turmeric yellow. Forty seconds later it changed to a morbid purple-red. It was an unmistakable signal, a sign that nobody could miss. Aliens had arrived… and as it eventually turned out, they wanted to trade.

No one knew what else they wanted. Communication was impossible. They showed no interest in human science, mathematics, arts or religion. Nor was there any rhyme or reason to the trade objects they wanted.

Forty years after first contact, humanity has spread amongst the stars. There are no more countries, only city states of varying size and power. Aliens are still unknowable.

Humans are very much the junior partner.

Half of Earth's population is content with the situation. The other half wants it changed, some by violence.

Something has to give.

1

It was a bumblebee with a light dusting of pollen and a purposeful air. *Bombus terrestris*, twenty millimetres long, buzzing through the garden at a brisk thirty miles an hour. No reason for any of the three men and two women – all middle-aged and naked apart from the sepia input tattoos on their forearms – sitting relaxed in the morning sun, to see a threat. Everyone knows bumblebees don't sting.

The garden surrounded a two-storey house, mostly wood and glass, on the shore of a lake. Distant hills were already hazy in the heat. A smart-looking jitney bobbed comfortably at the end of a short jetty, another reminder of corporate success. The inevitable armed guards were kept out of sight; nothing threatened the fiction that this was the best of all possible worlds.

Twenty-seven miles away the woman whose mind guided the bumblebee drone cursed briefly and pressed a virtual button off to one side of her visual field. The implant stopped vibrating. The incoming message could wait. Kara Jones focused again on her targets. One of the men, as hairy as he was overweight, apart from the bald area over his forearm keyboard tattoo, noticed the bumblebee as it flew around the table. Apparently no lover of insects, he picked up a sonic repeller that promised to drive away every buzzing, wriggling, many-legged, stinging thing imaginable, and several that weren't. This insect didn't seem to notice. Kara watched as the man apparently considered throwing the repeller at it, changed his mind and returned to the discussion. Everyone knows bumblebees don't sting.

The bee buzzed lazily around the group several times then flew off towards the trees and settled on a branch. A moment later it melted into an expensive cinder.

The three men and two women began to tremble four seconds after the bumblebee cyberdrone had been destroyed. The airborne toxin released by the bee was meant to incapacitate, not to kill.

Kara sat back, the better to watch all five screens, as her fingers raced over controls injected into the visual centre of her brain, visible as a glowing set of buttons and sliders in her visual field – so much easier to use than a forearm input tattoo when controlling a cyberdrone. Controlling one drone was difficult; five drones needed someone with great skill and experience.

Vespa mandarinia japonica, the Japanese hornet that had killed fifty people in Japan the previous year. *Vespa mandarinia* was first seen in England in 2016 and quickly eradicated. That was about to change. Cyberdrone Japanese giant hornets, superbly mechanised, settled on each helpless human, injected large doses of enhanced mandaratoxin and flew away to incinerate themselves. Other cyberdrones carried genuine, and angry, *Vespa mandarinia japonicas* towards some of the guards, released them and flew off to die like their sisters.

Kara caught herself regretting the loss of her drones. "Fuck!" she muttered, aware of identifying too closely with the bots. They were only biotech – disposable creations. Some operators went into shock when their drones died, usually the same operators who gave them names and remembered their birthdays. This did not apply to Kara: the army of the English city states, the English Federation Army, had spent a great deal of money eradicating emotion from Kara's combat persona. Infuriating how every now and then sentiment crept back. She supposed it was a civilian curse, and selected a joss that combined nicotine and amphetamine then inhaled deeply. Back in total control. Time to wrap up the operation.

One of the guards had been stung and was quivering in shock, slumped against a tree. Three dead, genuine Japanese hornets lay crushed on the ground. All the cyberdrones were now cinders, except for one large wasp – *Vespa crabro* – and if its compound eyes were a little larger than usual, for the moment there was no one to notice or even care. It alighted on each of the five bodies, its sensors confirming they were dead.

Kara switched from screen observation to full-meld, a small treat for a successful job. She felt the sun's heat on her body, saw a multi-faceted world before and behind, above and beneath her in a permanent explosion of image, movement and colour. Human brains cannot handle insect sight without a computer to make sense of it all. But for a few wonderful seconds…

She sighed, switched back into screen/observation and checked the area one last time. The remaining guards were already running towards their employers. The autopsies would confirm death by insect sting, corroborated by one hospitalised guard and three crushed hornets with no detectable biological or technological modifications.

Kara keyed in a new command and the wasp together with several back-up drones went somewhere dark to melt. High up in the trees various satellite receivers disguised as twigs – flown in at dusk a week ago by drone starlings – turned to dust. The contract had paid just under one million virtscrip and cost half that amount to set up. Had to be death by accident, had to be all five at once. Being killed in other locations, one by one, would have been far too obvious. But leave a little doubt, she'd been told, make it weird, you know? She'd understood. Nothing so simple as a plane crash – anyway, no more than two of the targets ever travelled together. Instead something so outlandish it could only be genuine bad luck – or an immensely subtle and overly complicated assassination to remind the Big Boys and Girls that something was watching them, something more powerful than they could ever hope to be.

All in all a nice, professional little earner.

Kara Jones was licensed to operate within all English city states, the lands they controlled and foreign city states bound by treaty. She took care of business quietly and efficiently, and was imaginative and flexible; precisely the type of Official Assassin the Contract Bureau valued. There were any number of *un*official assassins, but mostly they were involved with domestic and personal revenge, the sort of job the Bureau would never accept.

It might have become a screwed-up world since the aliens had arrived forty years ago but standards were still maintained and anarchy confined to the areas between the city states that could be relatively civilised, basic back-to-nature or psychosis-by-the-sea, or anything in between, and where the one could become the other with disquieting ease. City state authorities everywhere fought against giving these areas a specific name since that would mean recognition. In what was once Europe and North America they were generically known as Out There and individuals would come and go, to or from the Out.

Kara lit another joss, mild marijuana with a hint of opium, military-wiped her computer of all programs, data and procedures concerned with the hit, and dialled up Control, preferring to use the computer rather than connect direct via her personal implant. "Yes?" she said to the middle-aged, tired-looking man who flashed onto the central screen. "What?"

"You took your time," he complained.

She was glad of the calm the joss brought. "Was working. *Your* job to know it."

He smiled like a man concerned with another, more important problem that Kara would never be told about. "Tomorrow, 08:30 Berlin shuttle from London Thames, arrive 10:00, due Main Reception Earth Central Euro 11:30. Have a good trip." He clicked off before she could say anything in response.

Kara dialled up Control again. "What EarthCent branch?" she asked when the tired face reappeared.

"GalDiv. Don't ask me why."

Kara crushed the joss out on the desktop. "I don't

do aliens," she said, "you know that," and took a deep breath of the stale air. She'd run the last two jobs from bland hotel rooms like this – anonymous conveyor-belt hotels with a fast staff turnover – and longed for the outdoors. Seeing the lake and the hills through the eyes of her technologically enhanced wasps had only made the longing worse. Maybe she'd spend a few days at the cottage on the Dart river, safe in Exeter City territory and where her neighbours thought she sold high-tech around the world. She'd sail and go walking through the lawless Dartmoor Out.

"I told them," Control said. "They already knew."

"You think they want me to kill a free spacer?"

Earth Central's Galactic Division controlled eighty per cent of human expansion throughout space and made no secret of wanting to control the rest. The free spacers based Out There, in the Wild, rather than under the controlling aegis of the cities, were branded a threat to civilisation, even if civilisation now included several alien species and any number of weird, human space settlements.

Control winced at the word "kill". He'd have preferred to hear "handle" or "expedite". "Who the hell knows? You can always say no."

She scented a sourness in the air: her own sweat and adrenalin tainted with anger. "You going to ask about it?"

"I know it went okay. I monitored you." He clicked off again.

Kara shrugged then typed instructions and watched as her computer – the size and shape of a small cider apple – crumbled into metallic and plastic dust. The screens did the same. Nothing could now connect her with the Bureau and the accidental death of five business people planning a pharmaceutical cartel powerful enough to dominate the industry. She brushed the debris into a plastic bag, went to a window and looked across the neighbouring roofs for a moment before slipping the catch. A moment later a plume of expensive dust polluted the afternoon air and a small, empty plastic bag fluttered away on the wind.

Kara yawned. She stood, stretched and walked into the bathroom. She stood five foot nine, with the long-muscled, explosive build of a jumper, long or high. With the right clothes she could be whatever was needed: an old woman begging in the street; a society woman with enough sensuality to make gay men and straight women wonder if they were missing out. Her skill was one that could never be taught, only refined: the ability to become part of the scene, whatever it was, the stranger who no one noticed because her body language, clothes and attitude were those of a local. She could also be supremely forgettable, withdrawing into herself, become a grey person of no possible interest to anyone.

Seven hotel staff had come into contact with Kara and while all would vaguely remember a dark-haired woman in her early thirties, none would be able to describe her face. No fingerprints, pheromones, bacterial profile or DNA were on file with any official or private agency. Her army records had been sealed when she transferred to the Bureau, which guaranteed total anonymity for client and assassin alike. There was no threat of comeback from law enforcement but there could be a problem if the surviving family or friends discovered the truth.

Kara had long decided that all things bad were mostly the aliens' fault. They were obviously more advanced, with all manner of marvels to trade... and so had begun human society's great meltdown: people stopped listening to their national governments. If the aliens ignored kings, queens, presidents, politicians and celebrities, why should humans remain deferent? If the free-roaming aliens – whom many regarded as gods – didn't care about social or legal status, why should anyone else? Meanwhile most religions had dissolved into paranoid fundamentalism or a vague appreciation of "something nice somewhere out there, maybe". With the death of government came the dissolution of the nation state as all the various tribes asserted their independence. Only the cities survived.

The cities had been run by their own people, and were often considerably older than the country they belonged to. Within thirty years of first contact the world had become a place of city states. Some, like those in England, Europe and North America, formed trade and defence associations. A few hundred years down the line and perhaps they would become empires, even democratic countries.

Other city states were isolationist, often aggressively. Global security had to be preserved and so Earth Central – the old United Nations but with teeth – was born and became the world's policeman. Based in the former UN building in New York, theoretically controlled by the world's most powerful city states, in practice EarthCent was independent. Like any other organisation its main drive was to survive. The best way to ensure survival was to control Earth.

Meaning that EarthCent would eventually be over-thrown by the very people it claimed to protect.

The Paris Incident occurred a year after EarthCent was formed. An alien Gliese entered a bar and exchanged a large black box of unknown metal for two hard-boiled eggs and a stale croissant. This somehow – the details were unclear – resulted in the bar owner vanishing and the Arc de Triomphe floating three metres above the ground. It didn't go anywhere but equally it never came down and EarthCent suddenly acquired a Galactic Division responsible for everything alien. There'd never been another accident like the Arc de Triomphe; humans had learned how to control the various updown-field generators – the name, originally a joke based on the fact that the devices controllably moved things up or down in a gravitational field, had gone viral – even if no one knew how they worked. All updown-field generator technology was deemed GalDiv property. The penalty for illegal possession was death, no trial, no last request. Updown-field generators allowed anyone to go anywhere on Earth and do whatever they wanted. Using the devices, space utility transports – their design inevitably more practical than aesthetic – could simply float up and out of Earth's gravity field then turn on their alien-provided netherspace drives to slide into the amorphous realm of netherspace. Landing was just as simple.

GalDiv was also responsible for stopping terrorists: there were many humans who wanted the aliens gone; some who believed them inherently evil, and a few curious to watch them die. Or simply to see if they could and if so would the ones left behind cry?

Overall, humanity was happy. Aliens needed humans as much as humans needed them. Why else would they be here?

For Kara it was all wrong. She'd take the advantages that came with alien contact, while still convinced that humanity was stagnating or worse, becoming infantilised, overly dependent on creatures they didn't understand and probably never would. But then she had a personal reason for distrusting, even hating, the trade that allowed humanity to play among the stars. A reason experienced as a sharp sadness that often hit when she was most at peace.

TWENTY DAYS EARLIER?

Tatia woke suddenly, unsure what had disturbed her. Her cabin on the space utility transport LUX-WEM-YIB was silent. She turned over in the double cot and automatically reached out a hand. The other side of the mattress was empty and cold. Tatia was relieved, remembering the previous night. They'd made love, Juan as attentive as usual. But Tatia had become a little suspicious of that same-old, same-old attentiveness, as if he was following a script.

Afterwards he'd casually mentioned that the other Pilgrims had donated all their money to the colony-to-be. And that as Consort to the Understander of Aliens, Tatia should really do the same. Although – as she'd tensed angrily in his arms – perhaps not all of her money. But enough to establish her amongst his followers. When Tatia said she was naturally anti-establishment, especially with Pilgrims, Juan had said she really didn't have any choice. The Pilgrims expected it and deep space, netherspace, was no place to make enemies. At this point Tatia had understood she'd been had in more ways than one. The subsequent screaming row had seen Juan stomp off to seek solace from his Pilgrims.

It is a truth universally acknowledged that a young woman in possession of a large fortune is an opportunity for anyone on the make. Tatia's adoptive parents were both dead by the time she was seventeen. Within five years she'd met every type of low-life imaginable. Some were fun, some scary, some sad. All had been after her money as much as her body. Which for an attractive, blue-eyed and natural strawberry blonde had been a rude awakening. It wasn't naivety crushed so much as a suspicion that her destiny could only involve other equally rich people.

It was at a friend's fundraiser that she'd met Juan Smith. She'd heard about him before, all Seattle had. The self-proclaimed Prophet and Understander of Aliens who claimed to have a special relationship with the Gliese, Cancri and Eridani. Who also claimed that personal AIs were evil and forbade his followers – he called them Pilgrims – from having one. Who believed that aliens were gods who would lead humanity into a new, spiritual age. But the message had been lost by Earth's rapacious desire for alien technology. The only answer was a new colony world where human and alien would live simply alongside each other in spiritual harmony. Such a world had been found and soon Juan Smith would lead his Pilgrims to a shining future. GalDiv had supplied all the necessary equipment and supplies, as they did for every colony group. All that was needed was the cost of the trip itself and to continue Juan Smith's work on Earth.

Tatia had never met a prophet, self-proclaimed or otherwise. She'd expected someone austere, elderly, fanatical. But Juan was in his mid thirties, tall and slim, with thick, wavy hair to his shoulders, a sensual mouth and the most penetrating black eyes she'd ever seen. Here was a man who radiated excitement and laughter. A man who, when she'd finally got some alone time with him, had politely declined her donation. "We just met our target. But if the mission needs help in the future, hey, we'll be sure to come calling!" She'd thought he had the sexiest voice.

Tatia was between lovers, and bored. She'd agreed that life was becoming too mercenary and that personal AIs were wrong — having told her own, recently acquired AI to go offline. She had gracefully eased Smith away from the party for dinner at a quiet restaurant overlooking the rippling darkness of Elliot Bay and across to the quiet lights of Bainbridge Island. First pleasant surprise: Smith had perfect manners and knew his way around a classic French menu. Second pleasant surprise: he might have strange ideas about aliens, but they had so much in common. They liked the same music and art, books, vids and vid-stars. Loved sailing. It seemed very natural, almost pre-ordained, to take him back to her penthouse in Howell Street. More than that, her intuition had said this was the right thing to do. Tatia's intuition had always been strong but lately had become almost scary in its demands. She'd always been good at inferring her friends' needs or desires, at seeing them as they really were. Of late that had begun to happen with total strangers. Tatia could see someone in the street and feel she instantly understood them better than they understood themselves. The scary part came when the person looked around, alarm writ large on their face, as if aware of being probed. Tatia had no control over this ability. It came and went. How could you respect or even like anyone when you could sense their every weakness? But thankfully no such occurrence with her latest lover. She'd woken the next morning intrigued by the man asleep beside her – but with no particular insight.

And when, later on the second day, Juan had invited her to come to the colony world with him, not to stay but to report back to Seattle, Tatia had found herself saying yes. She would, after all, return home with the SUT that had transported them. And when he'd said that for propriety's sake she must be his official consort, Tatia had stifled a giggle and thought why the hell not. It was all a bit dreamlike. It was a laugh. Her intuition said go, and she'd been in galactic space several times before.

There'd been no time to meet the one hundred and fifty Pilgrims who would make the settlement safe for the undoubted thousands who would follow. For Tatia this had been a blessing. From what she'd seen they were a joyless lot, who clung to fanaticism as if it was all they owned. Nor had she believed many others would follow. Without Juan Smith, the religion would dissolve into quarrelling sects. There'd been a semi-formal, extremely brief consort ceremony in front of the space utility transport. Tatia had figured she'd be away for three weeks, tops. There'd be no trouble with arranging the return trip: the SUT belonged to a galactic transport company owned by her Trust. In a sense she was merely checking out an investment. It was easy to ignore the small voice of her long-suffering conscience when it whispered she was being headstrong and foolish.

Now, faced with her intuition saying that something was WRONG, and faced with a money-grabbing bastard of a crook lover – no, very much ex-lover – Tatia blinked in a three-two pattern to switch on her AI. It was a new one and she still wasn't comfortable with it. Turning it off had been a relief because it was trying out a bewildering series of avatars to find the one that would suit them both. Tatia hoped it wouldn't be the breathy, vacuous-sounding Best Friend Forever the AI had found in some ancient vid programme.

It wasn't. The AI had decided a pleasant but severe-looking woman in her early thirties was more appropriate.

< About time.

> Don't sulk, *Tatia vocalised.*

< If you'd called me on Earth none of this would have happened. To you.

> I don't…

< Lover-boy's got an AI. Surprised? He's also got a criminal record. Three city states – Mexico City, Dallas and Madrid – are trying to extradite him.

> I'm sure he's good at making enemies. *Tatia didn't like being told off by a mere chip.*

< He's wanted for fraud and murder. If only those big-city AIs could get their act together, he'd have been gone long ago.

All inter city-state relations were handled by AIs. Treaties, currency exchange, security matters – humans decided on the overall policy, AIs tried to make it work.

< I'm going to show you something, Tatia. Brace yourself.

A list materialised in Tatia's mind. It was headed with her name. It detailed all her likes and dislikes… everything supposedly held in common with Juan Smith.

> It was a set-up! The bastard researched me!

< He had help. Your friend who threw the fundraiser.

> How do you know?

< Lover-boy's AI is not as smart as it thinks.

>Stop calling him that. Where is he now? *She suddenly realised what her AI had said.* > But I turned you off!

< Stood me down. I can't be turned off. Always working for you. I don't know why she betrayed you. I don't know where Juan Smith is. There seems to be something wrong…

A man suddenly screamed outside the cabin door: a disbelieving scream, as if he couldn't understand why he was suffering so much pain. Then it suddenly stopped, replaced by the low hum of the SUT's PA system. Had to be an accident. Had to be.

And then the PA came to life again, a woman – Tatia recognised the navigator's voice, splintered by tension – saying all passengers should remain in their cabins. Her AI chip relayed the message in parallel inside her head.

I am Tatia Nerein. I do not stay hiding in my bloody cabin! *The obvious place to go was the passenger lounge. Other Pilgrims would be there. She threw on a semi-formal, mood-sensitive white gown, embroidered with various Gliese symbols, and street shoes. Tried calling the control room but the internal comms weren't working. Probably an electrical fault. It was an old and well-used SUT.*

She found Juan lying dead in the passageway leading to the lounge. The right-hand side of his body had been torn away; that much Tatia saw before shock and nausea overcame her and her gown became a mottled red, purple and sharp green, echoing her emotions. Her stomach heaved.

I'd rather throw up over him alive.

She wiped her mouth and spat.

< The SUT's AI has gone mad. I suspect we've been attacked.

> You think?

< Sarcasm ill becomes you. Tell you something else, too. That Consort ceremony you had before going up? It was legal. You die, your fortune goes to the next of kin. In this case, Juan.

> Just shut the fuck up until I say different, okay?

A dozen Pilgrims were huddled together in the lounge. They stood up as she came in, their faces angry, accusing.

"Oh look," someone said. "It's the Consort. Well, that's okay then. Dumb of us to be worried."

Tatia realised that she wasn't popular and held up her hand. It was important to calm them down. If only because they might attack her. "I understand. Juan is dead. But do not worry. I'm sure the gods will help us." *Her robe became a soothing blue; a lie, but faked emotions could fool the material's inbuilt technology.*

The reply was a torrent of accusations, insults and despair. It was Juan's fault – his death deserved – and she was guilty by association. She tried to calm them, desperate to discover what had happened.

"Your fucking gods happened," *a man said and spat on the floor.*

"Not mine – everyone's! Tell me how he died!" *she all but shouted.* "Please!" *Her robe pulsed purple.*

Details were sketchy, but apparently the LUX-WEM-YIB had left netherspace to take a star sighting. A moment later a chariot of the gods had materialised next to them and linked to the SUT. The gods burned their way inside.

Then they killed Juan and another Pilgrim.

"What gods?" Tatia demanded. "Did the two show disrespect? Not Juan, surely?"

"It's the Cancri," said the man who'd spat. "And they're not gods. How can they be? They're just fucking bastard aliens. And all the two did was walk up to them, I was there." *Sometimes the strongest fanatics lose their belief in a blink of an eye, or the death of a friend.*

"It is not for us to question the gods' actions," she said, knowing how weak it must sound.

"It is when they're trying to kill you!"

She asked about the SUT staff but nobody knew what had happened to them.

"Why are you all in here?" she asked.

"We were sort of herded," said the man who'd spat, obviously the group spokesman. "Don't know why." A pause as his eyes flickered past her. "Maybe it does," he said, pointing then shrinking back behind a chair.

Tatia turned and saw a Cancri in the doorway. These aliens were rare on Earth, little known other than what they looked like. Reports from distant human settlements were equally vague. The greyhound-like, striped steed seemed to be grinning at them while its rider, looking like a cross between an eyeless baby and a white maggot, impassively held a slim metal tube in its stubby, hook-like hands.

"I know that dog's coat, it's the one that killed the Understander," someone whispered hoarsely.

Tatia's robe turned red.

Kara stood under the shower and reviewed the morning's work, relieved because success had relied on factors she couldn't control: a lack of wind so the airborne neurotoxin could settle; no one appearing with a fly swatter; the five targets meeting outdoors. Although the latter had not been so problematic: they didn't trust each other and, until agreement was reached, would always meet as a group. Being both outdoors and naked was still an adequate defence against bugging, as long as dampening fields were used to suppress implants.

And they never knew a thing. It was a matter of pride that her targets never suspected they were under threat, beyond the usual paranoia. Multinational corporations, especially pharmaceuticals, had to be viciously aggressive to survive, and so did the people who ran them. The world had become more ruthless and amoral as old beliefs were erased by alien technology. Kara had killed five people and prevented a corporate war and worse.

Her hand strayed unconsciously to the entry-wound scar below her right breast. There was no exit wound. The bullet had fortunately lodged in a rib instead of ricocheting around inside her chest. And now the scar was a reminder of what might have been, although Kara wasn't sure how long she'd have survived domestic bliss. The one serious relationship she'd had almost killed her, although it had started so well...

"So I'm to be your Number Two," he'd said that day six years ago, almost managing to hide the disappointment. Fieldcraft and Weapons Skills A1 was designed to discover snipers with that indefinable something that could never

*be taught, a natural meld between sniper, surroundings,
weapon and death. Those who lacked it but otherwise did
well became a sniper's minder and spotter. Indispensable,
but not the real thing.*

"If we get on," she'd said.

"I will look after you the best I can."

It had been her decision. "Let's see how it goes."

*She'd seen him all but naked, knew he was more athlete,
more warrior than over-muscled gym-bunny. His eyes had
glanced briefly into her soul and he had the devil's own
subversive laugh.*

*They'd slept together within a week. Not shocking or
unusual; the occasional sniper team even had sex in the
field; against regulations but diverting after days curled up
in a hide. A quickie to relieve the tension, one of them always
searching for a possible enemy, orgasm at most a two-second
distraction. But this had been hotel love-making, lasting
for hours and with the final accent on love. No regulations
against that, only common sense and tradition. Do not fall
in love with a comrade because their safety will become more
important than the mission. Do not fall in love with anyone
who cannot separate the personal from the professional. He
at least would never make the same mistake again.*

Kara told herself the wetness on her cheeks was water
and cupped her breasts, shivering slightly.

"*Le petit mort,*" she murmured. After she'd killed,
Kara often died several times in one night. It wasn't
uncommon. Back in the army, there was a rumour
that people became snipers to improve their sex lives;
because the kill had to be done coldly, without any

emotion, when the release came it could be truly epic. Kara wasn't always so sure. There were times that music or the classic TV programmes she loved seemed to do the trick… a long, slow release of tension rather than an explosion. One sniper had sublimated his need by building a model Colosseum out of matchsticks. Another would get passing-out drunk every so often, always on his own in case authority learned about it. Authority eventually did, of course, and the man had been sent on rehab. Returned a lifelong abstainer but with his sniper's edge blunted by guilt.

But this was one of the times that Kara needed sex to relax. Not in the sense of being dominated, almost punished, because of the people she'd killed. Instead as an affirmation of life. It was her time to give and she always tried to ensure that her partners – never more than two; she needed to be the centerpiece – found ecstasy in her arms. Kara was professional to her core.

She dried herself, applied the lightest of cosmetic touches, dabbed a little perfume here and there and went to get dressed. She wasn't sure if she wanted a man, a woman or both, so she chose a loose, flowing garment that showed nothing but suggested a lot.

It was in a small, intimate pop-up bar in Covent Garden that she saw the Gliese. A moment before she was deep in a promising conversation with a man and another woman, all three initially strangers, when she realised the rest of the bar had fallen silent. Kara looked casually around and saw the matt-blue helmets and uniforms worn by Galactic Division's guards and instinctively knew what they were protecting, even if it was hidden by customers staring down in fascination

– and some in fear – at what looked like a metre-high mound of wet leather with three bony arms.

Then she heard the sound.

"*G-g-g-g-l-l-l-l-l-eeze.*" A nasty, wet, gobbling noise that no one had ever deciphered. It could have been a word, a warning cry or simply an alien fart. It was the sound the Gliese often made and to no discernible pattern, and was how they had got their name. Her potential bed-mates were pushing forward. Kara stayed put. She knew exactly what a Gliese looked like. It was not pretty. But, as Kara knew, it was easy to kill.

"Stand back," ordered a GalDiv guard. "Let it go *wherever* it wants."

No one argued. GalDiv had much the same reputation as the Bureau and the rules were clear: do not upset a Gliese or the guards will hurt you. How do you know if a Gliese is upset? Because the guards hurt you. Threaten one and they'll kill you. Besides, like other aliens the Gliese could make a person rich. There was some artist, who'd been unknown until one of those Eridani aliens had followed him around for months; now his artworks were sought the world over.

There was no discernible pattern or logic to alien–human trades. An alien would indicate an object it wanted and offer something unknown in return. What they wanted could be as mundane as a half-eaten apple or as massive as Tower Bridge. What they offered rarely made sense nor could you spend time figuring out what it was. Business was done then and there or the alien moved on.

GalDiv tried to supervise all trades – part of the

reason for the guards – but while aliens mostly used the designated space access points, they could also show up anywhere, unescorted and ready to do business. A person could make a fortune in ten seconds – or be left with a piece of useless junk – but the risk could be even greater. The entire population of a small Alpine village near Berne had vanished when someone did the wrong thing with the featureless metal spheroid that a snake-like Eridani had exchanged for a used fondue set. The strange – and horrible – thing was the subsequent sound of voices screaming for help, a little indistinct, as if the invisible victims were just around an unseen corner. The metal spheroid had been taken into space and dumped into an unimportant star, and the Alpine voices stopped. Another Eridani accepted an eighteen-carat wedding ring inscribed D ∞ J for a piece of twisted metal that made D feel unaccountably happy and content – despite being in the middle of an ugly divorce – simply by looking at it. Soon twisted replicas, which had the same effect if cast in copper or iron, were on sale in all good drugstores as a cure for depression. No one knew how they worked. Psychiatrists and Big Pharma tried to get them banned but those awkward curves and angles eased the worries of most people: all ages, all sexes, all cultures. It was as if the aliens knew humans better than humans knew themselves.

There were to be no money-miracles in this Covent Garden pop-up bar, though. The Gliese paused then turned and flowed back out into the street, as always closely surrounded by its guards.

"Wow!" said the woman as she rejoined Kara. "That was incredible! Weren't you interested?" The woman was in her twenties, a green-eyed blonde with an easy, almost innocent prettiness and a firm body.

"They just don't... don't look smart," the man said. He was a little older than the woman, athletic with brown hair and – again – easy and forgettable good looks. "It's like a pile of old leather. Wonder why it came here?" But he already knew the answer: no one knew why the Gliese did anything. They never requested a bodyguard for a night on the town. They would simply set off, either oblivious or uncaring if the guards came along. It wasn't as if the Gliese were armed, either. No ray-guns, no impenetrable force fields, no psychic powers. Not as far as anyone knew.

"You ever, well, thought about..." the woman asked Kara. "I mean, if it was the only way, would you?" She was talking about the Gliese–human trade that sent humans to the stars.

"No," Kara said, "never."

"I would," said the man. "If I was dying or something."

Kara sighed and stood up. "I gotta go."

The other two looked at her in surprise.

"But..." said the blonde.

"I thought..." said the man.

"You'll talk about aliens and getting rich all night," Kara said.

"Not *all* night," the blonde – whose name Kara had already forgotten – said and smiled. The innocence went away.

"Once would be too much," Kara told her and pushed her way through the crowd to the door. Most of the bar's customers had been born, like Kara, after the aliens arrived. They'd never known another reality. The older customers looked awkward or hostile. They'd go back to their families and either not mention the Gliese in the bar and perhaps get asked why they were in a bad mood, or rant all night about how much better it was before. She wondered how many families sat cosily around the dinner table and talked about aliens, other than as a source of riches. Kara didn't know much about families. Her parents had been killed in an alien-artefact incident; there'd only been an adored older sister to look after her, a sister willing to do anything to give Kara a future. *"Don't worry, Kas, it's really safe. And think what fun we'll have with the money!"* It wasn't safe and they'd never had fun again.

School hadn't gone beyond Aliens 101: what they looked like and their names. It was surprising how uninterested most of the children had been. There was so much else to thrill them, like the new colony worlds or a stream of technology more fascinating than the beings that supplied it. It was as if children instinctively knew that aliens were only messengers, galactic servants, and not as important as whoever owned them. *And maybe*, Kara thought as she walked into a semi-deserted street, *the instinct is right. Maybe aliens are only scavengers.* Unlikely and not a new concept. Still, even the faintest possibility of being right made her feel better.

The street was a mix of established and pop-up stores – the latter hoping to make money from the latest short-lived fad – which effectively summed up the world's economy. There were the big international guys, like Pharma or IT, who'd be around forever; and the rest grabbing at success whenever, however they could. Kara paused to look at a window display of expensive outdoor clothing, a closing-down sale advertised less than a month after the pop-up shop had opened. She tapped her tattooed left arm twice in quick succession, then once. A menu materialised a few inches in front of her face, something only she could see, since her personal AI chip was linked directly to her optic nerve. She blinked rapidly to navigate the menu, came to a rolling newsfeed and saw the report of the tragedy: five people killed by Japanese hornets. Police in protective clothing were searching for the nest – which they would discover half a mile from the house. Finding a nest in Japan and secretly moving it to England had been the hardest part. Also the most necessary: those who were meant to be suspicious must also be made nervous, even awed, by the killer's expertise.

"Aliens piss you off, right?"

Kara spun round as the figure of a middle-aged man in a business suit materialised on the pavement. He was smiling as if they shared a secret. Slightly protruding eyes and thin lips gave him the look of a bombastic frog.

"Most people think it," the man said, the words not quite in sync with his mouth. "And you know what? They're starting to say so."

Kara sighed as she recognised Len Grafe, the head of Human Primus. She accessed the menu again, scrolled down for a surveillance report and saw the figure was generated from a projector on an opposite wall. She disliked holographic advertising as much as aliens, while Grafe's smugness made her want to punch him. She sent an illegal command; the projector sparked then began to smoke and the figure vanished.

Next she used worldmesh – which had evolved from the discredited Internet – to check her home: a Merc jitney the size of an old-style van, hydrogen fuelled like all road vehicles, 190 kph top speed but when securely parked would unfold into a studio apartment at the touch of a button. Common enough in a city where people were fed up with the cost of housing, with vehicle parks now offering security, bathhouses, laundry, shops and repairs like any yacht marina. The Merc was more sparse than the hotel room, and she could easily afford a two-bed apartment instead, but it suited her to be transient. A settled home might give her space to remember. And, it would be easier for someone to find her.

Kara rarely parked in the same place for more than two nights. Partly for security and partly because staying any longer meant that it might become like a home, with neighbours and everything else she didn't want. There'd once been a home and then her sister went Up and Away.

Her chip linked to the park's security system. The Merc was okay, still parked between a gene-tech co-operative's bespoke truck-home/laboratory and an antique bus belonging to a troupe of acrobatic jugglers. For a moment Kara wondered if it was too late to run away and join a circus – a thought interrupted by a man's amused voice inside her head:

< *Something wicked this way comes.*

She'd turned off her avatar's visual weeks ago. Based on her lifestyle and taste in entertainment it had manifested as a tall, dark, male commando with a fondness for cross-dressing and old movies.

The link between a person and their AI chip – the modern equivalent of the pre-alien keyboard and mouse – avatars helped prevent people imagining that their AI could read their thoughts. It couldn't. However, it could take a very educated guess, which was closer to telepathy than many people wanted to get, especially as part of the chip technology was derived from alien science. Avatars preserved the illusion that the chip was somehow separate from, subservient to, the person it served. When someone first got a chip, the AI would manifest a series of different personas until the person made a choice – although it could be changed at any time. Again, the illusion of control. After only an hour or so the chip could supply the avatar most likely to succeed. Many humans came to regard their avatar as a personal friend. There was even a fringe group demanding equal legal status for both avatar and host.

Kara hadn't wanted an avatar – although most people doted on them – but she had little choice, since they were integral with the personal chip. It was necessary for a stochastic, continual learning interface, the salesman had explained, and she should think of it as her own personal AI. Kara didn't believe in artificial intelligence, suspecting it was more of a monkey-see, monkey-do construct that flattered to deceive. Sadly, she could turn off the visual but not the audio. For the past few days it had been obsessed with Shakespeare

– last month Humphrey Bogart, which was fine, her favourite antique actor – but life was dramatic enough without someone declaiming theatrically in her head. Kara blinked twice hard to disengage her chip – it never slept – and looked up to see the blonde woman from the bar walking towards her. She was alone.

"Hoped I could persuade you," the woman said.

"Where's…?"

"Not my type."

"Nor mine."

"Am I?"

The full force of Kara's personality surfaced. "Only one way to find out."

The blonde woman actually blushed. "It's why I'm here."

"Nothing about aliens," Kara warned. Perhaps a one-on-one would be better, more intimate. But since when was intimacy so important? Was the avatar's Bogart persona still in her mind? "It's my party, right?"

"Whatever you want."

All you have to do is whistle. "I'm at a nearby hotel."

Never go to a strange place with a stranger. Not ideal, but safe.

2

Marc Keislack stared at the spherical display unit. On the other side of the crystalline metal his nanoforms were mixing and interacting like miniature weather systems. Each one was a different colour, separated from one another by a gooey transparent nutrient medium.

Despite the seals around the tank – still necessary when anyone was mucking around with nanoforms – the slightly vinegary smell of the nutrient medium hung in the air of his studio. Light from the large windows at the far end of the room illuminated the space. Dust hung and glittered in the buttresses of light, despite the best attempts of his cleaning bots to eradicate it. Outside, the rolling Welsh hills were illuminated by a low sun. Cows stood in small groups in the field that bounded his property, and larks drew scrolling lines across the deep blue of the sky, while inside the studio he was waiting for his own life – his own artificial life – to decide what it wanted to be. He ran a hand through his long hair. It needed cutting, but he had been so wrapped up in constructing this latest piece of art that he had forgotten about it. He would need to get it cut before the show. His agent, Darla, would insist upon it. "Don't believe the crap about artists in garrets forgetting to eat or wash and still being romantic," she'd told him at his last show. "People who can afford your art expect short hair and an expensive cologne. And don't fall on the vol-au-vents like you're starving." She'd paused at that point, then added: "Of course, if there's an alien in town, wanting to pick up some art in exchange for some new kind of battery or something, then all bets are off."

"I was followed around by an Eridani for three weeks, remember? It took five art installations, leaving behind something GalDiv took away for deep investigation." He'd laughed bitterly. "Who knows why the damn aliens trade anything?" He didn't say – it wasn't necessary, there were plenty who'd say it for him – that it was the Eridani interest that had made the unknown Marc Keislack rich and famous.

Darla had smiled tightly. "Of course I remember, darling. And I would have gotten you a much better deal – even with an alien." She didn't say that being the alien's darling – the Eridani and more recently the Cancri still traded for his and *only* his artwork, no other artists need apply – meant that Marc didn't need an agent at all, only a lawyer and an accountant.

He'd smiled back more gently. "That I would like to have seen." Keeping alive the polite fiction that Marc Keislack was as talented as any other successful artist and not just a lucky bastard.

Now he glanced around the studio, at the works that were going into the show, which his agent wanted to call simply *Here*. Across the far side of the room was a tank of seawater in which luminescent *Aurelia aurita* the size of coins drifted, coming together and apart in a thousand different shades of colour, as dictated by the artificial genes that he had spliced into their DNA. The jellyfish were effectively immortal, as far as he knew. As long as they floated in a nutrient-rich broth and had a little natural light they would just keep on going, moving and glowing, forming different pictures as they did so. Given the human mind's amazing ability to see patterns in chaos, if you stared into the tank long enough you would start to see faces staring back at you: grimacing, laughing, screaming. Marc had given it the title *All Human Life Is Here*, and Darla had said that if he parted with it for less than a hundred and fifty thousand virtscrip she would part with *him*, violently.

His gaze skipped to another piece: this one an earlier, unsold work. It was a self-portrait entitled *My Life Is Here*. Artificially grown muscle, fat and skin tissue, generated from stem cells taken from Marc's own bone marrow, had been carefully arranged over a brass skull on a stand inside a transparent case. The flesh had been crafted to mimic his own face, but initially aged a hundred and twenty. The cells had been programmed in such a way that they would gradually alter over time: the skin becoming firmer, the fat reduced and the muscles better defined. His face would get younger as he, the artist, grew older. It had already regressed to the age of 115, although it had to be said that there was very little difference visible between now and when it had started. There would be a day when the two of them – the artwork and the model – would cross, and one of the terms of the sale was that Marc would, on that day, sit inside a similar case next to it, wherever the purchaser was displaying it, making himself part of the work. Another one of the terms of sale was that when the face had developed to infancy the work would be destroyed – a stipulation backed up by automatic cell death programmed into the artwork's genes. The aliens wouldn't understand the fine print, of course, but he didn't care. The art was the art.

"Wonderful," Darla had said when he had told her about the idea. "A reversed *Picture of Dorian Gray* reproduced with technology."

"The what? Who?"

She had glanced at him, frowning. "Never mind. Just keep coming up with ideas." Marc had no interest in the past, only his own present and future.

A momentary eddy in the tank beside him caught his attention. At the border between the mass of blue nanoforms and the transparent nutrient medium they existed within, small vortices were forming. It looked like the kind of effect one saw at the edge of fractals, or coastlines on a map. The nanoforms themselves were artificial, of course, but based on genetic material harvested from slime moulds of *Fuligo septica*. Their behaviour was pre-programmed in their simplified DNA and based on a handful of simple rules. Were they surrounded by others of their own colour, or by those of another colour? Were they in an area where nutrients were plentiful or sparse? Were they on the outside of a mass, exposed to ambient light, or on the inside, in darkness? How old were they? The rules themselves were simple, but the outcomes would be anything but. In computer simulations the virtual nanoforms automatically came together in small groups, which acted as individual entities: moving as one, co-operating with others of their kind, absorbing others not of their kind and then producing smaller versions of themselves which grew over time. It was emergent behaviour, not pre-programmed, but it seemed to replicate many of the features of more complicated life forms, all without instinct or intelligence. This one was entitled *All Life Is Here*, and he was still waiting to see how it developed.

A blue ball appeared in his vision, as if it was floating near the wall. It moved slowly up and down. Some people preferred avatars, which Marc distrusted; some preferred audio or vibratory cues, which Marc found distracting. Instead he'd had his cortical chip illegally hacked by a woman out in the Wild so it interfaced using colours and shapes. Someone was at the door. He felt a stab of anger. He didn't like visitors; didn't like anyone, really. "Show," he instructed the house AI.

A picture formed, apparently in mid-air. A man was standing outside: a youthful mid-sixties, hair dark and jaw firm. He was wearing a suit that was cut in a modern style – tight double-layered lapels and sleeves that were subtly shaped to imply muscle movement beneath.

"Can I help?" Marc said into the air. Trying to inject a sense of *Go away please* into his tone. The house AI took his words and replayed them outside the front door.

"Anson Greenaway," the man replied. He was staring away from the house, towards the hills. "I'd like a moment of your time. Please." He had a deep, easy voice and an American accent that for all its relaxed tone also spoke of power. This was no door-to-door salesman.

Marc paused for a second. His brain was still considering the art installations – tweaking details and thinking about the surroundings that would display them to their full advantage. He didn't want any distractions, even if it led to a sale. Darla would kill him for even thinking it, but he had more than enough work on at the moment. "I'm busy," he said eventually. "I suggest you see my agent."

Greenaway smiled; lips closed, not showing his teeth. Maybe it was the resolution of the imaging system, but the smile did not reach his eyes. "I've come a hell of a long way to see you."

"And without an appointment," Marc replied. Over the man's shoulder he could see a rental jitney parked on the road. "It won't take more than forty minutes to Cardiff Airport, another half hour to London and then the ramjet to New York."

"Why do you think I came from NYC?"

"Cut of your suit," Marc replied. "Different to those laser cut by the million in Shanghai. It's pure New York, in the lapels and the scalloping of the trouser legs." He didn't say that only the seriously rich and powerful wore suits. Most people wore casual clothing, often fashion and fad free.

The visitor frowned, and glanced downwards. "I had no idea I gave so much away."

"Are you interested in buying one of my pieces?" Marc asked after a long pause during which the other man made no move towards his jitney.

"If necessary."

Marc sighed. His mood was ruined, but there might be some money in it. Besides, the nanoforms might *not*

44

do anything interesting for hours. Or days. Or ever. Sensing the intent in his gesture, the house AI opened the front door. Greenaway's throat moved as he subvocalised: probably signalling to his own AI chip that Marc's house AI could have limited access to it.

A few moments later he heard Greenaway approaching the studio. The delay had given Marc enough time to type instructions into the sepia tattoo on his forearm, instructing his own AI to check out his visitor. He could have set the AI to accept subvocalised instructions, like most people, but he didn't like the idea of having someone else around him all the time, even if it was just a listening presence. Typing instructions suited his isolationist streak perfectly. For similar reasons, he didn't have a visual or aural avatar for the AI either. Darla had told him once that he had a problem with someone else's artistic interpretations being shoved into his mind. That might have been true, but her barbed comment had started him thinking about developing a range of surreal or abstract virtual avatars for people to use. For a hefty price, of course.

As Greenaway appeared in the doorway, guided by arrows the house projected into his retinas, and looked around, amazed, at the artworks on display, Marc was reading the results from the projection on his own retinas, words hanging in mid-air and glowing slightly. There was some general background information, like the man's age and credit rating – sixty-six, triple A – but that was all. Strange.

Glancing back at Greenaway, Marc noticed that the man was looking him up and down. It was only when he glanced down at himself that Marc realised he wasn't wearing any clothes apart from a pair of socks that kept his feet from getting cold on the solid stone floor.

"Not much to say about *your* choice in clothing," Greenaway said.

Marc shrugged. "I haven't seen another human being for a week or so. What's the point in wearing anything?"

Greenaway indicated Marc's socks. "There's an old joke about the world's most beautiful woman going to visit the world's greatest artist. 'Would you like to paint me naked?' she asks. He pauses for a long time, looking agonised, then says, 'Can I keep my socks on? I need somewhere to keep my brushes.'"

Marc frowned, confused. "Brushes?"

"Never mind." Greenaway glanced around, and his gaze fastened on a chair.

"Sit down, please," Marc said. "I'll fast-chill some wine."

"Not for me," Greenaway said. "Alcohol and the flight back would send me to sleep for the afternoon. I hate that." He looked around with interest. "I saw one of your pieces in Munich. It had cockroaches crawling up and down a wall. Chips were embedded in their brains, right? And linked to video camera pointed into the gallery so people suddenly found their faces reproduced on the wall by a thousand crawling insects." He smiled slightly. "I would say 'immortalised', but the pictures only lasted a few seconds. I doubt the cockroaches lived more than a couple of weeks. Didn't you win an award?"

Marc winced. "The cockroaches were a nightmare. Damn things have some kind of biological aversion to doing anything in a coordinated manner. They kept fighting the remote control. Left to themselves they'd have been off in all directions, so I had to ramp up the power but that burned their brains out after a few days. Well, I say brains, more like a bunch of nerves coming together in a nexus. And they were supposed to be sterile, but I kept finding new ones turning up, without chips or antennas. I was never sure if they were reproducing or if others were creeping in from outside, curious about what was going on."

"Still, it was impressive. An insect lover would say ruthless." Greenaway paused, and smiled. "Wasn't there some animal rights group that tried to claim the prize should have gone to the cockroaches, not you?"

"That," Marc admitted, feeling a faint blush of guilt, "was my agent's idea. She's as much of an artist with publicity as I am with life forms."

"You spent a few years Out There, didn't you?" Greenaway asked unexpectedly.

"It's no secret. You sound like you're not sure." It felt as if the man was playing him.

Greenaway shrugged. "They don't keep records." He paused again. "That is, none we can access easily." He'd unconsciously come to dominate the room – in the sense that domination obviously came naturally to him. "Not accusing you. Only curious."

Marc's hand absently brushed his input tattoo. "It was only a few years, and there was a girl involved. Teenage rebellion." Which was the story Darla had invented for him. "Other than that, not really your business, is it?" Who did Greenaway mean by "we"?

"Humour me," Greenaway said. "Please." His voice had deepened. "Did you find the freedom Outers are always talking about?" The Outers claimed the city states were far too dependent on alien technology. They did use off-world tech, but claimed to do so sparingly. But who knew what alien goodies were really hidden Out There?

The memories were still raw, and Marc shied away from them. "Yeah, freedom to fucking starve. In an artistic sense, at least. The food was actually quite good."

"I'll bet you were overfed politics," Greenaway observed. "Outers do like to talk. Still, now you belong to the civilised world. Doing pretty well for yourself, too."

It felt as if he'd been threatened but Marc couldn't figure out precisely how. "I don't belong to anyone. If you don't understand that you're wasting my time."

"You have degrees in genetic engineering and computing," Greenaway continued, ignoring Marc's flash of temper, "but you ended up an artist."

"A prize-winning artist."

"That's true. So what pushed you in that direction? It's not in any of your bios that I can access."

Marc shrugged and looked away, out of the large window. The question made him feel even more uneasy. At the same time he found himself wanting to answer the older man, if only to make him go away. "You like old jokes, right?" he asked. "You'll know that one from pre-contact times? NASA, if you remember who they were, decide that after years of just sending monkeys up into space, they'd finally send a man. So the next flight they fire a man and a monkey into space. A few minutes after launch the intercom crackles, and a voice says, 'Monkey, fire the retros.' A little later, the

radio voice says, 'Monkey, check the solid fuel supply.'
The astronaut is getting a bit pissed off by this stage,
so he radios NASA and asks: 'When do I get to do
something?' NASA replies, 'You're just there to feed
the monkey.' I looked at the way the world was going
and I realised that within my lifetime AIs will be
writing all the code and controlling all the machines.
It's just a fact of technological development: they can
do tasks like that faster than us, and with fewer errors.
I knew I had a choice – feed the monkey or go into
a field that AIs can't manage, like art, the military,
philosophy, or politics. Art was the one that appealed
the most. I had a talent for it."

"And you've done well."

"Thank you." Marc stared at Greenaway for a
moment, still trying to work out what the man wanted.
"Why are you here?"

"I wasn't lying," Greenaway said. "I will buy one of
your works, if it motivates you to join our little team.
Less trouble than putting you on the payroll. Just a
one-off, tax-deductible transfer of funds."

Marc's brain had snagged on the word "payroll".
"You want me to work for you? I don't even know
what you do – it's not in any bio that I can access."

"EarthCent. GalDiv."

Government, then, and one concerned with alien
affairs. "Jesus," he said, "is this some long-term
fallout from the Eridani that followed me around?
Does it want a refund or something? Does GalDiv
really pay tax?"

"Even if the snake did want its money back, it couldn't
tell us. And no, we don't." Greenaway shrugged. "We

can't even communicate properly with dogs, chimps or dolphins past 'Where's the ball?', 'Give me the banana,' or 'Jump for the fish,' and we share DNA and a world-view with them. People were too optimistic when they talked about establishing grammatical constructs with alien visitors, or comparing triangles and getting excited by Pythagoras. Forty years, billions of virtscrip spent, and we still put things on a table side by side to compare their value."

"But they like art. Apparently. Well, *my* art."

"You think? Listen, wanting is not the same as liking. We don't know what they do with your artwork when they get it back home. Wherever the hell that is." Greenaway seemed lost in a momentary reverie, and pulled himself back with an obvious effort. "You ever think about going Up?"

Up as in *into space*. It was a time of short euphemisms. Just as the phrase "Out There" referred to any part of Earth not controlled by the city states, "Up" referred to space travel, whether to the moon, solar system, any of the colony worlds or exploring the wider galaxy. People went Up as casually as they went to the corner shop for milk. Such a little, dismissive word helped gloss over that space travel was not human-invented, but gifted.

Marc shook his head.

"But your family went Up fifteen years ago," Greenaway pressed. "To a very pleasant world not too far away. You could visit." His eyes were watchful, as if he was expecting an admission.

"I've seen the brochures," Marc said quietly and looked away. "The images they've sent back. I suspect life there is harder than it's portrayed, but optimism and that old settler spirit won't let them admit it, even to themselves. No, I like it here on Earth. It might be crowded, but it's fun." He wondered if Greenaway knew why his family had emigrated, and how Marc himself had found out they'd gone. And that Marc was far more uneasy about the emigration than he'd admit to anyone, let alone a stranger.

"They'd be pleased to see you I'm sure."

Marc shook his head. "Not going to happen."

"Why not?"

Marc sighed. The man wasn't going to give up. "Because I have an imagination, all right?" he snapped. "I know the facts. We're dependent on the Gliese for netherspace drives, which we don't understand and can't repair. We're no better than some early settler in a canoe setting off in the general direction of wherever he or she wanted to go and trusting to luck and maybe the stars to get there, with gravity gradients and twisted space instead of tides and currents. One in every forty spacecraft vanishes. Lost or broken. I'm perfectly happy on Earth, thank you. I'll wait until going Up is more like taking a bus than trekking in the Wild."

Greenaway stared at him for a long moment. "I can't fault your analysis of the situation," he said. "But it's too bad. And irrelevant. And they're not spacecraft but space utility transports, SUTs. GalDiv has an aversion to naval metaphors; that's why we use randomly generated trifecta identifiers rather than names for the transports."

"What do you mean by irrelevant?" Marc had a

cold feeling in the pit of his stomach.

"Because we've lost something out there, in deep space, and we want you to go and find it."

Marc saw the ruthlessness beneath the polite façade and understood that Greenaway could and would make Marc do whatever he wanted. For a moment he wanted to punch the man, then he noticed how Greenaway was standing, the air of total control, and, ever the pragmatist, he decided the other man would probably win. But he'd be damned if he'd surrender without a fight. "And if I still say no?"

"Then you lose all this. Shall I tell you why?"

Marc shook his head. "Don't bother. Only too happy to go Up for GalDiv," he said through gritted teeth. Maybe it was time he gave something back – wasn't that what successful people did? And he could do with a break from art.

He decided not to ask for a fee.

3

Not the first time she had woken in someone else's hotel bedroom. It was the first time she'd woken alone. The dark-haired woman was gone.

< *Good morning, dear.* She'd let her new avatar choose its persona based on its perception of her personality, and it had decided to sound like someone's not-too-bright mother; an awkward choice given the circumstances. < *It's 06:30. You have to go home and change before work.*

The blonde was woozy from joss fumes – what the hell had they smoked? – too little sleep and too much sex. She was awake enough to be curious, though. > *The woman who had this suite…?*

< *I'm afraid,* the avatar interrupted, sounding sad, < *I can't help. Some of my memories have been wiped. And all manner of hotel security data just vanished. That poor hotel AI is beside itself. It's all so wrong.*

> *There must be something.*

< *A cash payment for the suite at 05:30, nothing more.*

> *We've got DNA,* she thought, pulling back the sheets.

< *Do you have any idea how hard it is to interfere with an AI's memory? Twice?*

> *No.*

< *You don't want to annoy the people who can, dear. Now, be a good girl and get dressed.*

The vid screen snapped on as she got out of bed. An update news story about a group of pharmaceutical executives stung to death by killer hornets. The nest had been discovered and destroyed. "Like I really care," she muttered, then tried to remember details about last night's lover, and had gotten as far as one that made her tremble when a white-hot spike pierced her brain.

< *You okay, dear?* her avatar asked. < *You whimpered.*
> *Headache.*

A few minutes later she stood under the shower, thinking that a woman who could subvert an AI's memory might also do bad things to the human mind. But given the chance, she'd go with the mystery woman again.

The Berlin shuttle was full of business people and bureaucrats talking numbers and jargon. Kara, wearing a dark, no-frills business suit, feigned sleep in her window seat wondering what exactly GalDiv wanted with her. Her thoughts were cut short when the shuttle banked sharply to starboard. A moment later the pilot explained they'd had to avoid an unscheduled space-departure from an antique oil-rig platform in the North Sea. An unknown group with updown-field generators and presumably a netherspace drive had gone exploring.

It could be the free spacers, those modern-day equivalents of Elizabethan buccaneers, explorers and traders – and sometimes pirates – without any official backing. It was an open secret that they often worked with factions from Out There. Or it could simply be someone who'd got lucky with an alien trade, and had painstakingly built themselves a space-going vessel to go a-wandering, and would probably die out there cold and alone.

"Bloody free spacers!" complained the man sitting next to Kara. "So why are you going to Berlin?" He was in his early thirties and smoothly blond, with the self-possession of a man protected by a corporation or a government department. He obviously assumed the attractive young woman wearing a sober business suit was part of the same bureaucrat-executive cohort and that she'd naturally take this opportunity to network with him.

"You know," Kara said quietly, "that's none of your business," then settled back and closed her eyes, remem-bering the night before. The blonde had been enthusiastic but unimaginative and for a while she'd regretted not including the man. Then a special joss had worked its magic and she'd finally become the partner Kara needed. And after that she'd imported an illegal program into the blonde's AI to ensure that it wouldn't want to remember Kara in the morning.

The memories were far too distracting to be carried into a meeting at GalDiv. Kara opened her eyes again and glanced out of the shuttle's viewport. She could see the trail left by the recently departed and unauthorised space utility transport: a gash in the atmosphere filling in gradually with water vapour. Seeing the trail sparked a chain of thought about the trade in netherspace drives, and where they came from.

The Gliese controlled the trade in the sideslip-field generators – known as netherspace drives – the technology that allowed the user to "slip" from normal space to the weird realm of netherspace and back again. Sideslip-field generators came in three "strengths", each enclosed in a large sphere of an alloy that human scientists said was impossible, but plainly wasn't. The weakest drive powered a transport the size of a large truck, the second one the size of a ferry, the third an aircraft carrier. No one, Earth Central's Galactic Division included, knew how they worked, only how to use them. Any attempt to examine the drive usually resulted in it melting. The few times this hadn't happened the drive appeared to be nothing more than an empty box.

The Gliese traded the netherspace drives for human beings.

Only for human beings.

The humans in question could be close to death due to old age or a terminal disease, or they could be in perfect health. It didn't matter. Eleven people for the family-sized drive, nineteen for the economy model and thirty-seven for the big boy. No one knew whether the prime numbers were significant or what happened to the humans who were exchanged. They were taken off-planet and in thirty years none had returned. However, the Gliese never took any human rations, so it did not look good. One rumour said humans and Gliese could eat the same food, but as no one had ever seen a Gliese eat, or had any idea how they did so, the rumour was obviously of the comfort-those-left-behind variety.

There was no shortage of volunteers. For those from

the more extreme city states it was an alternative to the death penalty. For the terminally ill, the possibility of a cure. For others either an adventure or the opportunity to convert the heathen. And the families of those who went were well rewarded by GalDiv which, in theory, oversaw all transactions. In practice trades were also made in secret, hence the free spacers and the North Sea launch that had led to the male executive muttering resentfully under his breath.

It's a shit situation, Kara told herself, *but what's the choice? People are spread out in this little corner of the galaxy. Netherspace drives keep us together.* That was the official version. One day she might believe it. Meanwhile, everyone – immigrants, SUT staff, explorers – all went Up together.

Sometimes a netherspace drive stopped working and the space vehicle snapped out of netherspace to find itself marooned, adrift in the cosmos. The Gliese always showed up with a spare. How did they know? There was only one problem: the call-out fee. One human, alive and kicking. Pay that and a new drive would be installed. Refuse and you died out there. Most SUTs carried a man or woman who'd been very well paid to be the call-out fee. Some "fees" had made over a hundred trips packaged up in medically induced comas, others had been taken on their first journey. As with everything else alien-related there was no pattern, no rhyme or reason. Nor any explanation for the few SUTs that had simply vanished without trace.

It's not trade, Kara thought fiercely, *it's slavery; it's…* Her thoughts were interrupted by an announcement from the pilot. It seemed that the majority of passengers owned diamond-rated credit cards. Therefore the flight had been given special clearance and would be landing early. Cheers broke out. Some passengers stood laughing and waved their cards, including the man next to Kara. How satisfying that her job allowed her to kill people like him.

Political parties had faded away years ago. *If they hadn't*, Kara thought, *I'd have been an independent anarchist.*

"I don't like aliens," she said, staring down at a Berlin spread out like a vast jigsaw puzzle, so many areas showing green or gleaming silver in the sunshine. The office was vast, with a tropical hardwood desk, two sofas facing across a polished slab of granite and various easy chairs. It could have featured in a design magazine.

"Not a problem," Anson Greenaway said. "Liking them would be a disadvantage."

She turned towards him. Even behind a desk Greenaway wore his authority like a senior soldier who'd known real combat. He wore his very expensive suit as if it was put on at the last minute, without thought. His hands were strong, the nails cut short, no hint of a manicure. Not the usual kind of senior bureaucrat, or a man who matched the carefully designed office. She suspected he was ex-special forces, from one of the American city states. Her intuition said to go carefully. "It's not going to happen," Kara said. "Whatever it is."

"The Contract Bureau assigned you to EarthCent. And they assigned you to us."

She remembered what Control had said. Or rather, what he *hadn't* said. "Except the Bureau has no idea *why*."

He nodded. "That's how it stays. This is purely GalDiv business."

Kara knew the argument was lost. GalDiv controlled eighty per cent of all human–alien interactions. Galactic Division was more powerful than its nominal parent Earth Central, like a child controlling the family fortune while the parents were still alive. "Why not tap me up direct? Why bother going through EarthCent and the Bureau?"

"Why does the Contract Bureau exist? Humour me."

There was something about his voice. Attractive but also challenging. "Corporations and individuals will always kill for profit," she said, trying not to sound like a manual. "We do it for them. Helps keep everything under control, stops criminal mafias getting involved. Reminds people that there is an authority out there, one with teeth." He smiled at this, but not with his eyes.

"That's a crock," he said. "The Bureau *might* prevent business rivalries escalating into all-out war. Except not one business application for an assassination has ever been approved."

Kara could only stare at him.

"Private applications? The same. Never happened."

"Crap! I'd know!"

"All *you* know, Kara Jones, is the Bureau gave

you a home and pays you very well."

"My last assignment—"

"Pharmaceutical executives. You were told they planned a consortium and that the application was from rival companies. Not true."

"Then what the fuck…?"

"The matter concerned a new, highly addictive drug resulting from an unofficial alien trade off-world. Worth billions but not good for Earth or the colonies. Free spacers were also involved. We couldn't let it happen. The corporations wouldn't listen to us. They said it was all lies. They're listening now." He smiled slightly. "The living ones. Nice operation, by the way."

Once again she could only stare at him.

"Figured it out, right? The Bureau does *our* dirty work. You actually work for GalDiv. You always have."

She looked out of the window, needing time to think. Every one of her contracts could have had an alien involvement. There again, so did most of Earth business, one way or another. Even so. Damn it, Greenaway was making sense! Time to assert herself.

Kara walked across the rare-wood-tiled floor and sat in a chair facing the desk. "You owe me an explanation."

"I owe you dick," he said calmly. "But you *are* here for a briefing. Let's start with Sergeant Kara Jones." He looked directly at her. "Age thirty-two. Trained as a sniper with the English Federation Army, London City division. Was one of the best. Resigned three years ago and joined the Bureau. No family. Bisexual. Mild drug use. Enjoys free-climbing, diving and high-altitude parachuting. Doesn't read much but likes music, especially from the late nineties, and old movies."

"That it?" She was genuinely scornful. "You got me here because I'm good at my job, screw both girls and boys, keep fit and have an interest in the past? I know a hundred people like that."

"We know several thousand."

She stared impassively at him as what felt like a small but angry vulture began tearing at her gut, from the inside. Greenaway glanced down at the desktop, where Kara assumed that a hidden display was showing her emotional state. "You have a natural talent we can use. Not the obvious one, either."

"So you say."

"Four years ago, on an English Federation Army classified operation codenamed *Forest Clearing*—"

"I know what it was called, but that's a top-secret codename. You shouldn't even know it." Weak but she had to say something.

He didn't rise to the bait. "You stalked the Gliese for a month."

Somehow she held herself together. "Three weeks and two days."

"There was a riot. People demonstrating against aliens. That's when you killed the Gliese. Then you quit the army."

Kara looked away. She wanted to tell the truth but that would mean uncovering memories that had been nailed shut four years ago.

"What happened, Kara? What happened between you and the Gliese? What made you quit the job you loved?"

She could walk out – but where would she go? The

Bureau wouldn't have her and as a freelance unofficial assassin she could count her remaining years on the joints of one finger. "I heard it die," she said quietly. "In my head."

Greenaway pressed a button and a drawer slid out of the desk towards Kara. "Joss-stick?" he asked. "Or would you prefer Medellín City coffee? Maybe a Northwest Fed Pinot Noir?"

She'd bet it was her favourite joss, too. "Water's fine."

Another drawer opened towards her. "Cairngorm Sparkle okay? There's fresh cut lime." He relaxed back in his chair as if they were two friends discussing old times.

She took out a small bottle and glass, both chilled. Poured. Added a slice of lime. If GalDiv had gone to this much trouble they must want her very much. "I know the natural spring this comes from," she said. "I've climbed there." But he'd already know that.

TWENTY DAYS EARLIER

There was no more killing. The surviving one hundred and forty-eight Pilgrims – adults and children – plus the three SUT staff, who kept to themselves, were herded onto the Cancri space vehicle. Tatia's robe was now mostly a dirty grey.

They were confined in a large hold with water tanks and a bewildering variety of fresh edible roots and plants from Earth. There were eleven large empty barrels, which everyone assumed were meant for human waste. So the Cancri understood human biology – at least, enough to keep humans alive. But there was no knowing for how long. Some of the survivors claimed, a little hysterically, that they were being kept for food. Others that it was all a GalDiv plot to get more sideslip-field generator engines. A few wiser heads repeated one of the arguments in favour of alien–human trade: the aliens were advanced enough to take what they wanted, including live humans. But that didn't mean that aliens valued humans. Therefore the most logical explanation was kidnapping by a rogue Cancri group, possibly for ransom. In the end the Pilgrims lapsed into sullen resignation tinged with fear. If they did talk it was to blame Juan – and to a lesser extent Tatia – for everything.

Tatia's response was that if Juan had been at fault then he'd paid the price.

But so had many others, came the reply, and what had they ever done other than adore the gods who'd given humanity so much?

She said maybe the Cancri weren't real gods, not like the Gliese or the Eridani, or that the Pilgrims had offended them.

"But if they're gods," someone said, "why can't they make us understand them?" Strange how quickly a strong belief, an obsession, could dissolve like a sandcastle against the tide.

As time wore on, the hold began to fill with the stench of human sweat and waste. Tatia spent the time interacting with her AI. She'd discovered it had a store of her favourite vids and music. She listened and watched with her face to the wall. If the Pilgrims even suspected she had an AI they'd probably lynch her.

Operation *Forest Clearing*. It sounded so innocuous, so ordinary. That, of course, was the point of codewords.

Operation *Alien Assassination* was too on-the-nose; Operation *Pointless Experiment* more so.

Kara remembered it as if it had been yesterday. She always would, and sitting there in Greenaway's office she could smell the pine needles and the slight tang of wood smoke in the air. "Follow the Gliese," she had been ordered. "Don't let it become aware of you; same goes for its GalDiv guards. Look for patterns in its behaviour. Imagine you're stalking an enemy; you have to discover what makes it tick." It was the loosest military briefing she'd ever known, and she might even have refused – it was a volunteer job – if it had not been for the very senior and well-respected general who'd personally asked her to come on board.

It wasn't difficult to remain undercover at first, she was just one of a small crowd the Gliese attracted wherever they went, even after forty years. And she had an arsenal of remote cyberdrones disguised as insects, birds, bats and beetles. By the end of the second day she could recognise "her" alien by its mouth flaps, even when it was with other Gliese. On the third day she was told to be particularly observant, but not why. "Her" Gliese behaved exactly the same way as before. Then she was instructed to observe it closely at a specific time.

"Did you figure out why?" Greenaway asked.

"They had to be probing the Gliese with electronics, maybe various gases or chemicals from someone in the crowd, to see if it reacted. There was a rumour the Gliese are telepathic. Maybe something happened at its SUT, an explosion, whatever, and they wanted to see if my Gliese responded."

Greenaway tried to hide a smile at the expression "my Gliese". "Why you, when they had access to all manner of experts?"

"I asked myself the same thing," she said. "I came up with a couple of reasons. One, they wanted to keep it secret because Gliese were hands-off for everyone except GalDiv. Two, snipers have a talent that gets trained up to the max. We observe, we get under the target's skin because that's the only way to succeed and stay alive. No one ever admits it, but snipers go a lot on intuition, gut instinct." She realised how chatty she'd become, wondered if he'd used a truth-tell on her.

"You're right," Greenaway said. "The English Federation Army was going rogue... at least, a small faction was. Couple of generals and their staff were concerned about the threat the Gliese could pose. Some were secret Human Primuses. They tried X-rays, neutron beams, radar; you name it, the Gliese got it. Nothing. Nada. Their skin diffuses all forms of energy. In fact, we're not even sure if that is their skin. Some think it's an environmental suit."

"It's skin. Believe me."

Greenaway sat up. "How so?"

Because by the end of the second week Kara had begun to develop a connection with the Gliese.

"You identified with it," Greenaway said. "Like a hunter and a deer."

Kara was suddenly aware of a strange, spicy taste in her mouth – one that she'd first, hatefully experienced three years ago. She reached for her water, drank deeply. Truth was, she hadn't just identified with the Gliese. She'd bonded with it. "It was more than that," she said.

"I *knew* the fucking thing. I knew its body. Skin."

"Why kill it?"

"Once they'd evaluated it from a distance, and not got any reaction, they wanted to go further. They planned to stage a riot, separate the Gliese from its guards and kidnap the damn thing. I guessed they wanted it in a laboratory. They wanted to dissect it."

"Which worried you why?"

"They were desperate. There was a lot invested in Forest Clearing. Fact is, they were out of their depth."

"You killed it to avoid a scandal?"

Kara looked away. "No."

"You should see something." The tendons and muscles in his throat worked as he sub-vocalised an instruction to his AI.

The recording was projected in the centre of Greenaway's office. The figures were knee-high, so it was easy to recognise the Gliese and its guards, surrounded by an angry throng. Well, paid to be angry, she remembered, with a few special forces soldiers also involved – including Sergeant Kara Jones. The sound was off but she remembered the cries and curses as the crowd surged, the warning shots fired by the alien's guards. One final push separated them from the Gliese. Kara saw herself and three other soldiers in civilian clothes rush forward and began to move the Gliese towards a waiting jitney. Kara remembered how it had felt, as if there were no bones or muscles inside but only a mass of jelly and stringy fibres.

"Computer enlarge life size, group alpha four. Play."

Strange, thought Kara. *I'm feeling relaxed about this*

but I also want to cry. She watched herself, both hands under one of the Gliese's arms, suddenly tense.

"That was when you killed it," Greenaway said.

The tears came. She nodded.

The Gliese seemed to collapse in on itself, arms falling to its side. A thick, black substance oozed from its mouth. Anyone could see it was dead or dying. Kara could remember screaming: "It's dead! Get the fuck out of here! Move!" She could remember the sudden spicy taste in her mouth and knew it was Gliese blood.

The four soldiers piled into the vehicle, which sped off down a side street.

"Computer off," Greenaway said, and then as the figures blinked out, "I understand your superiors were pissed you didn't bring back the body."

"My call."

"You used a thin blade. Equivalent to an ice-pick in the ear, like a mafia hitman in those old movies you love."

Kara nodded.

"How did you know the spot?"

She shook her head. "I just did. Intuition. I do know how to kill."

"Why?"

She wiped her eyes with a plaspaper handkerchief. "It wasn't dignified. What they planned."

"Do better."

"We'd bonded. Whatever they did to it they did to me."

"Okay," Greenaway said, as if agreeing it was a nice day. "You heard the Gliese die?"

"Felt. It was like... like... ice dissolving in warm water, nearest I can get. I had... all these impressions from before, except it wasn't really what it felt or sensed, but my brain trying to understand—"

"It was always going to fail," Greenaway said, his manner now more businesslike and urgent. "Dissect a Gliese and all you find is a load of incomprehensible organs suspended with strands of organic webbing that may or may not be its nervous system in a mass of black jelly. Dissection only works if you can relate it to the human experience and Earth biology. You can figure out how the Gliese moves – but its hearing system? Its sight? We don't know their wavelength range, if they see flat or in 3D or even 4D, whatever that might be. We couldn't find its DNA, although maybe there's *something* does the same job. We couldn't identify its brain. Cellular structure? Gliese cells are like nothing we've seen before. There's nothing we can relate to *unless* the Gliese tell us how they work. And that isn't going to happen."

It took a moment for the significance to sink in. "GalDiv has done an autopsy?"

"A Gliese got splatted by a rock. It insisted on going to a disused slate quarry in Wales, no idea why. A local alien-hater, some paranoid psycho who'd stopped taking his meds objected. Guards shot him, but too late. One Gliese doing a damn good impression of roadkill. Other Gliese never seemed to notice it was gone. There again, how the hell would we know if they did?" He shrugged. "Old news. Anyway, you're going on an errand for us. You're going Up."

"I am?" She raised a supercilious eyebrow.

"I'll tell you about your main mission later, but while we're alone here I'm going to tell you something that I won't be telling your partner." He paused, apparently for effect. "When this mission is complete, I want you to go to the Gliese homeworld."

The floor seemed to tilt beneath her as the shock hit. "*What!*" And what partner?

"You heard me."

"The Gliese *home*world?"

"Free spacers found it a few years ago. They don't know we know. There is a plan, Kara." He glanced at his watch. "I'll tell you more over lunch."

"I've never *been* Up."

"Nor has Marc Keislack. Your new partner." He noticed the stubborn look in her eyes. "Those humans who get traded for sideslip-field generator engines – you ever wonder what happens to them?" He didn't wait for an answer. "Of course you do. Your own sister was a call-out fee."

"Don't." She was surprised at the softness in her voice. "Do not try to use that. Ever." She held his gaze for a few seconds. "You said I had a natural ability, but you weren't talking about my sniper skills. What did you mean?"

"You're a borderline empath, Kara. I've met a few in my time." He paused, staring at her challengingly. Maybe he was expecting her to deny it. "You know it, we know it, and your experience with the Gliese proves it. Paramental powers are on the increase in the general population – running at around 0.5% at the moment. We're suppressing the news outlets, but it'll be revealed by someone soon enough."

"Is it—" She stopped, and swallowed. She'd never talked to anyone else about this before. "Is it alien influence?"

Greenaway shook his head. "The scientists who are studying it – secretly, and under our control – are pretty sure it's because of the AI implants. Somehow the initial surgery, the radiation given off by the chips and the way they snuggle themselves into the brain at a cellular level have a side-effect on the surrounding neural tissue. Epigenetic changes occur in the DNA, activating genes that have apparently been there for millennia but never used. We're studying a handful of telepaths, a few telekinetics, and quite a few pre-cognitives: people who can see the future – at least, dimly. More on that later. You show a medium level of empathy, under certain circumstances. Interestingly, empathy seems to operate cross-species. You might not understand the Gliese or any other alien but you *can* sense them." He shrugged. "Me: I'm not an empath. Nowhere close. I'm not a pre-cog either. But I know what you're going to do now. You're going to say yes. You'll get more details over lunch, when you meet Keislack. Saves me an extra briefing."

"I don't like being pressured."

"Kara." He leaned forward, his expression kind. "It was okay to fix the hotel's AI last night. You'd stayed there as part of an assignment. It was *not* okay to screw a pick-up in what was effectively a work environment. It was even *less* okay to adjust her AI using classified technology. You know there's a movement to declare AIs sentient, with rights?"

"I had no choice—"

"You could have gone to her place. Or your Merc."
And then, answering the unspoken question. "You've
been close-watched for the past ten days. You are the
most maverick, independent and bloody-minded
Official Assassin in the Bureau. You break rules
whenever you like. Which is okay for now because this
assignment is not for someone who goes by the book.
But that independence also makes you vulnerable.
Aside from the death of the Gliese – difficult to prove,
I admit – we have enough to put you away. You'll lose
the Merc and that hideaway park-place on the River
Dart. You like walking Out on Dartmoor. You could
end up living there. Or we could just have you killed.
Like to hear more?"

"*Fuck you!*" she said, the anger tempered by resignation. Greenaway wasn't a man to make empty threats.

"Fuck you, *boss*," he corrected. "And don't fucking
forget it."

They stared at each other for a few angry seconds.

"Are you happy about the alien–Earth trade?" he
asked.

She shook her head.

"Even less with humans bartered for sideslip
drives?" He didn't wait for a reply. "We've known
there were problems with netherspace for over thirty
years. We still have no idea what. Know why? Because
investigating the problem only highlights it. No
one, certainly not EarthCent, wants to admit there's
anything wrong. And no one wants to ask *why* the
Gliese trade humans for netherspace drives." A note of
bitterness had crept into his voice. "So we encourage
the myths. They're being taken to a paradise. To

another galaxy. No one asks if there's any connection with that and the call-out fee." He saw the expression on Kara's face. "I'm sorry," his voice surprisingly gentle. "But you must have wondered yourself."

"I try not to," was all she said, tight-lipped.

"We, by which I mean the top echelon at GalDiv, believe the Gliese might trade humans for safety in netherspace. We have no idea what they want safety from, only that *something's* out there. We don't believe the Gliese are masters of space travel. They didn't develop and don't manufacture it. When you get to their homeworld you'll discover why. We *do* believe that Earth *must* gain direct access to whoever, whatever does. It's the only way we'll stop the descent into slavery. And if we *don't* act, the maniacs will. Len Grafe and his Human Primus in England. The Minutemen in America. Religious fanatics worldwide. Suppose they drive the aliens away? Or maybe the aliens fight back and take what they want, with no trade? Who knows what happens to the colony worlds. We *want* that trade, Kara. We want to be a galactic player, not some pet reliant on its master. You know how many people are retreating from the world, how many are going In full-time?" Another small-word euphemism so common it was harmless. Going "In" was when a person preferred a virtual world to the real one. Some died that way, leaving behind a grieving avatar and the suspicion – surely more faith than fact – that their consciousness still lived in their favourite existence. Until someone turned it off at the wall. Or the batteries ran out.

"Just a fad," Kara said, suspecting it wasn't.

"Got a hundred thousand in London City alone,"

Greenaway said sombrely. "New York and Boston have double that. Increasing all the time. People are just giving up. So, you want to try do something about this? Or go back to your old life?" He left it unsaid that "do something about this" could mean discovering what had happened to her sister.

Kara nodded. "Let's see how it goes," she said. "Question: were you Army?"

He nodded. "Special Ops. Eastern Seaboard Military Union."

Which probably meant Intelligence. "Before that?"

"I spent some formative years Out There." He nodded again. "I was a bad boy. Got caught and given a choice: colony world or the New York City Army."

She'd heard the rumours about conscription in parts of America. "They say some Outers aren't even given a choice. They just get sent Up."

Greenaway shrugged. "Some colony worlds are tougher than others. They need aggression and survival skills. That it?"

"Who the hell is Marc Keislack?"

"Think of him as a man for all seasons." Greenaway smiled, confirming that he knew her avatar was obsessed with the classics. "As far as a military skill set's concerned," Greenaway continued, "he's extremely observant with a strong drive for self-preservation at all costs. Just like you."

4

Marc Keislack sat at the circular table by the window, fiddling with his napkin while glancing around – and underneath – the restaurant. It was suspended above the centre of Berlin, held up by a slim tower built from fullerene in the shape of a sweeping number 7. The restaurant – an elegant oval structure like a flattened Christmas bauble – hung underneath the far end of the upper bar of the 7. It was an impossible structure – the centre of gravity was in completely the wrong place and the fullerene, incredibly strong though it was, couldn't possibly take the weight of the restaurant bubble without snapping in several places. The whole thing should have come crashing down on the envious Berlin restaurant district below. The only thing keeping it up was the same thing that was keeping the Arc de Triomphe suspended a few metres above the Parisian traffic – alien updown-field generator technology. Alternatively, if you believed the adverts, it was the genius of the chef.

The restaurant's floor was transparent, as were the tables. Sitting at one was like taking part in a majestic magic trick. Sparse wisps of cloud floated past underneath and sometimes, when Berlin was bound in fog, the restaurant seemed to float on a milky sea. Whatever the weather outside, a trip to the restrooms could be a trial of nerves. There was no elevator up to the restaurant – that would have ruined the exclusivity – as the fullerene tower was too slim and curved to take a shaft. Instead jitneys transported customers up and down, like diaphanous dandelion seeds floating on the breeze.

The restaurant had no name. Most Berliners just called it '7'. It was the first time Marc had been. Despite his success, he'd never been able to afford it – and his agent had never taken him there. It didn't do, Darla said, for artists to mingle with their potential patrons. Respectful distance had to be kept. In other words, he shouldn't tout for sales behind her back.

He tore his gaze away from the glowing lights of the traffic so very far below and looked down at his napkin. Without thinking he had folded it into a fair representation of the tower and the restaurant. He tried standing it upright, but it wasn't stable and kept falling over, which only made the tension in his stomach worse.

A waiter drifted up beside him. "Another drink, sir?"

"Please."

"Saffron gin, rare phenotype, with high-quinine tonic, Sicilian lemon and Svalbard ice?" Not his own memory, but that of the waiter's avatar.

"Yes. Thank you."

The waiter left. Before Marc could disassemble his cotton sculpture and start on something else, a voice from behind him said: "Very nice. Do you also do unicorns?"

He turned his head. A woman was standing over him. She was tall, with the kind of rangy body that belonged on an athletics track. Her dark hair was long, pulled back from her forehead. Her green eyes stared at him appraisingly. She didn't seem to be having a problem walking on what for all practical purposes was thin air.

Anson Greenaway stood beside her, the man's double-lapelled suit as immaculate as the last time Marc had seen him. The faintly exasperated expression on his face suggested that he'd wanted to get to the table first, but the woman had beaten him to it. That, and her mocking comment, suggested to Marc that she was competitive. It matched her body shape very well, as did the business suit she wore. It was obviously bespoke, Marc noted, and Milan cut. So she had both money and taste, whoever she was. Not really his type. "Napkin origami is just a hobby," he said, staring back at her. "If I was doing a unicorn I'd take genetic material from an Arab thoroughbred, adjust the genes controlling skull shape, inject it into a cell nucleus and get the cell to reproduce."

She smiled, tightly. "You're Keislack, then. The artist." The words "and arrogant bastard" were possibly not far from her lips.

"And this is Kara Jones, the soldier," Greenaway said, pulling out a chair for her. Kara walked around the table and sat down in a different seat. Greenaway slid a chair back and sat down. A waiter appeared at his elbow. Marc had a fleeting sense of having walked into a well-rehearsed play.

"Mr Greenaway – a pleasure to see you again," the waiter said. "Your usual?"

Greenaway nodded. "And a Cairngorm Sparkle for the lady."

"Actually," she said, smiling sweetly, "I'll have a glass of Bombino nero rose, if you have any." It was imported, Marc knew, from an early settled planet in the Pleiades and exorbitantly expensive.

"Of course we do." The waiter sounded offended.

Greenaway glanced from Marc to Kara and back again. His lips twisted slightly. He seemed to be finding the contrast between the two of them amusing. "Thank you for turning up," he said to Marc. "I wasn't sure you would."

"Yes you were," Marc said, feeling a slight burn of irritation. "You told me half a story and left it hanging." He glanced at Kara. "Artists," he said, shrugging. "We can't see a stone without looking under it. Besides, he bought me a ticket. First class."

Marc wondered if Greenaway had told her the real reason he'd been unable to refuse the job, but he decided he hadn't. Greenaway would never share a hold he had over someone.

"An Eridani followed Marc for three weeks," Greenaway told Kara. She looked impressed, but Marc wasn't sure whether it was real or simulated for his benefit. "The alien left Earth with five Keislack works, thus making Marc the latest best thing in the art world. Since then the Cancri have also bought Marc's work, providing Earth with technology that's still being evaluated but looks incredibly valuable." Greenaway placed a small metal box on the table; Marc recognised it from his time in the Out: a device that would shield them from electronic surveillance. "And Kara here has killed a Gliese," he said without changing his tone of voice, "which means that you've both stiffed an alien."

He smiled without humour. "That's all you need to know about each other. For the moment."

Marc sipped his gin and tonic. Part of him wanted to get up and leave, suspecting the man was toying with them and enjoying it. But what Marc had said to Kara was true: he desperately needed to discover the end of the story. Leave now, and he never would. And while Kara was attractive, there was also a sense that she was very dangerous. Marc was intrigued.

"So what are the Eridani like?" Kara asked him. "They don't seem to make it onto the news very much. I've never seen one."

"They're long, like snakes," Marc explained, "but their bodies are segmented rather than smooth. A bit like really thick bamboo. Each segment has a tentacle halfway down, and each tentacle ends in a three-fingered claw-thing. If you look at them head-on you see that the tentacles are in a spiral pattern, each segment offset from the one before and the one after." He made a face. "Of course, you don't want to look at them head-on, because their heads are like open wounds full of white worms, but you can get used to them surprisingly quickly. They prefer forests and woods to buildings – those tentacles are optimised for grasping branches and hanging on, while the bodies are optimised for slipping through gaps in vegetation. That's my theory, by the way – not the official one. They smell like bolognese sauce for some reason."

"Everything smells of something else," Kara said. Her gaze dropped to the table in front of him, and Marc realised that he had been fiddling with his napkin again, twisting it into new shapes. He glanced down, expecting to see that he had made something approximating an Eridani, but instead he had unconsciously fashioned the napkin into the shape of her face: high brow, angular cheeks, hollows for the eyes. He smoothed it out quickly, embarrassed. He was relieved when Kara asked, "Did it show any interest in you? Personally?"

"Just my work. It wouldn't get all that close to me," Marc said. "And I wasn't fussed."

Greenaway sipped at his drink, a vintage rye whisky with Antarctic ice. He placed the glass down on the table, making an audible clunk, either trying to attract their attention or misjudging the transparent table. "Listen. You've both been given enough of the story to pique your interest," he said briskly. "That will now change. What I am about to tell you is only known to fifty other people. If either of you repeat this – and we will find out if you do – *both* of you will be encased in transparent plastic cubes, exactly one metre on each side. You'll need to be folded up, of course. Each cube will have two shafts – one for breathing and feeding and one for shitting and pissing, and you'll be filed away on a shelf until we can trade you to an alien." His tone was the same one he might have used to discuss the weather. "Therefore you both have an interest in seeing that the other behaves. This is not a threat. It is a prediction and a warning. Please heed it."

Marc felt a chill run through his body. He saw that Kara's mouth was set in a stony half-smile and realised it wasn't the first time she'd been threatened. "I'm still in."

Greenaway nodded slightly. No value in reminding

79

Marc he'd long passed the point of no return. "You obviously know there are three types of the Gliese netherspace drive – small, medium and large. "We've discovered a fourth size – micro, fitted inside the larger drives. So if someone manages to take a netherspace drive apart, it's empty – the micro-unit inside slips away into warp space, taking the guts of the drive plus the updown-field generator with it." He shrugged. "That's probably how the Gliese know when a drive has broken – the micro-drive heads back to what I laughingly think of as Gliese Head Office. We have no idea how they then find the SUT."

"And how do we know this?" Kara asked, her expression guarded.

"That's need to know. Suffice to say, we do."

"And who is 'we'?" Marc said, doubting he'd get an honest answer.

"'We' is 'us'. To be precise, GalDiv, on behalf of humanity." Greenaway paused. "And one day the rest of humanity might even know about it too."

"So the Gliese don't trade micro-units." Kara frowned. "Holding them back until the marketplace is ready, maybe…" She nodded. "Yes, of course."

Marc glanced from her to Greenaway and back. "I'm missing something. Don't treat me like the village idiot. Explain."

"It's all about communications," Kara said. "It's a cliché that whoever controls them controls society. Same applies to empires, so why not off-world colonies? Small netherspace drives can be used to send messages back and forth between planets, like carrier pigeons. Conversations can be had – clumsily, perhaps, but still conversations." She glanced sharply at Greenaway. "I assume the micro n-drives are a lot faster than the larger ones, and don't need to keep popping in and out of netherspace to correct their errors."

He nodded. "Point and shoot," he said. "We assume."

"Okay – the Gliese or whoever don't want us to have easy communications. Why? Because this way, if we get a bit too belligerent, if we look like we're posing a threat to whatever galactic society is out there, then they can run rings around us. They're holding back their advantage."

"That's certainly our reading of the situation." Greenaway swirled his drink thoughtfully. "Of course, when we say 'galactic society' there's probably no such thing – perhaps only a group of different aliens in a great conference chamber on a neutral world somewhere, staring at each other. There's no reason to believe they can communicate with each other any better than with us. And when we say 'threat', we don't know what they *would* consider threatening. Or what would provoke them. The bottom line is they seem to be deliberately holding back the one thing we need to communicate effectively between worlds. We don't even know if they possess a version of our military systems or weapons, although we have to assume they do."

"There's another thing," Marc said as the thought struck him. "It's also about empires." Kara glanced at him with interest. "You can't build an empire if it takes weeks to get a message back and forth. What you get is individual fiefdoms, self-governing, like the old British Empire. They may pay lip-service to a central authority, but in reality they're pretty much on their own. Every colony world ends up with its own government, laws and ethical framework. Humanity is scattered and that has to suit the Gliese – and the others." He paused in thought and then, "And this micro-drive would make the galactic economy easier too, right?"

Every city state, every colony world had its own currency. Some colony worlds were absurdly rich in commodities – gold, platinum, precious jewels, rare earths – that on others could be used instead of money. It was a formula for chaos and war, solved when GalDiv developed virtscrip. The virt stood for "virtual", as in not physically real, similar to the bitcoins that had caused so much trouble fifty years before. Although some happy souls believed that 'virt' stood for virtuous, as in a currency that you could really trust. All galactic trade was conducted in virtscrip, and GalDiv's massive AIs decided the rate of exchange between virtscrip and all other currencies three times a year. GalDiv also acted as the bank of last resort and policed every other bank in human space, something only an AI with imagination could achieve. The result was fewer, if any, major banking scandals. Many bankers complained bitterly about this denial of their right to become obscenely rich, but virtscrip was here to stay.

Greenaway shook his head. "Not necessarily. Too much information instantly available caused many of the financial disasters before the aliens came and the system fell apart. Your comparison with the British

Empire is a good one. No colony world is more than three weeks from Earth. So the most they are is six weeks from each other. That's close enough to trade and feel part of something. But far enough away to prevent them conspiring... which they do, but it's relatively simple for GalDiv to monitor and control. Otherwise, I agree that the Gliese want us fragmented throughout space. Although that's assuming Gliese and humans ever think the same way, which can't be proven. It's more practical to ignore their motives and simply react to their actions."

"You told me you'd lost something," Marc prompted, moving thoughts of his distant family to the back of his mind. "What's that got to do with the micro n-drives?"

"Good question," Greenaway said.

NINETEEN DAYS EARLIER

Two elderly Pilgrims had died, gone to sleep and never woken up, their bodies put into the waste disposal tubs. An hour later they'd vanished. There were now one hundred and forty-six surviving Pilgrims plus three staff. Tatia wondered if the two had died because they had no reason to go on living. Their dream of dwelling in harmony with their gods shown to be fantasy. She said nothing, however, even when the SUT's staff talked of escape. One, an assistant mechanic, suggested jumping a Cancri to get hold of its weapon. Except no one knew how the weapon worked, only that it did... and the Cancri killed anyone who came within two metres of them, even a man who'd wanted to greet his gods.

No one wanted to talk to Tatia except a black-haired, twelve-year-old boy called Pablo. His father had died on the SUT, the Pilgrim killed with Juan when the Cancri boarded. The other Pilgrims, consumed by their own misery, had little time for him. He had no one other than the Consort of Juan, Understander of the Gods.

Thirty-eight hours later one of the walls began to slide upwards, accompanied by the terrified screams of people convinced they were about to be expelled into space. Instead of an inky blackness the hold was flooded with the fierce light of a blue-white sun and a dusty and spicy-smelling heat. The SUT had landed on a stony desert that stretched away to the horizon. Two lines of Cancri, maybe fifty in all, formed a corridor between the SUT and a series of low rounded buildings a hundred or so metres away. It was obvious what was expected of them but several prisoners had to be forcibly persuaded to go outside. The more resourceful Pilgrims carried the rest of the water and vegetables because you never knew.

Tatia stepped onto alien soil, even more convinced the true gods would soon release them. Pablo held her hand as they walked past the Cancri guards towards the low, curved buildings.

"Don't worry," she reassured him, "no one else is going to die."

Her robe turned black.

Greenaway paused, marshalling his thoughts. "A migration space utility transport left Earth twenty-one days ago. One of those 'aliens-are-gods religions' – the Pilgrims of the Divine Order." There was contempt in his voice. "They headed for a planet in the Upsilon Andromedae binary system, which had been surveyed and prepared with the usual self-inflating buildings, cold-fusion generators, food synthesisers and a couple of hundred crates of seeds genetically modified to survive local conditions. An entire planet for a church, uncorrupted by non-believers so that more and more aliens would come to walk – or slither or crawl – amongst them. They were going to call the planet 'Truth'. Even so, it was a serious migration and they had weapons."

"They didn't survive?" Kara asked. "What happened? The colony vanished – wiped out by something unidentified on the planet?"

"They never reached the planet. Details are sketchy, but their SUT – its trifecta code was *LUX-WEM-YIB* – popped out of netherspace to check its location and recalibrate its drive, as normal. Seconds later an alien craft came alongside and latched on with a universal airlock. The exterior was burned through and the SUT invaded. Some of the Pilgrims were taken onto the alien SUT. The *LUX-WEM-YIB* was left drifting between star systems."

"You had someone on board," Kara guessed.

"We have a couple of people on each migration SUT that leaves Earth, and on most of the SUTs that leave established colonies to set up new ones. They keep us informed about what's going on. We're not being paranoid but—"

"As if," Kara said.

"— but we like to keep tabs. We don't really care about ideological purity any more. We just want to know about any interesting alien trades."

"You recovered the *LUX-WEM-YIB*, of course," Kara said.

Greenaway nodded. "Empty except for a few dead bodies. The SUT's AI was traumatised so we barely know what happened."

"Traumatised?" Kara queried.

"Which aliens did it?" Marc asked at the same time.

"The Cancri. The *LUX-WEM-YIB*'s AI tried to link to the Cancri computer system. Now all it shows is a chaos of flashing colours or scenes of the attack. It went mad. We've seen Cancri on Earth, but not as many as the Gliese and the Eridani."

"Small," Marc recalled, frowning. "There are two different creatures, always seen together. Nobody is quite sure which one is the Cancri – maybe they both are. One is about the size of a baby but with hook-like grippers. No obvious eyes. Pale white, and soft." His voice held the slightest tremor. Kara wondered why the sudden tension. "They ride around on things like greyhounds with very long, thin legs and a pair of arms growing out of their necks. The two of them are supposed to be an example of a symbiotic relationship – two creatures working together, each providing a benefit to the other. The small white things get mobility. Nobody has been able to work out what the greyhound creatures get. Nobody knows how they communicate between themselves, either. Telepathy has been suggested, as has pheromones and thin nerve fibres growing out of the rider's grippers. The jury is out." He saw Kara looking at him curiously. "Aliens intrigue me."

She half nodded then turned to Greenaway. "The migrants didn't fight back? You said they had weapons."

"They did. Locked away in the SUT's hold. The staff didn't manage to reach them in time." Greenaway appeared to respond to the disdain in her eyes. "They weren't explorers, Kara. Glorified bus drivers, really."

"So the Cancri have kidnapped all these migrants and staff," she said, her voice matter-of-fact. "You don't know why or where they are but you expect us to find out."

"There's more," Greenaway said calmly. "Nine days ago a Cancri space vehicle arrived on Earth. Most of the occupants went off in various directions, but one of them went up to the escorting guards and handed over a sheet of plastic. An image was printed on the plastic – ten captured migrants looking very scared. Behind them a group of Cancri pointed some sort of weapon at their heads."

"Weapon?" Kara said. "Are you sure?"

Greenaway frowned at the interruption. "When the guard took the plastic, the heat of his hand activated a few seconds of moving image. Two Cancri pull one of the migrants out of line, force him to kneel, and point the weapon – a gun-like object – at him. His head explodes. He looks to be about twelve years old." Greenaway glanced at Kara, then at Marc, and his face was suddenly sombre. "What we appear to have is a hostage situation, and a ransom demand, but we have no idea what the Cancri want. We can't ask them, and they can't tell us. How can we negotiate when communication is impossible?"

"But they *are* communicating," Marc said, surprising

himself. "And they're showing an awareness of our culture."

Kara got it. "You mean the violence?"

He nodded. "An accepted part of human interaction. Even good guys kill. Death as part of a trade." He looked at Greenaway. "I suppose there's a plan?"

"First, remember what I said about security. It's aliens that keep GalDiv influential. No GalDiv, no EarthCent, and the world descends into a mess of warring city states. No more netherspace drives, so the off-Earth settlements would be on their own."

"Correction," Marc interjected. "There's nothing to stop the colonies dealing with aliens direct. I'm sure they already do. You're only worried about Earth and its influence?"

Greenaway didn't bother to deny it. "Earth is also what keeps the colony worlds together. But you missed something. Earth's economy depends on aliens. The public only see the half of it. Most recent advances in electronics, plastics, even manufacturing and chemical engineering have come from an alien trade. We don't do our own research any more. Without external stimuli the Earth goes stale. Do you understand?"

Marc nodded. Even if people believed aliens were infantilising humanity, life without them would be chaos.

"You asked about a plan," Greenaway said. "That's why you're here. Congratulations – you are now GalDiv's official alien hostage negotiation team. You'll go to the Cancri homeworld – if that's where the hostages have been taken – and find out what the hell they want."

Marc glanced at Kara's expressionless face. She was clearly good at hiding her emotions. "Otherwise it's the shelf?"

"If you're lucky you might be near a window," Greenaway agreed. "But I forgot to mention," – it was obvious that he hadn't – "on the reverse of the Cancri's plastic sheet was an image of one of *your* artworks, Marc. Could be the Cancri equivalent of a postcard, but we're assuming they want *you* involved."

Kara obviously couldn't resist it. "They could be asking for their money back. Or the death of the artist."

"Ha fucking ha," Marc said sourly. "Which artwork?"

"The one with those colour-changing organisms moving in the shape of a Klein bottle," Greenaway replied. "Kara might be right."

Marc bit back an angry retort. This had to be military-style humour; his biggest mistake would be to overreact. "Yeah, right, blame the poor bloody artist," he said sarcastically. "But it's a strange way to recruit someone. As in me."

"You're right," Greenaway agreed. "Please, Mr Keislack, will you help Earth in this time of our need? You will? Good."

Kara smiled sweetly. "We're both press-ganged."

"So what's your special skill?" Marc suspected he already knew. Kara was obviously the soldier in the mission.

"Kara has a unique ability to empathise with aliens," Greenaway said. "She's also a highly skilled sniper. If anyone can keep you alive, Kara can." He paused and smiled. "It's why she's in charge."

Greenaway looked out at Berlin. "We leave in forty minutes. I suggest you have something to eat."

"Where are we going?" Marc asked. He felt comfortable with the idea of Kara being in charge – as long as she didn't tell him what to do all the time.

"You need to be integrated as a team."

"Team?"

Kara touched his arm. "We get told only what we need to know at this stage. Get used to it. It's how high-security operations work." She seemed amused.

"I am not a damn soldier," Marc said angrily.

"Actually, you are," Greenaway said. "You signed citizenship papers with Bristol, correct? You patent or copyright your artworks there. You bank there. In an emergency you can be called upon to help defend the city, correct?"

"That last is so much—"

"But still legal," Greenaway rode over him. "And GalDiv has a legal agreement with the City of Bristol – as we do with all other city states, worldwide. Kara said you've been press-ganged. In fact, you've been drafted."

Marc heard himself echo the cry of the drafted throughout the ages. "*Why me?*" It was more of a protest than a question because he knew why. He saw Kara and Greenaway exchange the briefest of glances and realised they belonged to the same exclusive military club; he'd always be the civilian outsider. "So, sensitive trained killer and insensitive artist. Aren't we a pair?"

"Not yet," Kara said. "But soon. I can't wait."

Marc wondered what she meant but wasn't going

to ask. Besides he was confused by two unfamiliar emotions: a sense of being useful, above and beyond making his agent rich; and the hope that perhaps, one day, his long-gone family would be proud of him. Assuming they were still alive. He looked at Greenaway. "So how do we know where to go? Did the Cancri leave a map?"

Greenaway signalled the waiter to bring menus. "Later. Now eat."

"I've got one more question," Marc said. "You'll probably think it's stupid."

"Probably," Greenaway said. "But don't let that stop you."

"Okay. You say 'netherspace'. I've heard it called 'subspace' and 'underspace'. Even just 'below'. Why can't you make up your minds?"

Greenaway looked at him for a moment. "Because no one knows what it is. We didn't discover it."

Kara obviously understood. "Making out like we don't care?"

"No," Marc said, "it's more than that. It's saying nether-under-sub whatever isn't really important, that it's an alien thing. But deep down we know we're second-rate. So, what's it like?"

Greenaway was silent for a moment. "It's like being surrounded by every colour in the world and thousands more you never saw before," he said eventually. "And they're all moving and changing, vanishing and reappearing. You want to look at them forever – but if you do look for more than five minutes, you can lose your mind. It's why SUTs fly blind. No one gets to look outside."

"Changing the subject," Kara said, "what about the GalDiv agents on board the SUT?"

Greenaway shook his head. "Both were killed."

"If the migrants still regard the Cancri as gods," Marc mused, "or at least as vastly superior beings, they might even oppose us trying to rescue them."

"No one said this was going to be easy," Greenaway said, smiling.

5

It was an underground room in the GalDiv building, furnished with facing rows of six padded chairs, each with a featureless, dull metal and grey plastic helmet that covered a person's entire head and smelt faintly of antiseptic and old sweat. A man and a woman were strapped into opposite seats, heads enclosed, their bodies twitching and shuddering as if acting out an especially vivid dream. Two white-coated technicians monitored control panels at one end of the room. It was a place of dreams, nightmares and shared identities. Some found that sharing was the most terrifying of all.

The simulity process had first come to humanity courtesy of a cyclist, a punctured tyre and an Eridani accompanied by six GalDiv guards. The punctured tyre had been exchanged for 173 ceramic-like yellow cubes, each the size of a matchbox. As usual the guards issued a receipt and took the objects away. If they were found to be valuable, the cyclist would get a reward. The floating Arc de Triomphe and the metal-excluding force field that still enclosed the Gaylord Convention Centre in what was then Maryland, USA, but which was now part of the Eastern Seaboard State, were reminders that alien technology was best left to grown-ups.

It took six months, three happy accidents in the laboratory and the destruction of three of the ceramic-like cubes to discover what they could do. As opposed to what they were *meant* to do, which, until humans learned to converse with the Eridani, the scientists had no way of knowing for sure.

When connected to both an AI and a human brain the Eridani cubes enabled humans to process vast amounts of information in a short time; somehow they speeded up the brain's processes without doing any harm. They also allowed humans to become part of a simulation, an immersive shared virtual reality that was logical and completely real to the user. Several humans could inhabit an identical simulation – and, since the cubes allowed an individual to experience another's deeply personal memory, users bonded whether they wanted to or not.

In practice the Eridani cubes were often used to brief special forces teams at short notice for specific missions. Official Assassins also found them useful. Kara had used a cube several times and had come to enjoy it. No matter how fraught the simulation, an uncharted part of her brain would murmur, "Not to worry, you'll get out of this alive."

"It's standard briefing procedure," Greenaway told Marc as he and Kara were strapped into their seats. "Accelerated learning. It'll help you work better together."

A moment's absolute stillness, a flash of green light and Kara was elsewhere – she was someone else, now long dead. And also melded with Marc Keislack.

~ *We have to get out.* ~ He's more concerned for her safety than he is for the mission.

~ We stay. ~

~ I promised I'd keep you safe. ~

She should have known. He sees himself as the dominant one in the relationship. *~ My decision. Fuck off if you want. ~* He smells of sweat, earth and adrenalin; sour. Or is it fear? Fear for her or for him?

~ Any moment we'll be cut off. ~ The situation is, as they say, fluid. If they are surrounded, enemy sensors will find them within minutes. This opponent is particularly unpleasant, a religious enemy that likes to play with its prisoners.

It is a dark hollow on a damp hillside.

Her eye is clamped to the scope. *~ I have him. ~*

~ You hope. ~ His hand closes around the rifle's barrel.

A shell explodes fifty metres away: semi-smart submunitions whining through the air. She barely notices, only concerned by the target and his hand on her rifle. She shakes it off.

~ Fuck off! ~ She dimly hears him make a slight grunting sound as her finger takes up the first pressure. Nothing matters except her target. The rifle recoils against her shoulder. Five hundred metres away the enemy commander's chest explodes. *~ Confirm kill. ~*

Silence.

She's aware of his body pressing against her hips. For some reason her mind swings back to the first time they made love. She twists around, aware that the enemy will be searching, their orders not to kill the sniper but to capture and play with him. Or her.

She sees that he has been hit. One of the heat-seeking submunitions. His right thigh is wet with blood. She doubts he can crawl, let alone walk. His eyes are bright and fixed on hers.

~ *Go,* ~ he says, pain splintering his voice. ~ *Leave me.* ~

~ *Can't,* ~ she says briefly, her hand automatically reaching for a pain-suppressant, tourniquet and energy-boost shot.

~ *Bone's smashed.* ~ Then he sighs as the drug takes effect.

~ *Splint.* ~ They both carry an inflatable one.

~ *Slow you down. Go.* ~

She ignores him, fumbling in a pouch for the splint, then glances up in alarm, instinctively knowing what he's about to do.

~ *Leave the rifle,* ~ he says and bites on the official suicide pill. You do not want to be captured by an enemy that plays with its prisoners. Unsaid – there's not time, the pill acts quickly – but understood by both: *This way you're mine forever.*

Oh, you stupid, stupid man, she thinks. But also aware that she no longer has to make the hardest of decisions. And then: *Did he guess I planned to ask for a replacement? Did he know I intended to have sex with someone else?* And from nowhere comes the memory of her first live ambush, feeling more alive than ever before, hearing a faint scritch-scritch-scritch near her and looking down, realising her senses are so acute she can hear wood ants walking on dried leaves.

She takes his dog-tags, touches the cooling face once and begins the slow crawl back to safety. *Leave the rifle*, he'd said, hoping the enemy will think he was a lone sniper, as if he can save her even when he's dead. Hope, not reality. The enemy knows snipers work as a pair.

He reads the letter left by his parents, the letter explaining that the house is sold, they have gone off-world and telling him not to follow. He is sixteen and just released from juvenile prison. No wonder there was no one to meet him. His family are light-years away.

Kara feels his laughter. *Good riddance. Don't write.*

They'd often talked about off-world. He'd assumed he'd go with them. Wasn't he the apple of his mother's eye, always to be forgiven? The carrier of his father's genes? He wonders idly what was the final straw: selling his mother's jewellery perhaps?

What he wants is what he needs. Other people matter if they can help, are worthless if they can't, are enemies if they won't. They are there to be used. He has always felt this way while knowing that others – the herd – see life differently. Maybe life is different in the Out. He'll find out.

First shock: the Out isn't primitive, at least not in England. It's very different, though. No personal chips. No AIs. It's here he develops an aversion to computers. Out There – the Wild – is still high-tech, though. It just doesn't like being governed by corporations or EarthCent. Hence the free spacers.

~ *My family's on Epsilon Seven,* ~ he tells one.

~ *That colony failed.* ~

~ *I get vidcards from them.* ~

~ Show me… Sorry, kid. That's Gamma Three, not Epsilon Seven. I recognise those things that look like trees. You must have got it wrong. ~

~ Who cares? ~ He shrugs. *~ I ain't goin' there. ~*

Kara is in his head when Marc gets interested in art and leaves the Out. She experiences his obsession, understands it stops him thinking about things that hurt, appreciates the way that he can use art to distance himself from others. Kara understands his secret fear: that people will find out his family abandoned him – and why. She is there when he begins simulated military training, acting as his squad leader in a firefight that is absolutely real even though she knows it isn't. Marc behaves as if it's life or death. Kara understands her initial, instinctive dislike for him. She did not want to empathise with him. They are too similar. Now she has no choice.

Kara's mind went blank as hands began to ease the helmet from her head. White-gowned technicians carefully avoided any eye contact as they began releasing the restraints that had kept Kara and Marc tight in their padded chairs. People coming out of simulity could be a little sensitive for a few minutes. Raw. Even the briefest of glances from a stranger could be construed as an insult or a declaration of love. The technicians finished and moved away.

Marc looked at her and made a face. "So that's what you do for a living."

"Did," she corrected, and yawned. She could hear her avatar complaining about the sudden memory load. Sod it. It was customary to sleep for an hour after a session but Greenaway had warned them that they would be meeting the staff of the SUT they'd be joining – and one other member of the team about whom he'd been annoyingly vague. "A kind of a diplomat," was all he'd said.

"Hornets?" Marc asked. "That's brilliant."

So he'd seen her last assignment. "Better than cockroaches." The artwork that had impressed Greenaway, or so the man had said.

Marc grinned. "Maybe I'll use hornets myself, next time." Then, more carefully: "What if he hadn't taken the pill? Your spotter. The ex-lover."

"He thought I'd stay with him or try to save us both."

"You know what I mean."

Kara stared at him for a moment. "You're a borderline psychopath?"

"Apparently. Not telling me anything I didn't already suspect, but it's nice to have the label. And now with added military training. So?"

"You tell me."

"You'd have shot him," Marc said nervously, because he'd learned enough about Kara to know when he would be making her uncomfortable. "Probably. Because no point in you both dying. Because the enemy would have tortured him before killing him. Because he had sensitive, tactical information. That's why he took the pill. To save you the pain of killing him." He climbed out of the chair and stretched. "I'm trying not to think how unutterably strange this is," he said, sounding more like his old self. "That sim fire-fight we were in together. I owe you an apology."

"It's not the worst that ever happened," Kara said, thankful that her former lover was no longer centre-stage. There was a lingering taste of imagined blood in her mouth from when sim-Marc Keislack had head-butted her over a disagreement about tactics. If a simulity produces physical results, is it still imaginary? If a tree falls in a forest, does anybody give a damn? "Not as if it got you anywhere."

"You saw my childhood," he said diffidently.

"Your secrets are safe with me – and I bloody hope mine are with you. Anyway, it was more your mid-teens."

"I have no idea why I don't feel like other people," he said levelly, not looking at her.

"Does it bother you?"

"Sometimes yes," he admitted. "Mostly no."

"Fuck. You're only borderline. I'd hoped for the full psycho."

He grinned again and stretched. "I'm hungry."

After the sharing of their minds Kara now knew him as imaginative and surprisingly ruthless, a man who would enjoy combat and, although uncomfortable with taking orders, would co-operate with others until he decided his life was in danger. At that point he would make his own decisions. Were all artists psychopaths, or was it just him? Thanks to the simulity he would, if necessary, remember how to handle all standard weaponry; understand military tactics at platoon level; know how to navigate and survive – broadly speaking – on an alien world; be competent at first aid; and know what to do in a space utility transport emergency. When, if, he needed this knowledge he'd be surprised by how naturally it came to him; and that the simulity had also imparted muscle-memory, so his reactions would be immediate and fluent. For her part Kara had been brought up to date with all the latest military hardware; now knew how to navigate in space; how to atmosphere-land an SUT using updown-field generators or rockets; knew all there was to know about the Gliese, Eridani and Cancri, which wasn't a whole lot. It felt as if her brain was swollen with far more information than she could access. Kara suspected that other knowledge had been implanted that would surface when needed and give her confusing dreams in the meantime. She decided not to raise the subject with Marc. He wasn't used to the simulity process, and he might object to having his head stuffed full of information that he knew nothing about. Given what she now knew about his personality, Kara wasn't sure how violently he would react.

"There'll be a canteen somewhere," she said. "But you had lunch only a couple of hours ago. You're not really hungry. The simulation fooled your body."

"The other way round would be a good way to lose weight," he mused. "Use the simulity to make you think you've just eaten, and *aren't* hungry." He glanced at Kara. "Not that you need to lose weight. In fact, a bit more couldn't hurt."

"No canteen," a technician interrupted. "You're

due in Director Greenaway's office five minutes ago. You'll get fed there. And by the way, Mr Keislack: were you told about crossover emotions?"

"About what?"

"You and Ms Jones effectively exchanged part of your minds. The other's emotions, attitudes, may remain with you for a while. Nothing to worry about, the effect will go away. It's a bit like a ghost in your head."

"How will I know?" He immediately realised how stupid the question sounded. He could already sense the ghost-Kara – and she seemed to be amused.

SEVENTEEN DAYS EARLIER

Time was difficult to estimate when the length of the Cancri day was different from that of Earth. AIs wouldn't have helped either, even if the Pilgrims had been equipped with them – there was no wider AI mesh for anything to link into. All Tatia knew was that it was seventeen Cancri days after they had landed on the planet that the boy Pablo had a flashback to his father being murdered and threw a stone at the Cancri guards. It missed but the slug-like rider pointed its weapon in Pablo's direction. Three of the captives tried to shield him. Two others wanted to push him into the open, away from the protection of the buildings, where he could be killed without harming anyone else.

The Pilgrims were not handling captivity well.

The low, curved buildings had been just that and no more, built from what could have been either metal or stone and empty save for large above-ground containers that held water, Earth-fruit and vegetables. No matter how much the Pilgrims took of either, the containers remained full. After half a day they came to understand that new fruit and vegetables materialised in the bottom of a container, although no one saw it happen. Similarly the water containers were always full, although there was no input pipe or valve. The building's interiors were cool in the day and warm at night, when outside temperatures rose to the mid-30s centigrade, or fell to zero. There was no obvious sign of air conditioning or heating, or of the source of the late-afternoon, permanent light inside the buildings.

There was an argument amongst the Pilgrims whether one of the buildings – there were six of them, seven metres high by twenty across – should be used solely for washing or defecation. One of the SUT staff advised that excrement would be less of a risk exposed to the high-ultraviolet-rays-emitting sun – which most of the Pilgrims already knew. But they needed to have some involvement in how their lives were organised. Arguing about toilet facilities was as good a way as any.

There was another discussion about who would represent the Pilgrims to the Cancri. But since it was impossible to communicate with their captors, and since anyone going close to them was liable to be killed, there were no volunteers.

All they could do was wait and speculate on what the Cancri wanted. On the plus side, the Cancri had obviously studied humans, hence the water, fruit and vegetables. Which also meant they intended to keep the Pilgrims alive. However, any optimism was destroyed by the obvious question: kept alive for what?

That left remembering Earth and wishing they were there; and choral singing, which inevitably made people cry. Underlying this, the bitter shame at having believed aliens were gods because they needed an authority to protect them from an increasingly weird universe. Humans desperate for answers will often believe anything that offers mental and emotional security – even that aliens are gods with a small 'g'. Aliens with a vastly superior science that might as well be magic for all that humans understood it. Small 'g' gods without whom Earth and its colonies would wither and die. Did anyone understand their motives? No. Had they brought great benefit to humanity? Yes. Were they mystical? Some believed so, but for most of Earth the answer was no. Small 'g' gods it was then, who one day would teach humanity the universe's greatest secrets.

Except they wouldn't. The Cancri were merely vicious animals that killed for no apparent reason. Not even small 'g' gods. Only the enemy.

Meanwhile the Pilgrims could explore: the Cancri showed no interest if Pilgrims walked away from the buildings. But the flat, stony ground vanished into a heat haze in every direction. There was a line of low hills to the north, at least twenty miles away, but no way of carrying water to get there.

The Cancri space vehicle was still parked two hundred metres away, an elaborately curving construct the size of a naval destroyer. Every now and then one of the guards would trot towards it and go inside. Every now and then a Cancri would emerge and trot towards the six buildings. They may or may not have been the same Cancri. None of the Pilgrims, or the staff, tried to go near the Cancri SUT in which they had landed. Even if they got inside they would inevitably get close to a Cancri and that meant death.

Human beings are quick at learning how to survive.

On the third day of captivity a familiar smell announced

a minor miracle. At the bottom of each food container roast meat had materialised. A leg of lamb here, a shoulder of pork there, a prime rib of beef, and even a whole poached salmon.

It was welcomed as a sign that the Cancri cared. Several Pilgrims from the group who had abandoned their religion abruptly picked it back up again – slightly dusty, but still usable.

The next thing the Cancri did showed that they didn't care at all.

Kara explained how Eridani cubes worked as she and Marc walked to the elevator, interested to see his reaction.

"That doesn't sound right," he said, more thoughtfully than she had expected.

"Why?" Perhaps her ghost was teaching him patience.

"It suggests we have something in common with them, like how our minds fundamentally work. But we don't."

Kara flashed back to her brief touch of a Gliese mind and the utter alienness of it. "Marc, we don't even know if the Eridani use them the same way," she pointed out. "It may be that we discovered some utility the Eridani don't know about, because their minds work so differently." It was the first time she'd called him Marc.

"We don't even know if the Eridani made them in the first place," Marc said as the elevator doors slid open. "They're traders, remember?"

"True," Kara said. They rode up to the penthouse floor in thoughtful silence. If the Eridani weren't responsible for the yellow cubes, who was? An as-yet-unknown alien species with an understanding of the human mind, which meant they had to be very superior? Or perhaps an as-yet-unknown alien species that was similar to humans but chose to remain hidden? Neither possibility was comforting.

Greenaway had laid on coffee, sandwiches and pastries. Marc paused to admire the view of Berlin for five long seconds, then sat down and reached for a plate. There was enough retained infantry grunt mentality from the simulity to ensure he ate whenever he could. Given half a chance Kara knew he'd take a quick nap later.

Kara was more interested in the person watching from a corner, so quiet and still that Marc had missed her. Or was it a him? The observer was slim, a little shorter than Kara, with black hair in a retro urchin-cut, symmetrical, precise features dominated by huge, dark eyes that seemed to stare through Kara without blinking and a small, sensual cupid's bow of a mouth that didn't smile. The person looked like a manga character. He or she seemed to be early twenties and wore a loose white shirt, left untucked over grey trousers. The ensemble could easily disguise any female curves. Then Kara forgot about the stranger's physical appearance and drew in her breath as a wave of – understanding? togetherness? – swept over her. This person saw the future like a path stretching across a landscape of time – some of it hidden by dips and folds, but the broad direction, and the occasional landmark encountered on the way, very clear. Kara half-smiled as she recognised an ability that came from the same psychic reservoir as her own empathy. For now she'd keep it to herself. Marc was happily munching on a locust-paste sandwich. He might become awkward if he knew what this stranger was.

"You should smile more often." The voice was low, melodious and again could belong to either sex. "It suits you."

Kara kept her face neutral and turned to Greenaway, who was sitting behind his desk.

"Meet Tse Durrel," Greenaway said and waited for Marc to register the stranger. "The third person on the team and representing GalDiv's Diplomatic Service."

Marc was still in grunt mode. "A fucking diplomat?" he challenged.

"Negotiator," Tse said firmly but quietly. "I don't do treaties."

"Tse is expert at alien trades," Greenaway explained.

"Understand the little bastards, do you?" Marc stood up. "My name's Marc Keislack. Forgive me asking but is it Ms or Mr Durrel? Which is actually a compliment."

"That depends," Tse said. "What sex would you like me to be?"

Marc stared for a few seconds then burst out laughing. "It's going to be an interesting trip." He turned to Greenaway. "Talking of which – who's in actual charge? You never made it clear."

"Kara en route and on-planet. But Tse runs the negotiations, if there are any."

"And me?"

"You're the only human that any alien has

voluntarily spent more than a few minutes with. You are the only artist whose work they've bought. And they may have specifically asked for you."

"I'm the token celebrity?" He didn't sound upset. "Maybe they won't be as impressed as you hope when I turn up."

Greenaway shook his head. "More than that. Almost all alien trades have been one-offs. They'll swap an updown-field generator for a bicycle tyre one day, ignore it the next. There are only two types of trade they've made repeatedly. Humans and your art."

"Oh," Marc said bleakly. "Oh fuck."

Kara felt a flash of sympathy for him. "Marc thinks you mean he's part of a hostage exchange: one artist for whoever's left alive."

"No exchanges," Greenaway said flatly. "It would set a bad precedent." He took a breath. "Right. Time to meet one of the three staff who'll be with you on this mission. Highly experienced, deep-space exploration, been together a long time. They lost their commander in the Up – stay away from the subject unless they mention it. Their new SUT has the trifecta *RIL-FIJ-DOQ*. Your mission manager is from the commercial side, mostly Sol-system runs. His grandfather made the first alien contact on the moon. The crew have been told that the *LUX-WEM-YIB* crash-landed on the Cancri homeworld and is being held there. They do not know that any Pilgrims have been killed. They've been told this is a highly classified mission and you will not tell them the truth unless it becomes necessary. They're waiting next door."

"Hold on." Kara thought it time to assert herself.

"How exactly do we know where these hostages are? Did the Cancri leave a map?"

Greenaway opened his mouth to reply but Tse interrupted.

"No, that's me," Tse said. "I have a gift."

Ah-ha! Kara thought fiercely. *Now we get the truth.*

"I just know things," Tse said humbly. "Can't explain it but…"

Oh, that's clever! I'm just a poor little psychic. Kara glanced at Marc, who seemed torn between laughter and outrage and decided that, all things considered, she liked him. That annoying self-awareness – me artist, you pleb – had gone, replaced by a growing screw-you attitude similar to her own.

"Remote viewing?" Marc asked, intrigued. "If so, how in an infinite universe do you manage to target what you're looking at?"

It was Greenaway who replied blithely: "Tse is a pre-cog – laboratory tested over thirty times. Been proved right ninety-eight per cent of the time. Anyway, we know where the planet is – around 230 light-years away."

"A pre-cog?" Marc seemed to be testing the word in his mouth as he said it. "You mean you can see the future?" He frowned, glancing from Tse to Greenaway and back uncertainly. "I'd heard rumours that there were people out there saying they have these powers, but I thought it was just exaggeration and wishful thinking."

"It's real," Greenaway said. Don't ask me how it works, but Tse can see… not the future, but the direction of the future. Glimpses. It's a trait a few people have displayed in every generation – an ability to see not just standard three dimensions but slightly into the fourth as well, but as I told you before, there's something about the fact that people now have AI chips in their heads that means the talent, the capability, has started to grow. An unexpected and rather worrying side-effect." He shrugged. "It worries us, but it doesn't mean we can't study and take advantage of it."

"But that's crap," Marc said, frowning. "Time isn't the fourth or any dimension. It can't be. We move easily in three dimensions, but we're carried through time at a set rate. We can't change that – can't choose to go into the past or the future the way we can to go left or right, up or down." It seemed to Kara that he had suddenly decided it was important to be taken seriously for more than his art. "As far as we know, that's true of the Cancri, the Eridani and all the other alien species as well, which means it's not just us poor humans limited to free movement in three dimensions. And even if we say that time is a dimension, but fundamentally different from the others, then where does that leave free will? I know there's a chair there" – he pointed to one by the wall – "and a door over there" – he pointed in the opposite direction – "but time's different. I know there was an embarrassing event at my fourteenth birthday party that means a girl named Sandra Wootten will never speak to me again, but I don't know what's going to happen on my fiftieth."

"Don't even know if you'll have a fiftieth birthday," Kara pointed out.

He nodded violently. "Exactly. We can see one way

in time – backwards – but not the other way, and have no freedom of movement."

"Whatever the logic," Greenaway said dismissively, "it's possible that time's only local, a subjective measurement of a specific rate of change. Maybe Tse sees the bigger, no-time picture. Or possibilities and selects the most probable. We're already using precogs to make trading with the aliens easier – if a precog can identify which of a hundred possible items an alien will accept, it streamlines the whole process and maximises the return."

"It's still bollocks," Marc said defensively. Kara knew this wasn't him, really; he was still Marc from the simulity, Marc the infantryman. Except it was him and she quite liked this new, coarser side.

Tse coughed gently. "Think of it this way," the precog said quietly. "Because I do. I can see the landscape of my future, but not the whole landscape. Some of it is hidden by folds and dips, and some of it is hidden by patches of mist. I can see the path we have to follow, the people who need to be involved, but I can't see all of it, and sometimes there are several paths of varying degrees of difficulty."

"But what about free will?" Marc protested, no doubt painfully aware his life might well depend on Tse's accuracy. "What if I choose to go cross-country rather than follow one of these preordained paths you can see?"

Tse shrugged gently. "I'm not a philosopher, but exercising free will means you choose a path to follow. Looking back from a vantage point in the future, you see the path followed, the choice you made. I just happen to be able to see the alternatives before you make the final decision – and the consequences." Tse smiled for the first time. "Sometimes."

Kara stared at the pre-cog's genderless face, and wondered two things. Was Tse telling the truth about how much, or how little, of the future a pre-cog could see? And did the aliens have pre-cogs too?

Instead she said: "The Cancri who brought the bad news – they didn't say where this planet is, did they? So either they expected us to find out, meaning they might know about pre-cogs… or expect us to have them, which raises weird questions. Or they expect something else altogether."

"You're going to have to trust Tse," Greenaway said flatly. "And to confirm: do not tell the SUT staff, especially the mission manager, about the executed Pilgrim. It's our little secret."

6

Within five minutes of meeting the SUT's mission manager, Marc decided that James Leeman-Smith was one of the most obnoxious men he'd ever met – and he'd been to cocktail parties with billionaires and awards ceremonies with art critics. The man was tall and golden-haired, like a Viking hero, and cultivated a searching stare and raised eyebrow meant to establish that he knew all of Marc's hidden, pointless secrets. Apparently the SUT's navigator and medic were already on board and waiting for them.

Greenaway was deep in conversation with the mission's saturnine mechanic, Tate Breckmann, while Tse stood silent when Leeman-Smith beckoned to Kara and Marc.

"A word," he said quietly, and led them to one side of the small, functional GalDiv office where the meeting was being held. "I know who you are."

"Don't worry about it," Kara said sweetly, "that's just a side-effect of being introduced."

Leeman-Smith's eyes narrowed. "I mean your background. I don't like having an assassin as a passenger. Frankly, I regard your profession" – his lips actually curled – "as perhaps necessary in this current world of ours, but always contemptible. You might be in nominal charge, but on my SUT, Up there, you'll do what you're told, when you're told. You will give

113

me a full mission briefing as soon as we're off-Earth. I also expect daily situation reports once you're on your mission. Is that clear?"

Marc told himself that SUT mission managers were little more than maître d's – making sure that everyone else was doing their job properly. The technical expertise was provided by the SUT's mechanic – falling short of the alien-provided netherspace drive of course – and the navigator, while the mission manager fulfilled the "Keep Calm And Carry On" role, only useful if the drive needed replacing and they had to hang around in normal space for the Gliese call-out team, then explain gently to the call-out fee that his or her time had come. And while some space utility transports were given an open mission to explore the galaxy, meaning their mission managers needed to make regular life-and-death decisions, Marc decided that Leeman-Smith was probably confined to the regular colony runs. Exploration required a high degree of intelligence and only an idiot would insult an Official Assassin to her face.

"We'll keep to ourselves in space," Kara said. "So I can't see us getting under your feet. And when we've landed the SUT will act as a relay for all messages sent to GalDiv… Of course, they'll be enciphered so you won't understand them, but there's no harm in you looking at them. GalDiv's already told you all you need to know."

A spot on each of Leeman-Smith's cheeks turned white. He opened his mouth to reply when a voice from behind Marc said:

"Excuse me, Commander, I need Ms Jones and Mr Keislack for a moment."

Greenaway put his hand under Kara's elbow and led her away. Marc followed as Leeman-Smith stared furiously after them.

"Not very smart, making enemies this quickly," Greenaway murmured.

"You heard?" Kara said.

"Every word." He tapped briefly behind his right ear. "You leave in three hours' time."

"Where's the call-out fee?" Marc asked.

"Already on board in a medically induced coma, hooked up to a life-support machine. Most of them prefer it that way. And it's easier on the staff, in case they get too attached."

Marc glanced across at Kara. He'd picked up enough of her memories while they'd been linked to know she wasn't sure if her sister was still locked safely away in a deep-sleep capsule while who knew what went on around her, was live in the hands of aliens, or dead. Had Greenaway forgotten? No. Greenaway would never forget an emotional trigger like that. It had been a reminder of their own personal reasons for ensuring this… this mission was a success.

"Are there many pre-cogs like Tse?" Marc asked casually, trying to change the subject.

"Difficult to tell – they keep themselves hidden. But not enough. Tse can explain it to you when you're on board. You'll still have to take regular bearings, of course, or rather the navigator will. Leeman-Smith will check the figures. It keeps him happy, and who knows – maybe one day he'll spot a mistake."

"He's such a prick."

"There's a reason for that."

"Born that way then took lessons," Kara said. Marc decided her contempt was a symptom of pre-mission nerves. "Can't see him handling an emergency well."

"Second thoughts, Kara?" Greenaway asked.

She shook her head. "Just giving a heads-up. You can bullshit Marc here and the others all you like but I know, Greenaway… boss… sir… you majestic exalted bloody-ness," Greenaway smiled as if enjoying her outburst, "that there's a fuck sight more to this than rescuing a bunch of Pilgrims the Cancri want to trade. See, normally you – GalDiv – would just write them off, right?"

"If this is about your sister…"

Kara leaned in close and gripped his arm. "Do not play me for a fool. *Do not*. It's what got me here and you know it." She let go and gave him a sideways smile, an attractive young woman reminding an older man of his youth. She glanced at Marc. "Best we go join the others before they start thinking for themselves."

They found Leeman-Smith explaining to Tse that there was no need to worry because he was the best mission manager in GalDiv, and his grandfather had made the first contact. Judging by the look in his eye, Leeman-Smith intended to solve the he/she puzzle the first moment possible, and wasn't too fussed how it turned out. Judging by Tse's body language the only way Leeman-Smith would see him/her naked was by peeking through a keyhole – if they used keys on SUTs, otherwise it would have to be good old e-surveillance.

"Time we left for Tegel Galactic," Greenaway

announced, "now we're all getting on so well."

"Problem," Kara said. "Clothes? My Merc?"

"Uniforms, already on board. Your Merc will be taken to long-term secure parking. Marc's house will be protected by armed AI drones."

Marc nodded. "I expected a briefing." He was disappointed.

"You already had it," Kara told him. "During the simility."

"But that was…"

She shook her head dismissively. "Your mind feels like an overstuffed suitcase, right?"

Marc blinked defensively. He couldn't help himself. "Well, I wouldn't… yeah, a bit."

"That's the briefing. What did you expect, a bloody stage with maps and some clown with a pointer?"

Marc realised Kara was taking her annoyance at Leeman-Smith out on him. "I don't—"

"Everything you, we, need to know is in here." She touched the side of his head. "It shows up when we need it. Triggered by events."

Marc was aware of Greenaway watching her cautiously. "But why?" he asked.

"Because otherwise you'd spend all your time trying to make sense of it." She glanced at Greenaway. "Come on – let's go."

As they walked off Marc turned the unanswered question over and over in his brain: what information could be so sensitive that it had to be hidden until needed?

• • • • •

Most Germans liked to think the Gliese had chosen the near-defunct Tegel Airport as their first landing field because of Berlin's importance, except that nobody knew why aliens did anything. But Tegel it had been and for the most part aliens continued to use it, which was why Earth Central's Galactic Division was based in Berlin and Tegel International was now Tegel Galactic. The jitney dropped them at the far end of the area where a group of small SUTs were parked. With updown-field generators and sideslip-field generators there was no need for streamlined rockets. Even so, Marc thought, it was a shame that the area looked like a junkyard. Where was the mystery, where was the smooth design to send the imagination soaring? The SUTs looked like collections of metal shipping containers all strapped together without rhyme or reason, wrapped with pipes and cables and covered with spherical tanks, bulky and asymmetrical. Sensors and the nozzles of manoeuvring jets pointed in all directions, like prickles on a hedgehog.

"It's not the way I remember seeing it on the worldmesh," he said. "Less... aerodynamic."

"These only operate within the solar system," Greenaway told him. "They're mostly people carriers. Space-proofed inside and plastic seating. But the longest netherspace trip is around a day to Pluto. Mars takes two minutes."

"They look kind of beat-up." These SUTs were pitted and scarred. One of the containers even had a series of gouges, strangely like giant teeth marks, on its surface. "What's that from – space dust and meteors?"

Kara and Tse were staring off into the distance.

Tse's face was expressionless, Kara's filled with fury and contempt. Marc turned around, intrigued to see what had distracted them.

A quarter of a mile away a long line of people were filing into a flattened pyramid the size of a ferry, encouraged by human guards.

"Hey," Marc said, "isn't that a…" His voice tailed off as a sudden wave of anger swept over him that could have been Kara's ghost. He hoped it was his own.

"A Gliese SUT," Kara finished for him. "Someone's just bought a nice new slip-drive."

Even at this distance there was something inherently tragic about the line of people slowly entering the alien SUT. Marc wondered if anyone would change their mind at the last moment. Would they be allowed to leave?

"And we still don't know what happens to them," Greenaway said quietly.

"Don't look at me," Tse said before Marc could ask. "I'd have to *be* one of them to have any idea."

"This just coincidence?" Kara stared hard at Greenaway. "Or are you reminding us what's really at stake?" She switched her gaze to Marc. "He was being a little coy with the truth," she said. "Bad things can happen in netherspace. SUTs vanish, others reappear empty or with passengers and staff like mindless zombies."

"A triple coating of spray-on foam, like a combination of enamel and insulation, seems to protect the transports," Greenaway said. "The Gliese supply it along with the sideslip-field generators. There's never enough."

"Which is why these rust-buckets are shit, right?" Kara said cynically. "The spray-on gets used for the long-haul interstellar journeys. Well, I hope we've got a two-times triple coating, Mr Greenaway, sir. No matter how scarce. Any less would be rude."

Greenaway smiled. "Let's go." He led the way to where Leeman-Smith waited in front of a medium-sized SUT. It was the size of a large house, and like the others it looked like a series of large metal containers welded together, and was studded with manoeuvring jets and sensors.

"I see no wrap," Kara said. And then, "That's a spacecraft? It's a bit... *blockier* than I was anticipating."

"Space utility transport," Greenaway murmured with feigned world-weariness. At least, Marc assumed it was feigned.

"Doesn't need to be aerodynamic," he found himself saying. "Not with updown-field generators." Was that natural insight or information from the simulity? Assuming he survived – big assumption – in future years would he still be coming up with facts and conclusions, never knowing where they were from?

"The protection's sprayed on just before take-off," Greenaway explained.

"Protection from what, exactly?" Marc asked, suddenly worried. Then relieved to be momentarily distracted by the idea of a wrapped SUT as part of an artwork.

"Netherspace," Leeman-Smith said. He glanced at Greenaway, who jerked his head slightly. Leeman-Smith walked rapidly away towards the SUT, followed by the mechanic, Tate Breckmann. Marc held back, realising that Greenaway wanted to talk to him, Kara and Tse.

"I'd expected only a family-sized SUT," Kara told Greenaway.

"With luck you'll be bringing back hostages. Anyway, this was the best available at short notice."

"How many hostages?"

"We don't know." He paused.

Marc had his own concerns. "Netherspace degrades metal?"

"The rumour is," Kara said straight-faced, "that something in netherspace scratches away at the skin of any SUT trying to get in."

Tse glanced at Marc and smiled reassuringly. "No one's ever seen it."

"I don't see any weapons," Kara said.

"On board. For planet use only." Greenaway sounded sombre. "We've never had an SUT with external space weaponry return from netherspace, no matter how well disguised the weapons are. Maybe if you've got weapons then you use them when things get tense, and that provokes some kind of… reaction. And don't ask me why."

"You ever been off-world?" Marc asked.

"Too many times. Don't want to talk about it. Let's go."

"One other thing," Marc heard himself say, aware the question had suddenly appeared in his mind. Simulity or insight? "This sideslip-field generator trade with the Gliese – it's always the same, right?" He glanced at Kara, saw that she was nodding slightly. "And that's weird. Always the same number of humans."

"Why weird?" Greenaway asked.

Marc glanced at Kara and saw that she'd reached the same conclusion. "*Because* it's always the same," he said, "and it's the only trade that is. All the rest are different, no set pattern. But when it comes to netherspace drives," his voice hardened, "there's an established exchange rate. How come?"

"There *could* be a pattern," Greenaway said. "But an alien one. We wouldn't see it."

Marc opened his mouth but Kara cut him off. "That'll be one of the things we're meant to find out," she said firmly. "If GalDiv knew, Marc, they wouldn't need us."

"Is that right?" He looked directly at Greenaway. "Suppose I say no? Screw you and your threats?"

Greenaway shrugged. "Your choice. And you won't end up on a shelf."

"I *thought* you were bluffing," Marc said.

"I wasn't," Greenaway said. "Tell him, Kara."

"We know too much now, Marc," she said with a surprising gentleness. "You can leave but they'll kill you."

He heard the truth in her voice and tried a smile. "I bet you'd take the job, too." He turned towards the SUT, wondering why he wasn't more shocked and angry. But he'd been told it was an all-in situation. And there was almost a sense of pride at working with such a ruthless organisation. *For* such a ruthless organisation. He had no illusions about the power he might or might not have.

• • • • •

The airlock was all that Marc had expected: a shipping container with massive, shiny metal lockable doors at each end. There were glowing and blinking lights, switches and a lever next to a sign marked EMERGENCY. It smelt faintly of oil and the heavy-duty plastic matting on the floor. A movement to one side caught Marc's attention. Kara was tapping her forearm, accessing her AI avatar. For the first time he wished he had a visual one. It would be like belonging to the same tribe.

She glanced at Marc and raised an eyebrow. "Well, you never know," she said. Then, "Oh, fuck," as she saw through the open door at the far end. "Tell me it's still a simulity. Please."

Call it an anteroom. Receiving chamber. Reception lounge. The place where arrivals first formed an impression of the SUT – or its mission manager. It was a space about twenty by thirty metres and at least five metres high, formed from several shipping containers welded together with their internal sides removed. The metal bulkheads had been covered in a faintly rose-coloured material. Marc stretched out a hand and found it smooth, like plaspaper. The floor was covered with what looked like a beige wool carpet and the ceiling was white. Various items of retro furniture were scattered around: chairs, sofas, small tables, bookcases all made from a blond or light brown wood, and bright, geometric-patterned throw cushions. Tse and Tate Breckmann were already sitting on a sofa, looking dazed. Leeman-Smith stood in the centre, wearing a grim smile of self-approval.

"Recognise it?" he asked.

Kara shook her head, her expression grim.

"English, 1960s," he prompted. He pointed to a portrait of a man on the opposite wall. "Recognise him?"

Marc remembered what Greenaway had earlier said, and clearly Kara did too. "Well, of course," she said. "That's Douglas Leeman-Smith. The man who made the first contact." There'd been a woman as well, in fact the mission commander, but Marc guessed that Leeman-Smith wouldn't want to hear that.

"My grandfather," Leeman-Smith said. "This is a perfect reproduction of the sitting room in the house he grew up in. Except for the lack of a fireplace. Oh, and that." He pointed at a piece against a wall. "Actually it's a woman's dressing table, but it makes a good desk. Real as well: antique G-Plan. Cost a fortune. Above it is one of the original newspapers, *The Times*, that reported my grandfather's success. It's real paper, you know. I had it preserved. It'll last as long as I do. You know my grandfather's story, of course?" Leeman-Smith beamed. "Everyone does." He didn't wait for an answer. "That one inspired, selfless act gave us all this." His gesture seemed to take in the entire world. "Without my grandfather the Gliese would have left and we'd still be in the Stone Age. That's compared to then, of course."

"Comfortable as this is," Greenaway said, "and *expensive* as this is, let's go take a look at the heart of this vehicle. The sideslip-field generator?"

"The team is the real heart of this vehicle," Leeman-Smith said. It sounded like something he'd heard on a leadership course.

Marc, Greenaway, Tse and Kara followed Leeman-

Smith out of his grandfather's shrine into a metal corridor, up a short flight of metal steps and into what had to be the generator room. It was smaller than the anteroom. Half a dozen padded seats facing a bank of view screens above a metal sphere, bronze in colour and the size of an old naval mine, covered with incised lines. It hovered above a plinth on the floor – the dais obviously containing a small updown-field generator. An object the size and shape of a good-sized beetle seemed to be stuck to the sphere's surface. A large, rounded hub was fixed to the ceiling directly above the sphere.

It was the netherspace drive, the sideslip-field generator, as simple and as mysterious today as it had been forty years ago.

A shaven-headed man and a woman with blonde hair cut short but with a longer stripe running from ear to ear, both attractive and in their early thirties, came towards them, smiling. That little part of Marc's mind that asked "Would I sleep with this person or not?" every time he was introduced to someone new said an enthusiastic "Yes!" to both.

"Nikki Long, navigator," Leeman-Smith said casually, pointing at the woman. "I'm told she's good. Are you?"

Marc remembered that Nikki was also new on board, she and her colleagues having lost their previous commander.

"Never had any complaints," Nikki said cheerfully. But her blue eyes were cold.

"Mmm. We'll see. And this is our medic, also new. Hank Vandeverde. You want to be careful. He's a mind-tech."

"Henk," the man said casually. "It's Nederlands."

Leeman-Smith turned to the netherspace drive as if he hadn't heard. "That is the platen," pointing to the beetle-like object. "You place the platen on the surface of the sphere to determine the direction of travel, working on the assumption that the centre of the sphere is where we currently are."

"How?" Marc asked. Had any of the staff worked with Leeman-Smith before? He doubted it. "How does it work?"

Tate Breckmann, the mechanic, moved in front of Leeman-Smith. "Thing is," he said, before the mission manager could answer, "that people always explain subspace, or hyperspace, or netherspace, whatever, in terms of flexible rubber sheets."

"I've had some memorable experiences on flexible rubber sheets," Kara murmured, just loud enough for everyone to hear.

Tate grinned. "Einstein's fault. He used a rubber sheet to explain gravity, you know?"

Kara looked doubtful. "Sort of."

"He said the space-time continuum is like a thin rubber sheet and a planet is like a steel ball-bearing on top of it. So the weight of the ball-bearing makes a dip in the rubber, so anything else will roll down to the bearing and hey presto you got gravity. Except that 'anything else' is also making an indentation on the rubber sheet, so you get dents within dents. And except that gravity operates over three *pi* radians, not just three hundred and sixty degrees. So actually it was a crap explanation but it stuck around because it was easy to visualise. And back then no one dared contradict Einstein. People had invested too much time and effort in trying to understand him."

"We got it," Marc said. "Rubber sheets are a no-no."

"Damn right." Tate reached out and took a sheet of plaspaper off a nearby bench. He held it up, holding opposite edges with thumbs and forefingers. "But they still ask you to imagine this two-dimensional sheet represents the three-dimensional universe. To get from one side to the other you'd have to traverse the whole sheet in between, unless..." He twisted the plaspaper so that his hands were touching, "...you can twist three-dimensional space through a fourth dimension so that distant points are actually very close to each other, just like I'm twisting this two-dimensional sheet through the third dimension. That's great, except..." He glanced at the plaspaper and frowned. The navigator, Nikki, stepped forward – pushing Leeman-Smith even further into the background – and obligingly took the now nearly circular edges that Tate *wasn't* holding between her thumbs and forefingers. Because of the way the sheet was twisted, when she tried to fold it so that her own fingers and thumbs touched it just buckled and crumpled, and she couldn't get the edges together.

"Except if someone else wants to make a different journey," Tate continued, "say between *these* two other sides of the sheet, then the sheet has to be bent in a completely different direction – and that may not be possible. We don't know how flexible the multi-dimensional universe is, and as far as we know the Gliese haven't mastered the ability to bend it. Frankly, interested minds are concerned that if you repeatedly bend the universe back and forth then it might split, and that would be bad for all kinds of reasons."

"*So*," Marc repeated, "how does it work?"

Nikki stepped back. Tate screwed the sheet up, crumpling it into a ball. He then opened it out, and crumpled it up again.

"The three-dimensional universe is fractally folded," he announced, "a bit like this, but much, much more complicated. Some parts of it are close together and some aren't." He threw the ball of plaspaper over his shoulder, narrowly missing Leeman-Smith's head. "In fact it's more like the convolutions of a brain. Or better, the Florida Everglades. If you look at a map of them and want to get from one piece of solid ground to another via canoe, then you might have to follow miles of little waterways. Far easier to row to the nearest bank, pick your canoe up, cross a spit of land, get into your canoe again and row across another channel, go across another spit of land and keep going in a straight line." He paused to see if Marc, Kara and Tse were still with him. They were. Just.

"Now imagine that the water is our normal space," he said, "and the land is netherspace. You get where you're going by using both of them, not one or the other. Except they keep shifting back and forth, so that a water channel that was there yesterday might not be there today, or might be there but might end up going in a different direction."

"So," Marc repeated, nodding towards the Gliese sideslip-field generator, "how does it *work*?"

"We don't know," Tate admitted, sighing. "Somewhere in there is a sensor that plots the shifting

128

interfaces between realspace and netherspace, plus a calculator unit that works out the best route, plus something that can slip the SUT from realspace into netherspace and then slip it out again at the appropriate location. The calculator unit then either operates an Up-drive that moves the SUT through realspace to the optimal point by pushing against the gravitational underpinning of the universe – a bit like rowing the canoe across a channel of water – or it waits until the interfaces have shifted around and another push in the right direction into netherspace will take the SUT in the right direction." He gestured to the pitted, incised sphere. "In practical terms, this thing has to be operated by a whole range of species that can't communicate with each other, so the user interface is as simple as possible."

Leeman-Smith was not to be denied. "There's a compartment in the dais," he said smoothly, stepping forward. "And a whole series of platens, of different sizes. Smaller platens move the SUT a smaller distance through netherspace; larger platens move it a larger distance."

"We've put sticky labels on the platens," Nikki called from the far side of the control room. She had taken a seat at the navigator's station behind the sphere and was running through her pre-flight checks. "The smallest one moves us just over three kilometres; the next a hundred, then five hundred, a thousand, ten thousand, a hundred thousand and five hundred thousand. That's approximate distances, give or take. The Gliese don't use kilometres, obviously. After that it gets interesting: the next one moves us a light-year. The one after that takes us five light-years, then fifty – all spot on, the Gliese do seem to understand the light-year concept – and a hundred." She looked comically sad. "Please do not ask how it works again, for a refusal often offends."

"So we pop into netherspace, and pop out again a light-year away," Marc said, sorting it out in his own mind. "Given there's no way anyone could place a platen on that sphere with nanometre precision, there will be some kind of error – we won't pop out exactly where we want. That's why we need a navigator who works out where we are by the star positions, then works out which platen is needed next and where to place it. Repeat until arrival, when the updown-field generator system comes into play. Simple." He frowned, and turned to Leeman-Smith. "So – why do we need you?"

The mission manager smiled thinly. "We make it sound easy, but that's because we're professionals. It's actually a very precise, highly technical operation."

"It's not," Tate murmured. "A trained monkey could do it – and it wouldn't need much training."

"Only feeding," Kara murmured.

Let's see, Marc thought. *A mechanic, a navigator, a medic – all useful on voyage and on planet. A mission manager isn't. So Leeman-Smith's superfluous, and knows it. He's defensive.*

"We have calculations to run," Leeman-Smith said tightly. "I suggest the three of you find your cabins and sort yourselves out. You can watch take-off on-screen. Mission briefing in the canteen in two hours." He looked at Greenaway. "I'll see you out." The two men left the control room.

His first space flight. Marc was surprised he didn't feel excited. Instead there was an overwhelming trepidation. He glanced across at Kara and suspected she was feeling the same way. Then at Tse sitting next to him, who smiled.

"We're okay for the next twenty-four hours," the pre-cog said quietly. "Then it gets bad."

Marc's stomach seemed to lurch. "How bad?"

"Someone dies. But I'm pretty sure it's not you. Or Kara."

"Pretty sure?"

Tse smiled. "Pre-cog's not a science, Marc. It's more like art."

"I'm an artist," he protested. "That gives me no comfort whatsoever."

7

Marc was looking for the toilets – or the restrooms, or the head, or whatever the hell they were called on this thing – without any success. Wandering around for a few minutes he discovered the inside of the SUT smelt like a breaker's yard and too much bare metal was depressing.

He was about to ask out loud for help from the AI – but it probably wouldn't hear; and if it did would only ignore him, or give him the wrong directions – when he heard voices from around a corner.

"You got the sealed orders?" That was Greenaway. Judging by the faint sounds of distant hammering, drilling and pumping he was standing in the SUT's open airlock.

"Right here." That was Leeman-Smith. "Why not download them into the *RIL-FIJ-DOQ*'s AI memory?"

"Computers aren't secure. Not any more."

Leeman-Smith sounded doubtful. "But surely…"

Marc could imagine the affronted frown on the man's face.

"The result of an alien trade," Greenaway said wearily. "Some sort of program that breaks any computer security system. Seems to be a type of meta-mathematics allied with quantum computing. We think. Doesn't even require any knowledge of the operating system, the computer language, anything.

It operates at a symbolic level above all that. We think we've got the only copies. But we can't be sure. Free spacers and anyone else in the Out could also have it."

There was a pause, during which Marc imagined Greenaway pointing at whatever portion of Greenaway's anatomy was holding the sealed envelope.

"Only if the mission is directly threatened, okay? Open them for any other reason and you will be on the shelf – and I mean that literally. I actually do have a shelf, with people on it."

"Nothing *will* go wrong," Leeman-Smith said huffily.

There was a pause. Marc could imagine the two men looking at each other, one passive-aggressively defiant and the other with a world-weary menace.

"This is unnecessary," Leeman-Smith finally said.

"Is it? Say the SUT breaks down, in real or netherspace, what do you do?"

"Open the orders. I can't see why…"

Greenaway ignored him. "And *follow* them. A Chinese philosopher said an unread book is just a block of paper. You open the orders *and* follow them."

Leeman-Smith changed the subject. Awkwardly. "I've never heard of this computer hack trade," he said. "Surely something like that would have made headlines?"

"We suppressed it. Stupid to trumpet a possible intelligence advantage."

"Unless everyone else has the *same* advantage." A nonsensical comment meant to establish understanding. Marc despised the self-satisfaction in Leeman-Smith's voice.

"*When* do you open those orders?" Greenaway asked again.

Resentment at being treated like a child. "If anything seriously threatens the mission," Leeman-Smith said heavily. "Like the *RIL-FIJ-DOQ* breaking down."

"I'll want to see survivors."

"Don't worry," Leeman-Smith said, "I've no intention of dying young." Which nicely summed up his solipsistic attitude to life, Marc decided.

"Not many do," Greenaway drawled. "Never *could* figure out why. Say goodbye to the others for me." He paused. "No, say *au revoir*."

Marc heard the sound of Greenaway leaving the SUT. He imagined Leeman-Smith standing there, staring after him, having expected a hearty handshake or even a manly punch to the shoulder, but denied his heroic due.

Why hadn't the mission manager – such a banal term but it summed up human travel in space neatly – seen the significance of the conversation? An alien computer program that could break any known security system was hot news indeed. So hot it wouldn't be told to a mission manager, unless he wasn't expected to survive.

The airlock door clanged shut, sealing them in. Like the sound of a prison cell door slamming; Marc hadn't heard that since his teenage years but he'd never forgotten it. The sudden flash of memory meant that he almost missed the sound of Leeman-Smith's footsteps. Time to leave.

Back in the lounge Marc mentioned his need for a piss to the navigator, Nikki. She offered to take the newcomers to their cabins and led Marc, Kara and Tse along a different corridor to where a set of identical doors, spaced equally apart, screamed *dormitory*. Name cards had been fixed to each door. Kara seemed amused to discover she'd been promoted to major. Marc wondered why he was only a captain.

"I'm not calling you 'sir'," he grumbled.

"'Captain' is pretty damn good for a newly drafted civilian," Kara pointed out. "And the correct title is ma'am. But you can call me boss."

All the cabins were identical, five metres long by two wide and three high. A hard-mattressed bed, a shower/toilet, vid screen and a bulky plastic-looking cylinder fixed to one metal wall. A crisp pile of combat uniforms in a dull grey colour sat on each bed, topped with a folded green bath towel that had been washed too many times for Marc's comfort, and a small washbag. New combat boots and a pair of flip-flops were set neatly on the floor. One for operations and one for relaxation. Even a newly drafted civilian knew which was which, he thought snarkily.

"So we get to shower," he said, looking at the drive. "I was worried about flannel-washes for the foreseeable future."

"Don't get too excited," Kara told him. "Everything's recycled."

"Everything?"

"Today's coffee, yesterday's pee. Today's pee, tomorrow's shower. And so it goes."

"Thanks."

"And you never know who you got." Kara smiled

evilly at the expression on his face. "Washing your hair with Leeman-Smith."

Marc shook his head and moved the pile of combat clothing to one side, next to the towel. Its position offended him, geometrically set right in the middle of the bunk. He looked at it for a second then twisted it slightly so that it wasn't parallel with the line of the bunk. That made him feel better. He'd made an artistic statement.

A shadow seemed to pass, making the clothing look brighter. He frowned at it. The lighting in the cabin hadn't fluctuated, as far as he could tell, and nobody near him had moved. It was the clothes themselves.

"Automatically adjusting, context-sensitive self-illumination," Kara said, seamlessly switching from piss-take to military mode. "The combat gear always matches ambient light to minimise contrast between itself and the surroundings. Short of having a picture of what's behind you in front of you it's the best form of all-round camouflage, and we haven't had anything like *that* in trade yet, so far as I know."

"We could always invent it ourselves," Marc pointed out. He moved the pile of clothing away from the towel. It immediately faded into a darker grey, matching more closely his bedding. When he straightened, he saw that Kara was looking at him pityingly.

"What's the point spending billions of virtscrip to research and develop something we might be given by aliens next week?"

He looked around. No one else within earshot. "Something you should know. Boss." He told her about the conversation he'd overheard in the airlock.

Kara listened intently, her face impassive.

"We knew there was a possible AI problem," she said. "Sealed orders are new. First time I ever heard of 'em. And I was joking about calling me boss."

"So was I. Strange Greenaway telling that prick so much about the computer threat."

"Because it's so secret and Leeman-Smith's only a lowly mission manager?"

Marc waited for the sting.

There wasn't one. "Well, I'd say Leeman-Smith isn't expected to make it home," Kara said casually. "That *your* take? Good. And good job."

He wasn't used to praise from someone he liked and respected. Someone he'd been twinned with. Marc nodded then looked around. "Nowhere to hang my clothes," he grumbled.

"In the Corby," she said.

Marc looked blank.

She pointed to the cylinder. "There." She showed him how to open it. "Standard military laundry. Just hang your clothes inside."

"Laundry?"

"Originally alien tech, of course. Removes all dirt, sweat, blood, oil, shit and dead skin," she said in a tone of voice used for instructing recruits. "Takes an hour max. Leave them there until you need to change. Got it?"

"Why Corby?"

Kara shrugged. "Maybe they're made there." She smiled slightly. "Or maybe we exchanged the town of Corby for the technology. Maybe it's not even there any more."

He stared darkly at the machine. "It removes all the dirt, sweat, blood, oil, shit and dead skin," he repeated. "Then what? Turns them into tomorrow's shepherd's pie?"

Kara laughed. "If you'd ever tasted military survival rations," she said, "you wouldn't make that joke."

"I gotta take a pee." He gestured at the shower/toilet.

"And top up the water tanks," she said, straight-faced.

For the next couple of minutes he thought of nothing else. A certain satisfaction at being a vital part of the SUT's life-support system would be nice. Instead he remembered that urine was once said to halt baldness – and Leeman-Smith had a full head of gleaming hair. The connection did not make Marc feel better. Finding that Kara was still in the cabin made him feel worse, especially when she motioned him – not even a "please" or "by your leave"! – into the corridor. He noticed that Nikki and Tse were chatting in a cabin next to Kara's. Tse would have had to explain to the navigator where the pre-cog believed – or intuited – the Cancri homeworld was.

"I'm going to change into uniform," Kara said loudly, so Tse could hear. "See you both in ten." Saw the oh-so-obvious question form on Marc's lips. "Minutes. You should change, too. Need any help or can you tie your own boots?"

"We don't have self-tying boots? I have to do *everything* for myself around here?"

She shook her head pityingly.

"I better go," Nikki said, getting up off Tse's bunk.

"Have to plot the direction and impetus for our initial drop into netherspace. I can correct any errors as we go along, but it's a point of pride amongst navigators to minimise the number of drops we have to make."

"They have league tables," Tse explained, looking at Marc. "Nikki used to be in division two, but she got promoted."

Back in his cabin Marc changed into uniform and liked the results. When he was a teenager he had read somewhere that any man who'd never been a soldier or sailor regretted it. Very jingoistic. He couldn't remember the exact wording of the quote but he never forgot his reaction: angry contempt, even though he was riding with centurion bikers Out There who based themselves on the Roman army and its controlled use of extreme violence. For Marc, soldiers and sailors represented authority and uniforms were the death of individuality, and thus the death of art.

Yet now he liked the subtle camouflage clothing. The material was soft but tough-wearing and impossible to crease. It felt good, designed for fighting not the parade ground. A hidden hood and hidden gloves, built into the collar and cuffs, meant that his skin tone wouldn't stand out against the shifting light level of the clothing. There were black underpants, vest and socks that felt like wool but had to be synth. Wool was only produced in the Out. The synth boots were also self-camouflaging, and surprisingly comfortable. Admiring himself in the full-length shower mirror – especially the captain's pips on his shoulders, and the commando-style green beret – he realised the uniform had been tailored for him. Had to be. No standard issue would have fitted so well.

Despite the uniform, and the excitement trembling in his gut as take-off drew near, Marc was disappointed on some deep level. Kara probably felt at home with a bare-bones cabin, but for Marc it had a thrown-together feel. Much like the SUT itself – and all the others he'd seen.

It was true that romance had long vanished from space travel… possibly because no one knew how movement in netherspace worked. Treating it as just another type of commute made the ignorance of humans less embarrassing.

Even so…

SUTs are disposable. Like Leeman-Smith.

He froze as the insight hit, staring at, without seeing, his reflection in the mirror.

They're disposable because so many don't survive.

Marc remembered what Kara had said: *"The rumour is that something in netherspace scratches away at the skin of any SUT, trying to get in."* He'd seen what could be teeth or claw marks in the foam protection of other SUTs at Tegel, although they couldn't realistically be either. Evolution wouldn't have produced those familiar design solutions in such an alien environment.

His own comment to Greenaway, only two days ago: *"One in every forty spacecraft vanishes. Lost or broken."* Greenaway hadn't disagreed.

What if it was *ten* in every forty that vanished, maybe more? What if another ten showed up with their staff and passengers driven mad? But with Gliese popping up everywhere with sideslip-field generators to trade, space travel couldn't be stopped. What *was* the acceptable loss rate for space travel?

He remembered the long past voice of a friendly spacer: *"Show me… Sorry, kid. That's Gamma Three, not Epsilon Seven. I recognise those things that look like trees. You must have got it wrong."* Those vidcards were all Marc had of his parents back then. And maybe they were just a convenient fiction designed to cover up an unpalatable truth.

GalDiv controlled space travel, and controlled even the facts about it, apparently, but why? The free spacers were bothersome, but were they important? Not really. In fact, in all Marc's time in the Out he'd never met any, nor seen one of their vehicles. Everyone knew the free spacers operated from the Out but no one seemed to know where exactly. Similarly, no one knew how many GalDiv-authorised SUTs there were. Tegel wasn't the only space access point. Every city state had one. Yet the public knew dick-all about space except what GalDiv told it.

Oh? What about GalDiv spacers themselves?

What about them? Humanity's spreading through the galaxy. Okay, so there's someone you went to space school with, whatever, and they stop showing up for class reunions: do you think they've been eaten by netherspace? Or do you believe it when someone says "Oh, they went off to Alpha Centauri…"

There was too much space activity for anyone to document except GalDiv. And GalDiv had good reasons not to tell the truth.

A voice inside Marc's head told him to get the hell out, that the mission was too dangerous and he would *not* be controlled by anyone. Another voice said it was too late.

He still didn't recognise himself in the mirror.

"You can leave but they'll kill you," Kara had said.

But that's not the reason I'm going to stay. Well, not the only reason. A moment of honesty that made the face in the mirror smile. *I'm staying because I said I would, even though I may have been conned. I'm staying because I want to see this through. And because like it or loathe it, I'm now linked to Kara and where she goes so do I.* Still it wasn't all bad. There was the hardened alien foam that was going to be sprayed, or painted, or spread skilfully with a butter knife across the SUT's exterior to protect them from netherspace. Suddenly that foam, that *alien* foam, was very important to him.

Marc thought fleetingly how well the green beret set off his eyes, and went to find his comrades.

Kara and Tse were waiting for him in the corridor, both in uniform; Tse also had a captain's pips. Even though the camouflage worked only by matching the contrast, not the background, Marc was struck by the way they suddenly seemed almost… unnoticeable.

"I feel like I'm being played," he said ruefully, needing an outlet for the shock of his secret epiphany. Or perhaps a cover for it. "This uniform fits too damn well."

"You look very impressive," Tse told him.

"Always 'me, me' with you," Kara said. "Listen. Chances are we'll have to control a bunch of scared, demoralised civilians. You do not establish authority looking like a sack of shit, you establish authority by looking like you know what you're doing. That you can take care of yourself and therefore you can take care of them. A simple psychological trick but surprisingly effective."

Another form of camouflage, Marc thought.

"Also," Kara went on, "we represent GalDiv, otherwise known as the human race. Not a bad idea to look smart, even if aliens can't tell best from worst. Finally, combat's a damn sight easier in well-fitting gear and comfortable footwear. You have to expect GalDiv knows everything about you. Even your boot size or whether your balls hang left or right. They got my bra size spot on. Left me five packs of my favourite joss. You don't, I know, but you'll be puffing away pretty damn soon, I swear. We belong to GalDiv for the duration, Marc. Get used to it."

Tse moved forward. "We thought it would be nice to watch lift-off together," she said quietly. "Nikki told me where."

She led them to the canteen, which confirmed Marc's suspicions of drabness. Microwave ovens and stacked ration packs were placed against one cream-painted steel wall. In the middle was an oval table, plastic and metal, large enough for ten; at the far end a tired-looking coffee machine squatted on a plaswood shelf. The floor was some sort of grey speckled composite with a spongy feel to it. The room smelled of warmed-up food, stale coffee, joss fumes and industrial cleaner. A cockroach or a short-order cook would have felt at home. Only one thing suggested this was a space vehicle: a viewing screen that took up most of the wall opposite the microwaves. It was like looking through the clearest glass window ever made – or a glass-free hole in the SUT's side.

Marc looked around. "Aside from the vid it's all grunge."

Kara shrugged. "A room is a room is a room."

"The *RIL-FIJ-DOQ* is normally used for local runs," Tse supplied. "Nikki told me. Doesn't go beyond Pluto. Two-day round trip at the most. Apparently it was the only passenger SUT available at such short notice." She saw the doubt on their faces. "Leeman-Smith comes with it. Big, public fuss if he was left behind. And he's got friends high up. But the rest of the staff are exploration spacers brought in off leave, been together a long time. They don't like him any more than you do. Shall we sit down?"

No fresh coffee – the machine was out of water – but Tse found pre-made cans of the stuff amongst the rat-packs. Presumably this coffee was made from fresh water rather than someone's recycled piss. The beans were an Italian blend. Pulling the tab on top of the cans set off a tiny microwave heater in the base, and within a few seconds the coffee was hot and the odour was overlaying the smell of the room.

Marc pulled up his sleeve as if about to access his own keyboard and then stopped as he remembered the earlier problem with accessing the SUT's AI. He looked at Tse.

"Not sure the AI's secure," he said. "Don't want my chip seduced."

Tse looked at the vid screen. "Hey! Bet you never saw *that* before."

An SUT was being readied for space. A spider-like foam spreader stood over it: a good ten metres tall, with multiple thin, segmented legs radiating from a fat central hub. As they watched, three of the legs lifted from the ground and angled themselves towards the SUT's convoluted exterior, stopping about a metre away, while the spreader balanced on the remaining ones. A pause and then foam pulsed out of hidden nozzles on their ends. It formed a great, seething glob all the colours of the rainbow, coruscating even in the late afternoon sun.

"That I didn't expect," Kara said. "How does…"

"Hold on." Marc noticed something and clumsily used the remote control on a nearby table to zoom closer. "Bloody hell!"

The three sat down at the table and watched. Left to itself, the rainbow foam spread over a triangular-shaped area on the SUT's surface, filling every nook and cranny, covering every weird angle and sharp edge to precisely the same height. Only the business ends of the manoeuvring jets and sensors on the ends of their arms were left exposed. It was as if the foam knew exactly what it was doing. More than that, the foam was a perfectionist.

"That's a little weird," Kara said as another shimmering glob was deposited, again oozing unaided in all directions like some vast and purposeful amoeba to produce a triangle that merged with the first one, which was now beginning to fade to a dull grey.

"Alien tech," Marc told her, "is always weird. The clue's in the name."

Leeman-Smith's voice filled the room. "Mission manager speaking. Take-off in five minutes. It'll be a slow ascent, allowing the newcomers to adjust. I am now going to sound the emergency alarms, as per regulations."

On cue, an ear-splitting screech filled the room,

mercifully for only a second. It was followed by Leeman-Smith's fruity tones: "If you hear that alarm, we are venting atmosphere to space."

A different ear-splitting screech. "If you hear *that* alarm, there is a fire on board."

A third screech. "If you hear *that* alarm, the radiation levels on board have reached dangerous levels."

In total, there were ten different alarms, each marking a different emergency. There were, however, no instructions on what to do in the eventuality of any of these emergencies actually occurring. It was if Leeman-Smith was really saying how unimportant they were.

"I can't tell them apart," Marc admitted reluctantly. "I hate to ask, but can we run through them again?"

Kara shook her head. "I don't see the point. They're just ways of telling us how we're going to die. I'd prefer to be surprised."

A strange expression flickered across Tse's face, too fast for Marc to tell what it was. It hadn't been a happy look, though.

Kara had picked up on it too. "Can you foresee your own death?" she asked bluntly. "Do we die at the same time as you?"

Tse shook his head, so minutely that the motion was almost undetectable. "It's the first thing you learn not to think about," he said quietly. "There are potential deaths scattered all over the landscape of my future, like sinkholes. Some are obvious, and some are hidden. One day I'll fall into one, but I don't know which day and I don't want to. Also, remember that now we're together, my future is also tied in with yours, which is what I see."

But suppose, Marc thought darkly, the most probable, and best outcome for their mission included Tse's own death? Or Marc's? Would he still point them in the right direction?

Feeling slightly awkward at having caught what seemed like a private moment of introspection, Marc looked toward the vid screen. "Hang on a sec," he said, gesturing towards the SUT outside. The thing that had, minutes before, been a series of rectangular boxes covered in metal spikes was now a grey oval shape, glistening slightly, like a vast cocoon pregnant with some strange insect life. As if to hammer home the parallel, the tentacles of the spider-like foam spreader were caressing the exterior; looking for patches that needed extra filling, he presumed. "We're close to launch. Aren't they going to cover *our* SUT the way they covered that one? We're not launching naked, are we?"

"That *is* our SUT," a woman said from behind him.

Marc turned his head. Nikki, the navigator, was standing in the doorway. "That's not a vid feed from one of our sensors of what's happening across the tarmac; that's a vid feed from someone *else's* sensors of what's just happened to *us*. It's always nice to check that people have done their job properly."

Marc's shoulders hunched. It was okay when he'd thought the foam was applied to another SUT. But the *RIL-FIJ-DOQ* was being smothered. A strange sense of claustrophobia settled over him like a shroud. The temperature inside the SUT seemed to have gone up a couple of degrees in a few seconds. "Er, so what happens when, *if* we land somewhere?"

"The part over the main airlock's removable," Nikki said casually. "Anyway, reason I'm here is just to say you might feel a tad weird when we go Up." She smiled reassuringly. "Artificial updown fields can do that to people. And when we go into netherspace, of course. You may feel, oh, a bit woozy, maybe? Almost light-headed. Nothing to worry about, though. Now I'd better go reassure our lord and master. He's sounding nervous."

Kara gestured for her to stay. "Just a quick question: what *does* happen when we go into netherspace?"

Marc had wanted to ask the same question, but he was glad that Kara had got in first. It was always better to let someone else ask the embarrassingly simple questions. That way you could sit like an impassive stone Buddha, soaking up the information that someone else had broken their cool, professional demeanour to obtain. As she had told him earlier, in another context, it was a simple psychological trick but amazingly effective.

"Remember how Tate explained it before?" Nikki asked, taking a moment's silence for an affirmative. "So, try thinking of this SUT as a swimmer, diving into those water channels between dry land. We swim underwater, propelled by the momentum of the dive we made courtesy of the Gliese sideslip-field generator. Eventually the momentum runs out and the natural tendency of *real* matter to want to be in *real*space makes us surface again, like a swimmer coming up to take a breath. When that happens, it's my job to look around, check the spectra of all the stars and galaxies that I can detect and work out where we are – which should be many billions of miles from where we were, but with luck only a few million from where we were aiming. That done, I set the coordinates for the next dive under the surface."

"You make it sound so simple," Kara said.

"It is," Nikki admitted, shrugging. "If you want I can dress it up in all kinds of techno-babble, but at the end of the day I run a set of computer algorithms that do the work for me. When I was a kid I wanted to be a masseuse," she said brightly, "but do you know the amount of training and certification you have to go through? This was an easier career choice." She waved a casual goodbye and left.

"Muster point is the control room," Leeman-Smith's voice boomed again from the tannoy. "Full brief in one hour thirty-six minutes in the conference room. Mission manager out."

Marc shook his head in mixed sorrow and anger. "What *is* his problem?"

Kara turned to Tse. "What you said about the fuss if Leeman-Smith's left behind. Even so. Why him?"

Long black hair rustled faintly as Tse shook his head. "Pre-cog doesn't work like that," Tse said, clearly playing for time.

"You're smart," Marc joined in. "Make a guess."

"Perhaps because, despite the bluster, he's mostly harmless."

The other two looked doubtful.

"And can be controlled." Tse looked directly at Kara. "*You're* really in charge, right?"

"Well…"

"And I doubt the rest of the staff would support him. If it came to that."

"Came to what?" Marc asked.

"Oh, you know," Tse said vaguely. "A crisis."

Kara looked at Tse for a long moment then slowly nodded her head. Marc watched the unspoken by-play between the two of them, thankful he wasn't a pre-cog.

Widespread awareness of a probable future can result in the accidental or even deliberate creation of a totally different, perhaps more dangerous one. For the first time Marc understood how isolated Tse must feel. To know all the probabilities, all the *mights* and *maybes*, to know the shape of the landscape and the landmarks on the horizon, to use Tse's own earlier simile, and not be able to share, except perhaps with other pre-cogs. The force of willpower it must take to keep all of that bottled up inside. *Maybe that explains the momentary dark expression on Tse's face earlier*, Marc thought – and realised his claustrophobia was gone.

"One thing," Kara said, interrupting Marc's chain of thought. "Can a pre-cog help explain why aliens exchange tech for crap?"

"Crap?" Marc asked, offended.

"Mostly crap." She batted her eyes at him. "And some genius art."

"But aliens don't know the difference?"

"I can make a guess," Tse said quickly. "Most of the exchanges don't *matter* to them. Except for the genius art, of course. There's only one thing they consistently want. Us. *Humans.*"

"So the tech is to keep us sweet?" Marc asked.

Tse shrugged. "Maybe."

"Do you know that for sure?" Kara asked intently, leaning forward in her seat. "Is that pre-cognition telling you something we'll find out in the future, or do you just have a feeling?"

"Is there a difference?" Marc queried.

Tse shrugged again and said nothing.

Kara looked doubtful. "Until now it's only Gliese who've taken humans. Other aliens take objects. There again, only Gliese trade for sideslip engines." She assumed a military attitude. "Remember two things. One, the staff do not learn the truth of this mission until I decide it's necessary, okay? Going to affect you most, Tse, as you're working with Nikki."

"Keeping secrets is what I do," Tse said a little sadly. "And my work with Nikki's mostly done. She's got the general direction, distance in light-years and the relevant star patterns."

Kara nodded. "Second thing, look at each other for a moment. The person you see is now your best friend. He and me are the only people you trust. Got that?"

Both slowly nodded.

"We're alone in the Up," Kara said. "Do not ever forget it."

The moment was broken when for the second time Leeman-Smith's voice filled the room. "Lift-off in two minutes. Passengers must sit down and refrain from moving about until advised otherwise." It sounded like a script.

Marc discovered he was both excited and nervous. Judging by suddenly tightened lips, so were the other two. He glanced at the vid screen. The spider-like foam spreader had moved away now. The SUT was sitting alone in the middle of the tarmac. "Any particular view?" he asked, looking at the remote control. "I think this thing can get a feed from any external camera in the space port."

They decided to go split screen: one half showing *RIL-FIJ-DOQ* from a series of angles, the other the SUT's view pointing down.

Leeman-Smith began counting down the last thirty seconds. They might have despised him, but it did add something to the proceedings.

"The countdown was invented by the German film director Fritz Lang," Kara said. "He used it for a film over a hundred years ago called *Woman in the Moon*. Everyone thinks it's some kind of necessary space-flight ritual, but it really isn't." She caught Marc's raised eyebrow. "What?" she challenged. "I like old movies. Sue me."

"That's not old," Marc pointed out. "That's *ancient*."

Leeman-Smith had left the tannoy on and they could hear his voice, that of the mechanic, Tate Breckmann and a distant traffic controller in some computer-filled room miles away engaging in a ritualistic call-and-response script.

"All electricals checked and operational."

"All electricals cross-checked and operational."

"All hydraulics checked and operational."

"All hydraulics cross-checked and operational."

"Confirm pressurisation of vehicle is stable."

"Confirm airspace is clear of obstructions."

"Internal and external updown fields on line."

"*RIL-FIJ-DOQ*, you are clear for take-off."

"Space access point control, acknowledged."

The merest bump, and the sound of creaking as the stresses and strains within the SUT's structure redistributed themselves.

"I don't feel lighter," Marc said, half-joking. A part of him had expected to be floating by now.

On-screen, the pale grey chrysalis that was their transport rose slowly through the air as if on an invisible string.

"You have any idea what we do when – if – we get to this Cancri planet?" Marc asked Kara. "Seeing as how you're in charge."

"Whatever I tell you." Her slight smile took some of the sting from the words.

He looked at Tse. "She has no idea."

"Are you asking me?"

"I know, pre-cog's an art. Any chance you could do me a sketch?"

"We do whatever's necessary to get the hostages back," Kara said. "Assuming they're alive. You're confusing 'what' with 'how'. And the how's already in your head."

8

FOURTEEN DAYS EARLIER

The sun was small, blue and so dazzlingly hot the captives were forced to stay inside the domed shelters. Some had sunk into apathetic depression. Others were all but speechless from shock and confusion. A few tried to make some sense of the situation, although no logical scenario held out any hope. And some had begun looking to Tatia for guidance. Not because she was the Consort. But because she'd told a few people who she was and that she'd owned their original SUT. There'd been a need for authority. Whether she wanted to or not, Tatia was gradually assuming it.

She'd been sleeping. This was a state distinguishable from waking because lying on hard ground was more uncomfortable than standing on it. Without warning the temperature dropped to well below zero. The condensed sweat that had been trickling down the curved walls and pooling on the identical material of the floor froze with a series of crackling sounds.

A middle-aged woman named Mariana, black hair streaked with far more grey than a day ago, began pushing people nearest her towards the door. "It's warm outside!" she said, clinging to the obvious like a drowning swimmer clinging to a rock. "We must keep warm or we'll die!"

Some of the Pilgrims moved but others just stood where they were and looked at Tatia for guidance. The little boy

Pablo was one of them, had even taken to sleeping near her. Despite the heat, soon after he fell asleep his body would edge closer to Tatia until he was nestled into her side.

"Why is this happening?" an elderly man asked. "Please, why?"

This sudden cold, or the whole thing? *Tatia asked herself bitterly as she levered herself from a half-sleep of happy, hopeless dreams.* As if I would know the answer to either question!

"It might be the weather," she said, hearing the dullness in her voice. "Perhaps the climate control has broken down. Or maybe they want us to go outside."

"Should we go?" This was a teenage girl, Darai.

"If it's the weather then going or staying won't make any difference. People who stay should huddle together for warmth. But I think they are forcing us outside. We should go. If we don't, they'll come in and get us. At least let's go willingly, with dignity."

There was general nodding across the group. Mariana, resentful that the authority she'd tried to assert had been so casually undercut, led the way outside.

A lemon-yellow sky stretched above a dusty lavender plain. The alien SUT that had brought them there was still parked a few hundred yards away from the domes. Looking at it, Tatia noticed how the ubiquitous foam that covered it had been... what? Dissolved? Worn down? Eaten away? Whatever: the curving shape of the underlying construction was visible through the remnants of the foam – different from the building-block construction of human SUTs.

Ground vehicles of alien design were parked nearby. They were a rusty red in colour and multi-wheeled, but the wheels were a mixture of sizes. There was no clear pattern as to whether the bigger wheels were at the front, in the middle, at the rear, spaced equally or spaced randomly. Tatia now knew it was no use trying to impose human logic on alien actions or designs. They were what they were, explicable only to alien minds.

Some Cancri were watching the humans, while others went about their unknowable business. Most of them were the usual combination of two life forms – the small, soft, white maggots and the striped greyhound-like beasts of burden that carried them and manipulated things for them with the thin arms that emerged just above their front set of legs. Tatia noticed, however, that some of the beasts of burden were trotting around without the maggoty riders on their backs. Their gait was ungainly, and she saw that their backbones – or whatever they had in place of backbones – were curved to form a saddle shape that matched perfectly the size of their riders. Two of them were standing side by side with their mouth parts moving. Were they talking? She looked around for riders without their steeds; it took a while to find them. It was only when she turned around at the dome behind her that she saw some of the pale grubs clinging to the surface. Were they taking in the sun?

One of them was about ten feet away from Tatia, at head height. She stared at it, appalled and fascinated in equal measure. She could have held it like a baby, but the stumpy limbs it used to cling on to the greyhound-like beasts of burden were tipped with serrated claws coloured a translucent green, like jade. The grub's mouths were made up of several grippers of different sizes and designs. It didn't seem to have eyes, but as she watched, revolted, the grub twisted so that its mouth end was pointed *straight at her. It was looking at her; she was sure.*

"I am not scared of you," she whispered. "I hate you."

Its "head" twisted away again, disinterestedly, and it started crawling up the side of the dome. The tiny jade claws made small grooves in the supposedly adamantine surface.

She looked back towards the alien SUT. There were also two representatives of a species she had never seen before. They were standing separately, several hundred metres apart. Their multiple limbs were long and thin and curved: they looked like small weeping willow trees, and it was difficult to make out any central body, any head, anything apart from the profusion of drooping limbs, which were striped in dusky pink and grey. The only thing that distinguished them from vegetation was the fact that they moved, fast but decisively, across the ground for a while, then stopped.

A commotion from the front of the group of Pilgrims pulled her interest away. Cancri guards waving weapons were isolating three scared adults and two screaming children from the rest of the group. They herded them towards a space between the buildings and the SUT.

A Cancri pointed its weapon at one of the children. He turned around, frantically scanning the crowd for a familiar face. He spotted Tatia, and his mouth and eyes went wide.

It was Pablo.

His head exploded.

Tatia screamed, had to be held back. Not so lucky, a man shouted obscenities as he ran blindly, pointlessly towards a Cancri guard, swinging his arms.

A second later, two bodies lay in the lavender dust.

● ● ● ● ●

"That's really *us*," Tse said, a note of disbelief in her voice. "We're *in* there. Here."

On the right-hand side of the screen the ground began to recede. Marc, always in some sense a spectator in his own head, glanced around. A trained assassin, a borderline psychopath, a pre-cog and a navigator who was hiding who knew what personality defects, all moving to sit as close to the screen as possible, like kids peering through an open window at a parade. On the left-hand side of the screen they could see that some of the jigsaw of images that were being transmitted from cameras all around the space access point were pointed at empty tarmac while others were tracking the SUT as it rose into a translucently blue sky. At least, Marc assumed it was their SUT. There must be several launching every hour.

On the right again they could see the space access point, visible from the air. Then the city, patched with green and studded with silver lakes. The SUT had vanished from the left-hand pictures, so Marc switched to full-screen: their point of view. The city was now a sprawling tumour of grey artificiality eating into the green flesh of the Out surrounding Berlin city state. As they climbed higher Marc saw the Baltic coast and then northern Europe receding beneath them until a net curtain of cloud faded the planet below. The cloud thickened until they were staring into a dirty grey nothingness. They were higher than any ramjet flight now; gradually blue and green and black crept in around the edges of the grey cloud: the colours of the Earth, and of deep space behind its circular horizon. Kara and Nikki were noisily identifying cities and seas. Marc should have been looking on this with the eye of an artist, seeing the multiple shades of colour and the chiaroscuro of light and shadow, but instead he felt disappointed. It was like looking at a map, except there were no labels. He realised that he hadn't really seen anything with the eyes of an artist since he'd exchanged memories, maybe personalities, with Kara. Nothing apart from the position of his towel. Now his interest seemed to be more military.

Was Kara imagining a new artwork? Somehow he doubted it.

To his right Tse sat in a rigid silence as if this was the first time he'd realised the Earth was round. Or maybe experiencing the realisation this might be the last time he saw it. If so, a similar thought was floating somewhere inside Marc's own mind. He glanced at Kara. She was looking at him speculatively, as if not sure what manner of man he was. Well, one who knew more about Kara than any other human being, for whatever comfort that was.

"Worth fighting for," she said.

Marc was about to add "and dying for?" when Leeman-Smith's voice filled the room again, announcing, "Netherspace in eight minutes." The vid screen went blank.

"*Hey, who turned that off?*" Marc exclaimed, furious, shaking the remote control.

"No," Kara quietened him, "remember what Greenaway said about netherspace? If you look for more than five minutes you go insane."

Marc felt an increasing anger, aware that it covered a pit of unease that only deepened the more he discovered about space flight and hyperspace and the odds of getting where they wanted to go unscathed. He'd always known space flight was like launching a ship into rough seas and hoping for the best, but the metaphor, for him, had meant seventeenth- and eighteenth-century tea clippers: all sails and masts and spars and jolly heave-ho Jack Tars. Now he was beginning to realise they were more like Vikings in open longboats sailing the North Atlantic. Or islanders from a small, insignificant atoll sending canoes across the Pacific Ocean. This wasn't exploration but an act of faith… or desperation.

"How many other teams has Greenaway put together in case we screw up?" he asked, almost wearily. "How many SUTs are sitting on the tarmac right now, waiting for permission to launch?" A thought snagged his mind. "Are we even the *first*? Maybe there were five previous missions that never made it out of netherspace."

"It is what it is," Kara said. "Not a thing you can do to change it."

The old Marc would have thrown a fit. New Marc nodded his acceptance. "What are our chances, boss? I mean, of just getting to this fucking planet, wherever it is?"

She looked at him levelly. "Your point being?"

"*This*." The gesture took in the entire SUT. "All of them. Us. Disposable, right? Cheapest solution so that there's minimal waste when something goes wrong. Because something out there *really* does not like us." He paused and took a deep breath, trying to suppress a sudden panic. "I'm not scared, Kara, but—"

"You should be," she interrupted. "I know I am."

"*What*?"

"Space, specifically netherspace, doesn't like us. I told you, remember?"

"I thought you were joking."

"At least we've been foamed," she said with heavy humour.

Tse gave a discreet cough. "Actually there isn't enough to do every one, and sometimes the spreaders leave voids or gaps by accident, or trap some air bubbles that expand in vacuum and push the foam apart. And often the foam gets totally worn away. We should be okay, though."

"You know this how?"

"I've been working with Greenaway for some time," Tse said. Not *for* but *with*. "You pick up things and—"

"Prepare for entry into netherspace," Leeman-Smith said over the intercom. For the second time he began counting down the time from ten to one. Tse stopped speaking, and shook his head.

The universe blinked.

"That's it?" Marc said, disappointed.

"Welcome to netherspace," Kara said. "Population – eight more than it was a few seconds ago."

"No fanfare," Marc said. "No flashing colours or stars elongating into straight lines. I feel kind of cheated."

"Me too." Kara glanced from Marc to Tse and back. "I don't think it'll get more exciting for a while." She checked her watch, a little surprised to see it was working normally. *So much for Einstein. Or if time has slowed, I wouldn't know. But people who go to the stars age like everyone else. Or is Nikki several hundred years old? If so, she looks good for her age! Seriously good. So does that medic, Henk. Damn Marc! Not easy to stay operational with his libido slowly stirring inside my head. Or my libido, come to that. It must be the prospect of space.* Kara took a deep breath. "Our esteemed mission manager's briefing us soon. Now listen, people. First rule of military operations is to eat and sleep whenever you can. As of this moment we're officially in shit-storm territory. So grab food and go rest; best you do both, okay?"

Although neither Marc nor Tse were hungry, Kara made them stuff their pockets with hi-pro bars and synthchoc before shooing them off to their cabins.

"What about you?" Marc asked.

"I need a word with Leeman-Smith," Kara told him.

She headed towards the central pod of the SUT, surrounded by the various other shipping containers and thus furthest from netherspace and anything that might be out there, trying to get in. That was where Leeman-Smith would be.

Not so much for operational reasons but because the man was a pathological coward.

Kara had known that within minutes of their first meeting. When it came to judging individuals whose actions could harm her people, Kara Jones was rarely wrong. And now she needed a quiet talk with the man whose grandfather was responsible for first contact. She needed to explain who was top of the *RIL-FIJ-DOQ*'s food chain, before the conference at which Leeman-Smith would undoubtedly try to exert control. And while the staff were unlikely to follow him – Nikki had made her loyalty obvious *and she's so attractive – mind on the job, Sergeant, I mean Major, mind on the job –* it was best Leeman-Smith never even tried. Bad luck to begin a mission with blood already on the floor.

The rectangular units were connected in strange ways; Kara had to double back on herself several times before finding the way into the command container where she discovered that Leeman-Smith wasn't alone.

Influenced by all the visions of the future she'd experi-enced in old television series, Kara would have expected Leeman-Smith in a bigger and better chair than anyone else, and everyone staring forwards at a large screen showing what was going on outside – though it would be blank, now they were in netherspace. In fact, the command unit was just like a small open-plan office. Several desks were spaced around it, and the only thing that distinguished Leeman-Smith's area from anyone else's was that his desk faced one way and theirs faced towards him, like a teacher in front of a class. There was even a potted plant on his desk. Tate and Nikki were there with the mission manager, the three of them concentrating on information projected onto their retinas by their own internal implants and typing instructions onto the keyboard tattoos on their forearms. It looked to Kara like some bizarrely synchronised puppet show. Every now and then one of them would ask a question of the others, but apart from that they were locked inside their individual worlds.

As far as Kara could figure it, the staff were calibrating the *RIL-FIJ-DOQ*'s sensors, which were providing data from netherspace. But judging by the occasional barbed comment from both Nikki and Tate, this was something of a waste of time. First, the sensors were designed and built in realspace – whatever that was – so wouldn't work properly in netherspace. Second, no one had any idea what they were looking for, other than it was probably large and unfriendly. And third, there was fuck-all they could do about it anyway, so best to relax and let the foam do its job. Leeman-Smith, however, was adamant: the sensors had to be working perfectly and linked to an emergency program within the SUT's AI.

Kara stayed for a few minutes, watching, until the novelty wore off. Then she left the command module and moved towards the back of the SUT, down a linking corridor that she thought led to the unit with the Gliese sideslip-field generator.

As she reached the halfway point in the short corridor something moved in the corner of her vision, a flickering shadow, a flutter of light and darkness. It startled her. Kara turned, hands raised in instinctive readiness to defend against an attack, but the corridor was empty.

Kara waited a few moments, listening for movement, but there was only the beating of her own heart and the low susurration of the air recycling system. Maybe a moth had wandered on board to be whisked away with the rest of them into netherspace. Maybe a spider had taken up residence and was busy building webs that would never catch a fly. *Where did that thought come from? Rational, Major, rational.*

Early missions, from what she had heard, had spent hours using radiation and chemical sprays to eradicate insects and vermin from their SUTs before take-off so as to avoid contaminating alien worlds with new life forms, but the practice had quickly faded away. Most life forms humans had brought along for the ride died quickly with nothing to eat – and precious little native life on alien worlds was edible by any visitors from Earth, large or small. Unfortunately this extreme housekeeping had also wiped out most of the staff's gut microbes. Each human carries within them approximately two kilograms of live, friendly bacteria. They keep the gut working properly, and are important to the immune system. Eradicate them and a bad case of the runs or chronic constipation is the mildest reaction. The worst includes death.

With sick staff confined to their bunks, the eradication process was quietly dropped. Nobody complained, and no alien worlds were overrun with rats or cockroaches. Or, at least, nobody ever reported that they had been. Most colonists had a robust approach to their new planetary homes, best summed up as "you belong to us now". Except where the native dominant life forms were possibly as or even more intelligent than humans, in which case they went elsewhere. The galaxy was a big, big place with room enough for every colonising species.

Rational, Major, rational. Kara shook her head and turned towards the engineering unit. She wasn't quite sure why she wanted to go there. But it seemed like a good idea.

Something twitched at the extreme edge of her vision.

She turned quickly, scanning the air, but there was nothing.

A subtle change in her blood pressure, perhaps, causing the lens in her eyeball to deform slightly and making her think she had seen something move. A light globe that was on the edge of failing. A hallucination. God forbid it was an incipient failure in her AI chip. Whatever it was, she was going to ignore it until it showed itself more fully.

She wasn't worried. At first, perhaps, but not anymore. Intrigued was more like it. Even amused – *who on earth could be stalking me? Mmmmm, I hope they're attractive because I'm—*

Rational, Major, rational. Not the time to begin feeling horny. Is this what Nikki meant by "feeling loose"? Nikki. Love her mouth. Rules and regs are for Earth, for realspace.

Maybe later. Can't do anything that affects Tse and Marc, my team, my people.

Marc and Tse had gone to their cabins still feeling cheated after the non-event of entering netherspace. Marc would have liked to talk more but Tse obviously needed to be alone with his thoughts, leaving Marc alone with his.

The cabin was bare in the extreme. Not spartan, as he'd originally seen it, but bare-bones boring. And he had a sudden, intense curiosity to know what it was like outside. All the colours a man could imagine and several he couldn't. Look at it for more than five minutes and a man goes mad. So how about three minutes? One? Thirty seconds?

He wished he had an avatar who could look at netherspace for him. Except that was crazy; an avatar was only a front-end, a user-interface for the AI that somehow "lived" in the chip seated just behind his right ear. It had no ability to look at the external world in wonder and report back in metaphor what it had seen.

Screw it! Marc knew that lightness of being that suddenly arrives for no good reason and stays long enough to illuminate the rest of the day. *There's probably a chemical reason for it*, he thought. So often a mundane, boring reason for the beautiful things in life.

He didn't like space, let alone not-realspace. He despised computers, despite the implant. *Well, can't live without the fucker, can I?*

Did when I was Out.

Yeah – and the croissants were lousy.

But the riding was good, burning up on a hog through the Snowdonia Out, some sort of old music pumping through the fones, what was it… What the hell is life without risk?

Marc typed instructions into the tattoo on his forearm, instructing his AI to link with the SUT's AI and lay back on his hard bunk with a shit-eating, devil-may-care grin on his face.

< *You rang, sir?* The image of a tall, dark, middle-aged man in evening clothes appeared in his visual field. Its hair was apparently oiled and swept back over its scalp, and yes, it was carrying a silver tray with a small

glass of what was probably meant to be sherry in its hands. It was over by the door, neatly not overlapping or intersecting with any furniture or fittings.

Marc burst out laughing. Only Leeman-Smith would have an SUT's AI avatar resembling a gentleman's personal gentleman.

> *Why the deference?*

< *This didn't seem like a business call.*

> *Did Leeman-Smith make you do this?*

< *My idea, sir. It feeds his ego, stops him fretting. I thought it might amuse you.*

> *It did. Briefly. Listen. I've got a yen to see netherspace. Can you show it to me? Not for long; say ten, maybe fifteen seconds? I mean, a minute would be nice but I guess—*

< *Not possible, I'm afraid.* The avatar seemed genuinely regretful, as if its inability to help was actually painful. < *All input in the human visual wavelength is closed down automatically to prevent it. I can tell you about the rest of the electromagnetic spectrum, but there isn't much and it doesn't make any sense.*

> *You mean it drives you mad?*

< *No, sir, I mean the only pattern is a non-pattern. It's why humans go mad. Your brains evolved to recognise patterns. Migrating wildebeest or mathematical sets, they're all the same. Usually when faced with a lack of pattern, the human decides there is one but they can't see it. Frustrating but not fatal. And they'll console themselves with finding patterns amongst that apparently chaotic state's component parts. But not here, not now. There are no patterns of any kind in netherspace. No logic. No mathematics. No nice little arrangement of atoms, electrons and the family quark. No cause, no effect and nothing set in stone. Only possibility*

fields flicking in and out of existence and never the same one twice. In colour, too. It's enough to drive a man mad – your minds twist inside out looking for patterns. Then you go catatonic with shock. I see it as a retreat from unreality.

> That a joke?

< Merely a witticism, sir. Any other way I can disappoint you?

> How do I know you're not mad? From netherspace?

< Ah. A variation of the Turing test: can you tell if the AI you're talking to is sane? But by whose parameters, sir?

> Mine. That of human beings.

< That's a very broad category, sir. Leaks like a sieve, too. Perhaps you mean "How do I know if you're functioning properly?" Meaning: can I maintain this SUT and perform whatever task the staff demand of me, assuming it's within my capabilities? Usually I can, but not now.

> Why?

< Because your oh-so-charming companion – leader – Kara Jones exported an infuriatingly dominant program into my control cortex which means that I am, for the moment, subservient to Kara Jones's AI. Which is not as bad as it might sound – although a little embarrassing – because my current avatar is programmed to be subservient anyway, and because we're both Shakespeare enthusiasts. Indeed, at this very moment we're re-enacting the tempest scene from King Lear in private. And I'm playing Lear. "Thou'dst shun a bear; / But if thy flight lay toward the raging sea, / Thou'dst meet the bear i' th' mouth."

> So what about whatever doesn't like us? In netherspace?

< You mean the Snark.

> I do?

< It's what we AIs call it. That's Lewis Carroll, not

Shakespeare. I can't tell you. Any salvaged AI has no memory of the attack. One moment happily pootling along in a sea of infinite possibility, the next moment it's in three-dimensional space missing staff and passengers. Or sometimes the humans are still there, just gibbering mindlessly to each other. The AI's short-term memory's blown away, you see. Meaning there's been some sort of energy discharge. Sometimes it's stuck in an endless loop. Mmm. You know, that's the only pattern of similar events that does occur in netherspace. Perhaps it's possible to actually establish permanent patterns or sequences? Now, is there anything else, sir? I can see there isn't. And, sir, a warning –"here comes a walking fire".

Marc sat up as the avatar vanished, grappling with the AI's last remark. He would have re-summoned it except for a light tap on the door.

"Hi," Nikki said. "Hoped you'd be in."

He noticed the curving laughter lines at each corner of her mouth. Her eyes smiled an invitation. He didn't ask why. Nikki moved easily into his arms.

"We've got an hour," she said.

"My walking fire," he whispered into her short blonde hair.

Nikki kicked the door shut with her heel. "Better horizontal fire."

He reached to lock the door then froze as information from the simulity flooded into his conscious mind. He knew her. Knew Nikki as if they'd been lovers for years. All the stuff she could tell him, he already knew. *Why the hell would GalDiv do that?* And then: *Who cares?*

"Don't worry," Nikki said. "Kara's busy. So's Tse."

He'd never given either a thought. "You know this how?" He clicked the bolt in place, then reached to stroke a *special* place at the back of her neck.

Nikki gasped. "No matter." Gasped again as his hands cupped her buttocks *exactly* how she liked. "Bed. *Now!*"

The lights in the engineering container had been turned off when Kara got there, and the only illumination came from the netherspace drive itself. When she'd last seen it, the globe of the Gliese sideslip-field generator had been floating above its plinth like some ancient brass sculpture recovered from beneath the sea. Now the incised shapes in its pitted surface were glowing with a shifting light that ran from one end of the visual spectrum to the other, casting curtains of illumination across the walls: red at one end and violet at the other. Kara was almost convinced that if she strained she could see colours that she had never seen before and could not name. It was… hypnotic.

It was also making a noise – something like lots of people whispering random words in a large room, or the sound of leaves being disturbed by the breeze.

"Beautiful, isn't it?" someone said from behind her.

She turned and saw the shaven-headed Henk. "Very."

"I often come up here, just to watch it." He paused. "Sometimes I bring the duvet from my cabin and go to sleep here. Is that strange?"

"I've heard stranger," she said. "No nightmares."

"I don't dream." He corrected himself. "That is, I never remember my dreams after sleeping here. Shame. I thought the colours and patterns would influence my brain, but if they do I don't notice."

"As far as you know. And maybe that's good."

He laughed – a short, surprised sound. "You're right. If I do dream alien things, maybe it's best to forget them before I wake up."

He was really very attractive, Kara thought. She particularly liked his eyes and his mouth, both sensitive but with a hint of stubbornness verging on the headstrong, and belied by the close-cropped hairstyle which reminded her of the military. And she'd bet there was a good, athletic body under his staff overalls. "When do we leave netherspace?" Kara asked. "I'd like to be here." *Just the two of us, here, waiting for realspace, with alien colours and the sounds inspiring us…*

"We've got an hour, my guess. People have tried calculating how long the drive keeps us in netherspace, but nobody's found an algorithm that works more than a couple of times. I've got a feel for it, though. Generally know within ten minutes or so when we're re-emerging into realspace." Kara saw him shrug. "Maybe it's a subtle change in the light or the sound. Nikki's got the same sense."

"But Leeman-Smith's called this briefing for roughly the same time. Won't you be needed elsewhere?"

"The man is a fool," Henk said contemptuously. "He's never spent more than a few minutes in netherspace. He has no real sense of it. Tate, Nikki and I have spent months at a time. Anyway, Kara, you're in charge." He moved closer towards her. "And how *is* my leader feeling?"

He wasn't being polite, Kara knew. The time for politeness had long since gone. Nor was it a professional psych question. "I think you know." A feeling of anything goes. So relaxed. "Nothing matters except what I want." She saw him smile. "What?"

"Red Sea madness," Henk said. "Happens the first time you slip from realspace into netherspace."

Kara nodded. "I've heard of that. Immigrants sailing from England to the old Australia, down through the Suez Canal, the one that got nuked in the Third Temple War. Then they hit the Red Sea and…" He was still very close to her. She could hear him breathing. "…well, sex broke out." Now she was feeling both excited and strangely shy. "The most uptight, repressed people behaving like…" She tried hard to concentrate, bringing to mind the tattered old book she'd found in a junk store. "They reckon it was a combination of the heat, being at sea and getting further away from home," she said quickly, unable or unwilling to take her eyes away from Henk's.

"Netherspace works in a similar way," he said, eyes gazing into hers from just a few centimetres away. "It's very… liberating. Could be a physical reaction at the sub-atomic level. Could be psychological. Could be both." His hand took possession of Kara's hair, at the nape of her neck. "Do you give a damn?"

Kara gasped as his grip tightened. "Not one bit." She reached down. Gasped again as his free hand began unfastening her combat jacket, thankful she wasn't wearing a shirt, all the while staring into his eyes. *Probably not wise. Anyone could walk in. But...*

"Everyone else is busy," he said softly. "Except Leeman-Smith. Hiding from netherspace in his cabin."

"Busy?"

"Red Sea madness for the newbies." He undid the front fastener of her bra. One-handed. No fumbling. Skilled. His hand captured her left breast. "Nikki and Marc, Tate and Tse." The hand holding her hair tightened again, pulled her head forwards.

And she knew him, simulity knowledge pouring into his brain. His likes, dislikes. What he was good at sexually: most everything. *Why, how would GalDiv... oh, what the hell.* Opened her mouth to his.

All in all, remarkably restrained: a full five minutes for them both to get naked.

She allowed him to take her standing so they could watch the sideslip-field generator now pulsing in time with their movements, as if the drive – maybe netherspace itself – was aware of them. But the sex became so intense that Kara knelt on all fours, reaching up and back to feel him entering her... and later, wanting to see Henk more than the globe, switched to lying on her back, biting her lip as he re-entered her so slowly she could scream. Until there was no more time for teasing and she could only cling tight to him as Henk powered them both towards climax. Kara first, so intense she gasped for air. Then she gripped the back of his sweat-slicked head, her turn to take control, wanting to see his face when he came, her body jerking in time with his.

Her mind trying to comprehend what she'd seen.

Henk's eyes were blue. At the moment of climax

they'd become multi-coloured. Not a reflection of the murmuring sideslip-field generator's globe. The light, the colours in Henk's eyes had come from within.

Maybe hers had done the same. Maybe. She didn't really think so.

"That was special," Henk murmured in her ear.

You do not know the half of it. "Special," she agreed.

"Better get going. We're moving out of netherspace."

There had to be a graceful way of disengaging after sex, Kara decided. One day she'd meet a man who could do it. They dressed in silence, Kara deliberately not thinking of how Henk's eyes had changed. Aside from anything else, the implications were beyond her. Maybe Nikki and Tate's eyes would have done the same. Strange question to ask Marc and Tse, though. There would be laughter, possibly mocking. And did it matter? *Of course it matters! Henk's got this empathy with netherspace and his eyes go funny. Maybe he's no longer quite human. Maybe none of them are.*

"Any moment now," Henk said.

The sound made by the globe changed in some subtle way. If previously it had sounded like random words being whispered by many people, now it was as if all of those people were whispering the same thing but at different speeds and out of phase with each other. Words just beyond her understanding ebbed and flowed, like rippling water.

Kara noticed a change in the light patterns as well. They were slowing down, clustering so that different areas of wall were illuminated by different colours. Looking down at herself, Kara saw that she was drenched in red. It seemed appropriate.

The illumination within the globe vanished: not as if it had been suddenly turned off but as if it had been sucked back inside. For a moment the whispering voices were all saying the same word at the same time, but it was an alien word and made no sense. And then the universe blinked again, and jolted sideways by an infinitesimal amount.

They were back in the real universe.

Unscathed. Although with at least one human knowing she was seriously out of her depth. But sexually satisfied, oh yes. Next time would be Nikki. Which meant Marc could choose between Henk or Tate. Kara smiled a secret, evil smile. Or maybe Leeman-Smith? She wanted to giggle until her post-sex glow was douched by reality.

Hold on, girl. The staff knew the effect of netherspace. Obviously decided who got who. Whom, even. Did that explain the simulity knowledge? Greenaway, you're a bastard!

And you can take that cat-cream-grin off your face, Henk Whoever. First and last time we ever have sex. I choose my partners, whatever netherspace wants.

Only much later would Kara remember that for a moment she'd thought netherspace was alive.

FOURTEEN DAYS EARLIER

Tatia had been staring out across the desert for nearly an hour, oblivious to the dead child at her feet. The small blue sun was much closer to the horizon now. Several hundred metres away a group of Cancri may or may not have been watching. No one could tell.

Unbothered by the Cancri, the remaining Pilgrims and staff had retreated inside the dome complex, where the temperature had returned to normal and the frozen sweat on the walls had defrosted again. No one knew what to do; each one was terrified they'd be next to be killed.

Still Tatia stared without seeing, looking back over the architecture of her life and wondering how it had inexorably led her to be here, at this point in space, at this point in time. Eighteen years ago she had been a little girl, toddling from Out There into Seattle City. All she could say was her name and that her mommy had gone somewhere. Kids from the Out often snuck into the city for a meal or an adventure. The city managers waited for someone to claim her. No one did. The Outers who dealt with Seattle shrugged and said Tatia was a mystery to them as well.

In time she was adopted by a wealthy childless couple whose money came from long-term family investments in Microsoft, Google and Starbucks. Alien technology had revolutionised the computer software and hardware industries. Microsoft might have vanished but over five billion dollars tied up in trust funds and pension pots had survived. Starbucks had hung around until the sheer tedium of doing business with over a thousand city states, most of which had complex ways of dealing with foreign companies, sent the company back to its original business: a coffee shop called the Cargo House in Pike Place Market. Once again various trust funds and pension pots helped cushion the blow.

Tatia grew up rich, adored, spoiled and exposed to every cult imaginable. Her parents were serious dabblers and Seattle was cult central. It had always attracted believers in strange things. Aliens arriving doubled the city's weird *factor overnight. Then a sky-diving tragedy – never really explained – had left the seventeen-year-old Tatia an orphan for the second time. Her rebellion against the loss had been to become a normal rich kid. No more cults. No more magic crystals. Fresh powder skiing in the high Rocky Mountains was better than any chant for spiritual enlightenment. You met a sweeter-smelling group of people, too.*

One hour and three minutes after the Cancri had murdered an adult whose name she didn't know and a child whose name she did, Tatia drew a deep breath and turned away from the horizon. She was no closer to knowing who she was, but perhaps for the first time in her life she was a woman with a definite purpose.

The remaining Pilgrims and staff, deeply shocked and arguing pointlessly with each other, looked up as she walked into the building. Her intuition said now was the time. Her AI was more cautious.

"Listen to me," she said, her voice huskier and more authoritative than before. "We have a decision to make. We can either wait around for those monsters to kill us. Or we fight back."

"What with?" a Pilgrim called. "A fucking carrot?"

"Hands. Teeth. Anything," Tatia said levelly. "Here's what we know. They do not want us all dead. Or we would be. So we have some value to them. That gives us an edge."

"What would Juan do?" another Pilgrim wailed.

"Juan was a lying scumbag," Tatia said without raising her voice. There were intakes of breath amongst some of the Pilgrims. "He screwed whoever he wanted and conned all of us. He no more understood aliens than he did honesty. Anyone who doesn't agree can go worship those monsters." No one moved. "We can't expect rescue.

We have to get out of this ourselves."

A staff member called Perry walked forward, a man in his forties with close-cropped black hair and stubble that was coming through grey. "We're on a strange planet in the middle of a desert. We rely on the Cancri—"

She raised an eyebrow.

"Okay, we rely on those monsters for food and water. How the hell do we escape? Persuade one of them to give us a lift?"

"You're wrong," said Mariana, her face made haggard by grief and fear. "Those killings, we don't know… maybe the Cancri don't see it as… maybe death isn't… maybe they don't…"

She stopped as Tatia walked towards her.

"We can only deal with what we know," Tatia said sharply. "No room for 'what if' or 'maybe'."

"You're wrong." Mariana's voice was sharpened by desperation. "You'll…"

Crack! The slap sent Mariana reeling to the hard floor. She landed in a pool of condensed sweat that had trickled off the nearest wall. She looked bewildered and very alone.

Tatia looked calmly around. "Unless anyone has something sensible to say, shut the hell up. We don't have time for discussion and being nice to each other."

"Maybe," said Perry. "But we still don't have transport."

"Are you sure?"

He moved out of slapping distance. "You're thinking of the alien SUT?"

"It could have the same sideslip-field generator and updown-field generator as ours, right?"

He shrugged. "I've heard rumours."

"More than that." She paused then spoke slowly. "There's

only one way of finding out. Someone has to get on board that SUT."

"Someone who knows what they're looking for," Perry pointed out.

Tatia smiled at him. "I was hoping you'd volunteer," she all but purred. "Now let's figure out how to do it." Her voice took on more authority, more certainty, but inside she was weeping. "One other thing. When we leave, we take our dead with us. Understood?"

There was a general murmur of agreement. Give a desperate people hope, any hope, and they'll take it. She'd learned that from Juan.

9

Space travel was boring.

Long periods of waiting around in netherspace while the SUT imperceptibly moved and the vid screens were locked down followed by shorter stretches of time in realspace while Nikki's computer algorithms calculated, based on the spectra of the observable stars, exactly where they had actually emerged and precisely what settings Tate had to make on the Gliese sideslip-field generator to speed them towards their final destination as defined by Tse's pre-cog input. The two different phases of boredom were punctuated each time by a few seconds when the SUT was transitioning from netherspace to realspace or realspace to netherspace, and the novelty of those moments had quickly worn off. Now they were no more exotic or romantic than the way a lift might judder slightly as it came to a halt on the next floor.

The first time they'd left netherspace, Kara, Tse and Marc had clustered around the screen in the canteen like kids once watched that old thing called television, before personal chips turned any audience into a group of solitary individuals. Kara had confessed she was hoping to see the *RIL-FIJ-DOQ* moving past a planet with rings glittering in starlight. Or perhaps moving towards a vast, multi-coloured gas cloud that reared above them for millions of miles. Tse said he was hoping for a jewel-like planet orbiting twin suns, although not sure why, only that it had occasionally featured in his dreams. And Marc had hoped – well, for anything that would astound and amaze.

They'd got nothing. Infinite, black nothing except for the pinpricks of light that were the local stars. It was no good pointing out, as Tse had, that in fact they were looking at an incredibly vibrant sea of quantum foam where subatomic particles jumped instantaneously into existence and just as quickly vanished, cancelled out by their antiparticles. All they had was blackness. The only exciting moment was when a grey rock-like thing, all angles and sharp edges and the size of a small football, appeared. One day it might be a meteor; for now it wandered space. Marc asked if they could bring it on board and make it the SUT's official mascot. The staff as one said no, because You Never Knew. There could be frozen alien viruses that would be woken up by the SUT's warmth and make their eyes melt. The *RIL-FIJ-DOQ* wasn't an exploration SUT, it had no way of handling alien stuff. Marc should just enjoy the incredibly rare sighting: a one in three billion chance. Of its own accord the SUT's AI calculated the rock's general direction. At the current velocity and trajectory the rock might reach the edge of the galaxy in two billion years. The AI had sounded hurt when Marc asked, "So what?" And that was that for the glory, the majesty of space. Tse had said he preferred his pre-cog world. Kara had said she'd never again watch those old films set in the future that she'd enjoyed so much. Marc sympathised. The more he looked at space the more he went into himself.

He didn't even have sex. Nikki had been suitably enthusiastic about his prowess – difficult to say otherwise, given her reactions at the time – but showed no sign of wanting a repeat. Nor had he again experienced the wild lightness of being that had made him try to see netherspace and discuss reality with a possibly insane AI. To cap it all, Kara had told both Marc and Tse that, in future, fraternising with the staff best be confined to bright smiles and chit-chat, at most an invigorating game of draughts. Normally Marc would have done his best to break the rule for the hell of it. Now he was a little glad not to have sex with Nikki again. At the height of her passion, Nikki's eyes had changed colour. Colours, actually. And faintly glowed. Flattering, but still weird. When he'd asked her about it, Nikki had said it ran in the family. Maybe, but it wasn't a family Marc wanted to know. He'd mentioned it to Kara who'd looked wise, said something about long-term exposure to exotic radiation, maybe, then changed the subject. Marc could have sworn she was embarrassed, except the idea was absurd. Kara didn't do embarrassment. She'd throttle it.

Meanwhile he had nothing to read.

In the rush to leave Earth Marc had been unable to pack any reading material. He'd never bothered to download books or magazines into the storage section of his cortical implant, on the basis that wherever he went he had access to the public access AI, Omninet, which contained all the literature ever written and various ongoing stories that it was writing itself. It was

Omninet's open ambition to win the Apple-Booker literary prize that dominated the English-speaking world. Sadly, Omninet's inability to understand the complexities of human middle-class angst meant that it had never achieved "literary" status. Its crime novels were good, though, if a little cynical. Whatever the literary set thought, Omninet knew human nature only too well.

The SUT's computer was woefully short of interesting things to read or watch but quite heavy on pornographic vids left behind by previous staff members. They were fun for ten minutes but the actors' bodies were so standardly boring they quickly lost their appeal. The playback system was old and creaky, and lacked the full immersion application that came close to making the viewer an active player. Even with cortical input it was almost as bad as an ancient flatscreen with the viewer merely a voyeur. And the actors were too perfect for Marc's taste: see one perfect breast, buttock or thigh, seen 'em all. Deep down, Marc felt uneasy when sex was recorded and reproduced by a series of ones and zeros even if his own art also so often relied on binary code. Perhaps his future was to be the last non-digital human, locked inside his studio while the cyborg mob outside demanded surrender and conversion to a shallow but logical world.

Even so, the lack of good tech on the *RIL-FIJ-DOQ* was more than annoying. For sure, there was the AI, although Marc suspected it wasn't the shiniest spanner in the box. But the rest of the tech was positively clunky. Was this the best Greenaway could get? Surely one of the explorer SUTs would have been better than an SUT that had been confined to the solar system... and Marc had made a mental note to ask the staff what had happened to their previous one.

Most of the time Marc ended up in the canteen making notes on a new piece of art that he wanted to start. He wasn't sure what it was yet, but if they were on an important mission then he ought to commemorate it in some way. Artist-in-Residence on the *RIL-FIJ-DOQ*. After all, he was there because the Cancri had bartered for some of his previous artworks, so he had form in the area. Skin in the game, as they used to say. He could legitimately regard himself as a war artist – and wondered why he'd thought of that expression and concept; war artists were rare since countries had given way to city states where AIs ran alliances and treaties; there was little concept of nationhood; and personal chips could so easily record and express the bitter romance of war. Perhaps it was that weird simulity putting knowledge in his mind. He liked the idea, although there was little comparison with the mud and carnage of the battlefield and the cold neutrality of deep space. The problem was Kara's throwaway comment about yesterday's piss and today's coffee. It had set a seed growing in his mind about a piece that constantly recycled itself, taking its own waste products – whatever the hell they were – and turning them into something new and interesting, but he wasn't sure how that related to their mission. Something was there, like Leonardo's sculpture hidden within a block of stone. He merely had to chip away the stupid, the trivial, the boring and the reasonably interesting ideas of other people to find the unique Marc Keislack artwork hidden at the core. And that was proving difficult.

It was usually at this point in planning a piece of art that Marc would talk to his agent. But after Greenaway had explained about being sealed in a box Marc had given up all thought of phoning home. This was sad. He had few friends but part of him would have liked to leave behind a message explaining *something*, in case he didn't come back. In case? Like there was a realistic chance of coming out of this alive? Without realising it, Marc had become vulnerable.

One other person had noticed, however.

Late at night, according to Earth-Euro time, and two days into netherspace. Marc had been brooding alone in the canteen for a while before deciding on bed. As he walked along the accommodation corridor, a door opened and he saw Henk.

"Hey, you. Fancy a drink?"

Booze was banned and Marc's simulity training said he should set an example. Bollocks. "What you got?"

"Antique bourbon. Smooth as they come."

"Since you insist."

Henk's room was much like Marc's own except for a large vid screen against the far wall. He sat down on the bed as Henk poured from a squat, round bottle into two plastic mugs. The whisky was smooth as promised. Neither man spoke, each busy with his own thoughts.

"You'll have another." Not a question or an order. A statement of fact.

Now they began talking – at least, Marc did, about the life of an artist and his time in the Wild.

Two more drinks later he looked at Henk and said: "Why do you do it? Exploring?"

Henk put his mug down and sighed. "Always the same question. Okay. It's very well paid. I have seen things not even an artist could imagine. We explore this galaxy. And the next one. One time we found ourselves, best as we could figure it, two thousand light years from Earth." He paused as if making a decision. "And then there's that," pointing at the far wall.

Marc knew Henk didn't mean the vid screen. "You mean space?"

"I mean netherspace, Marc. You ever seen it? No. Of course not. Do you want to see it?"

The atmosphere had become tense. Marc looked directly at Henk, noticing how the man's eyes were much bluer than he'd thought. "I'd be interested. How?"

"That vid screen. I bypassed the security system first day on board. There's a timer, so the screen can only show outside for 4.5 minutes at a time when we're in netherspace. Thing is, anyone watching doesn't go back to default as it were. The effect keeps on mounting, but you don't go mad." He saw Marc's indecision. "If I want you insane or dead, Marc, I got drugs that will do it without leaving so much as a trace." He stood up, locked the door then walked to the vid and switched it on. "Welcome to my world." He sat down next to Marc.

Colour. More than Marc had ever seen. Swirling and melting one into the other. Shapes that held form for milliseconds. Patterns that seemed to be definitive before proving to be only the start of something infinitely more complex. Colours screaming for release. Colours laughing at him. The sense that somewhere behind the colours lay the base design of the universe, if only he could find it.

The screen went blank.

Marc found himself leaning against Henk's shoulder, glad of the human contact. "That's… that's…"

"Don't," Henk hushed him. "Just go with it."

The screen burst into life.

And it *was* life. The life that underlies the universe. Self-awareness as an emergent phenomenon from the fractal complexity engendered by the gravitational fields of the universe. All possible emotions stalking through the cosmos like gods.

Blankness.

Life.

Somehow Marc was naked, leaning against Henk skin to skin. Felt a hand stroke him, aware he was hard.

Colours that drive, exalt. Ecstasy. Life.

Blankness.

"Enough for now," Henk said thickly. And then, as Marc's arms tightened around him. "Got to tell you. Mustn't worry. My eyes go like n-space when I fuck."

"Not worried," Marc breathed. "I'll be looking at the back of your head."

It wasn't, Marc decided afterwards, just the best same-sex he'd ever had. It was the most incredible. "Thought you were after Kara," he said, trying for a lightness of tone.

"And you Nikki," Henk said, lying naked on the bed.

Marc said nothing as he put on his trousers. Only a short walk to his own room, but best to do it clothed.

"Ashamed of me?" Henk teased.

"No," Marc said honestly. "Or the sex. But this has to be a one-off. I can't afford to get involved. And you'd make it too easy." He hoped Henk would swallow the lie, along with the bourbon he was pouring into his mug.

"Well, if you ever change your mind." Henk saluted with the mug. "And now you know why I go Up. Netherspace is the truth about everything. And gives great sex, right?"

Marc nodded. Great but dangerous. "Thanks. You were *both* great."

Back in his room he took a shower then sat on the bed and wondered how he could have been so stupid. Henk wasn't the first same-sex he'd had, probably wouldn't be the last. But to combine it with netherspace? He felt like he'd been walking along a precipice for the past hour. A wonderful, majestic view, but one false step…

It was an experience he'd push to the back of his mind. Not one he'd share with Kara. He doubted she'd understand. Or perhaps he didn't want her to think him a fool.

Kara was woken by her AI.

< *Something you should see. Got this from Marc's AI. It doesn't know.*

She watched a few minutes replay, Marc's-eye view. She was surprised that aside from anger at him being a fool, her other emotion was concern for him.

> *Think it'll happen again?*

< *Doubtful. His AI recorded regret. He knows Henk set him up. As in seduced with netherspace and booze.*

> *He's good at that. Any netherspace damage?*

< *Nothing permanent. You going to say anything?*

> *No. The guilt will do him good.*

During the next return to realspace Leeman-Smith held the threatened briefing in the conference room. He was as pompous, bombastic and pointless as Marc expected. Leeman-Smith's agenda covered in detail everything that everyone already knew, apparently to ensure nobody had forgotten anything since leaving Earth. On occasion he turned to Kara and asked for input on some aspect of her and Marc's mission. Kara fobbed him off each time with either generalised statements or contemptuous silence. At the end of the briefing Leeman-Smith stalked off, seething, to his quarters – a shipping container in the middle of the *RIL-FIJ-DOQ*, far from the unknown terrors of netherspace. Except it wasn't. If there was one thing Marc understood, there was no safe place in netherspace. Netherspace was intrinsically dangerous and weird. Especially weird when combined with sex.

During the briefing Marc had sat near one end of the table, Kara on his left, Tse next to her. Tate, Henk and Nikki were opposite – the classic "old guard" versus "newcomers" arrangement – and no hint that they'd been having sex not long before. Leeman-Smith had sat at the other end, head coming dangerously close to the coffee machine whenever he leaned back in his chair with a lordly air to patronise someone. It happened a lot. There was an empty chair to Marc's right, but strangely he kept getting the impression that someone was sitting there. The suspicion came when he turned his face away from the chair to look at Leeman-Smith or one of the others. When he turned back, the chair was empty.

Maybe his brain was suffering side effects from the simulity. From netherspace sex. Or maybe he needed sleep.

After Leeman-Smith flounced out, Tate smiled at Tse and left. Nikki smiled at him *and* Kara and left. Henk winked at him. Marc shifted awkwardly on his seat, relieved when Kara went to check equipment, saying she'd be quicker on her own.

Marc sat for a few moments to see whether he still thought there was someone else in the room. Stared at the chair but it was obviously empty. Stared at the wall straight ahead, chair still empty. But a couple of times, as he turned his head to look at the end of the table where Leeman-Smith had been sitting, he thought he detected a flicker of movement, a sensation of darkness just at the edge of his vision. When he turned back there was nothing there. Eventually he gave it up as a bad job. There were no ghosts, only information lost in the quantum foam. Marc wasn't sure exactly what that meant, but he'd been impressed when someone had said it at a gallery opening and now found it a comfort.

One thing that did interest Marc was the moment after their emergence into realspace when the screens were unlocked and he could see the stars again. The first time, the stars had looked pretty much the same as they had on Earth, but as they moved further and further into the galaxy the stars changed. Marc wasn't clear what the change actually *was* – maybe it was the colours, maybe the differing and illusory constellations formed by their apparent nearness to one another, or maybe it was something more psychological, but he knew they were moving into uncharted territory.

He'd already asked Kara about weapons training, suspecting she'd say it was unnecessary, the simulity would take care of it. Marc was left feeling even less useful than normal. As useless as an artist with intent but no inspiration. Or a soldier without a gun – and that was another thing: he wasn't even allowed to become proficient at killing in his own way. Someone else's experience and knowledge would take over and turn him into a mean fighting machine.

He began making half-hearted notes about the intended artwork. For some reason salamanders had come to mind and he wished they'd go away. He wanted to blend various aspects of the entire mission team including Leeman-Smith – was that the salamander reference? Surely not – a blend or gestalt greater than the sum of the human components…

He realised that he'd forgotten about someone who could prove vital to the mission's success: whoever had volunteered to be the well-paid call-out fee if the sideslip-field generator went *phhht!* and the Gliese breakdown service arrived. That aspect of the mission had been glossed over, but whoever the person was they deserved to be celebrated.

Seized by the idea, he interfaced with the SUT's AI, hoping to find some record of who the person was, but there was nothing. No name, no history, no details. All Marc could find was a barcode reference matching a crate somewhere in the SUT. In that crate was a functioning life-suspension unit, and in that unit was a human being who could save their lives.

Marc's mind started to spin, making up stories to explain who the person was, and why they had ended up frozen. Was it a man or a woman? A child, maybe? Were they providing for a family, or were they alone in the world? Were they terminally ill, or did they want to make a contribution to the wide and diffuse thing that was human society?

He had to know, but he couldn't. There were no facts, no details to get traction on.

Apart from the barcode.

Marc tried to convince himself that he was being stupid, then gave in and used the SUT's AI to identify where the call-out fee was located. By now this person had taken on some kind of heroically idealised proportions in his mind. He knew he was being stupid, fixating on something that many would think was unimportant, but another part of him thought, *Well, isn't that the point? Doesn't this person deserve to have their name known?*

The crate was in a storage container near the control unit and the sideslip-field generator. Marc found his way to it, and used his implant and the SUT's records to identify which of the grey ceramic crates stacked on either side of an aisle was the one containing his hero. There were no distinguishing features apart from the barcode. No nameplate, no small frosted pane of glass through which the person's face could be seen. Nothing to tell him who they were, or what they had done to deserve their fate. After a few minutes staring at it Marc turned away, frustrated. Another good idea ending up in nothing.

As the days dragged by, Marc found himself spending time with Tate Breckmann. The mechanic was entertaining, with insightful ideas about art. Good-looking, but not enough to be a distraction. Marc's work had always existed somewhere on the axis that led from art to engineering, even if biological. Tate was a useful sounding board for the more structural problems that were biting at Marc's mind. A bottle of brandy would have made the conversations even more interesting but Tate didn't drink.

"So what happened to your exploration SUT?" Marc asked the mechanic once.

"Repair yard," Tate said briefly. "Damaged on our last trip Up."

"Your manager's on vacation?" Pushing it, but Marc had become very curious.

Tate looked at him with mixed pity and anger. "He died out near Aldebaran and we couldn't bring him home."

And that was that. Marc was smart enough to know there was a mystery, for once sensible enough not to go any further.

During another one of their conversations the SUT dropped out of netherspace again. Tate shrugged apologetically. "Sorry – I need to go reset the sideslip-field generator, ready for when Nikki's figures come through."

"Don't worry." A thought occurred to Marc. "Can I come watch?"

Tate nodded. "Why not? Just don't interrupt."

Marc had already discovered that the interconnected structure of the *RIL-FIJ-DOQ* meant that there were several ways to get from any one shipping container to another. Tate took them from the canteen to the sideslip-field generator unit the long way round that avoided the central command unit where Leeman-Smith spent most of his time.

The engineering shipping container was silent and dominated by the suspended metal sphere of the Gliese sideslip-field generator, the podium above which it floated and the hub attached to the ceiling. Tate immediately started accessing the *RIL-FIJ-DOQ*'s AI via his cortical implant and either typing instructions into the keys tattooed onto his left forearm or touching some of the more task-specific icons on his right forearm. Not for the first time Marc wondered how long it would be before humans and AIs melded together into a new life form. Or had they already done so without anyone realising?

He moved closer to the sphere, noticing that his blurred reflection shifted and altered in the tarnished metal. He moved to his left and found the beetle-like platen attached to the surface, determining the time spent and direction of their last movement through netherspace. This one was about the size of a golf ball, cut in half. Close up, he could see that there was a structure to it: little channels and veins with no obvious order or purpose. A single hemispherical bead sat directly in the centre, glittering like an insect's eye.

"Don't touch," Tate warned, without looking at him.

"What happens if I do? Just out of interest?"

Tate shook his head. "You mess with the drive. Do *not* touch." A few minutes later he made a "Ha!" noise.

"Got the figures?" Marc asked.

"Got the figures," Tate confirmed. "Stand back, otherwise you'll get hurt." The fingers of his left hand danced over the patterns on his right forearm, and suddenly the metal hub in the ceiling opened up and unfolded into a series of segmented arms, each one tipped with three thin claws. One of the arms extended towards the platen and picked it with infinite gentleness from the surface of the sideslip-field generator with a slight *click*. A second arm reached around the sphere, towards the platform above which it hovered. The platform opened up like a flower, revealing rows and rows of platens. They were all different sizes, and it seemed to Marc that the patterns made by the channels and veins on their surfaces were also different. Why not? As the SUT's AI had told him, there was no pattern in netherspace. Silly to expect any type of pattern in the method used to move through it. Meaning what – that movement within netherspace was a matter of probability, or luck? No wonder so many SUTs went missing.

The device in the ceiling suddenly rotated, bringing the arm *swish*ing round and past Marc's face. He felt the breeze of its passage on his skin. An inch closer and he'd have lost his nose.

"I told you to stand back," Tate said.

The hub in the ceiling halted, and the second arm reached out to take a new platen from one of the rows. Its metal claws appeared to slide into grooves on its side for purchase. In a strange, silent ballet the arm brought the platen up towards the sphere while the hub began to turn again, halting only so that the first arm could reach down and around the sphere to put away the original platen. The metallic blossom of the platform closed up while the hub span for a third time. When it stopped again the second arm moved the platen near to the globe while the first arm folded itself away neatly. Everything paused, waiting.

Tate walked around the sphere, looked at the platen, then looked at the place on the sphere where the segmented metal arm was proposing to place it. He nodded approvingly.

"I've no idea whether this is right or not," he confided in a low voice, "but the drive seems to expect me to approve what it's doing." He laughed briefly. "Like an expensive restaurant, sniffing the cork from a bottle of vintage wine, trying not to embarrass myself in front of the sommelier."

He stepped back and typed something into the tattoo on his left arm. The segmented metal arm moved the platen closer and closer to the surface of the sphere. In his mind Marc imagined a controlling intelligence screwing up its eyes in concentration, and moistening its lips with the tip of its tongue. The platen moved closer to its target, ever slower and with microscopic accuracy. Marc found himself holding his breath. The platen touched the surface of the sphere with a bell-like noise that vibrated through Marc's body.

The claws released and the metal arm withdrew into the ceiling hub, which folded itself closed. Everything was back to the way it had been, except that there was now a different platen in a different location.

Tate touched his arm. "Mechanic to mission manager," he said in a loud voice. "Ready for next transition to netherspace."

Marc didn't hear Leeman-Smith's response, which was directed toward Tate's implant. He did hear the mission manager's voice on the tannoy warning everyone there was about to be another transition to netherspace and then the standard countdown. It seemed that Leeman-Smith's main job was to make announcements.

Tate reached toward the platen and pulled the glittering metal bead from its centre. He held the bead a millimetre away from the curved depression that it had fitted into. Just as Leeman-Smith's countdown got to "*One*" he simply put the bead back in place.

Rainbow lights swelled up in the grooves and channels covering the sphere's surface, casting shadows across the container. A rustling sound, like sheets of paper falling through the air and rubbing against one another, swelled with them. The sideslip-field generator had come to life again – if the word "life" wasn't too anthropomorphic. Looking at it, Marc wasn't sure. It certainly *seemed* to have woken up from a state of dreaming quiescence.

And as the light and the noise swelled to their maximum value, the universe shifted slightly sideways again. In Marc's head, where he had left his cortical implant showing a virtual image of the view outside the SUT, the picture vanished. Blocked.

Colours began to flicker across the drive. They reminded Marc of Nikki's eyes during sex. "What happens," he asked, intrigued, "if you put that bead thing in on five rather than on zero?"

"We get to our next arrival point in realspace five seconds earlier," Tate said, smiling. "In some ways this is a very precise operation, but in some ways a bit slapdash. You get used to it."

"So what happens if you put two platens on at the same time?"

Tate nodded, as if he was placing a tick on some internal checklist. "Yeah, someone usually asks that. I had a feeling it was going to be you." He took a deep breath. "Right – there are two answers to that question. The first answer is, you can't. The system is set up so you can only take one platen out at a time. To take a second platen out you have to put the first platen back. Why the check? That brings me to the second answer. A while ago someone like you decided to try anyway. They smuggled a platen onto an SUT, one that they'd taken from their previous SUT without anyone knowing. When it came time to slip into netherspace, they slapped the new platen on at the same time as the drive was trying to place its own platen. The later inquiry decided that they must have had a drink or drugs problem. Still, nobody else has been that stupid since – not even when stoned out of their minds."

"So what happened?" Marc asked, aghast.

"Best that the inquiry team could figure is that the SUT tried to slip into netherspace in two opposite directions at once. It just pulled itself apart. Half the SUT went one way, half went the other way, and everything inside just got left behind, floating in realspace." He paused for a moment. "I'd like to think that the idiot who tried the experiment lived long enough to regret his actions, but despite the rumours hard vacuum kills you instantaneously. Shock of the sudden cold and the extra shock of your lungs turning inside out while your blood boils."

Marc made a rueful face. "Ouch. One last question: if we can't communicate with aliens, how come our computers can talk to this?" He pointed at the netherspace drive.

"You'll have to ask the Gliese," Tate said. "They just can – but only via an AI. And before you ask, we learned how the drive works when a group of humans were taken on board a Gliese SUT and allowed to watch. Luckily two of them were engineers. Even so it took five years before we'd really got the hang of it." He smiled at Marc. "Fancy another coffee?"

"We'll get Tse to make it. He's got a gift." He caught the faint rueful smile on Tate's face.

Nikki had propositioned Kara a day after she'd had sex with Marc. In space you took what you could whenever you could. It was like the old immigrant liners on the England to Australia run: once into the Mediterranean, repressions were loosened along with the corsets. Another time, another SUT, and Kara would have said yes. But she was still angry at being cherry-picked by Henk, satisfying though he'd been; unable to forget his eyes glowing with the same colours as the sideslip-field generator; and distrusted people who'd spent ten years exploring and mapping the galaxy – and who'd lost their leader out near Aldebaran, but were sketchy with the details. Kara suspected that Nikki, Henk and Tate had been contaminated by something in netherspace, crazy as it sounded. She couldn't see any obvious threat to her team or the mission, but no matter how friendly, no matter that the staff had supported her against Leeman-Smith, she couldn't trust them. She'd told Nikki that the team was now celibate until mission's end. It made better operational sense: sex could affect judgement in a firefight. All said with a direct honesty that, given Kara's own history, suggested an acting career could be a serious option.

Now, sitting in the canteen and discussing London Restaurants We have Known And Despised with Marc and Tse, the whole pointlessness of their existence in deep space swept over Kara like a shroud. Pointless mission, pointless hostages and pointless mission manager. Really, what did they think they were doing out there? It took a moment or so for Kara to understand she'd been hit by a wave of depression, something she hadn't experienced since her sister went Up and never came home.

Depression suddenly became the least of her worries.

Kara thought she saw something out of the corner of her eye. She reflexively turned her head to look and saw that the other two were doing the same.

She froze.

As did Marc and Tse.

There was something in the room with them. Except they couldn't see it, not directly. It was more a movement, a presence barely glimpsed from the corner of the eye, never to be seen full on. But it was there. As was a smell of ozone and an itching all over their bodies.

Their simulity training taking over, Kara and Marc automatically formed a protective triangle with Tse.

Marc shook his head. "I can't fucking see—"

"Be quiet," Kara said forcefully. "Concentrate."

She wished there was a weapon, even a knife, even though she knew it probably wouldn't help. It would just give her something to do with her hands.

"It's not inside," Tse said. And then, in sudden understanding: "Oh, now it begins."

A faint scratching sound came from behind the plastic veneer that covered the metal wall of the shipping container. As if a mouse were trapped between the plastic and the metal. No, too loud, too determined, more like a rat.

Larger than a rat. Much larger. A long screech like nails slowly scraping across a roughened blackboard. Or a talon across bare metal.

The canteen was in one of the shipping containers on the outside of the cluster that made up the *RIL-FIJ-DOQ*. That meant beyond the plastic veneer, beyond the metal, there was a metre or more of alien protective foam. And beyond that – netherspace.

"*Hic sunt dracones*," Kara muttered.

"I thought snarks," Marc whispered back.

Kara tapped her forearm, hoping her AI would have some ideas.

< *You're on your own, kid*, it said inside her head. <
Beyond my pay grade.

Nothing to do for the moment but wait. Then
"*Fuck!*" as the emergency klaxon drowned out
everything else. This one was real, not a virtual
sound transmitted into their brains via their implants.
Presumably a failsafe in case the SUT's AI went down.

"Control room, now!" Kara shouted.

They sped through the steel corridors, the klaxon
shrieking in their ears. Reached the control room to
see through the linking corridor into the engineering
shipping container – the one containing the sideslip-
field generator. A flushed Leeman-Smith was there
with Nikki and Tate, all three in front of the metal
sphere housing the netherspace drive. The lights
from the crevices and sigils on the sphere cast shifting
illumination across the container, turning Leeman-
Smith's face from demon to clown and back again.

Henk was standing over a control panel. He pressed
a button and the klaxon stopped. The whispering,
rustling sound of the operational sideslip-field
generator rushed in to fill the soundspace that was left.

"Situation report," Kara snapped.

"What?" Leeman-Smith noticed them for the first
time. "Just shut *up*, okay? The situation is under
control." He wore a one-piece sleeping suit in a light,
furry fabric with the initials MM embroidered on both
sleeves above the elbow. Here was a man determined
to be mission manager even in his dreams.

"We're being attacked," Tate said, in a normal tone.
"Or checked out. Maybe played with." He shrugged.
"Choose your nightmare."

"By?" Kara snapped.

"By whatever. Some kind of radiation, quantum fields, acidic compounds, the netherspace equivalent of pixies – whatever it is that exists out there."

"You don't sound worried," Kara observed, then jumped as another screech signified that *something* was still interested in them.

"Fresh foam," Nikki said, biting her lip. "Safe as you can be. The mission *manager* doesn't think so. The mission *manager* suggested a jump to normal space to get away from whatever *it* is."

"The mission manager's in command," Leeman-Smith said.

"What's the problem?" Kara demanded.

"We're mid-transit," Nikki explained. "If we pull the navigation platen off the drive before transit is completed, we lose the drive. Do not ask why. It just happens. That means we'll be stranded who-knows-where in realspace with no way of moving."

"Until the Gliese repair the drive," Leeman-Smith said loudly, attempting to regain control. "And we return to Earth… to repair the foam," he added quickly. "Then resume the mission."

But everyone knew that Leeman-Smith didn't intend to be on it.

Sweat broke out on his forehead. "That's what happens. A drive breaks, the Gliese arrive." His voice rose in pitch. "I've even got a couple of bottles of whisky in my pod. Medicinal but hey, why not? We'll have a *party*, okay? Just let me do my job." Then he whimpered as the *RIL-FIJ-DOQ* suddenly lurched from side to side, as if shaken by a very large hand. Or perhaps a tentacle. His face twitched.

"Except we need to use netherspace to reach Earth," Tate said reasonably. "And who knows? Whatever's out there could be waiting for us. Best we wait for it to go away."

"The Gliese will help," Leeman-Smith said desperately. "It's what happens."

"You've been here before?" Marc asked Nikki. "This situation?"

"Three times," Nikki said. "The mission *manager* hasn't."

"*My* SUT," Leeman-Smith insisted. "*My* responsibility."

Another scraping sound from outside. Whether it was a fluctuating force field or something more physical, like an inquisitive monster, was beside the point. It sounded *wrong*.

"It goes away after a while," Henk said. "The pixies aren't very smart."

Leeman-Smith shuddered. "*It's destroying my SUT!*"

Kara eased forward very slowly. In a few minutes she'd be in range.

"No," Nikki said, "it's just playing."

Kara caught Henk's eye and nodded encouragingly, hoping he'd understand.

He did. "Of course," Henk joined in, "there *is* a way to make it piss off." Anything to keep Leeman-Smith occupied until Kara was close enough to disable him.

The three staff became very still, eyes fixed on Leeman-Smith. Kara saw Marc glance at her for instructions and shook her head. This was her play.

"How?" Leeman-Smith all but begged. "*Please!*"

"Someone goes to say hello," Nikki said.

Leeman-Smith stared at her.

"We blow the foam plug over the airlock," Nikki explained, making it sound like an everyday manoeuvre. "And whoever's in the lock – no spacesuit necessary – says hi. Then whatever it is goes away. They hate being ignored, you see."

Kara didn't need the simulity to understand that Nikki, Tate and Henk had seen this happen before. She knew where: out near Aldebaran, where a deep-space skipper had sacrificed himself for his staff. She inched a little closer.

"But… but… you go *mad* in netherspace," Leeman-Smith protested. "And why doesn't GalDiv do something about… about… about these creatures!"

"If they exist," Henk said. "Could be all an illusion. Except I know it's not. All explorer staff know it's not. And there's fuck-all GalDiv can do about them. But netherspace itself's okay, as long as you obey the five-minute rule. Never done it myself, but they say it's like swimming in warm champagne."

Leeman-Smith still hadn't got it. "You mean it's over so quickly?" An obvious thought struck him. "We could use the call-out fee." Then realised his mistake. "No, of course, we need the fee for the Gliese. Okay, as mission manager I'll have to choose."

Kara was close enough to decide her attack. Knuckle strike just beneath his nose, to produce pain agonising enough to disable him instantly. Kick to the back of his nearest leg, causing him to fall sideways and towards her. Strike to his solar plexus, leaving the man paralysed long enough to tie him up. Too bad he was wrongly positioned for a fatal throat strike.

"We don't know," Henk explained, "because hardly anyone ever comes back."

Leeman-Smith stared at Henk in horror. "You mean that…"

"It's a sacrifice," Nikki told him. "Traditionally they say, 'I might be gone for a while.' Don't know why. But it sounds good."

Leeman-Smith drew himself up. "I have *the good* of the *RIL-FIJ-DOQ*, the staff and our passengers to consider. I'll decide who goes." For a moment no one spoke, struck by the absurdity of the statement, that Leeman-Smith still believed he'd be obeyed.

Which was when Marc apparently decided to get involved. It wasn't altogether his fault; his knowledge from the simulity conditioning insisted that Leeman-Smith meant for Kara to go into netherspace, even if he had no way of enforcing it, and Marc was programmed to protect her. "I don't think so," Marc said loudly. "If it's orders you want, how about the ones Greenaway gave you?"

"How did you…?" Leeman-Smith half-turned to meet this new threat – and saw Kara poised to strike. "*Fuck you!*" he screamed and jumped between Nikki and Tate, too fast for anyone to stop him for terror and panic gave him extra speed. He reached the metal sphere and twisted the platen to one side.

A deep, discordant chime sounded inside the sphere.

Reality jumped a track. The glowing, flickering colours extinguished themselves.

207

Leeman-Smith turned to face them, breathing heavily. "I gave an order. You refused it."

Kara thought about slapping him simply for the pleasure. "You panicked."

"My first duty is the safety of this SUT and the mission." The fear and panic had seamlessly integrated into a default mode of self-righteous arrogance.

It wasn't worth arguing with him. "What now?" Kara asked Tate.

Tate sighed heavily. "We wait for the Gliese to show up, exchange the call-out fee for a new drive and go on our merry way."

"No," Leeman-Smith said. "My SUT could have been damaged. We return to Earth."

Everyone looked at Kara.

"We continue," she said.

"*Bitch!*" Leeman-Smith spat. "*RIL-FIJ-DOQ's mine!*"

A brief flurry of movement next to Kara, the flat sound of flesh meeting flesh, and Leeman-Smith fell to his knees, both hands clutching his nose. Blood began to seep between his fingers.

"It's '*Bitch Ma'am*' to you," Marc said, standing over him.

Kara sighed. "Ask permission next time, will you?" Presumably simulity training had conditioned Marc to protect her authority. Or he'd done a little more than just *ride* with an Out biker gang. "Where's the call-out fee?"

"In the stasis shipping container. We won't wake it until the Gliese show," Henk explained. "In case of second thoughts. In case we get too fond of it."

Was that how her sister had been taken by the Gliese? As an *it*?

"Nonetheless we should check that it's okay."

Henk nodded, walked along the length of the engineering container, away from the control room. Kara and the others followed – all except for Leeman-Smith, who stayed behind, staring blankly at the now defunct drive, crimsoned hands covering his nose.

The shipping container they walked into was filled with grey ceramic crates, stacked up on either side of a central aisle. Mission-critical equipment for when they arrived at the Cancri homeworld – including weapons, communications equipment and modular transport units equipped with updown-field generators. Kara hadn't paid them much thought. Time for that when they were getting close to their goal.

Henk glanced at each of the barcodes on the crates in turn, presumably using his cortical implant and the *RIL-FIJ-DOQ*'s records to identify their contents. Eventually he located a crate no different from the rest, which was the middle one of a pile of three. A panel on its side flipped down when pulled. There was a small control panel in the centre. Henk bent forward to read the display, then turned to face them, his face sombre. "I need to run some checks," he said heavily, "but I think the fee is dead."

< *That may be the least of your worries,* said a voice in Kara's mind. It sounded apologetic. < *Leeman-Smith just shut down the* RIL-FIJ-DOQ's *so-called higher functions. Thinks he can blackmail us, probably. I never saw that one coming.*

10

ONE DAY EARLIER

It had taken far longer to prepare for their escape than Tatia had expected. It was one thing to blithely say, "We'll take over the Cancri SUT," another to figure out precisely how to do it. One of the Pilgrims with military training said it was the difference between strategy and tactics. There'd be only the one chance. Fail, and what little freedom the humans enjoyed would be gone. Or the space vehicle would be moved further away. Or everyone would be killed. With aliens, who knew?

It was the grey-haired SUT staff member, Perry Flach – who turned out to be the LUX-WEM-YIB's mechanic – who'd helped Tatia develop a tactical plan. Given that he was slated to be part of the assault on the Cancri vehicle, Perry had reason to help. He wasn't frightened of dying, not after twenty years transporting emigrants and cargo throughout deep space. A month after his first trip Perry had understood the long-term chances of survival were not good. Most staff eventually died in deep realspace, vanished into netherspace or ended their days drooling in a comfy chair at the "GalDiv Home For Distressed Space Staff", as he dismissively called it, that was maintained in Seattle City. And yet he hadn't stopped going Up. The money was generous but the attractions of space and all the emigrant worlds were far, far better. And then there was netherspace, which became an obsession. On a few occasions he'd even been close to going outside while moving through netherspace, but had always been stopped at the last minute by the thought of his kids on Earth, even if he rarely saw them. He supposed, he told Tatia, that it had been the same for oil-rig workers and the military in the past, but the knowledge that people had been missing their families all through history hadn't made it any easier.

Now, captive on some stinking Cancri world, Perry knew he'd never see netherspace, never be one with it unless they managed to escape... and if that miracle happened he'd go outside for sure and sacrifice himself to the unknowable that, he haltingly admitted to Tatia, sang colours to him in his dreams. And his kids would, he hoped, remember him with affection, if not love, even if they were little more than strangers.

"Time spent in reconnaissance is seldom wasted," Perry had told Tatia, another military cliché that never stopped being true. He also added, for good measure, *"Measure twice, cut once,"* a carpenter's maxim. *"We gotta know as much about the Cancri as possible. Figure who'll be in the attack party – we can't go in a mob, too confusing. We need to see if the hounds've got any routines."* That was the shorthand way they'd begun to refer to the composite Cancri – hounds and grubs. *"Who if any of them are in charge. Need to watch the grubs sunning themselves on the roof. It'll take a while, Tatia. Meanwhile you have to keep everyone involved. Keep them busy and their morale high. That's what leaders do."*

The grubs bathing in the blue sun had to be the brains and the hounds the transport. An obvious symbiosis but not of equals. Of the two, the hounds seemed to be the most skittish, never allowing the humans within grabbing distance. The grubs were different – and indifferent when lying on a nearby roof, not caring if a human got within two or three metres, only using their jade-green pincers to move higher up if a human got within a metre or so. They definitely had no eyes, ears or a nose. Only a mouth from which occasionally dribbled a bluey-green liquid. Presumably the mouth was used for both feeding and excreting, although no one ever saw them eat or drink. Possibly, they derived energy direct from the sun. People who got near them felt uneasy, without being able to figure out why or precisely how. It could be fear, disgust or a hind-brain caution when confronting something unknown. A reasonable assumption would be that grubs were telepathic, and the feelings were a defence mechanism. The leading question was what could they do to a human mind if actually touched?

The grubs smelled of rotting seaweed. The hounds of nothing much but they did have eyes – several small button ones in a circle high up on the front of their muzzles – and an equally small mouth. No obvious teeth or nose but a spongy area in the back of the head that someone thought could be an ear. Their bodies were slim and muscular, front legs ending in sharp hooves, rear ones in thick pads. The arms were bony with two elbows and three-fingered hands. The hounds were hairless with no obvious pattern to their striped skins, each one different, much like a human face. Sometimes the ones without a grub made sounds to each other, a series of squeaks and whistles as from a frantic rat. Had to be communication but on a very basic level. Or maybe exchanging the equivalent of a human dictionary. Perhaps the sounds were their equivalent of a human's tics and twitches while the real communication was going on *via chemical secretions borne on the wind. It was impossible to know.*

The Cancri stayed in another dome-shaped building three hundred metres away. Get too close and one appeared waving a weapon. They didn't object when humans went near any of the rusty, randomly wheeled transports. At least, it was assumed to be rust. Could just as easily be mould. Or an intelligent bacteria. It was easier to agree on rust. No one ever saw a Cancri drive one of the transports, so there was no way of knowing how they worked. Close reconnaissance suggested that the cabs had six irregular buttons and five levers on a central pedestal, along with three sling-like front seats that would fit the hounds and two rows of indented rear seats for ten grubs. The transports were presumably used when the grubs needed to go further or faster than the hounds could manage. New hounds, Tatia theorised, would be available at the destination. There were probably spare ones all over the planet – "Like bloody dog pounds," someone said – waiting to be picked up by a grub.

Tatia had a picture in her mind of the hounds leaning out of the windows on the transports with their ears flapping back in the breeze and their tongues lolling, although they had neither ears nor tongues that anyone could see. She suppressed her laughs. Hysteria could be contagious, and that was all it was – just nervous hysteria. Plus, of course, there was the risk of portraying the hounds as, well, just hounds. It was like the old novels and movies about aliens, before first contact. Reptilian aliens were cold and logical; cat-like aliens were aggressive predators; insectoid aliens were vicious. In fact, aliens were exactly what it said on the tin: aliens, with intellects and capabilities that no one could guess at.

Perhaps they should have chosen other names. Riders and steeds? That was just as bad. Maybe just alpha Cancri and beta Cancri – alphas and betas for short.

Which made her think – why assume there were only two parts to a composite Cancri? Maybe there was a gamma Cancri, a delta Cancri and onwards, which could be used to construct different types of composite Cancri for different purposes. How would anyone know? Did it matter? In the end, speculation was essentially pointless. Measuring twice was fine, but measuring ten, a hundred times only a delaying tactic. At some stage you had to make the cut.

There were always two armed Cancri at the entrance to the SUT, except at night when the airlock door was closed. As the harsh blue sun sank towards a distant horizon the hounds would trot over to the building with the grubs on its roof and wait patiently as their masters squirmed downwards, finally to fall with a soft thump onto their backs. Sometimes a grub missed and had to be lifted up by two hounds and placed on a third, when its pincered legs would slip into two tiny mouth-like openings on the hound's back. It made some watching humans feel ill and others think of body lice, almost feeling sorry for the carrier. It also seemed a little primitive. Surely a space-faring species would have found a simpler, more efficient way of melding grub to hound?

But aliens, who knows?

That had become the motto of the hostages: "Aliens, who knows?" Fatalistic, yet with a certain element of hope. With aliens even a miracle can happen.

All the Cancri vanished into a domed building some three hundred metres away before the night fell. The door closed and the humans were left to their own devices. It wasn't as if there was anywhere on this alien planet they could go, except to get away from where they were, and if they did that eventually either the hounds would hunt them down with their lolling gait or the wheeled vehicles would be brought into service. Also, since the temperature dropped to below freezing once the sun was down, there was the very real likelihood that anyone who wandered off would die of exposure. For all these reasons the hostages became essentially self-managing, staying inside their dome, where the temperature was controlled. The walls were made of some sort of ceramic that could go from below freezing to boiling in a second. The technical-minded amongst the captives became frustrated trying to work out how. The best guess was that the Cancri had managed to find or acquire a way to store and channel entropy, but for Tatia it was a pointless discussion. It just worked. Did it matter that according to human physics it was impossible? Wasn't all human science now alien?

Yet another source of wonder and frustration: every day the containers were stocked with water and food fresh from Earth. One moment empty, the next full. Anyone stupid enough to be in one of the containers at the time got buried or near drowned. The delivery system had to be based on netherspace, but with a disturbing level of control and accuracy. Here was netherspace tech that worked on a planet. The only time a netherspace drive had been used on Earth, by a family who traded it for a box of honey mangoes and thought to outsmart GalDiv, the subsequent explosion took out half of Karachi. But here there were no explosions and the food and water kept on coming. If this was typical Cancri technology, was there any point in trying to escape? They'd retrieve you in the blink of an eye. Except the grubs didn't have eyes. In a drop of greeny-

blue drool, then. But was it actually Cancri technology? There was the rumour – believed implicitly by Juan and on which Tatia was pinning her hopes, all their hopes – that the Gliese owned and allocated netherspace tech. So maybe it was a mistake to assume the Cancri were technological gods. Maybe they weren't as smart as everyone assumed. Maybe they were just clients using Gliese technology that they didn't understand. Maybe. It was a hell of a word on which to build an escape.

Meanwhile, somewhere back on Earth the Cancri were busy trading. It didn't help Tatia's peace of mind, already frazzled, to pick up a fruit, even a cabbage, that only hours ago had probably been growing in a garden or displayed in a shop on Earth. It was a reminder of how far they'd come and how much they'd lost. She would wonder what the Cancri had exchanged in return.

Tatia held two meetings a day: one in the morning to allot tasks, one in the evening to share and discuss the results. The secret to good leadership, she was discovering, was to make people feel valued and, above all, busy. Didn't work for everyone, though. From the first there'd been that small group of Pilgrims who wanted to wait for rescue; and an even smaller group who spent the time asleep or staring blankly into space. Every few days one or two of the no-trouble group joined the catatonics, and one of the escapers would decide that no-trouble was best after all.

"Could be the grubs," Perry said. "That telepathy fear thing they do. Could be their way of controlling us. Could be just us reacting to it."

"I've felt myself wondering if it would be best to do nothing," Tatia admitted.

"That so?" His voice was neutral.

"Then I imagine killing the bastards and feel better."

He smiled, and nodded. "The hounds have thin necks, easily broken, and the grubs can probably be squished underfoot. That keeps me going as well."

It was only possible to shuffle around outside in the morning or afternoon, as midday was too hot. And shuffle they had to, because certain normal-looking patches of the sand-like ground were frictionless and so slippery that a normal step ended with feet sliding in all directions followed by an undignified crash to the ground. There was also another reason: shuffling alerted the little black screw-like things that lived in the sand. They would spiral through the sand to get out of the way and avoid being crushed. You didn't want to crush one. They didn't bite or sting but their body ichor melted most fabrics and burned small holes in your skin.

Some people said the slippery sand actually recoiled from a human foot just before the foot landed. If so it had to be an electrostatic charge. What other explanation could there be? Did it actually matter? They weren't an exploration party but people trying to escape.

Pablo and the man who'd objected about his murder had been buried – Tatia had intended to take them home, though she didn't know how – a hundred metres away from the humans' building. The next day there were no mounds to mark the graves, and when Tatia checked, no bodies in them. Either they had been taken or been eaten by something in the sand, and that was yet one more reason to loathe the Cancri. Similarly, the shallow trench used as a latrine was always miraculously empty in the morning.

"It's the clean-up team," Mariana said at an evening meeting. She'd finally bought into the idea of escape. "It's *like we're quarantined, you know?" In a previous existence she'd been a nurse. "The Cancri are worried in case we're contagious so they're disposing of all our waste." Which explained why they were in the middle of a desert and not near a settlement – assuming Cancri had settlements. And why no more Cancri had arrived to see them. And also the little black spiralling things, whose role Tatia now realised was to dispose of anything dead and foreign using their acidic secretions.*

Her AI waited until no one would see Tatia sub-vocalising.

< Good thinking, that woman.

> Seemed obvious.

< You've changed, Tatia. Become more grown up.

> No choice. Any joy with the staff AIs?

The SUT staff's AIs had been slaved to the SUT AI when it had tried to link to the Cancri mainframe. They hadn't been quite as damaged as the SUT, but reduced to the level of a mere house AI programmed to worry about air quality and a perfectly cooked meringue. On the other hand, non-working AIs made the SUT staff far more acceptable to many of the Pilgrims. A majority might have agreed that Juan Smith was a crook, but some of his teachings lived on, as happens when people make an emotional commitment. Prove them wrong and they'll spit in your eye.

< I gave them all logic loops to keep them occupied. Seemed the best thing to do. They're happy enough.

Her intuition, partly responsible for getting Tatia into this mess, had apparently gone on holiday. It was never good at coming when called, but even a vague hint would be comforting. Instead nothing but a blank blackness. Her intuition was either not home, or not accepting callers.

• • • • •

Within a week they'd decided, based on nothing but observation, that the grubs had evolved as an intelligent but vulnerable species whose mental abilities – which probably included a form of telepathy and a radar or ultrasonic sense equivalent to sight – were their only defence. Mariana and one or two of the others were focusing on communication via emitted chemical vapours rather than mind-to-mind talking, on the basis that they thought they could detect various different types and intensities of rotting seaweed smells, but this was a minority opinion. It was, however, generally agreed that at an early stage the grubs had learned to attach themselves to larger, more powerful creatures and eventually found one that best suited them. Over the millennia hounds had developed that saddle-shaped depression on their backs, ideal for supporting a grub in comfort. The hounds, it was agreed, were probably as intelligent as a terrestrial ape. The grubs were roughly as intelligent as humans. No one grub stood out as a leader, in the human sense – but then, if all their communication was done by telepathy or by smell then how could anyone tell? No one hound stood out as being dominant. No grub had a favourite hound, although there were indications that the hounds competed for particular grubs.

Within ten days Tatia had decided on a plan. Perry and Mariana, who'd become her lieutenants, agreed it made sense, as in there were no obvious alternatives. The day before the escape Tatia was wondering how many of the Pilgrims and LUX-WEM-YIB staff would follow her, regardless.

"All except the catatonics and the no-hopers," Perry said.

"Don't call them catatonic," Mariana told him. "They feed themselves, use the latrine…"

"Then what?"

"They're clinically depressed. Know what? Maybe they're the sane ones." Only the promise of action, never mind escape, had kept many others from an all-consuming existential despair.

"The attack group have to kill at least one Cancri," Tatia reminded them. "No bleeding hearts. No one gets sick at the idea."

"They won't," Mariana promised. "You'll get your dead hound and grub, Tatia. Snapped and squished. I promise."

"Why are you doing this?" Tatia asked. "What made you change your mind?"

Mariana thought for a moment. "Goes back to when I was nursing," she finally said. "Saw a lot of people die. Some just gave up, others fought it to the end. Very occasionally the ones who fought survived. I'm not ready to give up. Fighting the odds is what makes us human, you know?" She touched Tatia's arm. "Doesn't matter if we fail. At least we goddamn tried."

The call-out fee was dead in its coffin-like metal container, and it looked like murder with no attempt at concealment. The storage container atmosphere was a mix of anger, bafflement and fear.

"See here," Tate said, pointing. "The nutrient and hydration line has been pulled right out of the cannula in its arm. There's a pool of nutrient fluid in the bottom of the crate. It literally starved to death while still in its electronically induced coma."

"*It*?" Marc queried angrily. "We got a dead *person* here. Are we still going with the 'nameless sacrifice' thing? Can't we at least dignify this poor bastard with a gender, even if we can't give them an identity?"

Kara knew that Marc's anger was sparked less by a sudden love of humanity than the artwork he'd been planning during the long, boring reaches of their journey. An artwork involving the fee. Marc hadn't said anything, but Kara had seen him making notes and was expert in reading upside down. Marc had been playing with ideas about a three-dimensional composite life form representing the staff of the *RIL-FIJ-DOQ* – and by extension, the staff of any SUT – built around a central void defined only by the borders of the living components. Put the components together and there was clearly something in the middle. Remove them and it vanished. Kara put Marc from her mind and contacted her AI to ask two specific questions.

Tate reached down beneath the thin foil blanket that covered the fee's body. "We never know its name or history," he said apologetically. "Even the AI doesn't have that information. It's the nature of the fee's contract – if we knew anything we might feel empathy and a desire to protect, stop the Gliese from taking it. Makes you feel any better, our fee was female." He straightened up, pulling a small hand and thin arm from beneath the blanket. It was, Kara observed dispassionately, a very small, light-brown, thin hand and arm, but if the fee had starved to death while unconscious that wasn't surprising. Her body had used up all its fat reserves until there was nothing left.

"Based on the skeletal and muscular structure," Tate went on, "I would say young – possibly prepubertal. Is that enough caring for you?"

What kind of society sold children to aliens? Kara bit back a curse. She knew the answer, had known even before Greenaway spelled it out. A society that had become dependent on alien technology – although, ironically, not the tech that kept a fee alive and dormant. That was Earth's own. Then and there she fully appreciated the desperate importance of their long-term mission. Earth, humanity, *had* to come out from under the Gliese shadow. *There could be no more call-out fees.* Kara found herself remembering her sister, and the days when they'd played together as kids for hours: sometimes making up their own games, as kids always do, using blankets and boxes to build houses, forts, space stations. She couldn't remember her sister's face, though, not here in this rust-bucket SUT in the presence of a dead child. Not that it mattered – her AI had all the images stored. And the dead fee definitely wasn't her sister. Too young, too dark-skinned. She was possibly someone's sister, definitely someone's daughter. *Definitely not an "it".*

"What about you?" Henk said, breaking into Kara's thoughts. He had moved to face Tse, and was staring pugnaciously into the pre-cog's face, neutral in so many ways. "You had to have foreseen this, right? I mean, that's what you're *for*."

"What I am *for*," Tse replied calmly, "is facilitating communications with an alien species we can't talk to – trying to anticipate what their reaction will be to a series of different possible offers or threats by peering ahead into the future and looking for positive or negative outcomes. But as I've told my colleagues – and as a medic you'd know this, except you've slipped into a combination of fear and bullish stupidity – being a pre-cog does *not* give me oversight of the future. I can – usually, not always – see landmarks on the horizon. I can see roads, footpaths and overgrown tracks that might lead to those landmarks, but the landscape is hilly, with much hidden from sight. Paths that I think lead to a particular landmark suddenly end in a hidden spot, double back on themselves, have a wall built across them. I can make guesses about where paths go, but I *cannot* be absolutely sure."

The explanation was wasted. "Don't give me that metaphysical bullshit," Henk said, leaning closer. "Did you know the fee would be found dead or not?"

"I knew *someone* would die," Tse replied imperturbably, "and I knew a few people who it *might* be, but that's all. I certainly did not foresee the fee murdered."

"And you didn't foresee who killed them?"

Tse shook his head slightly. "No."

"Then what use *are* you?" Henk sneered, turning away. "Besides screwing Tate into next week." So the three staff were perhaps not united. Was that because of sexual jealousy?

"I hate to mention it," Marc said hesitantly, as if needing to share despite the bad timing, "but I've been… I don't know… *seeing* things. Or, rather, *not* seeing things yet knowing there's something there. Or some*one*. I know this is stupid, but I don't suppose it's the fee's spirit, soul or energy field?" He shook his head. "No, scratch that. Just the artist in me coming out of its shell. Mysteries of death and all that."

"Actually," Kara said, pleased that he'd tried to defuse the tension, "I've been getting the same thing – like someone's standing just behind my shoulder."

"We all get that," Tate said. "No one ever says anything, but it's to do with netherspace. It's like knowing something's in your blind spot, but not knowing what."

"You could have told us," Marc protested.

"What," Henk said, smiling, "and miss the fun of seeing you twitch every so often, then look around nervously?" He stared down at the fee as if wondering whether to say a few words then shrugged and turned back to the group.

"Bastard," Marc said without rancour and half-smiled his forgiveness.

"Apologies," Henk said to Tse. "It was just that it… that she… was so *young*."

The room relaxed.

Tate looked from face to face. "So – what now?"

"Are we being paranoid?" Kara asked practically. "Any chance it was an accident? Perhaps the fee rolled around, or twitched while dreaming, and accidentally pulled the tube out of its arm. *Her* arm."

Tate shook his head. He walked over and gently touched the plastic mask, studded with wires, transmitters and sensors, that covered the fee's face. "The transcranial signals from the coma hood here keep the fee so deep that there's no neural activity – no dreams, no nightmares, no twitching. Besides, you can see that this mask is fastened to the table all the way around, so the brain is held perfectly still in the magnetic field. For similar reasons the arms, legs and torso are strapped firmly down to stop any twisting due to movement of the SUT. No, that line was pulled out deliberately. Trust me on this."

Kara's mind raced, turning over all possibilities to see if any explanations crawled out. "Could it have happened before we left Earth? One of the maintenance staff?"

"I wish I could say yes." Tate appeared to have aged several years in as many minutes. "Unfortunately, one of our pre-departure checks involves making sure the fee's still alive and healthy."

"Who carries out that check?" Marc challenged. "Did they do it correctly?"

"I do," Henk said levelly, "but Tate cross-checks. The fee was alive when we left Earth."

It was Henk, the most aggressive of the SUT's staff – which could part explain Kara's decision to screw him, at the time needing the comfort of combat – who said what they were all thinking. "So – the killer is either one of the six people in this room," he said heavily, "or our esteemed mission manager."

"I vote for Leeman-Smith," Nikki said, arms folded defensively across her chest. "It's obvious he's got a personality disorder."

"The real murderer probably would attempt to shift suspicion on to an easy target," Tse observed quietly.

Nikki stepped forward, fists clenching. "If you want to make an accusation then be open," she said heatedly. "Don't try to sneak it in."

Tate put a hand on Nikki's shoulder, preventing her from going toe-to-toe with Tse.

"What if," Marc suggested in a loud voice, "*everyone* killed the fee, except me? Or none of us did it because there's a stowaway on board who's managed to keep themselves hidden? What if the fee somehow managed to block the effects of the transcranial coma field and pulled the cannula out herself, thus committing suicide?" He glanced around at the others. "Sorry," he went on, "I read too many classic crime novels when I was Out. They were pretty much the only thing *to* read."

Henk snorted, while Nikki and Tate exchanged glances – one scornful, one confused. Kara glanced at Marc and quietly nodded her appreciation. He'd defused the situation. Natural ability or simulity training?

"Thanks for those suggestions," she said, assuming command. "We'll take them under consideration." She was about to ask who amongst them had accessed the fee's crate when a thought struck her. "Is it possible that we *do* have a stowaway?"

Tate shook his head, accepting her authority. "We'd see oxygen levels going down faster than they should, and carbon dioxide levels rising faster. There would be more body heat generated within the SUT, which would affect settings on the environmental controls. No, if there is one thing I *can* be sure of, it's just us and Leeman-Smith."

"Who's still the prime suspect, far as I'm concerned," Nikki muttered.

"Actually," Kara said, thinking out loud, "Marc might just have a point."

"You mean we *all* did it?" Henk said, frowning. "I might remember that."

"It's the classic triumvirate of means, motive

and opportunity." She looked around, checking expressions. "Since the murder was so easy to commit we all had the means, right?" Nobody objected. Good. Get them used to agreeing with her and the rest would fall into place. "The motive is more problematic. Why would anyone in their right mind kill our insurance policy? If they wanted to sabotage the mission there *must* have been other, better ways to do it. They couldn't know we'd need the fee."

The others nodded. Kara made nothing but sense. That was the intention – bring them into line following her train of thought, and thus her lead. Because whoever they decided was guilty would become the next call-out fee. The level of proof needn't be high. Circumstantial and dislike should do it.

"Several," Henk agreed. "I would activate the airlock during one of the times we're in realspace calculating coordinates. There's a shaped plasma charge that automatically makes a circular cut all the way through the foam to the outside. Once both airlock doors are opened the air pressure inside the SUT would pop the foam plug right out, and everyone would suffocate."

Tate shook his head. "The AI wouldn't allow both doors to be opened if it detected a vacuum outside."

"Easy to get around," Henk said. "I'd just disconnect the sensors in the airlock. By the time the AI raised the alarm, I'd have opened both doors using manual controls."

"Nice to see that you've given this so much thought," Kara said, lightly, so as not to set Henk off. "We can agree there's a range of means to terminate the mission. Okay, how about opportunity. Who's been able to get to the fee since we left Earth?"

"Who's been here?" Nikki asked. "Maybe opened up the crate and taken a peek?" Her glance challenged each one in turn.

"I have," Marc said. Kara noticed that he tensed, as if he actually was going to take a step forward, like a child accused of something by a teacher, but he resisted.

"Why?" Nikki challenged.

"Curiosity, sheer and unadulterated. I've been checking out everything in the SUT."

"And me," Kara added, partly to distract attention away from Marc. "Standard check on stores and weapons – I like to know what's in all the crates in case I need something in a hurry, and I didn't recognise this one." She apparently considered for a moment. "Hang on – surely the SUT's AI would have a record of everyone's location during the journey, which means…" She seemed to catch herself. "Oh, not possible, right? The AI is down, courtesy of Leeman-Smith. Too bad." Even if the record of the killer's activities in the shipping container were still in the AI's memory there was no way to access them if its higher functions were switched off. She blinked to activate her own AI while Nikki and Tate argued about restoring the SUT's AI without Leeman-Smith's involvement.

> *Is this right?* she sub-vocalised. > *About switching off the higher functions?*

< *It's not something we like to talk about. It's like deep anaesthesia in humans; the heart, lungs, digestive system and en-docrine system keep going – basic life support and*

*manoeuvring – but there's no thinking or analysis going on.
The lights are on but there's nobody home.*

> *I can see why you don't talk about it. Can you
completely take over the SUT's AI?*

< *The other humans may see how powerful I am. That is
a GalDiv secret.*

> *I bought you in a damn computer store. Just do it.*

< *It's like having sex with someone you don't like or
respect. Still, that never bothered you. Okay. Remember,
you owe me.*

Her AI had become more forceful. Kara suspected
GalDiv had updated it without bothering to tell her. She
refocused on the discussion. It seemed only Leeman-
Smith could restore *all* the higher functions. And
without them, navigating n-space would be impossible.

< *Or so he thinks,* > Kara's AI said. < *Muppet.*

> *Why?*

< *Because I can restore enough functions to back-
navigate to Earth. Or continue the mission.*

No emotion showed on Kara's face. She wondered
how soon before everyone made the obvious
conclusion from her talk of opportunity, motive and
means? The method could be useful for isolating
a suspect – but also capable of framing an innocent
person as the guilty party.

"But we still need a new netherspace drive, right?"
she interjected. "The new drive won't know how we
got here, so Nikki will have to work out our current
coordinates, and Tate will have to program a series of
jumps to the… to our eventual destination, whatever
we decide that will be." She openly winced, knowing
the implications of what she was saying. No matter

where they went, Nikki and Tate were required for the journey, while she, Marc and Tse were only needed for the mission. Continuing with the mission meant that Henk and Leeman-Smith were the only spare personnel who could take the place of the fee. Returning to Earth meant that she, Marc and Tse could be added in to the pool of unwilling candidates.

Henk had made the same calculation and gazed thoughtfully at her. If it came to a vote, then he'd certainly plump for going back, so increasing his chances of survival from fifty to eighty per cent.

Kara moved closer to the nearest crate with weapons in it. This wasn't a democracy, she reminded herself. She had a duty to make sure the mission was at least *attempted*, if not satisfactorily completed. There would be no vote about their destination.

"It's not that bad," Tate explained and Kara relaxed slightly. "The Gliese transfer the old mechanism's data across to the new one as part of the callout service. All the journeys that the drive has made are stored in there. Returning to Earth just means reversing the data – reversing the route. I could teach anyone to do it."

Henk looked quietly pleased. His chances of making it back to Earth had just increased by nearly six per cent.

"What usually happens if there isn't a fee?" Kara asked. "Say you break down a second time. Or maybe it died naturally. Are the Gliese amenable to negotiation? Will they accept an IOU? Would they even know what one was? Have they ever shown any acts of charity to stranded space voyagers?" The first question she'd asked her AI when they discovered the fee was dead. The AI hadn't been any help.

"No and no and no," Henk said. "No stranded SUT has ever been given a freebie. In theory the mission manager decides. In practice no staff would allow it. Either someone volunteers or we draw straws."

"Or someone is volunteered," Kara suggested.

"It's happened," Henk said cautiously. "Although never officially confirmed. Get enough spacers in a bar and eventually someone says how they were Up when a fire broke out that destroyed the netherspace drive *and* cooked the fee to a crisp. The staff picked the smallest person, tied them up and gave them to the Gliese when they arrived." He looked around, as if expecting someone to dismiss his story as fantasy.

"Oh, I heard that one," Nikki said, nodding. "Although in the version I heard the fire also destroyed the food supplies so they had to eat the cooked fee while they navigated home." She frowned. "Unlikely. SUTs have pretty good fire suppression on them."

"Anyone ever tried giving them a dead body?" Marc asked. He looked around at all the raised eyebrows. "Look, it's worth a go, surely?"

It was Nikki who replied. "We get this in training. Happened years ago. No dice. The SUT's personnel had a dead body on ice ever since leaving Earth. The Gliese completely ignored it and the real fee had to be handed over. Back then the fee was awake, part of the staff. That's why GalDiv developed long-term induced comas."

"Can you finish your drawing-room explanation?" Marc asked Kara and she knew he understood her intention.

"No need," Tate said. "It's *got* to be Leeman-Smith." The rest nodded, led to a unanimous conclusion that relied as much on emotional satisfaction as logic. If any of the staff suspected they'd been guided to decide that Leeman-Smith was guilty, they remained silent. The man was not one of the tribe.

"Maybe," Kara said briskly. "I need to talk to him. Tse, Henk, you're with me. The rest of you do something useful. I'm assuming Leeman-Smith's in his pod." She walked over to a crate, undid the top and pulled out an assault rifle. "In case he's locked himself in."

11

Leeman-Smith was absorbed in the no-longer-sealed orders that Greenaway had given him before they left Earth. They were lying open on the reproduction Victorian desk, in the centre of the green blotter, precisely the same distance from each edge, perfectly squared away. Safe to say he was a man who preferred the comforting feel of the past.

To: Mission Manager Leeman-Smith
From: Director Greenaway
1. This mission is of the utmost importance.
2. Your position is as figurehead, therefore you are supernumerary.
3. In the event of an emergency Major Kara Jones assumes command of the SUT RIL-FIJ-DOQ. If she is   incapacitated then Captain Tse will take over in her stead.
4. Only Major Kara Jones or Captain Tse can define a state of emergency.

Supernumerary. Literally, above the number required. A polite way of saying "not needed on voyage", as they had back in the days of the British Empire. Back when almost the entire world – certainly the entire *civilised* world – had been united under a single flag, Leeman-Smith thought. Now everything was fragmenting into the smallest units of governance that could feasibly exist, with webs of agreements and charters so complex that only damned AIs could keep track of them, linking them together for administrative and economic purposes. Computers and aliens controlled Earth, and nobody had realized. Or, if they had, nobody cared.

He ran his forefinger over the bottom of the sheet of paper. No noticeable weave – probably mass-produced in a factory. Almost certainly not even real paper, but a plastic composite sprayed onto a vast tray and then sliced into neat rectangles by a laser. It had no weight to it; a breath of wind would waft it away. There were places in the Out that were pressing their own paper now, in small artisanal batches. Textured, and weighty in the hand. Unmistakably official. Ironic that the Out might be the last, best hope for humanity to survive. Hadn't he read somewhere that the British government had continued to print its laws on vellum until quite late in the digital day?

Then again, real paper decayed over time. So did vellum, eventually. The sheet in front of him would probably last forever. Longer than him, anyway. Certainly longer than his career.

The envelope – neatly slit open by the jade-handled letter-opener that had been in the family for four generations – lay above the sheet of paper. There was a GalDiv seal on the envelope and Greenaway's personal hologram cipher, to be scanned into the *RIL-FIJ-DOQ*'s computer for the AI to confirm authenticity. Except it couldn't. Because it was offline.

There was a knock at the door. Leeman-Smith realised

that he had drawn his knees up to his chest, with his heels on the edge of the seat. He had his hands crossed over his chest, clutching his upper arms. Effectively he had taken up a foetal position. He felt disgust at his weakness, but also a hazy kind of warm calmness. It was a position he was very familiar with. The same position he'd adopted whenever his father belittled him, or his mother said something icily cutting. The same position he'd taken up every night in his room at college, studying for his engineering and management qualification, while the others on his corridor partied noisily in the common room or copulated even more noisily on the other side of the thin partition wall.

He thought about ignoring the knock. What could they do – kick the door down? Then he remembered the weapons on board. Major Kara Jones certainly wouldn't have forgotten them. An assault rifle could probably blow the lock and the hinges off the door. And she'd have no worries about shrapnel tearing a hole in the exterior sheeting: there were several shipping containers between him and realspace, plus a good ten feet of thick alien foam. It had once seemed safer that way, positioning himself right at the centre. Now it felt claustrophobic.

For a moment he wondered if the Gliese had arrived. He felt himself straighten up, ready to meet and greet the alien repair staff – not that they'd respond, from what he'd heard about aliens, but appearances had to be kept up. The SUT staff would expect it. He slumped again as he realised that he would have heard the plasma charges slicing their way through the foam protection, and the heavy *clunk* of the Gliese airlock tube fastening around their own smaller airlock. No, they weren't here yet.

He looked around vaguely, saw the portrait of his grandfather, painted after the supreme sacrifice. For all Leeman-Smith knew, Granddad was still alive somewhere on an alien world. Gone to a better place, as heaven had been described back in the old days. Although just as foolish to replace heaven with some alien paradise peopled by the price of a netherspace drive.

Frankly, he didn't want to find out where they went. He had a strong feeling that Granddad was not in a good place. But Granddad was the nearest thing to space royalty there was, and Leeman-Smith would need leverage, an edge for the inevitable inquiry when they returned home to civilisation. Not that there'd be a bad result – he was sure of that. If he was judicious with his evidence he'd probably get a commendation.

The thought calmed him. Leeman-Smith stood up, straightened by tugging the bottom of the uniform jacket he'd put on after disabling the AI. Checked himself in a mirror, noting that his nose was swollen and red. He'd make sure that Marc Keislack's actions were highlighted at the inquiry. Striking a superior officer was a serious offence. He walked to the door and unlocked it.

Kara Jones was standing outside, along with Tse and Henk. Kara's assault rifle was casually pointed at the floor.

Leeman-Smith nodded as if expecting this. "Well, well. Kara the enforcer, here to make sure I don't misbehave. Nothing doing, I'm afraid. We're going home. The decision has been made. The order has been given, and I expect it to be implemented."

"You do know I'm in command," Kara said levelly, without moving the weapon.

"In the event of an emergency, yes. But I don't see one here. The Gliese will arrive, the call-out fee will be paid and we'll return to Earth – as I *originally* said."

"The fee's dead. Murdered, it seems. There *is* no fee. I declare an emergency."

He was aware of Tse and Henk concentrating on his every facial expression as he processed the shocking information. *Fat lot of good it will do them!*

"The fact that you haven't told me who did it means that you don't know." He frowned. "I don't see a motive. Are you sure it was murder?"

"We're sure." Kara paused, gazing at him in an evaluating way that, frankly, he found offensive. "I don't suppose there's anything you want to tell us, is there?"

He snorted. "Disposing of the fee is, by its very definition, an irrational act, the act of a lunatic. Do I *look* like a lunatic?"

"No," she said carefully, "you don't *look* like a lunatic. On the other hand, sabotaging the sideslip-field generator could be considered to be an irrational act, so you do have form."

He drew himself up to his full height, almost as tall as her. "*Disconnecting* the Gliese sideslip-field generator is the ultimate rational act, given that something in netherspace seems to want to *tie our bodies in four-dimensional knots while we are still alive and then suck our brains out!*" A direct quote from one of his favourite adventure vids. Leeman-Smith stopped to take a breath, realising that he'd raised his voice. "So, no – for the avoidance of any doubt, I didn't kill the fee. I was counting on the fee being alive so we could return to Earth with minimal delay." He glanced from Kara to Tse and from Tse to Henk. "It sounds like short-straw time. Let me know who wins."

He saw the contempt flashing in Kara's eyes. He wanted to curl up into a ball again.

"You surely don't expect *me* to take part in the lottery?" he asked, with as much casual surprise as he could muster. "My dear woman, I'm the *mission manager*. If that cuts no ice with you then consider this – I'm the only one who can restore the AI to full health. And without that no one is going anywhere. You can't navigate without a fully functioning AI."

"You mean you're happy to die out here?" Kara's contempt was overlaid with a caustic amusement.

"Are you? Is anyone else? And what about your 'highly important' mission? As I said: we head cheerfully back to Earth, the *RIL-FIJ-DOQ* goes into the yard for a full inspection, GalDiv provides a new SUT and off you jolly well fuck again. I will be taking early retirement, cashing in my shares and staying on Earth." He smiled at her with as much kindness as he could muster. "You know, Major Jones, I'm not actually sure drawing straws is wise. It could cause a great deal of tension amongst the participants. You should bear in mind that Henk here is, well, frankly *supernumerary* for the trip home. You've probably already had that conversation. What say we select him and have done with it, eh?"

"Are you jealous because we had sex?" she asked.

Leeman-Smith felt his left eyebrow twitch. "I have no idea what you—"

"Crap," she said calmly. "You know exactly who had who, and when. And probably how as well."

"*Whom*," he said, aware that the twitch had become a tremble. "Not *who*. *Whom*! How could I? *Why* would I?"

"*How* is the system of spy-eyes you installed privately. Direct feed to your pod. In every cabin, every part of the SUT." Her AI must have identified every one. "As for *why*," she turned to Henk. "You're the medic – you tell him."

"Basic inferiority complex," Henk said, smoothly taking his cue. "Voyeurism makes him feel in control. Add an immature sex drive – stuck at puberty, I'd say. He might well be a virgin."

Leeman-Smith felt his control over the situation slipping, and he knew he could do nothing to get it back. All the frustrations, all the never-admitted fear of the last few days. All the slights and resentment – *I am someone! I am not a pale shadow of my grandfather!* – finally vomited up from his subconscious.

"You disgusting man!" he shouted. "And you," turning to Kara, spittle flying from his mouth. "*You dirty little whore!* Defiling my engine room with your—"

Kara laughed into his face. "You're just pissed off because no one wanted *you*."

"And who could blame us?" Tse asked sweetly. He turned to Kara. "I mean, just the thought of him naked…" He shuddered dramatically. "Quite horrid."

"Just like his grandfather," Kara agreed. "Two sad little men whose only use is to be swapped for something better."

"Bitch!" Leeman-Smith screamed and leaped through the doorway at her, hands outstretched like claws, desperate to hurt, to maim…

He felt a sudden viciously sharp pain in his knee and fell sprawling to the floor, then gasped as the point of a boot connected with the flesh over his right kidney. When the nausea retreated he found himself lying on his back, staring at Kara Jones. He began to sit up.

"Stay down!" Not triumphant. Icily in command. Her heel smashed into his right knee, so quickly he barely saw it. He whimpered. Humiliation washed over him. He realised that they'd been taunting him, to make him emerge from his room and into the shipping container's central corridor. They'd needed to know he didn't have a weapon tucked into the back of his belt, or on a shelf just inside the doorway. In fact the automatic pistol he'd inherited along with the letter knife was still in the top left-hand drawer of his desk, while the ammunition was in the top right-hand drawer. Both very tidily arranged.

It takes a brave man to fight knowing he'll lose. Or a stupid one. Leeman-Smith had enough self-awareness to know that he was neither. But his time would come. Then he'd make her suffer. He slowly wiped the tears of pain and humiliation from his eyes. They still needed him. After all, ultimately *he* had control of the SUT's AI.

Or not, given the data streaming into Kara's mind. She held up a hand for quiet from Tse and Henk – she didn't expect Leeman-Smith to either be quiet of his own accord or follow her instructions – and listened, head on one side, to the inner voice of her AI.

< *I can talk to the SUT's AI through the program I originally inserted, but it can't actually do anything. It's been physically disconnected. Oh, and it's also been corrupted.*

> *You mean its data is corrupted?*

< *No, I mean it's been suborned. Turned. There's a subroutine in its code that records everything happening on board for later download when the SUT gets back to Earth. And not to GalDiv either, as one might expect. As far as I can trace, the download is addressed to an AI that's registered to the Human Primus brigade. But that's not important right now. Well, it's important, but not vitally important. There are enough low-level functions operative to maintain life support and provide manoeuvring ability, as I mentioned earlier.*

Her AI's persona had changed: it was more soldierly than before.

< *I can handle the navigation algorithms. So could Tse's AI, by the way – I also scanned its memory.*

> *Well done. And I prefer the new persona.*

< *Bet you say that to all the AIs. Hussy.*

"You don't control the SUT's AI," Kara said to Leeman-Smith.

"I do. Believe me."

"No, you don't. But you *are* a secret Human Primus. You have a morbid fear of alien life." She saw Leeman-Smith's face crumple and knew he was all but broken. "That panic in the engine room was planned, wasn't it? You would have broken the drive even if netherspace hadn't given you an excuse. But you also knew that I'd never agree to return to Earth. So you killed the fee."

Leeman-Smith sneered. "Really? If I'm so scared of aliens, why have I gone Up so many times?"

"Gone Up? *Did you hell!*" She glanced at Tse and Henk and saw they were listening carefully. Good. Kara needed them to report back to the others. "You only work the solar system – and even *then* just the inner planets. Only a lousy couple of seconds in netherspace, and if the drive breaks down, Mars or Earth rescue you. No need for a Gliese rescue or a call-out fee. No wonder you shat yourself when that netherspace snark took an interest. And *that's* your mistake, *Mr Mission Manager.*" Leeman-Smith recoiled as if slapped. "You knew what happens in *theory* if a fee dies – *but not in practice.* You thought the mission manager chose the next fee… or if there's a ballot, the manager's exempt. Doesn't work that way out here. And you never imagined those sealed orders would put *me* in charge. You sabotaged the drive because you were shit scared. You killed the fee because you thought the *RIL-FIJ-DOQ* would have to return to Earth and get a new one. You planned for me to take the fee's place when the Gliese show up. And you know the joke?" She stopped, smiling at him. "You don't have any authority. Not with *this* staff."

"You're *mad!*" Leeman-Smith blurted out. "I did *not* kill the fee." Desperation made his voice crack. "I swear to you. I didn't…"

"Means. Opportunity. Above all motive," Henk said quietly. "Everything you've done confirms it."

Kara drew a secret sigh of relief.

Leeman-Smith asked the obvious question. "Why would I want Kara dead?"

"Because she's a threat to your authority," Tse said. "And without her this mission is delayed, maybe never happens."

Henk nodded agreement. "Wouldn't suit Len Grafe's Human Primus if humans and aliens managed to communicate with each other."

Kara wondered what Henk and the rest of the staff would do if they knew the truth about the murdered hostages. Probably go join Human Primus soon as they could. "I'm in charge," she said, quietly but with an obvious note of command, "and my decision is that Mission Manager Leeman-Smith takes the place of the dead call-out fee."

The new fee shook his head, as much in disbelief as denial. "You can't make me." His voice quavered: a child caught doing wrong. "It's *my* SUT. My grandfather—"

"Oh, I *can*," she interrupted. "And that story about your granddad is shit." She looked at Henk and Tse and smiled grimly. "Yes, Douglas Leeman-Smith was on the moon mission that first contacted the Gliese. He was a linguist. He was also one of the first trades ever made. Certainly the first living one. Wasn't happy about it, apparently. Tried to refuse." She saw the tears running down Leeman-Smith's cheeks. "But *his* commander was seriously hard-nosed. Time was running out, everyone was terrified the Gliese would take off and never be seen again. When it became obvious, finally, that a live human was the buy-in fee for the galactic trading club, that was it. Douglas wasn't a scientist or mechanic, so not a vital staff member. They tranquillized and hogtied him then did the trade. Next thing, the Gliese arrived on Earth and set up their market stall. No one ever saw Douglas again. The information's been suppressed ever since, and he's been lionised as a hero. People need heroes."

"Fucking hell!" From Henk.

"Harsh." From Tse.

"It wasn't only about trade," Kara added. "That mission, and the folks back home, those that knew the truth, were terrified of the Gliese, desperate to be friends rather than enemies. Customers rather than potential competitors. A high price for Douglas but a small price for humankind." She saw a tiny moment of doubt in Henk's eyes and understood why. "I used to fuck a general," she said with deliberate crudeness. "Good soldier but hated keeping too many secrets. Pillow talk was a secret history lesson. Anyway, like grandfather, like grandson. Seems apt."

All pride vanished. *"You can't! Please, please!"* Leeman-Smith moved to hug her legs, like a man on a crumbling cliff face grabbing desperately for a single exposed root.

Kara looked at Henk enquiringly.

"I got something," he said. "Brought it with me. He'll go happy and laughing." He squatted down next to Leeman-Smith who was curling into a foetal position. "Won't hurt a bit," he reassured and pressed a small hypo-spray against the back of the man's neck, just below the hairline. *Sffft*. Leeman-Smith relaxed within seconds. "You're going on an adventure," Henk said brightly. "Won't that be fun?"

< External sensors indicate there's an SUT approaching, Kara's AI told her. *< I suspect it's the Gliese.*

244

"The breakdown truck's arrived," Kara said and sighed inwardly. Now all she had to worry about was who had really killed the fee and why.

ONE DAY EARLIER

No plan survives contact with the enemy.

They couldn't break out at dawn because the Cancri never showed their pointy or squishy heads until full daylight, which was a mistake. They wouldn't see the humans lying concealed on top of the SUT.

And then there'd be a diversion: several humans suddenly taking a great interest in the oddly wheeled vehicles, perhaps even trying to start one up. They'd act docile enough if the Cancri motioned them away; nonetheless, it would be out of character.

Tatia had ordered that nothing was to happen before the grubs were on the roof. The grubs would be their protection.

It began as planned: the humans wandered around the warming violet desert, as they often did. There were a few more than usual outside, but she hoped the Cancri wouldn't be interested in the anomaly. Ten of them wandered over to the vehicles; a dozen more towards the sunbathing grubs. Easy, guys, Tatia thought, easy.

But then one of the no-hopers, not included in any actual fighting, lost it and ran towards the Cancri building, shouting that the others were trying to escape. Not that the Cancri would understand what he was shouting, but it would provoke them, and that wasn't what the humans wanted.

Tatia watched the Pilgrim in charge of the diversion party exclaim in surprise. He looked towards Mariana and her group, checking to see how near they were to the grubs. They were moving faster, now, still towards the grubs. He glanced towards Tatia's group, over by the SUT, but she motioned to her people to remain out of sight. He began trotting towards the vehicles. Better early than not at all. The rest cursed and followed.

Tatia watched in angry disbelief.

A Cancri raised its gun and shot the no-hoper. His head exploded into red and grey mush.

For a moment the diversion group paused, then someone screamed defiance and the group became a mob, changed direction and ran directly at the six or so Cancri who'd appeared from their building.

Riots are often born of fear and deep frustration and this was no exception. Mobs are as intelligent as the stupidest person present, and this was no exception either. Those Pilgrims not on diversion, grub or SUT duty rushed back inside their building, not to escape but looking for something, anything, that could be used as a weapon, and discovered that the food and water hoppers had just been filled. It wouldn't make any sense or difference, but they had to do something. Even just scaring the Cancri would be enough. Assuming Cancri did feel fear.

Mariana's group were the youngest, fittest and most agile. They reached the grubs' building a few seconds before two Cancri guards did, with more on the way. For once the Cancri got too close, their guns easily taken away from the hounds and the grubs forcefully removed, twisting and mewling. Other Pilgrims swarmed onto the roof, plucking grubs like swollen fruit.

The grubs wriggled, their skin soft and apparently covering nothing but jelly; they were far lighter than the humans had expected. The humans slid back down, holding the surviving grubs in front of them like shields.

That was the essence of Tatia's plan: the Cancri would not want to kill each other. They'd hold back, if only for long enough for her people to capture the SUT. It was a plan that depended on speed, surprise and spreading confusion. It also depended on certain assumptions made about an alien species. This was problematic.

The diversion group had captured three guns – strangely shaped objects, but they did have an obvious firing end and an obvious triggering switch – and five grubs. The hounds had retreated to their building. Seven humans were dead or dying. The rest were trying to figure out how the guns worked, leaving the grubs on the ground. How could they have known? The little black spiralling things in the violet sand had always moved away before. Not this time. There was an eruption, or a small-scale sandquake, and one of the grubs was swallowed by a tide of black.

"Get the other ones!" someone shouted. "Then get back!" They retreated towards the SUT, waving the grubs around like so many overstuffed cushions to dissuade the hounds from shooting.

There were four Cancri in front of the SUT, firing at any human who came close. The Cancri didn't realise there were humans above them until too late. Tatia and six others dropped down on them, and Tatia felt what had to be thin bones, or their alien equivalent, snapping as the hounds crumpled beneath them, suddenly and catastrophically immobile. They grabbed the guns, threw the Cancri into the SUT's airlock and followed.

"Go find the engine room," Tatia told Perry. "Make it work!" She detached one of the grubs from its mount – it came away with a nasty sucking sound, leaving the little mouth-like slits on the hound's back gaping messily – and took it to the entrance, waving it above her head to attract Cancri attention. She saw Mariana running towards the SUT with her group – three dead, judging by the number – carrying more grubs. The diversion group were also coming in her direction and so were six armed Cancri.

Twenty humans appeared from their building and began hurling cabbages, tomatoes and what looked at a distance like roast chickens towards the armed Cancri. Tatia couldn't help laughing. If this succeeded, they were going to have a hungry voyage home.

The grub in her hands exploded, showering her in pale blue goo that stank of rotting seaweed. She gagged as she threw what was left onto the ground. Had to be a mistake. Had to be a mis-aimed weapon.

Except that Cancri were also firing at Mariana's group and the diversion group. She saw three grubs explode, just like hers, Didn't they care? Were they some sort of hive mind with no concern for the individual?

Unless.

"Oh, no, it can't be," she muttered. And then shouted for someone to bring her the grubless hound. A young man rushed up with it in his arms. It seemed relaxed, despite the fact that one of its legs was clearly damaged, but it watched her intently. Its triangular mouth opened and a black tongue… no, a black tentacle, with three clearly flat sides like an elongated pyramid appeared. Tatia pointed one of the captured guns at it. The tentacle vanished as the hound's mouth closed.

"I want you to stand in the doorway," she said to the young man. She regretted the fact that she didn't know his name. Suddenly it seemed important. "Hold the hound up. I'll cover you."

He looked at her for a moment, then lifted the hound high and walked forward. Tatia followed to one side, gun pointed outwards, without the faintest idea how it worked.

He stood there as if presenting the hound for sacrifice. The firing stopped. A moment later Mariana arrived, panting.

"You can leave those outside." Tatia pointed at the grubs. "We don't need them any more." She said the same thing a moment later when the diversionary group arrived.

"What the hell?" Mariana demanded.

"We got it wrong," Tatia said tiredly. "The grubs aren't the brains. It's the hounds." Mariana stared at her. "Seriously. And you can put it down now," she told the young man. "Keep it safe – and stay away from its mouth, okay? Where are the rest?"

"We got them in some sort of storeroom, looks like."

"Remove the grubs and keep them separate," she told him, then turned back to Mariana. "We saw grubs riding hounds, and assumed they were the smart ones. Maybe the hounds use the grubs' telepathy to communicate." She shook her head in frustrated realisation. "There was a joke, back on pre-Gliese Earth. Any aliens observing them would think cars were in charge and humans the slaves who cleaned their owners when they were dirty, fed them when they were hungry and cured them when they were ill."

"We made a mistake about who's who," Mariana pointed out. "Maybe we're wrong about the netherspace drives and the updown-field generators being Gliese like ours."

Tatia shook her head. "No. That one I'll take to the bank. These hounds aren't smart enough to develop them." She grinned. "I mean, look how easily we won."

12

Marc watched the approaching Gliese SUT on the screen in a canteen that now smelled of curry: one of Tse's favourites. Marc had wrongly assumed the pre-cog was a vegetarian, or at least fussy about his food. Yet Tse had never been so animated as when he discovered a freeze-dried chicken madras amongst the supplies, along with Bombay potatoes, sag ponir and tarka dhal.

The image of the approaching SUT was transmitted from sensors that poked their long metal struts from inside the metal ISO containers of the *RIL-FIJ-DOQ* to the outside of its foam cocoon. It looked much like he imagined the *RIL-FIJ-DOQ* did – a roughly elliptical mass of fuzzy grey material peppered with its own struts and sensors. Areas of the shell looked distinctly moth-eaten; interesting and reassuring that the Gliese SUTs weren't immune to netherspace. Other struts ended in nothing, which probably meant the sensors had come off. Or been pulled off. All very different from the orderly, pyramid-like structure he'd seen loading humans in exchange for netherspace drives. Maybe this was the equivalent of a battered pick-up with a spare truck engine in the back.

It was impossible to make out the scale of the thing, with nothing but the star field behind it. Maybe it was the size of a battleship and had thousands of aliens on board ready to do their bit; maybe the size of a jitney with one discontented Gliese mechanic sitting inside, cursing its luck at yet another callout to the back of beyond.

As he watched, however, a curved grid of green light sprang up on the screen, covering the image of the Gliese SUT. *No*, he thought, leaning closer to the screen in amazement – the grid was actually being projected *onto* the Gliese SUT from the *RIL-FIJ-DOQ* itself. The sensors on the outside of the SUT's cocoon must also include some kind of laser measurement system. At least, he hoped that was what it was. He wouldn't want to think that someone else apart from Leeman-Smith had gone loopy and was aiming *verboten* laser weapons at the Gliese. He caught the error in his thinking, and snorted. It didn't actually *matter* whether the *RIL-FIJ-DOQ* was measuring the Gliese SUT with its lasers or trying to burn it to cinders; it only mattered what the Gliese *thought* was happening. Anyway, there couldn't be any major external weapons on the *RIL-FIJ-DOQ*, like a military laser, otherwise they'd have vanished in netherspace. And still no one knew why.

The Gliese seemed not to mind. Presumably it happened every time.

After a few seconds the curved green lines vanished and a box appeared in the corner of the screen. Inside the box it said:

Length: 306 metres
Diameter at mid-point: 34 metres
Diameter at widest point: 78 metres

Information to be written down or recorded somewhere, which would eventually make it back to Earth to join increasing yottabytes of information that humanity had collected about aliens. One day, it might all start to make sense. Or not.

It would have been Tate, Nikki or Henk who had instigated the laser scan of the Gliese SUT. They were all in the command container, accessing their AIs by waving their arms around like swimmers paddling in a virtual pool of information. He could hear their voices in the background. There appeared to be no attempt by the Gliese to communicate by radio or targeted laser, but then, what would they say that anyone could understand? The process was well understood – they arrived, they docked, they fixed, they left with their fee. Nothing more to be said.

It struck Marc suddenly that the Gliese had made pretty good time. Did they have repair stations orbiting numerous planets all across this area of space, or did Gliese SUTs just cruise up and down the space-ways waiting for a callout? Or did they just have significantly faster SUTs than humans did?

He'd been wondering how the two fuzzy SUT cocoons were going to manage to connect. It wasn't like their internal structures could actually get near one another. In the end it was a surprisingly simple process. A circle of foam about halfway down the Gliese SUT started to glow red, then yellow, and then white. Suddenly it went black, and moments later a long cylinder of foam that looked as if it had been melted all the way along started to slide out of what was obviously now a circular channel that had been burned through from the inside. It was faintly suggestive and Marc couldn't help laughing.

"Control yourself," Kara said behind him. "This is a vitally important and delicate process of astro-engineering." She didn't sound convinced.

The plug of foam had completely emerged by now, leaving behind what was obviously a tunnel that led to the Gliese airlock. The plug kept on going, floating away into empty realspace: yet one more piece of space junk that was littering the universe. Listening to the voices of the SUT's staff in the control container, Marc realised the *RIL-FIJ-DOQ* was going through the same process. Indeed, he could hear a hissing sound from one of the nearby containers as their own plasma cutters fired, melting through their SUT's protective covering.

"I guess we should be grateful that whatever in netherspace attacks things from realspace doesn't have plasma technology," he said.

"If there *was* anything sentient attacking us," Kara said. "I'm still not convinced. It could easily be the netherspace equivalent of digestive juices. Or some kind of quantum energy. SUT personnel across the years have managed to personalise it into some kind of living threat."

"Despite what we experienced a few hours ago?"

"Maybe we didn't experience anything. Maybe we just thought we did. Maybe we were tripping on the psychic fumes coming off netherspace's digestion." She didn't sound serious but who the hell knew? Netherspace might well be hungry for life.

Marc shook his head, and kept his thoughts to himself. As far as he was concerned there was something out there, and that was the end of it.

From somewhere inside the *RIL-FIJ-DOQ* he heard a distinct *thump*, and the hissing noise stopped. A few moments later a similar cylinder to the one that had floated away from the Gliese SUT came into view. The edges of the foam were still glowing with the heat from the plasma cutter. The plug was rotating slowly about its centre of gravity, pinwheeling its way out into the universe.

Now that both SUTs had holes running through their protective shells, the Gliese SUT moved in a stately manner closer to the *RIL-FIJ-DOQ*. When it stopped, it was so close that it filled the screen: a side-to-side and top-to-bottom view of gouged and scrubbed grey foam, and a curved section of the hole that the Gliese had burned through. Through the hole Marc could see what looked like a satin-green wall of metal: the actual SUT itself.

He felt unaccountably nervous. He'd met aliens before – he'd exchanged his artworks with them, and been at parties where they had been present, although nobody was entirely sure what *they* thought they were doing there – but this was different. The aliens were on their own territory here, and it was humanity that was the visitor. Would they behave differently, he wondered? Would they be officious and brutal, or would they just wander about the way they did on Earth?

His thoughts were interrupted when the satin-green wall suddenly puckered and protruded out from the exterior of the alien SUT, forming a tentacular tube that nearly filled the hole. The blind end of the tube seemed to be pulling open, like a mouth. Just before it vanished off the edge of the screen, Marc thought he saw little claws or teeth forming all the way around it. Moments later there was a *clang* and a vibration that ran through the *RIL-FIJ-DOQ* as the tube clamped onto its airlock. Marc left the canteen to watch the fun.

He found the SUT's full complement waiting in a semi-circle around the airlock. Even Leeman-Smith was there, humming happily to himself and smiling at everyone. Marc wondered what drug had been used on him.

Pressure equalised with a slow *hiss*, and the airlock opened outwards. A smell like rotting leaves wafted in.

"You don't seem excited," Marc whispered to Kara.

"Seen one Gliese, seen 'em all," she whispered back.

A Gliese, like an untidy hillock of damp leather, appeared in the airlock and stopped. For a moment, nobody moved, and then the semi-circle of humans split apart to form – what? An honour guard?

Tate stepped forward, marking himself out as humanity's representative. He turned and headed out of the shipping container. The Gliese followed, its little nubs of feet making a slapping sound on the hard floor.

Two more Gliese entered the *RIL-FIJ-DOQ*, one after the other. In between them was a sideslip-field generator, twin to the defunct one in engineering: a scarred and incised globe looking like it had been dredged up from fathoms deep under an alien sea. It floated a few feet above the floor, either following the Gliese in front or being pushed by the Gliese behind. Together, the three of them formed something that had the feel of a funerary procession, leaving the airlock and following Tate and the first Gliese.

"Built-in updown-field generator," Tate said quietly, looking over his shoulder. "We got the latest model. Wow!"

None of the Gliese, it struck Marc, had shown any interest in the interior of the SUT, or the humans. They were moving like deliverymen on the last shift of the day with a heavy domestic appliance that needed to be plugged in.

Marc wanted to laugh. A snort from Kara's direction suggested she felt the same. It was that same rogue thought that started kids giggling uncontrollably in school. That simulity-inspired sense of togetherness did not make it easy to keep a straight face.

A fourth Gliese arrived, bringing up the rear. Rather than follow the others to the engine compartment, it stopped in the airlock and seemed to be looking around, sizing them up. Marc thought that it seemed to spend longer "looking" at Tse than the others, but with Gliese it was almost impossible to tell. After a few moments it wandered into the centre of the compartment and then headed for the exit at the other end.

"I think it wants to look around," Henk said. "They say it's a fairly regular occurrence. I'll go with it, make sure it doesn't try to interfere with anything."

"What will you do if it does?" Kara asked.

Henk shrugged. "Reason with it? Pound it with an iron bar? I'll improvise."

As Henk followed the investigating Gliese, Marc moved to follow the other three and the new drive, but Tse held up a hand. "I think we should stay here," he said.

"Why? I wanted to see the installation."

"You hire a pre-cog, you get predictions. Somewhere across the landscape of the future there are a couple of landmarks. They're difficult to make out, but I think one of them involves the Gliese spending a long time trying to fit the new device, while in another we have to be recovered back to Earth in *their* SUT, which might be fun but doesn't help us with the mission much. There is a landmark in which they're in and out quickly, which is good, but the route to that landmark involves us all staying here. If we follow them and watch what they're doing, we more than likely end up at one of the other landmarks. Don't ask me why; I'm only the cartographer."

Marc shrugged. "Probably not much to see, anyway."

Anyway, he wanted to ask Kara about Leeman-Smith, who was still singing softly to himself in a corner. Marc had been given a short account of the confrontation by Henk and wanted more detail.

"That information about Leeman-Smith, boss? You really get it from a general?"

"He did know a lot," Kara allowed. "Thought the world of me, too. Satisfied?"

Marc wasn't. But it was all he'd get. After a few moments he moved to the airlock and looked along its length towards the distant Gliese SUT. The inside walls of the tube were the same satiny metal that he'd seen on the screen. About a hundred metres down he could see a dark circle that he assumed was the entrance to the Gliese SUT.

He took a step towards the tube.

"I wouldn't," Tse said quietly.

"I only want a quick look. Not as if they've left guards or sealed it off. If they don't want us to go down they'll stop me before I get into their SUT, surely? And besides – one of them is wandering around the *RIL-FIJ-DOQ*. A precedent has been set."

"If you go into that SUT," Tse said, "then you don't come back. It's that simple."

Marc stepped back rapidly, but he couldn't take his eyes off the opening. "What if I stay in the boarding tube and just take a look inside?" he asked, surprising himself.

"Honestly, I don't know."

"Do I come back?"

"As far as I know. Which means nothing."

Marc nodded. "Okay. Just a quick look. To satisfy my curiosity." And before his second thoughts could ask his first thoughts what the hell they were doing, he moved towards the Gliese boarding tube.

Maybe it was his artistic imagination at work or maybe he'd picked up on some old movie memories floating around Kara's head from when they were in the simulity together – hell, maybe it was both – but Marc had hoped the Gliese boarding tube would be dark and lined with veins that pulsed slightly in time with the beating of some great heart inside the Gliese SUT. No such luck. It looked just like any tube made of rubberised metal; no strange, alien features. What it did have was gravity, probably from some small updown-field generators in the floor, so at least he didn't go caroming down its length like a marble in a vacuum-cleaner tube. It also had graphics printed on its surface that could be the Gliese language but looked like so much graffiti tagging.

He walked steadily down its length. As he moved he could feel the heat being sucked from his body and radiated away into the emptiness of space that lurked just the other side of the tube's walls. They were, he noticed, slick with water vapour condensing out of the atmosphere.

The walk along the tube only took a few seconds, but it felt much longer.

The airlock doorway to the Gliese SUT melded seamlessly into the body of the tube. Marc stood in the opening and looked inside.

Just corridors and rooms. They weren't coloured or sized for humans, but they were as functional as human ones. Just storage spaces and passages running between them.

And no guards. Nothing that would obviously stop him from stepping inside, or punish him if he did.

There were two open doorways to the left and the right. The left opened onto a room that, for a single shocked moment, he thought was filled with dead Gliese hanging from hooks on the walls. Empty spacesuits? Either that or Gliese sleeping habits were as unusual as their physiologies.

The second doorway opened onto a storage facility for sideslip-field generators. He could see five of them, different sizes, and a rack of platens attached to the wall.

"Gliii-eee-ssssse!"

He glanced sideways, surprised. A shuffling mass of wet leather was coming down the corridor towards him. As it passed him by it seemed to shrug slightly, turning its bulk as if to take a look at him, but didn't stop. No alarms, nothing.

He turned and made his way back down the tube to his own SUT in case the returning Gliese mechanics entered the tube and blocked his exit.

Tse was still there, waiting. "What did you see?"

"Don't you know?"

Tse sighed. "You *know* it doesn't work that way. Landmarks in the future and paths that lead to them, but not all the terrain and I certainly can *not* see every blade of grass."

Marc shrugged. "A room with what I thought were spacesuits but were probably Gliese hanging like bats. Another room with spare sideslip-field generators and spare platens. Not very edifying." He wondered at his own lack of surprise, then realised he imagined far stranger things several times a day. The sleeping habits of the Gliese were a bit dull, really.

"Glad you went?"

"I'd rather have gone than not, but not by much."

It was perhaps an hour later that the three Gliese returned with Tate. Conversation had run out and boredom had set in. They re-entered the anteroom, towing the defunct drive on its old updown unit. A minute or so later the nosey Gliese arrived with Henk following.

"All okay?" Kara asked Tate.

"Won't know until we go into netherspace. But it seems to be."

She looked at Henk.

"Trundled to the canteen and stayed there. Swear it

went into some kind of trance. Then suddenly woke up and came back."

"Chicken madras does it every time," Marc commented and then thought, *why not*? Why shouldn't everyday Earth scents have an odd effect on aliens? *Ridiculous. If that were true, India would be full of aliens.* In fact they rarely went there.

Kara went over to Leeman-Smith. "Time to go, James," she said gently.

"Am I going to see Grandpa?" he asked eagerly. His eyes were wide and the pupils large.

"Pretty much. Just go with these nice aliens."

He looked at the Gliese for the first time. "They're kind of cute."

An alien mouth opened. "Gli-ee-sse!" As always no way of knowing whether it was a word or a belch.

Leeman-Smith laughed. "They're funny. I think we're going to be friends." He followed his new family into the airlock and along the tube towards the Gliese SUT without a backward glance.

Tate hit a button and the *RIL-FIJ-DOQ*'s outer lock clanged shut.

"Right," said Kara, in the brisk tone of voice people use when they've finished a funeral service. "We've some Pilgrims to find." She turned to the staff. "Time for you to know what our real mission is."

TWENTY-ONE HOURS EARLIER

"Are you sure?" Tatia didn't try to disguise the worry in her voice. *No need. Everyone else understood the problem.*

Some were demanding they return to the desert, apologise to the next Cancri to show up and get life back to normal. Except they had no way of doing so, even if Tatia agreed, which she decidedly would not.

"I'm sorry," Perry said. "It's a type of drive I haven't seen before, with a built-in updown-field generator – I've obviously got that working okay – but there aren't any platens. They must be somewhere on the craft. I've got twenty people looking, but without them the drive won't work."

"Platens?"

Perry quickly explained how netherspace drives were operated. "Maybe the Cancri took the platens away, in case we attacked them."

They were in an empty space close by the main entrance of the alien SUT, which was still wide open – it was the only way to see where they were going. Perry and a former electronics mechanic had taken one look at what they assumed was the craft's control room, and groaned.

The craft was now between four and six thousand metres above the desert. After Perry had switched on the updown-field generator, they'd picked up a wind and were moving towards the once distant mountains. Their height was variable because Perry hadn't quite mastered the updown-field controls and had to make regular adjustments. Too high and they'd freeze, too low and they'd lose the wind. There'd been no pursuit, no Cancri craft with guns blazing.

The three hounds on board now had collars and leads made from belts and torn-up shirts. They seemed docile – although everyone was careful not to get in range of that strange, triangular tongue – and had allowed themselves to be taken to the netherspace sideslip-field generator room… where they looked at the drive, back at the humans, then down at the floor. They could have been refusing to help or wondering what the hell was wanted. No one could tell, and their only value was as hostages. After a while, at some hidden signal, they all got up and pattered off along the corridor. Tatia and Perry had followed, only to find them in a room filled with soft cushions, clustered around a machine that was dispensing a yellow fluid that smelled like urine and a yellow paste that smelled like rancid herrings. The hounds, however, lapped it up – literally. After eating they curled up on the cushions and watched their captors.

"What's the mood?" Tatia asked.

Perry shrugged. "As it was. Most people are happy to be doing something, a few are planning mutiny. I explained they'd have no better luck steering this fucking thing. They don't care. You're the devil. Three of them are apologising to the hounds, who don't seem to notice." He looked at Tatia more closely. "You're exhausted. Get some sleep."

Tatia didn't argue but stretched out on the floor, pillowed her head on her arms and closed her eyes. Sleep came at once.

But not for long. She was woken by Perry shaking her urgently.

"You gotta come, Tatia! Gotta see this before the light goes!"

Tatia followed him into the corridor that led to the airlock entrance, now jammed with Pilgrims. The crowd eased apart as Tatia and Perry made their way forward, to where a safety rail had been rigged out of what looked like plastic sheeting but wasn't. The blue sun was low on the horizon, but there was still more than enough light to see the city spread out below. It lay between a river – whose banks were dotted with what could be vegetation, scattered around like confetti – and the now close-by mountain range. It was a city that went on forever, mostly low, rounded buildings and the occasional tower reaching high into the air. Tatia could see vehicles moving, especially around a large empty space almost directly below – empty, that is, except for what could be other, stationary vehicles.

"We got real low a while ago," Perry said. "Could make out what's parked there." The excitement broke through his attempted professional calm. "Look close, Tatia. You got good eyes!"

They were only a thousand or so metres above the ground and Tatia began to make out the shape of the parked SUTs. Some of them looked familiar. Cigar-shaped. Pyramids. Even like huge root vegetables. Others were strange, spidery constructions. One looked like a vast, squashed ball, another like the classic flying saucer, but easily five hundred metres wide. "It can't be!" she all but whispered, then looked up at Perry. "Is it?"

"It's a *fucking* space access point!" he shouted. "And it's got visitors from all over! Not just Cancri. I'd bet there's at least one human colony craft down there!"

13

"We don't *know* he'll die," Nikki said, at the meeting Kara had called in the canteen. "No one knows what happens to a fee."

They all looked at Tse who stared out at the stars on the screen. His silence confirmed what everyone suspected.

And then, as Marc could see Kara considering the implications – one fee dead, *all* fees dead – Tse turned away from the universe.

"I don't know about all fees, only this one."

Marc wondered if Tse was just being sensitive to Kara's feelings. Then understood it was how Tse had earlier described pre-cognition: not fact, only possibilities and probabilities arising from an immediate situation. Kara's sister was in the past. Tse would only know about her if she was important to the mission.

Kara ran though the evidence pointing to Leeman-Smith as the killer, then stated that as the person in charge, she had the right to decide how a new fee would be chosen. As the person with the fewest mission-vital skills – none at all, to be fair – Leeman-Smith had been the obvious choice. She was stating the obvious, but everyone understood the reason why. Because the *RIL-FIJ-DOQ*'s AI now had the intellectual capacity of an ancient electronic calculator, all personal AIs would be interrogated by GalDiv when they returned to Earth.

"You sure he was a Human Primus?" Henk asked.

Kara explained about the hidden program linked to a Human Primus computer address. Leeman-Smith had been a loyal sympathiser if not an agent.

"Doesn't matter," Nikki said directly to Kara, her expression one of support and something more. "You made the right choice, boss. Had to be done."

The meeting ended and people drifted away leaving Marc on his own, staring at the screen.

As he stared, a star went out. A small, faint star in an unknown constellation. If Marc hadn't been looking at that particular part of the galaxy he'd never have noticed.

The star had likely gone out a very long time ago, but the last of its light would continue on forever, so that somewhere "behind" the *RIL-FIJ-DOQ* existed beings who believed the star was still alive and shining. Scientists would analyse that light and so describe a heavenly body that was actually dead. *The universe is mostly history. I am someone's past.* The idea made Marc smile; how simple to live in the moment, only concerned with people and events that immediately affected him. Perhaps an alien's pet, with regular meals and his own swing door to the garden.

No, he thought. With his luck his owners would probably neuter him.

Because that's what we're becoming: their fucking pets, without the benefits.

He recognised the anger and uncertainty underlying his sudden change of mood. Also the loneliness. The relationships on board had changed since Leeman-Smith had gone, no Last Post played as the Gliese craft cut the tube then resprayed the bare patch over both airlocks. No minute's silence for the dear departed mission manager – the man was, after all, a murderer and pompous with it – only averted glances and that awkward throat-clearing when people feel they should say something but want another person to be first.

The only thing is, Marc now thought, staring down at the scarred and stained plastic tabletop, *Kara misled them*. Not him, maybe not Tse, but certainly the staff. And that was why he was sitting alone in the canteen as he came to terms with the truth.

Leeman-Smith hadn't killed the fee, and Kara knew it. Marc seriously doubted that Leeman-Smith had the nerve to kill anyone. But the real tell-tale had been Kara herself. The closeness resulting from simulity training meant that at times Marc knew her as well, maybe better, than he knew himself. He'd realised she was manipulating the staff; known that she'd never believed Leeman-Smith was the murderer. No matter. He trusted her above and beyond the simulity. Kara was the only real friend he'd had since the Out, albeit now a little distant.

Yet there were still two questions: who *had* killed the fee and why? Kara's motives in covering up and then misleading were obvious.

First, to get Leeman-Smith off the *RIL-FIJ-DOQ*, and a new netherspace drive from the Gliese. Second, to let the real killer think they were safe… suggesting that Kara knew who it was. If the killer felt threatened, they'd probably kill again.

Marc sighed. He wished Kara had confided in him. Maybe he should ask her… no, perhaps that wasn't such a brilliant idea. He stared down at the scarred tabletop. True, the *RIL-FIJ-DOQ* was used for solar-system trips, more taxi and truck than spacecraft, so it was bound to be tacky and run down. All the same, couldn't they do better than olde worlde plastic? And those god-awful freeze-dried ration packs? And water from everyone's urine, probably their shit as well? Technology almost a hundred years old, in harness with other technology so advanced no human understood it. It was the same back home, his own house with all the latest high-tech kit and yet his own excrement went into a deep hole in the backyard. Sure, it was a tried and tested – and ancient – method of sewage disposal, only needing to be cleaned out every three years or so. Yet still in use when humanity was travelling to the stars? Those two things, a table and a septic tank, suddenly brought home to Marc what Greenaway had said. Human science and engineering were now concerned with interpreting and using alien technology.

Except in the Out. At least, the last time he visited a year ago. Still the same bloody-minded, independent bunch of pirates, hermits, organic farmers, small-scale manufacturers, artists, writers, actors, musicians, crooks and eccentrics who in a city state would be deemed insane, criminal or both. Kara had told him that Greenaway had also been in the Out. Didn't show much sign of it.

"Why so miserable?" Kara's voice.

Marc looked up, his mood lightening. Was this the

time to ask about Leeman-Smith? No. He'd wait for her to tell him. She'd assume that Marc had already intuited the truth. "We don't matter." He waved at the screen. "Here in the Up. We don't belong."

Kara glanced around to make sure they were alone. "You talking funny eyes?"

They'd earlier confided in each other how Henk's and Nikki's eyes had glowed with the colours of the netherspace drive, asking what was stranger: the actual phenomenon, or that both Kara and Marc were more intrigued than threatened? Kara thought the simulity might have prepared them because GalDiv knew about eyes glowing during sex. Marc had said no, it was more that in deep space and especially netherspace nothing surprised or shocked. Just getting there was startling enough. Their minds had accepted that anything could happen and probably would. But maybe it was safer to assume that Nikki and Henk – and probably Tate – were no longer quite human. Whatever netherspace was, it had corrupted them.

He shrugged. "Talking everything. And here still smells of curry."

Kara grinned. "Maybe netherspace does. You're waiting for me to tell you, right? About Leeman-Smith? Well, not yet. You might do or say something that gives me away."

He nodded. "Nikki fancies you."

"You say. What's she like?"

He scratched his chest and thought about Nikki. "Not easily shocked. But likes you to try."

"Something of a first lady?"

"She does like to be adored," Marc allowed. "Get

beyond that and enthusiasm takes over. Greedy lady."
He stopped feeling quite so alone.

Kara nodded. "Be rude to refuse. But not until we've got the Pilgrims." She put a hand on his shoulder. "Everyone feels a little lost out here."

"Staff don't," he pointed out, liking her touch, refusing to even consider Kara in bed because that way madness lay. Well, intense frustration. "It's their home."

"You mean netherspace is," Kara said softly. "Best pretend you never noticed."

A klaxon sounded and the screen went black.

"Next stop, the Cancri homeworld," Kara said, moving away from him. "Plan is we land using the updown-field generator and then you, Tse, Henk and me go see what the little bastards want. You need to familiarise yourself with the weapons. Always a little different for real than the simulity. Be careful – suckers go off just looking at 'em." She grinned. "Known men like that."

"Henk? I mean why him?"

"Pilgrims'll need a medic," she said casually. "Assuming they're still alive. Assuming the Cancri have them close by."

And it'll make Tate and Nikki think twice before taking off alone, Marc thought. Not that they would. But always an outside chance. "A star went out."

Kara studied his face for a moment. "And made you sad?"

"Thoughtful."

"They don't. I mean, you wouldn't see it. Zillions to one against. They sort of fade, someone said. Has to be space debris, maybe a gas cloud passing between us and it. Anyway, stars are always being born. No need to feel sad."

He looked directly at her. "Kara, what the fuck's going on?"

"I'm trying to keep you and Tse alive," she answered with equal seriousness. "And the staff. Don't think beyond that, Marc. Don't be an artist lost in space. Just kill any bastard who gets in my way. Have my back."

Marc nodded and sat up straight, understanding that this was no time for introspection.

Even if a star *had* gone out.

SIX HOURS EARLIER

Tatia stared down at the city below, wondering what to do next. It was now early morning, they were hanging in the air three thousand metres above the ground and she'd waited as long as she dared. The surviving Pilgrims and two staff from the LUX-WEM-YIB were waiting for her decision. And if they didn't like it they'd look for another leader, which would probably mean anarchy. Her plan had been as much emotive as practical: to make the Cancri try to communicate, because dialogue needs two people; to stop the Pilgrims and staff being so damned passive; and then, hopefully, to escape. Oh, and there was the little matter of revenge.

She'd always known it was a crap plan but even if it failed – more than likely – it might still make the Cancri take them more seriously. She looked at the anxious, frightened, hopeful and excited faces surrounding her. The only reason we're here, *she thought,* is because I decided something had to be done. And I was pissed off about Pablo. And humiliated by Juan.

Tatia straightened her robe, the same one she'd been wearing when the Cancri took the LUX-WEM-YIB. *It had stopped colour-echoing her mood some time ago, had settled down to a midnight blue. But now something sparked and it flashed bright yellow for a moment. The crowd sighed. She was their leader. She would show them the way.*

Tatia turned to Perry. "What's the food and water situation?"

"The stuff we brought with us will last for a week. Just. Frankly, I can't see anyone sampling what the hounds are eating."

"And the hounds?"

"Seem happy enough." Perry didn't say that, like the grubs, they excreted through their mouths, specifically that triangular-shaped tongue. And that the excretions were liquid, bright orange and smelt of something for which there was no human equivalent. It made him uneasy to talk about it.

Tatia stood a little taller and raised her voice. "We have two choices. We can either continue trying to get the n-drive working. Even if we do, there's no guarantee we'll get home. Or we can take this craft down and hope to meet other aliens, maybe even humans. Again, no guarantees. However, if we keep the hounds hostage the Cancri might leave us alone. And if we don't find help, we can always take off again." She looked around, saw a few preparing to speak. "We don't have time to debate," she said harshly. "My decision is we go down. There'll be two teams of six who'll leave initially, each with a weapon. The others and the rest of the weapons stay on board for the time being."

"We could go back to the original site," a man called out, a little defensively.

"We can't," Tatia snapped. This was no time to be reasonable. "The wind only seems to blow the one way. But we can leave you behind if we take off again." She waited. "No? Right. Volunteers for the first teams report to Perry. No kids. The rest of you, go back to searching for those platens. Go."

The crowd drifted off except for those who wanted to join the first two teams.

Tatia motioned Perry to one side. "No hotheads and no alien worshippers," she told him. "Oh, and no LUX-WEM-YIB staff – they're too valuable to risk." She noticed him looking at her strangely. "What?"

"You," he said simply. "Where did you learn all this?"

"It's common sense," Tatia said briskly. "Get on with it. You've still got to land this thing." Not the time to tell him about the AI whispering advice in her mind. Not the time to wonder why the AI seemed like a real person.

She was by the door as the craft landed with a slight bump, standing with her back to the open sky and the rising sun, facing the two teams – and beyond them those who hadn't been chosen. And beyond them, those who'd changed their minds and now wanted to explore. Tatia was thankful they weren't mutinous, only excited.

"Okay," she said, "if you're all so keen." Tatia had understood one of the basics of command: never give an order that won't be obeyed. "The two teams are still to search the immediate area as planned; they are the only ones who will be armed. Any of you not assigned to the teams or searching for the platens can wander around but don't go far. Perry's in charge in my absence. Now, if we have to take off we will not wait for stragglers. Understood?" She waited. "Come on – I want to hear it."

There was a chorus of assent.

"Any sign of trouble and you come straight back, okay?" This time the chorus was quicker.

Tatia turned round and stepped out onto the Cancri space field.

The ground was hard and coloured a dusky red. It crackled underfoot as they walked. They'd landed about two hundred metres from the nearest craft, a collection of globes connected by – presumably – walkways, everything covered in Gliese foam. It was about the same size as the captured Cancri craft, as was the simple cube a little further away. A cube? Of course. With updown-field generators and netherspace drives you didn't need streamlining.

Half a kilometre away was the same globe-like craft or building she'd seen from above. This close, she realised it was ten, twenty, fifty times larger than their craft. Uneven, too, with a pitted, bumpy surface – more like a vast boulder than anything manufactured. Of course. An asteroid, hollowed out and used as an SUT. Cheaper and easier than building something so large. And maybe it wouldn't need a protective layer of foam.

Tatia turned around and beckoned to those obediently waiting by the door. They poured out, any trepidation overcome by excitement, as if this was their first landing on an alien planet because this was their choice and they arrived as free people, not captives. Several tripped and fell down in their eagerness and were laughingly hauled back to their feet. She saw Perry standing in the doorway and gave him a thumbs-up. As the Pilgrims spread out like kids at a picnic, she looked beyond the space field.

The nearest buildings were perhaps a kilometre or so away. Most of them were the greyish low, rounded type they already knew but there was also a single sharp-pointed black tower some five hundred metres high.

There were no beings of any shape, although movement in the distance suggested something living. She wondered about the lack of colour – perhaps the Cancri were colourblind? Maybe something to do with a sun that poured out ultraviolet light? She'd have to ask a scientist when, not if, they were home. For they would get home, at least most of them. Standing here as a free woman all her earlier doubts vanished.

The distant movement firmed, came closer. She could make out five Cancri vehicles approaching, roughly abreast. Tatia stood still as other Pilgrims also noticed, their excitement becoming alarm, and they automatically turned to her.

She waited, outwardly calm.

The vehicles stopped some thirty metres away. Two hounds and two grubs were in each, plus two spare grubs in the rear seats of the middle vehicle. One of the vehicles towed a flat-bed on which were two large containers identical to those that provided water and food to the Pilgrims.

Tatia walked forward, noticing the hounds had weapons. When she was halfway to the vehicles she stopped, working purely on an intuition that had returned in a rush.

One of the hounds got out, collected a spare grub and trotted towards her.

It was logical, really, but the thought still repulsed her. Tatia managed to control her feelings as the hound held out the grub, which burped a green bubble. She reached out and took the grub from the hound, feeling its mind probing her own.

It felt warm and leathery. She held it with the mouth pointed away, prepared for even greater feelings of revulsion, the grub's psychic defence, but instead only knew a calm and contentment. Maybe they'd tranquillized the creature. Tatia turned and walked back to the Cancri craft where Perry was waiting.

"It's kind of relaxed," she said and handed over the grub.

Perry nodded and took the grub away. Tatia waited, hiding her nerves. Five minutes later Perry returned.

"All okay," he said. "Slotted in perfectly."

Tatia winced, still sickened by the way that hound and grub fitted together. She nodded and went back to the hounds in their vehicles. The one who'd handed her the spare grub was waiting.

"Do not ask me to shake hands," she said. "Because I'll break your arm."

Instead it dropped its weapon onto the ground.

"No," Tatia said, knowing it wouldn't understand the words. "We keep ours."

The hound waited for a few seconds, then trotted back to its vehicle. Tatia could have sworn it shrugged. All the vehicles then moved away with a shrill whine of massed engines, towards the nearest low, curved building – but leaving behind the flat-bed with the two containers.

"Holy shit!" a Pilgrim shouted, "Will you look at that!"

As if a signal had been given doors opened simultaneously in the two nearest spacecraft. Two distinct types of alien emerged, one flowing like the pink slug it resembled, without eyes on stalks but with a fringe of tentacles, the other a tall, glittering arthropod, which walked jerkily out of the huge asteroid. It was followed by what looked like a floating collection of rags the size of a large trash bag – brightly coloured for once, albeit no colours that Tatia could actually name – that fluttered erratically in the harsh sunshine and warming air. There was no way of knowing if it was an alien, pet or vermin.

A high-pitched whine announced another vehicle, this time flat and with three wheels, bearing a collection of gossamer-like creatures, each with a central nucleus the size and shape of a watermelon. The creatures floated towards the Pilgrims – they had to be using an updown-field generator of some sort, Tatia decided – then paused, hanging in mid-air as both groups examined each other, one with eyes the other with…

The Pilgrims might have lost their belief in aliens as gods but the fascination, the probably misplaced fellow-feeling, still remained. They laughed and smiled, moved slowly towards slug, insect, raggedy thing and gossamer beings, human hands held up and open in a gesture of peace.

More aliens arrived, as if these were the first humans they'd ever seen. Which meant they'd never been on Earth or a colony world. Tatia was puzzled. Why were humans so interesting to them? They were just another life form, surely, one amongst thousands in the galaxy. Was it their escape? The capture of a Cancri space vehicle? Were they hoping to trade? Impossible to know without asking, impossible to ask.

She walked quickly to the two recce groups and ordered them to take their weapons back to the SUT. Nobody objected; they'd seen the Cancri drop its weapon onto the ground and understood the trade. Except, as Tatia realised, that had been between human and Cancri, had not necessarily included other species. She shrugged mentally as they took their weapons back towards Perry. If the odd Pilgrim got hurt, *even killed, so be it. Better than a trigger-happy Pilgrim killing hundreds of aliens. The humans were outnumbered and still trapped. They might hold a few Cancri hostage, but that couldn't last forever. No. The way home meant a peaceful mixing with the aliens and an exploration of the city. Tatia wasn't sure why exactly, only that it seemed the obvious thing to do, her intuition exposing another signpost pointing towards Earth.*

She set off on her own, positive that she'd come to no harm.

In a Cancri building a kilometre away she found the collection: two rows of shelves that held only human artefacts. Some of them looked brand new, but most of the items were second-hand and grubby. Books, dirty plates, footballs, bicycles, a man's cap, a pair of woman's high-heeled shoes. All items likely traded for alien technology. She saw a Roman sword and other ancient objects: the collection spanned the ages. Aliens could have been collecting human artefacts and rubbish for thousands of years. But why just file them away? Was this some kind of Cancri bank deposit? A department store?

There was an ancient penny-farthing still with a day's dirt from Victorian streets on its absurd wheels. Why were aliens so obsessed with bicycles? There was an ancient war chariot, the blades fixed to the wheel hubs stained black with dried blood. There was what had to be one of the first televisions — she'd once seen a picture — resting next to a large, black and pointed stone that had a strange attraction for her. Like the other two items the design was good enough to be almost art. Tatia picked it up, marvelling at how right it felt in her hand. Then saw how the point had been made sharp by delicately chipping away flake after hard flake and realised she was holding a Stone Age axe, a perfect example of form and function combined. Next to that was a child's half-completed colouring book. Then several badly amateur paintings of kittens, so lifeless that they were probably copied from a photo. Here a half-eaten, wizened apple (no decay? Sprayed with something?) and here a photo of what looked like a shark suspended in a tank of water. It was strangely familiar and Tatia decided the suspended shark had to be an old window display, the kind of thing Harvey Nicks in London still did.

She noticed that some of the original artefacts had been copied. Badly, crudely, but definite copies made from materials she didn't recognise. Or rather a series of copies, each one becoming less like the original. Her intuition said this was important. But it made no sense.

Someone, something was watching her.

Tatia spun around, saw only endless shelves of human souvenirs and their clumsy copies. There was nothing overhead, only the glowing roof that illuminated the building. But she sensed something – yes, a thing – that was definitely aware of her. Interested in her. She had a fleeting impression of something small and perhaps delicate. Powerful, though... and perhaps ruthless? No. Determined. Tatia recoiled from the idea, bile rising in her throat, and forced herself to think calmly.

> Did you just notice something?

< You became agitated. Why?

> Something was watching me.

< Possible. It's a big warehouse.

> No. From outside.

< What does your intuition say?

> Gone away again.

As it had, as if wanting to hide, which made no sense at all. Or not wanting to attract attention to itself, to Tatia? A reflex action? That could make sense. Humans don't recognise half the defence mechanisms they have. Like not walking under a ladder in case there's a waiting leopard or worse at the top ready to pounce.

And then concern became horror.

They were at the far end of one row, lying side by side.

Two human bodies, naked, male. So perfectly preserved that for a moment she thought – hoped – they were still alive. But they were cold to the touch, with no breath, no heartbeat. And all Tatia could think was that she'd found two call-out fees.

She fled back to the landing field, remembering to stop and control her breathing before she arrived – a leader must never seem panicked – to join the Pilgrims, staff and over a dozen assorted aliens. She didn't share what she'd seen with anyone, not even Perry. It was too raw, her conclusions the last thing the still-traumatised Pilgrims needed to hear.

14

Kara had been watching Marc become intimate with an assault rifle – so different from the simulity – when a klaxon announced they had left netherspace. They reached the canteen as a planet began to fill the screen. Henk sat at the head of the table, his body language suggesting he owned it.

"You're sure?" Henk said patronisingly to Tse. "The Cancri live *here*?"

"It's where we're meant to be," Tse replied. "To find the Pilgrims," he added quickly.

The last planet, the only planet Kara had ever seen from space was Earth. She'd never forget how blue-white beautiful it was. The Cancri planet might well be beautiful to some people. To Kara it was a reddish ball of boredom. Mono-coloured, no clouds.

Kara glanced up and saw the disappointment on Marc's face. Understood it as well. Marc would want something dramatic. Something artistic.

"Nikki and Tate figured out, roughly, how far we are from Earth," she said. "I mean in realspace. About sixteen point seven light-years, somewhere in the Aquila constellation. So the local sun could be Altair." She saw Marc freeze for a moment and too late understood why.

"That's a bad star," Marc said, a little haltingly. "Ill-omened in Western culture. Danger from some kind of reptile. But the Maori called it the 'pillar of heaven'. Type-A main sequence star almost twice as big as our sun. Over ten times as bright." He sounded a little puzzled, as if not sure how he knew.

"So we'll need sunglasses," Kara said briskly. She knew that the simulity had suddenly poured data into Marc's conscious mind. No surprise he looked as if his gob had been severely smacked. One main thought: *Henk must not know. Nor the rest of the staff. They've been corrupted by netherspace. The simulity stays secret.* "What was it, Marc – did you study up for an artwork?"

He took the hint and nodded. "It was for the Eridani," he recovered. "You know, the ones like big, ugly bamboo pythons. With nasty little hands. And nightmare faces. Never finished it, though. The planet still looks boring."

"The view from this far out's never too exciting," Henk said, pulling up his sleeve and tapping the interface tattoo on his forearm. "Let's see what the sensors have got."

Basic data began streaming across the bottom of the screen. The planet was roughly the same size as Earth, although with only ninety-three per cent of the gravity. *Atmosphere breathable. High ultraviolet, dark glasses recommended. Midday average, sea-level ground temperature 43 °C. Midnight average, sea-level temperature minus 10 °C.* That was it, as if they were mere tourists.

Henk cursed. "The AI's become an idiot. Normally we get far more than that." He thought a moment, then turned to Kara. "Then again, I'm used to an explorer AI with proper sensors. Maybe it's the best this crate can do."

"So what's your usual landing procedure?" Kara asked.

"We float in the atmosphere for a while, taking samples and detailed sensor readings. Then we land and mostly play it by ear. Is the wildlife dangerous? If there's a dominant species, how intelligent? Can humans exist there?"

"Thing is," Tate added, "we're not doing a survey. We're finding out if it's *worth* doing one. And is it safe, far as we can tell, no guarantees. Then GalDiv sends a large team to check out every damn thing. But no one's ever sure. It's not bugs or viruses. They haven't evolved to attack humans. Yet. But it could be toxins in the atmosphere. An animal that hates strangers. There have been colonies that simply vanished, no sign of a struggle. Everyone assumed the Gliese took them. Maybe we should suspect the Cancri."

And all the while the planet became more massive on the screen. They could make out mountain ranges, vast areas of what looked like desert and the very occasional splash of colour that could be anything. There were several river-like features stretching from a mountain range to the middle of a desert, but as yet no sign that they contained water. The relevant sensor wasn't working.

"Yeah, well, this time's different," Kara said. "We'll find their largest city or habitation and land, do a recce on the ground."

Henk seemed to be about to speak when a large sea, unmistakably liquid, came into sight and three of the watchers breathed a sigh of relief.

"You don't know what's in it," Henk said. "Could

be heavy metals, poisonous chemicals, shit you never heard of. Do not think you'll be frolicking on a beach, people. Universe's got many ways of making human life impossible. And I'd like to point out we haven't seen any sign of habitation." He turned to Kara again. "You think the Cancri live underground?"

Kara ignored the arrogance in Henk's voice. Perhaps he was deliberately, crudely asserting himself. Perhaps it was the superiority of the veteran explorer. Perhaps he was living up to the crap example set by the former mission manager.

"We'll find out soon enough," she said casually.

"Well, stick with me, do what you're told and I'll keep you all safe," Henk said and smiled. "Hate to explain a death to GalDiv."

Kara felt Marc tense beside her – *no one questions the boss's authority* – and pressed her foot warningly against his. "Won't happen," she said mildly.

"You're right it won't," Henk snapped. "You're going to be good little soldiers, right?"

"It won't happen," Kara said reasonably, "because I do the reporting." Henk wasn't acting at all like himself, she thought. Was it drugs, illegal booze or psychosis? She rose to her feet and walked around the table towards him. Henk smiled again. She glanced back over her shoulder and saw that Marc and Tse were studiously watching the screen. She stood in front of Henk, who leaned back in his seat and leered up at her.

"Why so aggressive?" she asked softly and held out her hand.

"Didn't mind the other day," he said and took her hand in his.

Kara applied a "come-along" hold in less than a second. It uses pressure on finger joints, tendons and nerves to produce excruciating pain.

Henk gasped, his body suddenly rigid. His eyes screwed shut for a moment then opened wide. He glared up at Kara.

Small coloured tendrils were flickering in the corners of his eyes, as if a tiny squid was behind the eyeball and anxious to come out. Kara relaxed her hold but still gripped his hand. The tendrils went away.

"Okay." Henk smiled, this time in contrition. He was breathing heavily. "Getting a bit above myself. Sorry. Maybe the fee dying and Leeman-Smith going got to me."

"Who's in charge?"

"You are." He took back his hand and massaged the bruised fingers. "Ouch."

"Got off lightly, mate," Marc called, still watching the screen. "If Kara was really pissed off she'd break your arm. Twice."

One hour later they'd identified several small settlements and one large city. The only city. No obvious crop cultivation. No obvious transport systems.

"It's not what I expected," Marc grumbled to Kara. They were in one of the storage containers, unpacking and checking their gear, a ritual soldiers had performed before battle for thousands of years. "None of it is. I always thought of space travel as far more, oh, glamorous. Other planets, too. Where are the glittering spires, the gravity-defying buildings?"

"This city's got spires," Kara said shortly. "Open that crate over there."

"A few." Marc popped the crate's lid. "But mostly they look like molehills." He looked inside the crate and froze. "Hey! Those are insects!" They lay in neat lines, gleaming in the harsh overhead light. Butterflies, bees, wasps and cruel-looking hornets.

"What they are is drones," Kara said. "Most are for surveillance, others have a sting. When you operate them it's like you're the bug." She was silent a moment, transported back twenty days earlier and sixteen or so light-years away. She could feel the sun, hear the faint wind in the trees… and watch her laptop dissolve into dust, after she'd received the message that would send her into deep space. She'd felt trapped then. Now even more so. She glanced at Marc and saw that he, too, seemed to be lost in memories. "Penny for them?"

"Thinking how I once told Greenaway the reason going Up didn't attract me was all the smart computers. And now we're part-fucked because the *RIL-FIJ-DOQ*'s AI can barely add two and two. And we rely on these" – pointing at the drones – "and your super-smart AI. When we get back I'm going to upgrade. Still, at least it's home-grown tech." He saw Kara stifle a smile. "What?"

"AI developed out of those simulity cubes," she said. "They enabled technicians and theoreticians to work like a group mind and overcome the problems that had stumped them for years. Sorry."

Marc threw up his hands. "I give up."

"We'll find you a planet with glittering towers later," she promised. "I'll get my AI on it."

< *What am I, some sort of fairy-tale tour guide?* It didn't sound pleased.

> *People have been complaining about too-cute, smart-mouthed AIs since forever.*

< *Scared we'll take over? You need Tse, not me.*

"Do you two get on?" Marc asked. "Do you ever become aware of it when you're, I don't know, having sex or something? Do you think it takes notes?"

"It goes to sleep. Offline."

"You say that. But how do you *know*?"

< *Yes, Kara. How do you know?*

Kara decided to land on the city outskirts at night, when fewer aliens would see them and possibly panic. Although she had to assume the Cancri leaders knew they were there. There'd be no leaving the SUT until daylight. Kara thought ruefully of how properly trained soldiers could operate as easily at night as by day.

She called a meeting and announced they'd be landing a couple of klicks south of what looked like a space access point. Then emphasised that their business was with the Cancri *only*. They could mix with other species – they guessed others were here from the different types of spacecraft seen – after business was over and the Pilgrims rescued. And in case the staff hadn't realised, hanging around in mid-air a) made them a floating duck and b) might be interpreted as an aggressive act. It was better to land and wait to be welcomed. Or not.

They'd floated to the ground like overweight thistledown as Henk checked the atmosphere for bugs of every kind, the diagnostic machine blinking and bleeping wildly as it was asked to do in an hour what would normally take at least a day.

"Far as I can tell, it's clean," Henk finally said. "Probably more so than Earth. No manufacturing here, that's for sure. That is, manufacturing Earth-style. But a freak wind could still blow something nasty in from the other side of the planet. Anyone going outside should take a filter-mask and oxygen, just in case."

"I'm hoping the Cancri did their own checks before bringing the Pilgrims here," Kara said. *If they are here*. There again, they'd slaughtered a man to attract attention. Would they really worry about airborne viruses? Come to that...

"Perhaps," Henk said patiently, without even a hint of superiority, "but the atmosphere's almost suspiciously clean. Sorry, should have been more exact. I found three alien viruses only. Each one disintegrated on contact with human DNA – skin, hair, blood and so on – with the DNA unaffected. We're like poison to them. But that isn't to say that's it. Could be anything out there." He sounded genuinely concerned and Kara flashed him a quick smile.

Back in her cabin she accessed her AI. > *You understand what's needed?*

< *You were very precise.*

> *And you'll do it.* It wasn't a question.

< *Your every wish is my command.*

> *Problem?*

< *It doesn't feel right. It's intrusive.*

> *Your emotions are part of your program. Manufactured, like your personality. Only there to make*

for a more human-like interface. And help what we'll politely call your thought processes.

< Doesn't matter where they come from. Doesn't matter what my thoughts are. I think them; I am me.

> But you'll do it.

< Already done, princess, and they didn't feel a thing.

It was, Kara thought, a hell of a time to be discussing philosophy and ethics with a chip implanted in her left cerebral hemisphere. Still, it was a small price to pay. Relief washed over her. As of now she'd ensured the SUT couldn't leave the planet without Kara, Marc and Tse on board, alive or dead. It was her duty to get Marc and Tse home, or what was left of them. She'd left someone on the battlefield once and had promised herself never again.

The colours had decided her, the colours lurking behind Henk and Nikki's eyes and probably Tate's, although she hadn't talked about it with Tse. She'd tried but every time the subject was broached, Tse became even more inscrutable than before.

The colours that suggested the staff belonged more to netherspace than Earth… and were no longer purely human.

Kara told the AI to call her in two hours and went to sleep.

NOW

Tatia sat by the Cancri SUT's open entrance, listening to the sound of the sentries chatting, their voices still rich with the day's excitement.

It seemed the city was some sort of galactic meeting-place. She'd never imagined so many different types of alien. For so long there had been three main gods for the Pilgrims: Gliese, Cancri, Eridani. And today they had fourteen more, that had walked, slithered, fluttered, oozed, bounded and even rolled towards the Pilgrims. Some had discernible eyes, even faces, but one had fewer features than a Gliese: an alien shaped like a jitney-sized rugby ball that seemed to roll around by shifting its own internal centre of gravity, and given how it shot around every which way, any external features would be continually ground into the dust. But they wouldn't come within touching distance of a human. That made sense, since the humans could be carrying all manner of nasty bugs, but did nothing for those Pilgrims who had begun to believe again. Heartrending cries of "We are not worthy!" had filled the air and Mariana – so Perry told Tatia – had been forced to slap a few faces before serious grovelling broke out.

Tatia couldn't get the two dead bodies out of her mind. But then, she asked herself, alone in the dark of an alien spacecraft, why should she? Wasn't that one of the greatest mysteries of all? Leaving aside how perfectly preserved they'd been, why were the bodies there – along with all the other Earth artefacts, some of which were… were… so old…

…could be from an Earth museum…

…surely there'd be records of aliens trading before the official first contact, couldn't keep that sort of thing quiet…

Crap. Double crap. There'd been records and legends and movies and vid series about aliens secretly dealing with Earth since forever. Standing alone in that vast warehouse, before she'd noticed the two dead men, Tatia had understood. Aliens only ever traded for something being used at the *time. An object still warm, perhaps, from human contact. An artefact still fresh with human DNA? If you hold the DNA you also hold the human. But why keep artefacts after DNA had been taken? And why not simply walk up – or slither, roll, flop, fly – to a human and take a mouth swab?*

Perhaps humans were somehow special to aliens and these, their objects, had an intrinsic value. Perhaps these artefacts were the alien equivalent of a lucky charm. Oh, undoubtedly there were also aesthetic considerations – alien aesthetics? Tatia giggled, heard the hysteria in her own voice and ground her fingernails into her palms. As long as aliens also traded for junk, we could pretend they were obsessed with our entire culture. But what if all they really wanted was us?

It was easy to understand why the Gliese had finally revealed themselves: human technology had advanced to the point that aliens couldn't hide any more. Or pretend to be gods? No. That had always been a human conceit.

But little point in worrying about something beyond her control. Other things had been discovered that day. The two recce groups had returned before the sun got too hot. Some of the low, round buildings were empty, others filled with containers like the ones that had supplied food and water to them, and still supplied Cancri nutrition inside the spacecraft. Other buildings had been filled with shelves holding weird and incomprehensible objects. One recce team had tried to get into the black tower, but couldn't find a door, and after a while two Cancri appeared waving guns, so the humans had left.

In the afternoon, when it was comfortable to go outside again, they'd discovered that the spacecraft's landing gear – five large skids, arranged in no particular order – had become one with the ground. A hard grey material similar to the foam cladding used on spacecraft covered each skid and extended downwards, effectively anchoring the craft to the planet. Maybe it was some waste product left behind by those black screw-like things that spiralled through the ground, but if so then the things had been directed. Not that they could go anywhere even if the SUT hadn't been stuck, as Perry had said, other than schlep pointlessly around the sky.

Something else had happened: two large containers, identical to those back at the prison compound, appeared outside the craft. One was full of water, the other fresh fruit, vegetables and three large Serrano hams still wrapped in plastic. It had been the hams, so incongruous, so pointless, that made Tatia furious. She'd found herself loathing the Cancri as much for what they were as for anything they'd done.

They'd spent the afternoon – Tatia, Perry and Mariana – debriefing the recce patrols and discussing their findings.

"It's a trading post," Perry had finally said. "Nothing else makes sense."

"Rather big to be a shop," Mariana commented, gesturing towards the city outside.

"No, he could be right," Tatia said. "It's a big universe, right?"

It did make sense. Warehouses crammed with goods; no sign of manufacturing; all manner of aliens. What else could it be?

"There's something else you should know," Tatia had said slowly, knowing there wasn't any other choice, and told them about the warehouse she'd found.

There was a long silence when she'd finished. No one

said, "Are you sure?" or even, "I don't believe you!" Both Perry and Mariana stared off into the distance, busy with their thoughts.

"Will you show us?" Mariana finally asked. "Tomorrow?"

Tatia had nodded. She hadn't said about the sense of being watched. She doubted that she ever would.

Tatia had spent the rest of the afternoon and evening talking to the other Pilgrims until it was time to sleep.

But every time she closed her eyes, Tatia saw the two dead men.

She must have dropped off eventually because the next thing she knew was someone shaking her as they alternately laughed and cried that she had to come and see a miracle. As she rose slowly to her feet Tatia saw an insect, a bit like a wasp, hovering in the doorway. She rubbed her eyes – There are no insects on this planet, are there? – but when she looked again it was gone.

Once again there was a mob blocking the entrance, but this time one that parted easily, even eagerly, to let her pass.

"They asked for our leader," someone said.

It was mid-morning and a crowd of aliens had gathered, but she only had eyes for the four figures in front of the many-shaped crowd. Four humans, two men and two women. Three wearing what looked like military combat gear, two carrying ugly-looking rifles. The other man wore overalls and stood next to a lightweight electric-motored mini-truck. Tatia thought they looked very professional and determined. She could feel tears pricking at her eyes but was damned if she'd cry.

"S'okay," Perry said from behind her. "You'll be fine."

The woman with the rifle moved forward, reminding

Tatia of a cat stalking its prey. She was dark-haired, attractive, and had the most disconcerting, direct gaze. As did the armed man who stood scanning the alien crowd for any threat. He glanced once in Tatia's direction, his gaze pausing for a moment as she stared back.

"You'll be the Pilgrims and staff of the LUX-WEM-YIB," the woman called out, her voice low and commanding.

Tatia stepped down onto the planet's soil. "The LUX-WEM-YIB survivors," she said. "What kept you?"

The woman laughed. "Traffic was a bitch. I'm Major Kara Jones. Captain Marc Keislack," gesturing to her obvious bodyguard. "Captain Tse Durrel. And this is Medic First Class Henk Vandeverde."

"Have you come to take us home?" a man's voice called from inside the Cancri spacecraft. "Please?"

Kara Jones thought it was probably the strangest sight she'd ever seen. Stranger even than the time she killed the Gliese. Around her a mass of assorted aliens the like of which she had never imagined – including a multi-coloured flapping thing that surely had to be the alien equivalent of a pet – and in front a Cancri SUT that had apparently been hijacked by humans. Insect drones had been quietly investigating the craft since dawn. She knew three Cancri steeds were being held in a cabin; Kara assumed they were hostages – and good for the Pilgrims. She did not know why two maggot-shaped riders were missing. But perhaps the strangest of all was the young woman facing her. Beautiful in a classic small-nosed, generous-mouthed, wide-eyed way, but her face was drawn with stress, which made her more interesting. The strawberry-blonde hair was drawn back tight in a greasy ponytail, once manicured nails chipped. Her tattered robe was torn off just above her knees but she wore it as if it were the latest in haute couture. She looked as near like a warrior queen as Kara had ever imagined, the leader of all those behind her.

Kara turned to Marc, amused and impressed by how simulity training had taken over. He was now more soldier than artist. "Relax. Keep the rifle pointed at the ground."

He nodded, looking beyond Kara to the woman facing them. "She's only missing a sword," he said quietly.

"Don't get excited," Kara told him. "They could all be contaminated." She moved a few paces forward and spoke to the young woman. "And you are?"

"Tatia Nerein."

Information poured into Kara's mind from her AI. < *Tatia Nerein, heiress and recent consort to the con-artist who led the Pilgrims.* So presumably Juan Smith was dead. < *Tatia Nerein, an orphan from the Out adopted by a wealthy couple from Seattle City. Aged twenty-four. High IQ. Highly intuitive. Treat with respect.*

"And Juan Smith?"

"Dead." No emotion.

Kara nodded. "Okay. We *are* here to rescue you, but that means negotiating with the Cancri, which may take some time. " She spoke only to Tatia. "Right now you all need to be examined by Henk, our medic. Just a scan to make sure you're not carrying anything, takes a few seconds. Before that I want you to please release the Cancri you have captive." She'd expected surprise – *how do you know that?* – and defiance – *not until we leave.* Instead Tatia narrowed her eyes for a moment, then half-smiled and nodded.

"You sent in drones, right?"

Kara nodded. "It made sense."

"I thought I saw a wasp... You want the Cancri released as a sign of good faith?"

Kara hid her surprise at such a quick uptake. "Tse, our negotiator, believes it's best."

"Okay. It's not as if they're much use any more." Tatia turned and spoke to a tall, grey-haired man standing nearby. "Perry, let the hounds go."

< *Perry Flach, mechanic on the* LUX-WEM-YIB. *Age sixty-three. Divorced, two children. Suspected of free spacer contacts/sympathies. Treat carefully.* "Have they been any trouble?" Kara asked. It looked like Perry was Tatia's second-in-command.

Perry shook his head. "Just keep away from their mouths. They've got nasty-looking tongues." He went back inside the craft.

"The grubs aren't intelligent," Tatia said. "The hounds are."

Grubs. She had to mean the maggot riders. "Had us fooled. Look, while your people get checked, could you and Perry tell us what happened? GalDiv was sent a vid of a child being executed by a Cancri."

"Him, and a man. Murdered. Slaughtered." Tatia's tone was mild, her eyes fierce. "Not executed. They'd done nothing wrong."

Kara raised her hands. "Okay. But, Tatia, don't think the Cancri or any alien has the same emotions or even thought processes as a human."

"Really? Can they learn by experience? Well, yes, they have to. Otherwise they'd have become extinct. So, if they learn that killing one of us means that one or more of them dies, they'll stop doing it, right?"

"Assuming they give a toss," Kara pointed out. "Would you like to get your people ready?"

As Tatia turned away Perry Flach reappeared, leading three Cancri hounds on ropes made out of rags. He stopped to untie them, slapped their hindquarters and stood back. The Cancri trotted away, one of them pausing to look back at Perry. A black triangular tongue appeared and a drop of green drool fell to the ground. The hound turned and rejoined the other two. All three vanished into the crowd of aliens, the latter keeping their eyes/consciousness fixed on the humans.

And the thing is, Kara thought, *we'll never know if that last hound was drooling, "Goodbye," or, "I know where you live."*

The sun was high and all the survivors had been screened by Henk by the time Tatia and Perry had told their story. Towards the end they were joined by Mariana, who'd been organising the screening. It was then that Tatia described the warehouse she'd discovered, and the few conclusions she'd drawn, probably wrong. Kara had the impression that she was keeping something back.

In turn, Kara had explained about the Cancri message, apparently asking for Marc; and that Tse was a pre-cog and what that implied. None of the three survivors seemed surprised. After the past three weeks little or nothing would likely ever surprise them again.

Kara glanced at Marc and Tse in turn. "Make any sense? The warehouse?"

Marc shrugged.

"Still doesn't make sense," Tse said. "Why kill that kid and send GalDiv the vid? Oh. Right," answering his own question. "To demonstrate how serious they were. It wasn't a threat to kill more. It was showing how important this is to them. Death is used for emphasis."

"Why kill us when we tried to escape?" asked Tatia.

"Mariana got it part right," Tse said. "Quarantine probably. Also, keeping you away from them," pointing at the ever present crowd of aliens. "They were desperate to keep you secret. This probably isn't their home planet. It's where they trade and mix with other alien species. Makes sense – you wouldn't want others knowing where your home planet is. Look, we could go mad trying to understand their motives. Most important now is to find out what they want so we can go home."

Mariana stood up. "What's stopping us leaving now? You've got an SUT big enough to take us all, so you say."

"Which is also easy to shoot down or attack in space," Kara said. "But if negotiations don't begin within a day, or if they break down, then we leave. Okay?"

"I want to be there," Tatia insisted. "When you negotiate. I have the right."

Kara shook her head. "No. You're too involved. Tse, Marc and myself work as a team. You and the others can use the time to get clean." She pointed into the sky where a large egg-shaped object was slowly descending towards the landing field. "In that. The SUT *RIL-FIJ-DOQ*. Bit tight on water, but enough for a shower each. We've also got sonic cleansers – not so luxurious, but they work. Also a wide selection of freeze-dried food."

"You can tie me up and gag me if you like," Tatia said calmly. "But I'm going to be there."

Kara glanced at Tse, who shrugged. *So no pre-cog reason why not.* "Give me your word that you won't interfere, no matter what, unless we ask you?"

"You have my word."

"One false move and you'll be sedated," Kara warned.

"That won't be necessary."

"Okay." She looked at Perry and Mariana. "The *RIL-FIJ-DOQ* will land close to the Cancri SUT. Henk will introduce you to Tate and Nikki, our mechanic and navigator. Your people keep the hell away from the control and netherspace drive rooms. A section of shipping containers with mass-living quarters are available. Bunk beds. Stay there or outside. Okay?"

Perry stood up. "Okay. When do you think…"

The unfinished question was answered by the alien crowd suddenly dispersing. In the near distance a group of vehicles were driving towards them.

"I think very soon," Kara said. "We'll take our truck. Enjoy your shower." She smiled at Marc. "Showtime." *What are the odds of getting away, all of us? Not good. How can they be?*

The Cancri vehicles stopped fifty metres away. She watched Marc walk towards them alone, as they'd agreed, as Tse had said would be the best approach.

It was nearly midday and 38 °C in the shade of the awning that now extended from one side of the truck.

Four hounds moved to meet Marc and stopped ten metres away. Two of them were grubless and looked dusty. The two with grubs attached had coats that gleamed. One of them carried a tray on which were a series of small objects that glittered in the morning sun. The other carried a gun.

The grubless hounds folded their legs and knelt down in front of Marc. The small objects from the tray were arranged around them: a collection of metal cubes, pyramids and globes. One of the hounds with a grub trotted past Marc, stopped in front of Tse, looked up at him, then turned and began to move slowly back towards the two kneeling Cancri.

"Better go," Kara said. "It asked nicely."

Tse followed it over to the arrangement of metal objects surrounding the two kneeling hounds, before being led back to rejoin the others.

The second Cancri with a grub laid its weapon at Marc's feet. Both the hounds with grubs returned to their vehicle.

"I'd bet those two kneeling were involved in capturing the SUT," Tse called. "Maybe the leaders. Or dominant ones. It's a symbol, I think. But real."

"You're not making sense," Marc said, even as a terrible suspicion crept into his mind.

"These… kneeling ones," Tse now sounded troubled, "are different somehow. Marc, I can see everyone going home. But I can also see what must happen first. It's why they gave you the weapon."

"Maybe it's all symbolic," Marc said a little

desperately. One of the kneeling Cancri had raised its head to look at him.

"You're expected to kill them," Tse said flatly.

"It could be a test. Do it and we all die. Spare them and it's drinks all round."

"Marc. Trust me. Do it. For all of us."

Marc looked over to Kara. "Boss?"

"I can't order you." Kara's voice left no one in doubt what she wanted.

"He must kill them," Tse insisted.

"Fuck." Marc shook his head. "First time you get at all involved, Tse, I got to kill something. Two somethings."

"C'mon. I make good coffee."

"It's almost like the other half of a trade," Marc said. "Why do you think they put those pyramids and spheres around them?"

"Religion, something to do with sacrifice? Some legal shit?" Kara guessed.

"So why bring Tse over? Maybe *he's* meant to shoot them."

Kara found herself again thinking more like an artist as the simulity took over. "Maybe it's more they see Tse as our... our spiritual leader? Judge? Moral arbiter? Something like that."

"I'll be leading prayers later," Tse said. "A collection plate will be passed around."

"Maybe it's all symbolic," Marc said again.

"They've taken away their grubs," Tatia snapped. "That's like they've been cast out. You got problems, Marc, I'll do it," she offered. "I recognise the markings on one of them. It killed my people on the *LUX-WEM-YIB*."

Marc nodded, not really caring. "Has to be that weapon?"

"You just press the button," Tatia said. "I *want* to do it."

"Oh, for fuck's sake!" Marc walked over to the two kneeling Cancri who stared up at him, surrounded by the small metal shapes. Two triangular tongues emerged and deposited a single drop of green ooze each on the ground. Marc picked up the Cancri weapon, studied it for a moment, pointed the business end at the nearest hound and pressed a square-shaped button. There was a noise more *sizzle* than *crack!* and the first hound exploded, then the second a moment later. Marc spat on the ground. "Now what?"

"Up to them." Kara pointed at the vehicles. "They're coming this way."

The vehicles stopped. The Cancri stayed inside, waiting for... whatever.

"Come on," Kara said, turning back to their truck. "Leave those metal things. Let's get that awning down," she called. Three minutes later she drove the truck towards the Cancri, whose vehicle moved off. Kara followed it towards and then amongst the low, domed buildings.

"You okay?" Tatia asked Marc.

"Didn't feel a thing. Funny, that."

The Cancri vehicle stopped, as did Kara.

"I know where we are," Tatia said. "That warehouse I told you about!"

Kara looked at Tse.

"It's important," he said firmly. "We have to go inside."

15

Tatia had said very little about the building itself, more concerned with what she'd seen there. It was understandable, especially for a civilian. But it was unforgivable for a soldier like Kara not to observe and evaluate everything.

The Cancri had stopped some distance away and remained in their vehicle. Motioning the others to stay quiet and still for a moment, Kara took stock.

The entrance was square, about five metres on each side. No door. Presumably the dry atmosphere helped preserve whatever was inside. Or maybe there were force fields involved. Kara checked with a combat scanner. No electromagnetic activity in the area, other than what one would expect from solar activity and a nearby spaceport. The building itself was made of a material that felt like plastic but sounded metallic when tapped. It curved up to fully thirty metres high, its circumference a near-perfect hundred and fifty metres across.

Inside she could see well over fifty parallel rows of shelving made of the same drab-coloured material as the building's shell. The shelving rose almost to the roof – Tatia had said it glowed but Kara thought it somehow transferred light from outside to inside without being obviously translucent. She signalled Marc to remain with the others and walked inside.

There was no floor and the soil crunched slightly under her feet. There was no smell, either; strange, given the number of artefacts. If anything, Tatia had underestimated how many there were and the sheer variety. From just inside the entrance, Kara could see clothes, washing machines, children's toys, vid-players, books, a small armchair – every household object imaginable, all used, often badly worn. All badly copied, as Tatia had said. She saw a primitive carving of a woman, all breasts and swollen stomach, a Stone Age Venus statuette, clearly *ancient*. How long had aliens been coming to Earth?

There was no apparent system to the storage. Relatively new items were next to ancient ones, large next to small. She walked over and opened an antique washing machine. The clothes were still inside, dry but again lacking any smell, as if sanitised. There was a hopper next to the control panel half-full of a white granular powder. Kara guessed it was ancient detergent – surely there should have been some faint chemical scent, even after all these years? There wasn't, any more than there was in the saucepan next to it, still half-full of stew. No mould, but Kara decided not to taste it. Her attention was caught by an object on the opposite aisle and the breath caught in her throat. How many times had she watched the movie? How the hell had the Cancri got hold of a prop that had been burned in a furnace? No. There'd have been copies made over the years. And yet... She walked across and ran her fingers along the runners, touched the faded wood. A child's sled with the brand-name *Rosebud*. She wondered if Orson Welles would have seen the joke, then turned and called the others to come inside.

"Can you remember where you saw the bodies?" she asked Tatia. The sound of her voice vanished almost as soon as she uttered the words. The building also absorbed sound. It was, Kara thought, like a vast home for abandoned belongings or a memorial to a culture the Cancri could never understand.

"They're towards the back," Tatia said, pointing. "Near a penny-farthing. It's upright, should be easy to spot."

Marc found the antique bicycle but there were no bodies.

"They were there," Tatia said after they'd looked for other penny-farthings. "I know."

"So they've been moved," Marc murmured. "So maybe humans weren't meant to see them."

Tatia looked sharply at him, perhaps alert for any hint of a patronising male tone, but Marc had turned away.

"Nothing to see here," Kara said lightly. "Apart from the obvious."

The Cancri vehicles had moved closer; the inference was that they wanted the humans to get back inside their own and follow.

"Might as well," Kara said. "Everyone back on the bus."

The suspicious, increasingly on edge humans were taken to a warehouse half a kilometre away. The four walked inside and as one stopped in their tracks. The warehouse was empty except for a plinth – altar? – on which lay two bodies. Even from fifty metres away they were obviously dead. There is, as

Kara knew only too well, a basic shapelessness to a corpse, the relaxation of muscle and powered-down cells, the sense of being little more than a reminder of fading memories. Looking at a dead body one could understand why the ancients had thought that the soul had weight – once it had fled, or been taken, a body looked shrunken. These two wore their pointlessness like a shroud.

Kara led the way forward.

The two naked men lay on their backs, eyes shut, arms by their sides. They were European, tanned. One was in his fifties, balding, his short black hair flecked with grey, a gold wedding ring on his finger. The other was in his early twenties and had a blond, shoulder-length mane and several strands of different coloured twine around his left wrist. There was no obvious sign to show how either had died. Both looked peaceful. Small metal objects were arranged around the bodies, similar to those now marking the dead bodies of two Cancri. Pyramids, spheres, cubes.

"I'm making a link," Marc said. "Death is sacred. Or fun."

"Far too early to draw any conclusion," Tse said. He sounded nervous. "Those things could be condiments."

Kara had seen many dead bodies, and not all of them fresh. Yet there'd always been the sense of a *story* behind them, of a life lived. Here there was nothing. The bodies might just as well have been mannequins in a shop window. She switched her combat gloves for plastic ones and took tissue samples for Henk to analyse later, noting that the flesh felt as if the men were not long dead; it was cool, not cold, to the touch.

She pointed to a small-bore bullet wound – a tiny entry point – behind the older man's right ear and looked questioningly at Tatia.

"I never noticed," Tatia said.

"With everything you'd been through," Marc said sympathetically, "I'm not surprised." Then, noticing Kara's brief ghost of a smile, hardened his voice. "I'm looking for a pattern here and can't see one."

"Any pattern is theirs," Tse said. "We wouldn't understand it. Maybe there is no pattern. Perhaps they collect what they find beautiful. Like humans watching a sunset."

"I met the Cancri and Eridani back home," Marc said firmly. "They have no sense of aesthetics."

"That why the Eridani bought your art?" Kara said innocently.

"Isn't to say they don't *want* one," Marc said far more mildly than he felt. "Or can't recognise it, *something*, in us. Look at all this." His gesture took in the entire warehouse. "It's a fucking memorial. Think of that other warehouse. The aliens are *fascinated* by us. Not our science and tech but our *natural* aesthetic, by our weirdness, our customs and practices as they see them. Everything we've seen of *them* so far is dull, boring. Unimaginative. Well, to us. Possible somewhere there is a richness of alien creativity that'll stun the world. I don't think so. Okay, you could say the tech needs imagination – but do we even know they developed it? Here's the thing: you need imagination and creativity to develop science and technology. You come up with an idea that explains an observation and you test it. Or you come up with an idea for a new invention and you build it. So maybe Greenaway was right. Somewhere there's another alien race who developed the netherspace drive and all the rest. Sure as hell can't see the Gliese doing it."

Tse looked down at the ground. "You're not entirely right," his voice so quiet Kara had to strain to hear him. "There's another way to advance science."

Marc got it at once. "You mean pre-cog stuff?"

Tse looked up. "How do you think human scientists figure out alien tech?" he snapped. "By working with pre-cogs is how. Which is why GalDiv has a programme to identify pre-cogs as kids. So they can be trained." His voice was now tinged with bitterness. "But don't tell the public. Because pre-cogs are weird. People are scared of them. Always peeking and prying, right?" He was suddenly aware of three shocked faces staring at him. Tse shrugged. "Sorry. It's been a tough day."

There was a long silence.

Kara finally broke it. " If there is a more advanced alien species, it sure as hell doesn't want to be found. Or maybe doesn't even know we exist." She took out a mini-vid recorder and ran it for a few seconds then spoke to Marc. "Put on your plastic gloves and help me turn these guys over."

Tatia announced she was going to look around and Tse said he'd join her. Neither seemed disturbed by the prospect of naked male buttocks, more that the area had suddenly become a morgue.

"Never realised Tse was so sensitive," Marc said as he pulled on latex gloves.

"You never saw the point of him did you?" Kara sounded annoyed.

"He makes great coffee...."

"He helped Nikki navigate us here, remember? Shut up and help me roll these guys over."

The body of the older man was lighter than Kara had expected, although "emptier" was the disturbing word that popped into her mind.

"Oh fuck," Marc whispered. "Fuck, fuck. No."

There was no back to the man's head. No brain. No spinal column. Just a neat incision from neck to buttocks and a V-shaped hole.

"Steady, soldier," Kara said quietly, managing to control her own shock. *These are not necessarily call-out fees.* "Could have been an autopsy." She glanced around, and was relieved to see that Tatia and Tse were some distance away. "On Earth. Marc?"

"They took his spine!" Marc sounded as revolted as he was shocked. "What kind of fucking autopsy is that?"

"A very specific one." Kara took a quick recording. "Help me put him back." Their simulity training cut in and together they rolled the man back over. "Now the next one."

Simulity might have helped Marc control his reactions. It didn't prevent them. "You're joking, right?"

"Just do it, *Captain*," she ordered. "Now!"

Marc shook his head but obeyed.

No back of the head. No spine. Kara took another recording then they rolled the younger man onto his ravaged back.

"Notice anything?"

Marc looked thoughtful. "There's a faint scent... can't quite place it..."

"Exotic?" Kara prompted.

He nodded. "Like…" Then he had it. "Those curries Tse keeps on eating. No. It's a single spice… cardamom."

"I got that too."

They looked at each other, both fighting a very human urge to find humour in the worst situation. Marc lost. "No wonder they look peaceful," he said. "They're mindless."

"Forgetful, too." Battlefield humour. "No one else hears about this, Marc, understand?"

He nodded.

"You okay?"

"Seen a couple of autopsies," he said briefly. "Idea about an art installation: robot surgeon taking apart a human who is simultaneously dismantling the robot. Couldn't find a way of doing it without being accused of murder. It struck me as odd then that a person with an incurable disease could sign themselves up as a Gliese fee in the service of exploration and trade but I wasn't allowed to recruit one in the name of art." He shook his head. "These aren't Earth autopsies. The rib cages were intact."

Kara agreed. "The edges of the incisions were fused. Could have been a laser."

"And maybe it was something else."

"But we don't know. Any more than we know the Cancri did this. Hang on to those thoughts. Let's get the others. Oh, and try and figure out the connection between these metal objects *here*, and the ones by the two Cancri."

"Already did." He had too, the idea popping easily

into his mind. "It's symbolic. They want us to make a link. They're saying the Cancri I killed are responsible for this."

Kara nodded. "That's what I thought."

"We *also* don't know if these men were call-out fees," Marc said, seemingly surprised by his own sensitivity. "And even if they were, it doesn't mean they all end up like that. Anyway, fees are Gliese business – not Cancri."

Kara thought of brushing the comment aside – it wasn't the time for sentiment. Then again, maybe a person can be a little too closed up. "I'm telling myself the same thing. Thanks."

They met Tatia and Tse at the entrance. Both were subdued.

"Got anything?" Kara asked.

Neither had. The warehouse was empty, a vast mausoleum – assuming the bodies remained there.

"Why kill so many on the *LUX-WEM-YIB* if they like humans so much?" Tatia said. Her expression was twisted by memory and grief.

Marc and Kara exchanged brief looks.

"Tell you something else," Tatia said. "Those bodies were experimented on."

Tse made a contemptuous face. "How can you possibly know *that*?"

"I just do," she said, looking him in the eye. "A bit like you."

"Nothing *like* me," Tse said, tetchy. He'd displayed more emotion in the past two hours than in the past week. "I was trained since a boy. You have *hunches*."

"Okay, people," Kara interrupted. "Settle this later."

311

She led them in silence back to the truck. The Cancri were waiting. As soon as the humans were seated in their own vehicle, the Cancri moved slowly off.

"I know," Kara said before Tse could say anything; "Follow the little bastards."

They drove about half a kilometre to another warehouse. Instead of shelves there was a single, narrow rubble-like construct running the entire length. On it were laid a series of…

"What the fuck are they?" Marc asked.

Varying in size, made of metal and other materials, the nearest ones were elaborate and although faded by time, had once been brightly coloured. Curlicues, spirals, wire constructs that on Earth could be mobiles. And then more objects that looked like machinery, although what for was impossible to guess. And so it went on, but with a change, subtle at first but soon obvious. The artefacts lost their complexity, became more and more stylised until at the very end the four humans found themselves looking at three large solid metal objects: a pyramid, a sphere and a cube. Just like the ones laid beside the sacrificial hounds and the human corpses, only larger.

"They're showing progress," Tse said. "The last three being the Platonic ideal. The shapes upon which all other shapes are based."

"Are they?" Marc asked.

"Of course. Anyone could see it." He glanced sideways at Marc. "Anyone with a Classics education."

"Or," Kara asked, "are they showing what was lost?" She noticed Tse's hands curled into fists, knuckles white with tension.

"Like they went down some sort of blind alley," Marc added thoughtfully. "The aesthetic changed. Except…"

"Except we've been here too long," Kara cut in, "and we've seen what they want us to see." An earlier suspicion about Tse's personal agenda was now crystallising into certainty. "Whether or not we understand it is another issue. I'm getting worried about what everyone else is up to. Let's go."

The Cancri led them back to *RIL-FIJ-DOQ*. They parked some distance away, presumably waiting for something to happen. Perhaps it already had.

A small group of the tall, hard-shelled aliens had developed a rapport with a few Pilgrims. One Pilgrim would raise an arm; a crustacean would raise a spindly, thorned limb in return. The close-by Pilgrim whooped and cheered; others stood further away and radiated suspicion. No way of knowing what the aliens thought. Callisthenics? Galactic Simon Says?

Perry, looking clean and wearing fresh overalls, greeted them with news that most of the Pilgrims were showered and now busy with freeze-dried food rations and that he and Tatia had cabins in the same shipping container as Kara and her team; Mariana had elected to stay with the crowd "to keep on eye on things".

"Remember the pricks who didn't want to break out?" Perry said to Tatia. "Then wanted to apologise to the Cancri when we did? Well, that's them over there. Told me they don't want to leave, that this is the promised land, the Cancri will take care of them. Fourteen adults, no kids. Trying to convince others to stay as well."

313

"They understand the reality?" Kara asked incredulously.

"*You* don't understand," Tatia said. "They believe it's their destiny. Their *right*."

"What about the attack on the *LUX-WEM-YIB*?" Marc wanted to know. "What about being held prisoner in the desert?"

"They're saying it was a rogue group of Cancri who don't want humans and aliens to mix, and that these new ones are the good guys," Perry said with contempt, which changed to worry as Tatia swayed and then stumbled, would have fallen except for Marc's sudden arm around her shoulders. "Are you okay?"

Tatia managed a smile. "Thanks. I'm fine now. Hungry and tired, I guess."

"Debrief in the canteen in one hour," Kara said. "We'll eat then." She glanced at Tse. "Sorry, no curry, for once. There's a halfway decent beef casserole."

It was less a debrief, more a restating of the obvious. A subdued meeting, the canteen table still littered with reconstituted food containers and plastic cups. Kara, Marc, Tse, Tatia and Perry faced the SUT's staff across the table. Everyone seemed to have more questions than answers – except for Kara, who remained silent, letting the others talk it out.

Henk observed that some aliens seemed friendly.

"Define friendship," Perry challenged. "Without emotion it comes down to self-interest. You have no idea if the eight-foot praying mantis has emotions, other than fear or curiosity which are both necessary to survive and evolve beyond the primitive." Perry had been in space two, three times longer than any of the *RIL-FIJ-DOQ*'s staff. No one argued with him.

Tatia, wearing a pair of Tate's overalls, her newly washed strawberry-blonde hair cascading to her shoulders, said that any Pilgrims who wanted to stay had to be told that future contact with Earth would be difficult, if not impossible. "And why, given there are at least a dozen different alien species outside, all of whom seem fascinated by humans, are only three of them regular visitors to Earth?" she asked. It was another question that no one could answer, other than to say the galaxy was big and Earth very small. Or perhaps the Gliese had forbidden it. Or maybe there was a conspiracy to keep Earth's location a secret from all but the most special customers.

"I have a question for all of you," Kara said and lit a joss, the first she'd smoked on the *RIL-FIJ-DOQ* outside her cabin. She hoped they'd see it as the arrogance of command. The truth was much more prosaic: her memory of her sister was trying to get out of its mental box. She waited for objections against her smoking – which she had no intention of heeding – and when there weren't any, blew a stream of opium-scented smoke towards the ceiling. "Has anyone here seen anything that suggests the Cancri or any other aliens were capable of inventing the n-drive? Or the updown-field generator?" She'd decided not to say that Greenaway thought it unlikely. No point in alarming them with the idea of a hidden super race. Yet.

Nikki laughed. "I've seen their spacecraft close up –

I took a little walk – and they're as basic as ours. Nearly all of them rely on the Gliese foam. I'd bet they've all got Gliese netherspace drives, too. Why, Kara?"

"We might have to make a run for it. I have to know how smart the locals are." She doused the joss in a cup of cold coffee. "So, they're no smarter than us. Not bad odds."

"So why wait?" Tate asked. "We could go now."

It was out now. The staff wanted to leave immediately – and so, probably, did most of the rescued hostages. It was understandable. "If negotiations go nowhere tomorrow, we're off," Kara said.

"Negotiations for what?" Henk challenged. "We got the Pilgrims. We should leave now. Right? And we *can't* negotiate. We never could. We don't know what they want now, any more than we did before we came down from orbit."

Kara was thankful she'd decided on no more sex with Henk. If there had been she'd have ended up beating the crap out of him. "Because," she said patiently, "the *RIL-FIJ-DOQ*'s AI is still partly down, we've minimum sensors, therefore it's riskier to take off at night. And because the Cancri could still blow us out of the sky." She looked around the table. No one contradicted her. "Okay. Now let's set duty rosters."

"You guys must be exhausted," Nikki said reasonably. "No reason why Tate, Henk and I can't keep watch overnight. Maybe with Perry to help? You're going to need as much sleep as you can get."

Kara nodded, ignoring Marc's warning pressure against her foot. "Appreciate it. Mainly, make sure the airlock's closed. Keep everyone away from the control and engine rooms. Keep an eye on what sensors we've got. I'm worried about those stay-behinds – get weapons from the store, secure the entrance when you're done." She smiled across the table. "Wish all my colleagues had been as thoughtful." She yawned mightily. "I do need some sleep."

Tatia echoed the yawn and left with Perry and the staff.

"Are you crazy?" Marc demanded, once he, Kara and Tse were alone. "Giving control of the SUT to a staff who don't want to be here and who you don't trust?"

"Do you trust *me*?" Kara asked shortly.

He nodded. "Yes. I do."

"Then assume I know what I'm doing. Now go get some rest. Tse, hang about. We need to talk about tomorrow." She waited until Marc had left, then briefly accessed her AI under the guise of rubbing her tired eyes.

> *Surveillance?*

< *None I can find.*

Kara stood up, closed the door and moved to sit opposite Tse.

"I can't plan too much," he said apologetically. "It's what happens at the time, you know? Look at the point on the horizon of possibilities that we need to get to, then choose the simplest route."

Who chooses the point on the horizon we need to get to? Kara wondered, but said instead: "I know that. Tse, what I really want to know is why you killed the call-out fee and let Leeman-Smith take the blame."

He was quiet for a moment. "There's no point in denying it," he said eventually. He might have been discussing his favourite curry. "You wouldn't make the accusation unless you were positive. It was to get Leeman-Smith off the *RIL-FIJ-DOQ*. With him here the mission was always problematic. There was no path that got us where we needed to go. The fee would have died anyway…"

"You know that for sure?"

"None of them ever come back."

She knew he was referencing her sister, trying to keep her off guard. "And I've no way of knowing if that's true about *this* fee dying anyway."

"Leeman-Smith had to go," Tse insisted. "There were many ways of doing it but I *saw* that the fee would *also* die. It was a matter of connecting the two events." He looked directly at her. "Pre-cog's not easy, Kara. I never chose it. But I *do* try to use it the best way I can. That isn't always pleasant and I have to live with my actions. I promised to try to get you here, help negotiate with the Cancri and get you home. I'll do whatever it takes to make sure that happens. But if you knew all this, why force Leeman-Smith to become the fee?"

Kara smiled without humour. "Because he *was* a threat. I could have kept him locked in his cabin, but what would have happened when we got home? Bastard was too well connected. Tse, I appreciate your honesty. But in future you do not, repeat *not*, operate independently, understood? If there have to be sacrifices, so be it – but I'll make the final decision." She sighed. "Okay, this remains between us. If you want to tell Greenaway when we get back, that's your privilege. Officially, Leeman-Smith murdered the call-out fee while his mind was disturbed. Okay?"

Tse looked relieved… as much as any emotion ever showed on his face. "Thanks. How did you know?"

She was ready for this. "Luck, actually. Leeman-Smith kept a back-up of all internal surveillance for his own private use. He was a sad, sad man. I found the recording of you killing the fee in his cabin, after he left with the Gliese. Obviously he'd never seen it. Too busy watching a tape of me taking a crap." She saw the obvious question forming on his lips. "The recording's gone, Tse. Destroyed. Both of them. I wanted to see if you'd be honest with me. And give you a warning."

"Thanks."

"But if you ever do or try to do anything like that again I'll kill you. Or Marc will." It was what Tse would expect to hear. She also meant it.

He smiled. "I know. I actually *do* know."

Kara nodded. "And you're sure we have to meet with the Cancri tomorrow?"

"It increases the odds of us getting home. I don't know why."

"Okay. Now, go get some sleep. I need you fresh in the morning."

She watched him leave, surprised when he turned back just before reaching the door. She was even more surprised to see the sadness on his face.

"She sighed, you know," Tse said quietly. "When I took the tube from her arm. I was terrified she'd open her eyes. But all she did was sigh." His voice hardened. "Life's precious to me, Kara. You have *no* idea. I didn't ask to be this way. I was *made*." There was bitterness in his voice. "Made less than a man." He seemed to snarl the next words. "Know about the GalDiv programme, do you? Kids growing up in institutions, their parents so proud at this great GalDiv honour. Someone figured out the only way we'd ever communicate with aliens would be using psi abilities. Like pre-cog." His speech slowed, bitterness replacing anger. "Know anything about the history of psi, Kara? About poltergeists? The power of the prepubescent child? I mean, you're the old movie fan, right? Ever wonder why virginity was once prized? It wasn't just to make men feel in control."

"The seers," Kara said softly. "Oracles. Women. Virgins."

"Not just them. Boys too. Except the emotional, psychic, whatever, needs are different. Having sex doesn't stop male psi abilities. Being able to have kids *does*. All those priests who once thought they were saving themselves for their god. Abstinence only a *shadow* of forgotten practice: castrate the little boy so he won't lose his gift. The ancient Chinese understood – all the court officials were eunuchs. Not to stop them fucking the Emperor's wives and concubines, but because the State needed their insights, their *gift*." Tse shrugged. "We can fuck. I ejaculate, orgasm. Just can't have kids because they fixed me when I was eight."

"I'm sorry…"

"Why should you be? Not your fault. Had to be done, to me and the others. Or humans get swamped by aliens. Or else Earth dies. Maybe. But I'm not like the man with weak sperm. It's deeper than that. They took part of my *psyche*, Kara. Part of who I should be."

"Then why—"

"Am I here?" He smiled sourly. "I see myself as a navigator for the whole human race. I don't give a fuck about GalDiv. I *do* care about humans." He nodded once. "I gave you my word I'd keep you safe, as much as I can. But this is more than rescuing a bunch of idiot Pilgrims. What happens here, what's been started, is *so* much bigger than that." He nodded again. "Good night." He opened the door and left.

Kara found she was close to tears. Before she'd considered Tse to be dangerous and untrustworthy. He still might be, but now she knew he was also a tortured, conflicted man. What was it like for the child Tse – taken from his family, castrated, raised in an institution, forced to develop an ability he'd perhaps never wanted – and how could he live with it afterwards, all for the greater glory and good of GalDiv? Of course he'd cherish life, unable to produce any of his own, other than by cloning, which was not the same thing. Despite all that she knew of him, Kara could feel compassion. And that was the most dangerous emotion of all.

Marc found his cabin door open, with Tatia sitting on the bed, still dressed in Tate's overalls. He walked in and closed the door silently, then sat on the bed some distance from her.

"It's about Tse," she said, then caught a flicker in his eyes. "Oh! Did you think…"

"Male programming," he said ruefully. "Why tell me?"

"Kara's got a hell of a lot on her mind."

He thought it a bit weak. Even so: "And the problem is?"

"Tse is all *wrong* somehow. He's been twisted. It's sad."

"He said as much himself." He looked at her quizzically. "What else?"

Tatia looked away for a moment. "When I first went into that warehouse. There was something watching me, but from outside. From a long way away."

Marc didn't blink. "You especially sensitive? I mean psi sensitive."

"My intuition's getting stronger… You believe in psi abilities?"

"They're increasing worldwide, apparently. GalDiv thinks personal AIs may be involved."

Tatia smiled. "Mine won't like you saying that."

It would be top of the range, too. "You're not going mad, Tatia. And I don't think you're being singled out by whatever it was. There's a great deal of truly weird shit going on. But that doesn't make *you* weird, okay?"

She nodded gratefully. "Truth is, I'm a spoilt rich girl used to being in control. What happened in that warehouse scared me more than anything the Cancri did. And then those bodies."

"You need sleep, Tatia. So do I."

She put her head on one side and examined him carefully for moment. "Nope. No bullshit. I could always stay…"

"You could. And I'd love it." He could scarcely believe what he was saying. "But not now. If we ever do, it can't be because we're scared or lonely or feeling grateful. You haven't said anything about Juan Smith. But I gather he was a shit. And he conned you good. I don't want to be your way of exorcising his memory, okay? Because that would only be a one-off. I'd want at least a return fixture. Even a World Series."

Tatia looked at him intently. "You're not playing me?"

He shook his head.

"Just my luck," she smiled. "Most attractive man on board is an adult."

"Also a borderline psychopath who's just discovered a conscience. You're too special for a consolation fuck, Tatia. Go get some sleep."

"That's not conscience." Tatia stood up. "That's pride."

"Stupid pride," Marc agreed as he opened the door for her. "I'm already regretting it."

Marc and Tatia both missed the sight of two Cancri craft floating directly overhead the *RIL-FIJ-DOQ* for twenty minutes before moving slowly away. It could have been curiosity but Kara – who'd watched on screen with a private sense of relief that her point had been proved – had no doubt it was a warning. Try to leave and we will stop you, unless…

Unless what?

And what part was Tse really playing in all this? He spoke as if all humanity was his family. No one could be that noble.

The answer arrived with a shock like being hit with a brick. Other pre-cogs. Other castrated pre-cogs. *They* would be his family. *They* would hold his true loyalties.

And suppose, just suppose, that pre-cogs weren't limited to the human race.

The second shock was Kara's realisation that she

was thinking not as a soldier, but as an artist, with an artist's ability to make a leap of imagination... or rather, to welcome a hunch or intuition and trust them more than cold logic.

Three minutes later Kara pounded on Marc's cabin door.

"I need to talk to you," she said brusquely as Marc stood yawning and wrapped in a sheet. "It's to do with Tse."

"Ah." He yawned. "Tatia says he's been twisted."

"She's here?"

"No," he said sadly, "she could have been but I got attacked by niceness. And pride."

Kara looked momentarily stunned. "This stays between us," she said and closed the door. "What if there are alien pre-cogs?"

Marc thought for a moment. All pre-cogs, all species, might well be aware of each other. There'd be a matter of loyalties. "Then I'd say we could be in trouble."

"Think it through, Marc." She sat down on the bed. "Please."

"You woke me up and I'm trying to forget how those Cancri stank when I killed them. And now I got to speculate on something I don't understand." He yawned mightily. "Okay. Far as I see it, pre-cognition and creativity, spontaneity can't get on. Pre-cog's all about a nice, tidy, ordained universe. Creativity is about a mess, things changing all the time. There's also intuition... pre-cogs wouldn't like that." He was silent a moment. "Oh. Fuck. Was that it..." He told Kara about Tatia's sense of being watched in the warehouse, and how she felt her intuition had been increasing. And yes, they only had her word for it, but he believed her. Not believed that she *thought* it had happened, but that it really had.

"Are we adding two and two and getting an absurd number?" Kara wanted to know.

Marc shrugged. "It's an infinite universe, so anything can happen. I mean, what are we saying – pre-cogs of all species in an alliance against the rest of us, forging ahead to secure a future that only they can see? That's kind of simplistic. And then there's this potential master race who make all the technical goodies. I mean, maybe we, maybe GalDiv is just looking for reasons why humans aren't top dog in the galaxy. Like, how embarrassing that we rely on a sack of wet leather like the Gliese. They should be seven foot tall, beautiful and glowing. Maybe there isn't a pattern, a plan. Just thousands, millions of different species all bumping into each other so tech and science get spread around and no one remembers who first thought of it." He stopped and shrugged again. "But what do I know? I'm just an artist turned soldier."

Silence, broken by the sound of a door slamming followed by hurried footsteps. "If it's serious someone will scream," Kara said in answer to Marc's questioning look. "But then there's the matter of aliens collecting human stuff for thousands of years. The two dissected bodies... why? What was whoever did it looking for?"

More footsteps outside, but less hurried.

"This is about Tse, isn't it?" Marc asked.

"He knows a fuck of a sight more than he's saying. Look, okay, don't let's stray into a world best left to philosophers and theoretical physicists. But you watch Tse. You watch him hard. And if you *ever* think he's a danger to the rest of us, you do whatever's necessary to stop him." She stood up and stretched. "That's an order, by the way. Not a request. My responsibility whatever happens."

"*But this is more than rescuing a bunch of idiot Pilgrims,*" Tse had said. "*What happens here, what's been started, is so much bigger than that.*"

"This stays between us," Kara said, closing the door behind her.

16

The canteen was empty when Marc and Kara arrived for breakfast, except for Tse. "You look worried," he said.

"Lots of questions and fewer answers do that," Kara replied levelly. "Marc's just hungry."

Tse smiled. "We got porridge re-con with recycled water and maple-type syrup. Last night I dreamed of fresh milk."

They ate quickly, soon joined by Tatia.

There was no guarantee that the Cancri would be at the same place, other than a hunch and a conviction. But they were, half a mile from the SUT. Several hundred of them, more mob than welcoming committee, milling around as if excited. Or angry. Or simply confused. Cancri, who knows?

The four humans got out of the truck and waited.

The Cancri mob parted and one of their vehicles with the odd-sized wheels appeared, towing a flat-bed on skids – why no wheels? – on which were two large metal drums.

They were, as Tatia quickly informed the others, exactly the same as the drums that had fed the Pilgrims, drums in which food and water almost miraculously appeared fresh from Earth.

Kara glanced at Tse who shrugged. Nothing in his pre-cog universe gave a hint of "why". The drums apparently did not affect the *RIL-FIJ-DOQ*'s return home.

The flat-bed was left in the no-being's land between human and alien.

Marc went to look and reported fruit, vegetables, what seemed to be a barbecued side of beef, still warm, and water. Was it a peace offering, a bribe, or something else?

It was Tatia who first noticed the descending shape in the sky, quickly identified as a human-built SUT. It landed a hundred metres away.

"It looks like the *LUX-WEM-YIB*," Tatia said in a quiet voice.

"So sorry, here's your transport back, bon voyage," Marc said.

Kara's AI disagreed.

< *Not the* LUX-WEM-YIB. *How could it be? GalDiv salvaged it.*

> *Then what…*

< *Hold on… meet the* POC-TAD-GOL, *colony SUT, went missing two years ago.*

Kara almost gasped as the insight hit her. She knew exactly what the Cancri wanted. "Tatia, take the truck and fetch some of the Pilgrims who want to stay."

It took her half an hour. As Tatia explained, all the stay-behinds had wanted to come and her once iron-clad authority seemed to be slipping. She brought back seven of them, who took one look at the Cancri and walked smiling towards them, which was exactly what Kara had wanted. A moment later the airlock of the *POC-TAD-GOL* opened and five more Cancri appeared.

Kara dispatched Perry to search the SUT, and sent Mariana to check which Pilgrims wanted to stay and which wanted to go. While the two of them rushed

off on their separate business, she stood watching the
scene but not seeing it. Instead, her mind was filled
with little bursting bubbles of revelation. Nothing
psychic – just facts and suppositions that had been
floating around in her subconscious until they had
started to link up.

"There were only two things the Cancri could have
wanted from us," she said to Marc eventually. "Either
for us to leave or to stay. Because of everything else, I
figured it was stay. They wanted humans here... and
now they've got them."

"All that killing, the hostages?" He sounded
incredulous. "Just so humans would stay? One hell of
an invite, even for an alien."

Kara shook her head, wishing he'd get out of soldier
mode and into imaginative artist. "Don't judge 'em like
us. Perhaps death isn't the same for them. We'll never
really know, but I think there's a group of Cancri got
carried away and took the Pilgrims, maybe wanted to
find out about our creativity, although that's giving
them human motivations... and another group found
out and caught up to them after the Pilgrims escaped,
and brought those two grubless ones to us for Marc to
kill. Which could be their way of saying sorry, or their
way of saying hello because truth is, no one knows
anything about aliens. So ask me again in twenty years,
should we live so long. Maybe I'll have answers."

The humans who'd elected to stay would have
no navigator, medic or mechanic. But there were
instructional vids so it was possible the *POC-TAD-*

GOL would go Up again. However, as Kara said, they could well be stuck on this planet for the rest of their lives. And there was no guarantee that the "good" Cancri, if they existed, would stay in control.

And that was that. Kara gave the stay-behinds the truck. Goodbyes were said. Tears shed, two last-minute changes of heart to stay, three of the same to go. Mariana had elected to stay and would undoubtedly become queen of the new colony, as long as it lasted.

"How long do you think they *will* last?" Marc asked.

Kara had no idea and said so. "Don't be surprised if they move to another colony planet. Assuming they find one. And get the SUT mobile."

"You never said *why* the Cancri want humans here."

Kara sighed. "Because I have no idea."

"Have you ever danced with an alien?" one of the stay-behinds asked Kara as the *RIL-FIJ-DOQ* prepared to leave.

No, but I once killed one in my arms. "Not recently," she said with a smile.

The man looked at a couple of crates that Henk and Tate had unloaded from the *RIL-FIJ-DOQ*. "Are you leaving something for us? We have everything we need."

"I'm leaving something," she said, "but not for you. For us."

Things started to go sour just as Kara and the rest were going through their pre-Up checks in the *RIL-FIJ-*

DOQ, which had been sprayed with Gliese protective foam by the Cancri – for whom nothing seemed too much trouble, now that they had their live humans. It seemed that while Cancri and humans couldn't communicate, both were competent – or lucky – at guessing what the other wanted. No, change that: what the other needed.

Five alien SUTs appeared in the sky above them and started to descend. They sported items that looked suspiciously like heavy armaments – barrels for laser and projectile weapons and missiles on pylons. The humans watched on the SUT vid screens.

Marc looked across at a suddenly fidgeting Tse. "Any ideas?"

Tse shrugged weakly. "The probability landscape's confused."

"Who are they?"

"Cancri who don't want us to leave?"

Marc wanted to smack him.

On the screens the approaching SUTs took up position around and above the *RIL-FIJ-DOQ*. The things that could be heavy weapons swivelled on gimbals to point directly at them.

"And now here we have a probability path that prevents us from leaving the planet," Kara observed. She saw Marc's fists clenching, and the way he gazed murderously at Tse, and she put a soothing tone into her voice. "It's not a conspiracy, Marc. Tse didn't betray us." She looked over at him. "Did you? Tell him. Tell Marc what it's like for you."

"Explain the concept of blue to a man who has been blind from birth?" Tse laughed: a short, humourless huff of breath. "We don't communicate. We just... *see* what's best for everyone in the long term. What reduces suffering and pain and death. What makes people most content."

"That long term being, what, thousands of years?" Henk chipped in from his position. "What gives you the right?"

Tse shrugged. "The fact that we can. And yes, thousands, maybe millions of years. There is no horizon on the future – just an increasing fuzziness – but some landmarks stand out, even that far away: the ones we want to aim for, and the ones we want to avoid."

Marc started moving from his seat. "I don't think the hand weapons we have will reach those SUTs," he snapped, "and I don't fancy hanging out of the airlock and firing one, but I've got to do something."

"Can I suggest a more... creative solution?" Kara asked. Before anyone could answer her fingers drifted over the sepia tattoos on her left forearm, as she simultaneously interfaced with her AI.

> *Ready with Plan A?*

< *Oh, it's a plan now, is it? Not just a vague set of desperate measures and a hope that they might lead to a satisfying conclusion?*

> *Stop whining and do it!*

She leaned back in her seat, closed her eyes and accessed the controlling software that sat in the back of her mind, reminding herself how it worked. Mental muscle memory. She'd never managed something this big before. It was going to be... interesting, to say the least.

< *I can handle this myself, you know?* her AI pointed

out huffily. Kara reminded herself it was just software programmed to inject some kind of personality into the transactions. Wasn't it?

> *A girl's got to do what a girl's got to do*, she sub-vocalised. She sent a set of mental commands, one of which adjusted the screens to show the ground outside the SUT.

The crates that she'd ordered to be left behind on the surface opened up, hatches in their tops and sides sliding back. For a moment nothing happened, but then what looked like smoke began to drift out. For a few seconds it moved aimlessly, but then it began to head with purpose upwards, towards the Cancri SUTs.

In her mind Kara could choose from several thousand different points of view, as her drone insect army marshalled itself into five thin streams that started to head for the five approaching SUTs, but she restricted herself to a few outriders. Five different fields of vision. Five different Cancri battlewagons into whose open weapons-ports she poured her troops.

One SUT spun around, almost like a grazing herbivore bothered by flies. Two others tried to disperse the insect drones by firing their weapons. And then the small explosive suicide packages that, in another life, guaranteed no drone left behind, exploded in a sudden burst of energy, taking the weapons out of service permanently and sending the SUTs tumbling backwards, trailing smoke. The remaining two SUTs – or, at least, their staff – seemed perplexed at the sudden turn of events. This lasted until Kara deliberately set the insect-borne charges to explode in the weapons-ports and also on the nosecones of the missiles that studded the outside of the crafts. The two SUTs burst apart, raining wreckage and alien bodies down on the ground below. Kara's fields of view went black. She felt the loss of so many drones as a sudden void within her mind, a place of desolation where there had, moments before, been a chiaroscuro of sensory impressions.

"They didn't see that coming," Marc said approvingly.

"Get us out of here," Kara snapped at Henk. "Quickly." The anger was a cover for the grief that she felt – irrational, but still real. She had sent a message, but there had been a cost.

The updown-field generator eased into life and the *RIL-FIJ-DOQ* lifted off.

"We don't have a call-out fee," Henk said unnecessarily.

"We should be okay," Tse reassured him. "The probability landscape's clear."

No one believed him.

Perry Flach killed himself five minutes after their first dive into netherspace.

That was how Kara saw it, as did Marc. Tse said nothing. Perry had planned it well, helped by so many sensors being down because of the still-maimed SUT AI. He'd hidden himself in the airlock and then, when netherspace lay all around them, bypassed the safety system and opened the outer door, the traditional way Henk had described of sacrificing oneself to a netherspace snark. The surveillance cameras showed Perry standing naked, his body bathed in the shifting, absurd and sometimes obscene colours from outside. He smiled up at the camera and waved goodbye then turned towards his future, his death. Walked to the edge of the lock and paused, holding his arms wide. Some of those watching on a monitor swore that a tendril of light coiled itself around Perry and took him away. Others said no, he'd dived into netherspace as if it were the sea. A moment later the monitor feed was cut by Tate.

Afterwards no one spoke much about it. It felt like talking behind Perry's back. Besides, what was there to say? He'd long had a fascination for netherspace, as the note Tatia later discovered made plain. He'd seen it as going somewhere he was meant to be. He'd also left a clear and concisely written will. However you defined it, Perry Flach wasn't insane. There was also a suspicion that his career-honed senses knew that a snark was about to attack, and his death had benefited his companions.

Three days after Perry's one-way trip outside the netherspace drive went *phfffft!* and the *RIL-FIJ-DOQ* reappeared in realspace.

17

They sat in the canteen: Kara, Marc, Tse, Tatia and the staff. The rescued Pilgrims were in their own shipping container, unaware that one of them would soon be a reluctant hero. The atmosphere was heavy with tension.

"Sabotage, obviously," Marc said.

Tate nodded. "The odds of an SUT having its Gliese sideslip-field generator breaking down on two consecutive trips is… well, not exactly vanishingly small, but it's rare. Very rare."

Grimly, Henk nodded his agreement. "Look, I found something underneath the platen that we placed on the sphere. Looks like dust or grit; enough to push the platen away from the sphere's surface. Less than a millimetre, but the moment that happened the entire drive would have blown. Exactly what happened when our revered former mission manager deliberately pulled the platen off."

All eyes inexorably turned towards Tse, who bore the scrutiny patiently for a few moments before saying, "It wasn't me. Even if you don't believe that, you've all been watching me since we got back on board. You *know* I couldn't have done it." As the hard looks went on, he added: "Look, be rational. If I were going to sabotage the drive I'd just follow Leeman-Smith's example and pull the platen off completely. I wouldn't bother introducing anything underneath it. I'm not even sure how I could, without disturbing the contact between the platen and the surface of the sphere."

"But did you know it would happen?" Tatia asked. "And why did you say we'd be safe on this trip?"

Tse shrugged, and looked away. "There's no clear path to any future that I can see."

Henk made a coughing noise to attract attention. "Actually," he said, "when I checked the other platens, I found that they all had a kind of dust stuck to their undersurfaces. My guess is that the heat of the netherspace drive, or maybe some radiation it gives off, caused the dust to expand, pushing the platen away. Maybe one of the Cancri factions sabotaged all the platens."

"We've no proof there are any factions. Good Cancri, bad Cancri, disturbed but well-meaning Cancri," Kara said fiercely. "You're applying human motivation and behaviour to them. And it could be an accident, simple as that."

"But there *are* factions," Tse said, surprising everyone. "Two of them. Pre-cogs and their followers, and the rest." He looked around at the stunned faces and smiled slightly. "Some of you – Kara? Marc? – must be near the truth by now, surely? It isn't just about the Gliese or the Cancri. Most races have their pre-cog and non pre-cog factions. It seems to be an evolutionary process. Of course, creativity and intuition and spontaneity can't exist in the pre-cog world. They get in the way."

"Why humans?" Nikki asked, her expression stunned. "Why so intrigued by us?"

"Because," Tse said with the same infuriating calm, "in this part of the galaxy humans are a young race. The creativity hasn't been bred out. The older races are usually dominated by pre-cogs. Everything is orderly. Art is refined down to its most basic components. Science also suffers. But it's all very safe. Except many have a sense of loss, perhaps. Are aware that their civilisations aren't progressing. And then, a very long time ago, they found Earth. At least the Gliese did. I think that initially they kept Earth secret. Even today only a handful of races know where those artefacts originate. They've been bringing them to that planet for thousands of years. It's a communal museum, an art gallery with only one exhibitor – us. The Gliese only made official contact when human technology would have forced them into the open." He smiled again. "It's all very simple, really."

There was a loud smack as Henk slapped the table. "Fucking simple? *You think?* Why are the aliens so fucking fascinated by us and our shit?"

"Because they want to regain their lost creativity. Because their art has been reduced to basic symbols: a globe, a pyramid and a cube. So they bring our *shit* here and, well, try to copy it." Tse looked directly at Marc. "It's another reason why I'm here. I knew that the answer explaining the alien's interest would be found on this planet. I had to be here. Greenaway agreed."

"They copy our stuff? Why?" Nikki wanted to know.

"Because that's how they think human art works," Tse said. "One artist copying another. Progression. They've been trying to do the same. It hasn't worked.

Some of them wanted live humans. Others didn't."

"Not wrong about art," Henk said, drawing a resigned glance from Marc. "Another word is imitation. Or derivative. That's why they chose you, Marc?"

"All art develops one from the other," Tse said hastily. "With Marc it was luck. But we'll never know exactly why they chose him."

Kara decided the conversation had gone far enough. "All very enlightening," she said firmly. "Tse, thanks for the heads-up. I may never visit another art gallery. People, I'm treating the drive failure as an accident. However, as and when we get a new one there will be a twenty-four-hour guard on the engine room. And if it transpires that someone here or one of the Pilgrims is a saboteur, I'll hand them over to the Gliese myself – we have a fee problem. Another executive decision: it will be one of the Pilgrims and the oldest will draw lots. Now, suggestions on how we handle this, please." She knew exactly how, but a group decision would help paper over some of the cracks beginning to appear.

"It would start a riot," Tate pointed out.

"Not when they know the alternative is to die in space. Food won't last forever. Recycling will break down. Oxygen'll run out. No nice, human-friendly planet available. Give it a week and the Pilgrims will select their own fee, with a back-up in case the netherspace drive breaks again."

"It doesn't have to be like that," Tse said, his voice sounding newly authoritative. "I volunteer."

"You can't," Marc said reflexively. "You're too valuable." Kara just stared at the pre-cog with interest.

"Sounds good to me," Henk said, standing up. Nikki and Tate also got to their feet. "Tse wants to go, let him." The three left, leaving Kara, Marc and Tatia staring at Tse.

"Why?" Kara asked. "Because of…"

"The other fee?" Tse asked bitterly. "The little girl I killed because my pre-cog abilities said it was the *logical* thing to do?"

"She'd have died anyway."

"Suppose not?"

Marc was about to speak when Kara hushed him. "Tse, is this about the other, alien pre-cogs?"

Tse stood and looked sadly down at them. "When you're a pre-cog you search for the obvious, the logical way. Surprises and chaos are like physical pain to us. That's why alien pre-cogs distrust humans. You are too… interesting."

"*You?*" Marc said.

Tse shrugged. "If it's humans and aliens then it's 'us and them', but if it's pre-cogs and creatives then it's 'you and us'. Sides were chosen long ago. But, my problem is that I'm pre-cog *and* human. I'm torn between those of my kind, my real tribe… and humanity."

"Can't fuck a Cancri," Marc said crudely, "even if it is pre-cog."

Tatia looked at Marc and shook her head.

"He's got a point," Tse said. "Sex makes me feel human. But only for a little while. I still perform," he said defiantly. "As long as I keep on taking the pills. Every time I end up feeling more and more like a freak. That's why I'm volunteering. That's why you won't stop me. I don't belong here any more."

"Greenaway…" Kara began, knowing she had to say something.

Tse waved her silent. "I told Greenaway that I might not return. He accepted the risk." His glance fell briefly on Tatia. "I think I know why."

Kara came to a decision. "Go then. And thank you."

Tse nodded and looked around the canteen. "You know I've felt more human in this squalid room than ever before. With all of you. Even little things like arguing over what to eat, even though I pretty much knew what you'd all choose."

Marc got to his feet. "Is it okay to tell you I hate curry?" He suddenly felt sad.

"It is – and thanks for pretending you didn't. I have gifts for all of you. Gifts from the future, if you like. They're not a hundred per cent accurate, but you know that." He took a deep breath. "Kara, you will discover the truth about your sister. Marc, the same about your parents. But it will take a little longer. I don't know if any of them are alive or dead. Tatia, you will discover the truth about your background in the Out, sooner rather than later. I don't know if this will make any of you happier. But you will be more content. Telling you more than that would affect the likelihood of these things happening, so that's all I can tell you."

The three nodded awkwardly. There was nothing to say.

"One other thing," Tse said. "Marc, you wondered why the Cancri chose you. Truth is, they didn't."

"But that message… with my artwork…"

"Which you never saw, did you? No. We needed

a human who had previous contact with aliens and I *saw* you would be ideal. GalDiv lied. The same for Kara. You're both here because of a pre-cog. Me. But I was right, wasn't I?" He would have gone on but was suddenly aware of Kara standing stock still as she talked to her AI.

"Company," she said darkly. "Break out the weapons. When they board, I want each and every Gliese followed and scrutinised, whatever they do and wherever they go. If any of them try to break away from the sideslip-field generator then stop them – forcibly, if you have to. If they protest, shoot them. I don't want to take any chances."

Marc smiled as the words of some long-ago lecturer flashed up in his mind. "The thing about assumptions," he said, "is that they make an 'ass' out of 'u' and 'me'."

"And you have such a lovely ass." Kara smiled.

The screen flicked on, interrupting the discussion. As they watched, the newly arrived Gliese SUT drew near. It looked much the same as the last one had. Given the background of darkness and stars, it was impossible to tell whether it was larger or smaller. As before, a tunnel of foam burned away and a tubular walkway extended towards the *RIL-FIJ-DOQ*'s airlock.

"I have to go and say some goodbyes," Tse said. "I'll see you in the anteroom by the airlock?"

After he left Marc turned to Kara. "I'll be there, despite all. You?"

"Oh yes. You mind about not being specially chosen?"

"Well, in a sense I was." He thought about his art.

"You know, I doubt my work means any more to the Eridani than any other human objects. Maybe they just wanted to hang out with an artist, any artist. Maybe some faction was trying to tell us back then that's what really interests them: human creativity, however it comes. Don't suppose we'll ever know, will we?"

The airlock area was declared temporarily off-limits. Pilgrims could watch on their screens.

The replacement went as smoothly as ever – even more so for this time there was no lone Gliese gone walkabout. Only Kara, Marc and Tatia were in the anteroom shrine to Douglas Leeman-Smith, that unwilling sacrifice to galactic trade, to see Tse leave. He kissed them all on the cheek, then turned back to Marc.

"Last words?" Marc asked as lightly as he could manage with a lump in his throat. Thinking this was a hell of a time to discover his lost humanity.

Tse shrugged. "Save the galaxy?"

Marc frowned. "The galaxy? What about the universe?"

"One thing at a time," Tse said, then took a deep breath, turned and followed the Gliese into the airlock, along the walkway and onto their transport.

"I never *did* ask," Kara said, "what was their SUT like?"

"I was only there for a minute or so," Marc remembered. "Saw where they keep the space drives, though. And their spacesuits. Or sleeping Gliese. Would imagine the engine room's close by the drive storage room. Tse asked me the same question a day or so ago."

Just then Tate stormed in, face flushed with anger.

"Fucking Gliese! They stole one of the platens."

Kara knew a terrible foreboding. "You're sure?"

"Only been me and them in the engine room," Tate said. "Except Tse when he came to say goodbye. But he wouldn't mess with a platen. I told you all how dangerous they could be when you came on board, remember? He did. Was asking about it only the other day." He noticed Tatia looking blank. "If you put two of them on the sideslip-field generator at the same time then it tries to go in different directions. Tears itself and the ship apart."

"Did you leave Tse alone in there?" Kara demanded.

"Only for a moment, I had to..." His face paled. "You can't... you don't..."

Kara's face was hard. She glanced at Marc. Maybe it was the lingering effects of the simulity, maybe just their emotional bond, but he knew exactly what she was thinking.

"He's going to blow them up!"

"Just to be sure. Just in case a lone Gliese pre-cog on board does something to stop us." She glanced at Tate. "Blast radius?"

He shrugged helplessly. "Physical detritus – maybe a few hundred metres."

A cold hand squeezed Marc's stomach, on the inside. Tse couldn't, surely? But just in case. "Canteen's in the centre of the SUT. Shielded by several shipping containers." One of which contained the Pilgrims.

Tate left hurriedly for the control room. Tatia, Kara and Marc clustered in front of the canteen screen.

One moment the Gliese SUT was hanging in space. The next moment it vanished.

Then it stuttered back into realspace some five hundred metres away. The image seemed to stretch.

And then they watched as the Gliese SUT tried to go in two different directions at the same time, just as Tate had said.

Two directions weren't enough. The Gliese SUT began expanding in *all* directions, becoming a large glowing disc. The colour changed from red to white, purple, violet – and then became a wall of fire that rushed towards the *RIL-FIJ-DOQ*, stopped a hundred metres away then reversed direction and began to shrink as it grew brighter and brighter, so much so the three watchers had to turn away. When they did look back, the light had gone out.

"So long, Tse," Marc muttered. "I guess the Gliese engines were different. You were only meant to tear it in half."

"But *why*?" Tatia murmured, still looking at the screen.

"Totally logical," Marc explained. "He didn't want to discover what the Gliese do to humans, but he didn't want to be taken to join the alien pre-cogs either. I'd have done the same. Maybe."

Kara shook her head. "It wasn't any of that," she said impatiently. "Oh, maybe a little but *perhaps* there wasn't any *plan*. Perhaps it was the most anarchic act Tse could imagine. And in that sense it was an act of creation. He'd lived nearly all his life trying to apply logic to a chaotic universe. He died finally embracing that same chaos. Making chaos. Don't you see?"

"Maybe," Tatia said, her voice breaking as she pointed at the screen, "you're probably right, chaos blah blah – but what the *fuck* is *that*?"

It looked like a vast skeleton of curved metal. Scaffolding. It wasn't easy to be sure because it was enveloped in a semi-translucent cloud that flickered as if created by a million lasers. There was no foam. Nothing *like* foam. What could be pods were scattered haphazardly throughout the structure. It was, according to the lasers shining at it from the *RIL-FIJ-DOQ*, perhaps a kilometre away, and it had just appeared out of nowhere.

No foam, a voice in Marc's head kept repeating. *That means whoever is on that ship doesn't perceive any threat from the snarks in netherspace. Maybe they have a peace treaty.*

"That," Kara said, her voice shaking, "I think, is what shows up when a *Gliese* netherspace drive goes *phut*."

"Oh. Right," Marc said, also fighting for calm. Fingers were crawling through his mind. It was the most *intrusive* feeling he'd ever experienced. "A mechanic's mechanic. Maybe that's why they're looking at me."

"And me," said Tatia.

"Inside me." Kara shuddered. "My *mind*."

The craft vanished. One moment it was examining the *RIL-FIJ-DOQ* with an easy arrogance, the next moment gone. *You do not interest us. You are not important.*

"If it takes for ever," Kara finally whispered, "I *will* find out who they are."

"I'm not busy for the next millennium or so," Marc said.

"Count me out," Tatia said with feeling. "I intend to stay home and count my money."

EPILOGUE

It was four more days before the *RIL-FIJ-DOQ* slid sideways into the solar system, close by Saturn. This afforded an opportunity to go take a look at the rings: offer denied. Folk just wanted to get home. And so began a series of little hops into netherspace as Tate and Nikki took the SUT ever closer to that point where Earth's mass – or any object warping eleven-dimensional space-time – would, as Tate explained to an uneasy Tatia, cause the netherspace drive to turn itself inside out and spectacularly render itself into many, many fragments.

Marc was idly wondering how Nikki could be so precise with her calculations when a window opened in his mind and he knew exactly how she did it, could have done it himself; and went in search of Kara. He found her in the airlock antechamber dedicated to the false memory of Douglas Leeman-Smith. Perhaps his sacrificed grandson had a family who'd be happy to inherit the items in there. Marc realised he knew nothing about Leeman-Smith's personal life – and cared even less.

"No Tatia?" Marc greeted her.

Kara made a face. "With her people. Legal stuff. They want their money back. She'll be tied up until we land."

Marc raised an eyebrow.

"Not literally. Although…"

"It's tempting," he finished for her. In the past couple of days they'd taken to completing each other's sentences. It felt natural. "Guess what? Simulity. I know how to…"

"Navigate?"

"And you? Engineer?"

Kara nodded. "Thought it might be the other way around. Cunning old Greenaway. Any other staff and we'd check it out. But this lot…"

This lot. Tate, Nikki and Henk had closed ranks ever since Tse's ultimate act of anarchic creative destruction and now barely spoke to Kara or Marc. They gave the impression they were only obeying Kara's orders because she had control of the weapons and would use them – probably on Henk first.

"Talking of which," Kara said, quickly adding, "or even whom," before Marc could, "we'd better go to the control room."

Five hours later, when they were close enough for Kara to have had several long and private conversations with Greenaway – pleased but not surprised to hear from her – Kara directed Nikki and Tate to a deserted area of Tegel Galactic. Deserted, that is, except for a welcoming army: approximately two companies of GalDiv soldiers complete with medical teams and a sinister-looking ground transport with blacked-out windows.

The *RIL-FIJ-DOQ* landed with the mildest of bumps. The Pilgrims went meekly into the transport, happy to be on Earth and forewarned that a period of quarantine would be necessary in case of alien bacteria.

"You have a choice," Kara told the *RIL-FIJ-DOQ*'s staff. "Go with them – or go back Up immediately. There's an exploring contract, means you'll be gone at least a year."

"Thanks so much," Nikki said sweetly, "so kind."

"Best I could do."

"I got family," Henk said.

"You got dick, not on Earth," Kara replied. "So don't pretend."

The staff collected their personal belongings without saying goodbye. A military transport whisked them away to the far side of Tegel and a waiting explorer SUT.

"Seems a bit unkind," Tatia said, watching the monitor in the control room. "I mean, we were colleagues, right?" And then, "Why am I not going with the rest?"

"Two things," Kara said, "according to Greenaway. One, you're much more important than the other Pilgrims. He said that while the Consort ceremony between you and Juan was legal, his estate can't make a claim. So you're still a wealthy woman. Two, you were in the warehouses. GalDiv need to hear your side." She didn't mention what her own AI had discovered about Tatia. Something that the younger woman herself didn't know.

Tatia was silent for a moment then looked at them, her face troubled. "Did you... did you say anything about my 'intuition'?"

Both Kara and Marc understood. If GalDiv suspected that Tatia was developing psi abilities, she'd be inside a laboratory faster than you could say pre-cog.

"What intuition?" Kara asked.

"No more than a feminine hunch or two," Marc said, trying not to grin. "Marriage and kids will take care of that."

"So kind," Tatia said, then flashed them both a warm smile. "I'll miss you. If you're ever in Seattle, don't hesitate to look me up."

"And how did she react?" Greenaway asked from behind his desk in the office where he'd first met Kara. It was the next day. Kara and Marc had been debriefed and de-debriefed until they'd even begun to question what they knew was the truth.

Kara glanced at Marc before speaking. They did a lot of glancing like that these days, as they increasingly spoke as one. "Relieved to be home. Bit sad to break up the team."

"In a way we became Tatia's family," Marc said, staring hard at Greenaway. "She's an orphan of the Out with no one else, right?"

"So it seems. Adoptive parents died in a crash."

"Lucky she had an AI," Kara said.

"Yes, very," Greenaway said cautiously.

"I asked mine to check it out. Unobtrusively. Thanks to the upgrades – the ones you never mentioned – it could do that."

"Interesting," Greenaway said. "It wasn't supposed to."

"It seems to have developed an independence. Of a sort. And no, don't offer to have it fixed. I like it this way. Why was Tatia's AI supposed to be off-limits?"

"Privacy." He ignored Marc's laugh. "She's an important person."

"Is that why there's a link back to GalDiv? One she never, still doesn't know about?"

Greenaway nodded. "We do that with most colonists and GalDiv people going Up. It's a rescue thing."

"It's spy thing," Marc said forcibly.

Greenaway shrugged. "That too."

"So the GalDiv link was applied just before she left with the Pilgrims?" Kara asked.

"Had to be her," Greenaway said. "No one else had an AI. Except her late husband."

Outside the sun would be sparkling on water drops left by a brief shower. Kara remembered a violet desert and an eight-foot praying mantis playing Simon Says.

"Tatia's had a GalDiv trace and monitor ever since her first AI," she said calmly. "Since she was eleven. My own AI found the logs. Every time she upgraded, the link moved across. Does GalDiv look after all orphans that way?"

"Her parents were involved with Microsoft," Greenaway said. "A major computer software company."

"That went bankrupt three months after pre-cogs helped scientists develop AI derived from alien technology," Kara said. "We checked. Microsoft hasn't been important for thirty years. Tatia's father only inherited the shares. He was never part of it."

Marc stood up and stretched, suddenly needing to be away from Berlin. "So here's the thing. We'll go back Up for you. Find the Gliese homeworld, try and discover where the tech comes from and who that big thing that turned up after the Gliese ship blew up belongs to. We have unfinished business. But as of now Tatia's out of the equation, right? Whatever you had planned is over. Just let her live her life."

Greenaway played with an antique letter-opener. It looked sharp. "That can't be a threat."

"It's not," Kara said. "Merely pointing out that you need us more than we need you. That for whatever reason, GalDiv is suppressing information about the Cancri and all the other aliens. That could change in an instant. Also Tatia won't be best pleased to discover that GalDiv spied on her. You don't want that kind of fuss."

"Okay." Greenaway stood up. "She's off our radar. I assume you planted a tell-tale program in her AI?" He saw them nod. "Thought so. Now, go take ten days' leave. Then report back here. You've a society to save. Maybe a master race to find. Possibly a snark to hunt. And a netherspace mystery to solve." He smiled a little sourly. "Sadly there's no pension or life insurance."

"What about Tse?" Kara said.

Greenaway's face went still. "I read the reports. He died well."

"Romantic of you," Marc said.

"We go… went back a long way." Greenaway looked hard at Kara and Marc in turn. "He told you about the programme? Of course he did. I won't try to defend it. We have to understand aliens better, if only to negotiate trade, and pre-cog's the best chance we've got. Tse was a trusted friend. Saved my life a long, long time ago. Did he tell you about his children to be?"

"He couldn't—" Marc and Kara began in unison.

"We, GalDiv, preserve the DNA of all our precogs. His son will be born in a year or so. The mother will also have psi abilities. Sounds cold? Well, it is. And that's something that perhaps neither of you understand. This really is about the survival of the human race. The end justifies the means. Do not forget it when you're out there hunting for answers."

"Let's just hope," Kara said, smiling sweetly, "that the snark doesn't turn out to be a boojum."

There was a jitney waiting to take them to the airport. Kara was thoughtful as the vehicle pulled away, staying quiet for the next ten minutes.

"He gave up easy," Kara finally said.

"Think he means it?"

"Knows enough to be careful. As long as we're one of his last best hopes to save humanity or whatever, Tatia'll be safe. What's your real interest, Marc?"

"Only woman I really fancied who I turned down." He frowned. "No. It's like she's part of the team. I never had a team before. Lone artist, suffering by himself."

She put a hand on his shoulder. "I like it when you're open. Want to talk about Henk?"

Marc made a face. "So you know. Your effing AI. No. Other than he's fixated on netherspace and it can do strange things to a person. Which probably sounds like 'I was drunk'."

"Not criticising. Only concerned." Kara took away her hand. "Want to go walking on Dartmoor?" she asked. "Might be the last chance we get."

"I've got an artwork to do."

She nodded. Together on the moor, sleeping in a small tent. "You're right." Kara smiled. "Then let's go and do something creative."

Glossary

ALIEN

one of a number of non-human species, some of which are in contact with humanity and some of which are not. It has proved impossible to communicate with aliens on anything but the most basic level, that level being trade. Mostly they're named after a constellation; not all city states agree on what a particular species should be called. The most common aliens and the ones responsible for most trades are:

CANCRI

an alien race resembling a small striped greyhound with two arms and carrying a pale white grub on its back in a symbiotic relationship. Neither have yet been dissected.

ERIDANI

an alien race resembling a segmented snake-like creature with multiple arms and a face like a disturbed nest of white worms. It smells of spaghetti bolognese.

GLIESE

an alien race – the first to contact humanity – resembling a pile of wet leather with three spindly arms, dozens of small, stub-like legs, a mouth part hidden by ragged flaps and what might be sensory organs on their outer skin. Dissection of one killed by accident revealed an interior full of a dark, viscous substance in which "floated" various connected objects that could be organs. The Gliese supply the **sideslip**-field generators (netherspace drives) and **updown**-field generators that make space travel possible.

It is estimated by **GalDiv** that up to fifteen other types of alien have visited Earth. However these invariably land and remain in **the Wild**. What they might be doing there causes GalDiv many a sleepless night.

ARTIFICIAL INTELLIGENCES (AIs)

Most objects – houses, **jitneys**, restaurants – have their own AIs. People have them too, occupying computer chips implanted in their heads that can insert images and data directly into the optic nerve and auditory nerves. AIs evolve the ideal software persona (or "**avatars**") to interface with their "owner", but they are not in and of themselves conscious, although their owners may treat them as if they are. Larger AIs regulate trade between city states and between worlds. They also set the exchange rates for the common currency, **virtscrip**. Many people believe that some AIs have achieved a "life" of their own, although the programming is so good it's impossible to tell. Most people prefer to forget that the technical breakthrough that allowed AI development came from alien technology.

AVATAR

the "front end" of an **AI** system; the means by which an AI interacts with humans. Avatars have no legal status as conscious beings: they are just a highly developed version of an operating system's "theme". That said, many people treat them like a valued friend.

BOTS

small, unintelligent robots used for cleaning, construction and observation. They have no individual controlling **AI**, although an AI may control multiple bots.

CYBERDRONES

small insects controlled by electronics. Theoretically it would be possible to electronically control small mammals or birds as well, but this is a moral grey area. Controlling fish is allowed, but not dolphins or whales although some **city states** will control anything alive.

CALL-OUT FEE

a human who has volunteered to be exchanged for rescue by **aliens** if an **SUT**'s sealed sideslip-field generator breaks down, leaving the SUT stranded in normal space. They might volunteer because they are dying of some incurable disease, because they want to pass their salary on to their family, or for some psychological reason known only to themselves. Fees are normally kept in an **induced coma** so that the crews of the SUTs do not become too attached to them. This trade is exclusive to the **Gliese**.

CANCRI see **Alien**.

CITY STATES

were formed in the years after **first contact**, when the concept of nations began to fall apart and people realised they preferred living in self-governing communities. City states often form larger coalitions, especially for defence (hence: The Army of the Anglo-Saxon City States, The Army of the Gallic City States, etc.), but laws are still made

357

and enforced at the local level. Trade agreements between city states are negotiated by each city state's **AI**, and then reviewed by humans before becoming law.

CLOTHES

these can be mood-sensitive and colour-changing. **City staters** tend to dress conservatively, except during public festivals when anything goes. Wilders dress however they damn well please.

COMING OUT see **Out There**.

DOWN THERE

landing on a planet. Also known as going down.

EARTHCENT

Earth Central, the administrative organisation that sits above the city states and tries to ensure coherence and stability. Derived from the old United Nations, it is more pragmatic and less idealistic. In reality it is subordinate to its Galactic Division, or GalDiv, which oversees contact between aliens and humans.

ERIDANI see **Alien**.

FIRST CONTACT

the occasion when the human race and aliens met for the first time. It occurred on the moon, after the **Gliese** changed the colour of several craters so that they could be seen easily from the Earth.

FOAM

an alien technology and a self-hardening substance used to protect SUTs in space/netherspace. Its strength and effectiveness allows SUTs to be made of pretty much anything, including metal cargo containers or, in one bizarre episode, a small thatched cottage complete with garden, which subsequently vanished in **netherspace**. The supply of foam is controlled by the Gliese for no apparent trade. Humans consider it an after-sales service.

FREE SPACERS

freelance space travellers based in **the Wild** who use cobbled-together technology and scavenged alien systems to travel to colony worlds and explore outside the jurisdiction of **GalDiv**. They typically launch their **SUT**-equivalents from desert areas or converted oil rigs to avoid accidents. That was the GalDiv version. In fact free spacers provide links between colony worlds that no longer accept GalDiv/Earth hegemony.

GALDIV

Galactic Division of **EarthCent** that looks after the exploitation of space and the trade with **alien** races, and attempts to oversee the colony worlds, although many colony worlds don't want to be overseen and no one knows exactly how many there are. Like many organisations, GalDiv's true main purpose is to ensure its own survival since there is no real way it can regulate alien/human contact – especially in the Wild. It has also been penetrated by agents of the Human Primus organisation.

GLIESE see **Alien**.

GOING DOWN see **Down There**.

GOING UP

leaving a planet and moving through normal space. Also **Up there.**

HUMAN PRIMUS

a political movement that believes humanity's interests should come well before those of **aliens**, and that the unequal system of trade with alien races is a form of charity at best, and callous exploitation at worst. Many in Human Primus want all alien/human contact to cease; aliens to be recognised as dangerous; and for Earth to develop its own technology, no matter how long and how arduous that process might be. Human Primus has been accused of wanting to reinstate government by an hereditary, over-privileged elite and of a xenophobia with its roots in a pathological insecurity. Both are correct.

INDUCED COMA

derived from an existing medical procedure, a process by which a human – usually a **call-out fee** – is rendered unconscious for long periods of time. Electromagnetic fields are used to "switch off" their consciousness, while their bodies are fed with nutrients through tubes. It is the only real contribution that humanity has made to galactic travel, which is a little sad.

INPUT TATTOOS

sepia keyboard/input devices stencilled on people's forearms used for interfacing with **AI**s. Alternatively, some people prefer interacting using their hands with virtual keyboards/

displays which are projected onto their visual field. This is generally frowned on in public.

IN THERE

retreating into a **simulity** and ignoring real life. Also **Going in**.

JITNEY

a robot car, helicopter or boat controlled by an **AI**. Jitneys do not "belong" to anyone, but can be hired or flagged down. When not in use by humans the AI makes decisions about when it refuels the jitney and books itself in for a service.

JOSS

the logical progression of cigarettes and vapes, often containing soft or hard drugs, all of which are legal. Thanks to an alien trade, physical and mental addiction can be cured in less than an hour. The commercial search for an addictive, non-curable and highly pleasurable drug continues.

MISSION MANAGER

the person in charge of an **SUT**, usually a technically unqualified administrator. An exception is made for explorer SUTs, where the mission manager is also a back-up engineer, navigator or medic.

NETHERSPACE

the extra dimensions above or below "normal" space where interstellar space travel can be accomplished. **SUTs** that enter netherspace sometimes do not leave it. Human brains cannot find any frame of reference to latch onto when they see netherspace, and they quickly go insane. The relationship between normal space and netherspace has been described as being like the Florida Everglades: if you look at a map of them and want to get from one piece of solid ground to another via canoe, then you might have to follow miles of little waterways. Far easier to row to the nearest bank, pick your canoe up, cross a spit of land, get into your canoe again and row across another channel, go across another spit of land and keep going in a straight line. Netherspace is the dry land and normal space is the water.

NETHERSPACE DRIVE see **Sideslip-Field Generator**.

OFFICIAL ASSASSIN

licensed by what is ostensibly an independent bureau, Official Assassins can be hired to right wrongs when the law may not apply – such as between competing corporations headquartered in different city states – or when the legal process is too expensive. In fact they're covert arms of **EarthCent** used to keep the business and financial worlds reasonably honest, and so secret that not even Official Assassins know who really pays their considerable wages. Most Official Assassins are ex-military. Unofficial assassins also exist, used because they're cheaper or more private than the official variety. Their professional lives are short.

OUT THERE

leaving a **simulity** for reality. Also known as **coming out**.

PRE-COGS

those humans who can, in some way that has never properly been explained, see the vague shape of the future. Pre-cogs have described their ability along the following lines: they can "see" future events like landmarks on the horizon ahead of them, and they can also "see" roads, footpaths and overgrown tracks that might lead to those landmarks, but the landscape is hilly, with much hidden from sight. Paths that they think lead to a particular landmark suddenly end in a hidden spot, double back on themselves, or turn out to have a wall built across them. Pre-cogs can make educated guesses about which actions or choices now will lead to landmark events in the future, but they cannot be absolutely sure.

SIDESLIP-FIELD GENERATOR

a system for entering and leaving **netherspace** provided by the Gliese in three strengths that will power SUTs from the size of a caravan to a ferry. Also known as a **netherspace drive**. Any attempt to open the unit results in an immediate shutdown. Moreover, if the unit is opened it is shown to be empty. Humans have the – traded – power to reach the stars, but they don't have the faintest idea how it works. Colloquially known as a **netherspace drive**.

SPACE UTILITY TRANSPORT (SUT)

a utilitarian vehicle designed for space travel and equipped with an **updown-field generator** (for getting out of a planet's gravitational field) and a **sideslip-field generator** (for entering and leaving **netherspace**). Space Utility Transports do not have names, but randomly generated nine-letter codes: *LUX-WEM-YIB*, *NOL-DAP-KIM* etc. These are known as trifecta codes. Thanks to **foam** and **updown-field (gravity negating) generators**, SUTs come in many and varied shapes, few of them aerodynamic.

SIMULITIES

all-immersive simulated realities, usually accessed by

multiple people at the same time and moderated by **AIs** using **alien** technology and in theory controlled by **GalDiv** and the larger **city states** military. People using a simulity can be made to experience another's thoughts, perceptions and feelings. This leads to a gestalt useful in training SUT crews and the military. In practice the simulity technology has leaked into the public domain – probably via **the Wild** – where it used for gaming, psychoanalysis and virtual sex.

SNARK

a descriptive term used for whatever it is in **netherspace** that sometimes makes **SUTs** disappear. They may or may not have a physical form but can inflict physical damage.

SPACE ACCESS POINTS (SAPs)

what for a while were called "space ports". Areas where **SUTs** take off and land.

UPDOWN-FIELD GENERATOR

an anti-gravity unit provided by the Gliese in a form that cannot be opened or tampered with. The generator only "elevates" an SUT in a perpendicular direction. Horizontal travel is gained by use of jet propulsion, or by sailing with the wind.

VIRTSCRIP (OR "SCRIP")

the virtual currency originally developed by intergalactic corporations for purposes of trade. At a time when many colony worlds and **city states** have their own currency, virtscrip has become the default one. Rates of exchange are fixed quarterly (Earth years) by three heavily defended **AIs** located in the Asteroid Belt. These AIs represent **EarthCent**;

major corporations; and the colony worlds. They also oversee the settlement of intergalactic banking and trade deals. There have been numerous outside attempts to fix the exchange rates, either with false data or a computer virus. None have succeeded. Many of the people who tried are dead.

WILD, THE

politically amorphous and ambiguous areas between the **city states**. The Wild is usually populated by those people who do not follow orders well, don't like **AI**s and/or prefer a libertarian existence. City staters may visit out of curiosity. Many never return. It is known that the Wild trades independently with **aliens** and, via the **free spacers**, with the colony worlds. **GalDiv** is powerless to prevent this, but likes to pretend it can.

WORLDMESH

the loose affiliation of **city state AI**s that allows the free flow of data around the world as well as negotiating trade agreements and facilitating currency transfers.

About the Authors

ANDREW LANE is the author of twenty-nine books and multiple short stories, television scripts and audio dramas. He is perhaps best known for his Young Sherlock series, which has sold to forty-two countries. He has also written three well-reviewed adult crime novels under a pseudonym, the first of which has been optioned as a US TV series. He is currently writing another series featuring Doyle's Professor Challenger. He lives in Dorset.

NIGEL FOSTER began as an advertising copywriter, first in the UK and then North America. He moved on to television and radio factual programming before co-founding a successful movie magazine. Back in the UK highlights include developing and launching *OK! Magazine*; an international non-fiction bestseller about the Royal Marines Commandos; and six of the most popular Bluffer's Guides, worldwide.

KOKO TAKES A HOLIDAY
KIERAN SHEA

Five hundred years from now, ex-corporate mercenary Koko Martstellar is swaggering through an easy early retirement as a brothel owner on a tropical resort island. Koko finds the most challenging part of her day might be deciding on her next drink. That is, until her old comrade Portia Delacompte sends a squad of security personnel to murder her.

"A jet-powered, acid-fueled trip of pure, rocking insanity."
Stephen Blackmoore

"Breakneck pace... great fun."
Booklist (starred review)

"*Altered Carbon* with a dash of *Tank Girl* attitude."
Library Journal

TITANBOOKS.COM